THE BLACKSMITH'S BOY

BRUCE BUCHANAN

A Wild Ink Publishing Original

wild-ink-publishing.com

Edited by Andie Smith

Interior illustrations by Tamara Horton

Cover Design and Layout by Abigail Wild

ISBN Paperback: 978-1-964885-21-6

ISBN Epub: 978-1-964885-22-3

To Dad.
You shared your lifelong love for books—and so much more.
This one's for you.
Love,
Bruce

PROLOGUE

THE FARMER WAS PLEASED—HE peeled back the dark green husk of the corn, the kernels inside as golden as the sunset cascading over the farm. His family would eat corn stew this winter, perhaps they could sell a few ears in the village for some much-needed coins. This small patch of corn served his family well.

He had no way of knowing it was where his life was about to end.

The farmer, his wife, and their two children tended their one-acre farm in the morning and evening. During the day, they helped tend the fields of a Noble Class land owner. Like their neighbors, they were members of the Serving Class, forbidden by law to enter certain trades, hold public offices, or own more than small amounts of property. That had been the way of life in the Kingdom of Imarina for centuries. The farmers, laborers, builders, and artisans did their share of grumbling, but as long as the kingdom was at peace and dinner tables remained full, few felt the need to press for change.

"Look, Papa! Rali wants to show off for you!"

The boy, around eight summers old, hurled a chewed stick through the twilight sky, sending the tail-wagging collie streaking toward the wooden missile. The dog snatched the stick in full stride before it could touch the ground, then raced back to the child to receive a well-earned pat on the head.

"Ha! That's a great trick!" the farmer said. "Now run along and get washed up for supper before your mother takes a switch after both of us!"

But instead of turning toward the house, the young boy pointed behind his father and screamed.

"Papa! Look out!"

The farmer spun around and could scarcely believe the horror before him. Row after row of his corn crop instantly disintegrated into black ash, as if an invisible inferno rolled over the fields. The wave rolled across the field, heading straight for the farmer and his son.

"Run, boy!"

The child hesitated, until his father yelled again. "Run!"

But the unseen force continued to consume rows of corn like dry kindling fed into a bonfire. Strangely, the rippling death made no noise. The only sounds in the cornfield were those of the farmer's footfalls and his gasps for breath.

He glanced over his shoulder. As fast as he moved, it was not swift enough.

The farmer, father, and husband screamed as the magical surge overtook him, reducing him to a small pile of black dust in a growing field of the same.

The boy, breathless and panicked, slammed open the front door of their small cabin.

"Mother! Come quick! We've got to run!"

"Where's your father. What—?" She looked out the cabin's lone window. What she saw terrified and fascinated her at the same time: A dark surge in a dry black ocean roaring silently toward their home.

The woman grabbed her daughter's hand, causing the child to spill her water cup. "Hurry!" she screamed, as much at herself as at her children.

She almost made it to the front door.

The spell crushed the small house into cold cinders. There, in the doorway of their own home, the Yult family died instantly.

Had they started moving just five seconds earlier, they would have lived. The killing black tide almost instantly dissipated after leveling the house, fading like a water mirage on a blazing summer day.

From a nearby hill, three people, all clad in black jackets over plain red clothes, dark hoods pulled low over their faces, inspected the scene. The Yult farm, which had been fertile and green just moments earlier, was now completely gone, erased in a perfectly square block.

The three—two women and a man—watched from beneath their hoods as the summer breeze sifted the black dust. They were pleased with their work.

"The spell worked—the Blight is a success!" said the shorter of the women. The trio stood around a neatly placed ring of red roses, nightshade sprigs, and charcoal lumps.

"You doubted it would, Neuragian?" the dark-haired, square-jawed man said. He wore the same black jacket over red clothes as the others, but red braids adorned the shoulders of his neatly pressed jacket.

"N-no; that is not what I intended, True Leader!" The woman offered a bow of apology for the unintended slight.

The other young woman intervened on her behalf. "I believe what she means is that the power of the Blight is beyond anything we could imagine."

The True Leader nodded. "Yes, Alaydrian. These magics have not been seen in more than 300 summers. Even the most skilled sorcerers do not know of their existence. But the Blight is real—we proved as much. And this is only the beginning."

"But what of the House of Magic? Won't they hear of this?" she replied.

"Yes. And King Isbiano? Will he not investigate?" Neuragian asked, apparently having recovered enough of her nerve to speak again.

The True Leader smiled. "Perhaps. The King will be alarmed when he hears of what we've done. I'm equally certain the sorcerers at the House of Magic will downplay the threat—they will never believe that anyone could threaten their supremacy, even when presented with irrefutable evidence to the contrary. And members of the Royal Council will pursue their own narrow agendas and scheme to win the King's favor.

"So yes—I'm sure the Crown will have some sort of response to our actions here today. But it will be insufficient. By the time our weak, ineffective leaders realize the threat before them, we will be standing in the Royal Palace and the Scions of Sonorian will rule the Kingdom for a thousand summers to come!"

Led by the True Leader, the sorcerers then walked through the black dust, three sets of footprints in what moments before had been a vibrant family farm.

CHAPTER 1

ON A SIMILAR FARM nearly 200 miles away, Bok Omat faced his own adversary and whispered a quiet prayer.

"Come on, please work with me, girl..." For 30 minutes, he had waved a spoon of metallic-smelling medicinal powder in front of the sick cow's nose, only to be ignored. Ministering to farm animals was an important, if routine, part of Bok's job as healer of Soleh Valley, a small, hill-covered farming community in southern Imarina.

Bok blew a breath out of the side of his mouth. As a healer, he practiced Folk Magic, enchantments handed down through generations of healers to heal and nurture animals, crops, even people. Folk magic worked to improve outcomes that already were possible in the natural world. It wasn't High Magic—the type practiced by sorcerers trained in Imarina's House of Magic. Unlike Folk Magic, High Magic harnessed mystical energy for a range of supernatural purposes, including devastating attacks and powerful shields. Only those from the Noble Class even had the Acumen—the innate potential to perform High Magic, and only a small number of Nobles were born with the Acumen, just as only a few in the Serving Class could employ Folk Magic.

It wasn't sorcery, but Folk Magic was an honest profession for a peasant. Unless Bok was dealing with an obstinate cow. *Now, if I can just coax Maka to take this spoon...*

"There, girl... that's it!" The cow finally opened her mouth and gulped down the copper powder. Bok then placed his hands on the animal's side and spoke a brief stomach-settling spell. The cow looked at him with oversized eyes, then turned away to consider whatever debate barn cows normally had inside their heads.

Bok exhaled, the job finally done. The young man of 19 summers dusted the excess powder from his hands—naturally dark and further tanned by long hours in the sun. His dark brown hair hung to the collar of his homespun white cotton shirt, which cost him a box of nails made in his family's blacksmith's shop.

"Just a sour stomach, Farmer Col. She should be fine now. But I'll stop back by next week." Bok rubbed his close-cropped beard as he spoke.

"Thankee Bok! I shore appreciate you comin' by so quick." The elderly farmer walked with Bok out of the small, unpainted barn. She patted Bok's thick forearm. "Without Maka, I don't have milk to make corn stew. And you know how much I love that ol' girl. But... I'm kindly short on coins..."

Bok smiled. "You still keep bees, right? I'll gladly accept a jar of your wildflower honey and call it even."

He only had been on the job for six months, when Weni Kon, his mentor and Soleh Valley's healer for 27 summers, retired to her farm. But so far, it was going well. Bok was proud he could help his neighbors.

He arrived home to his family's three-room pine-plank house, the smell of hot bread pulling him in from the road. Although such hearty foods were the reason he wanted to lose a few pounds around the middle, he could not imagine a more delicious aroma.

"Figured you'd show up right as I'm serving lunch, Bok!" His mother, Tana Omat, placed plain clay plates at the table in the home's main room, which housed its kitchen and dining area. At night, Bok rolled out a thin straw-filled mat and slept on the floor.

Bok kissed his mother on the cheek. "Widow Kara has a pretty bad case of the gout and then I had to go by the Col place and tend to Maka."

"You do this family—and Soleh Valley—proud, son!" a voice boomed from behind him. His father, Fin Omat, stepped into the small home, wiping his sweaty face with a handkerchief. "How an ironbender like me ended up with both a healer and the best blacksmith in Imarina—not to mention your amazingly talented mother—remains a mystery." A broad-shouldered young woman entered the house behind their father. Like Bok, Yata Omat had shoulder-length brown hair, tan skin, and powerful arms built by countless hours of hard work. But she stood several inches taller than her younger brother.

"Well, the finest blacksmith in Soleh Valley could use some help this afternoon. What little help my brother can provide!" Yata punched Bok in the shoulder on her way to the kitchen. He grimaced—Yata's playful jabs still hit like a mule's kick.

She tilted her head at Bok. "We've got to shoe Bron Akol's horses. Then we need to make around 100 more nails—the Drom family is building a new barn. Oh, and Japa wants her kitchen knives sharpened."

"In other words, a light day!" Fin gulped down a flagon of well water.

"I'll help, Father." Bok sighed. *So much for my plans to read this afternoon.*

Behind them, Tana deftly pulled an iron skillet off the potbellied, wood-burning stove, flipped the steaming griddle bread onto a plain clay plate and handed it to Bok in one smooth, well-rehearsed motion.

At that point, Noji, Yata's son, came barreling out of the back room he shared with his mother and grabbed a hunk of griddle bread that Tana already had slathered with strawberry jam.

"You are a messy creature, aren't you? I guess you take after me!" Bok playfully mussed the dark-headed little boy's hair with his left hand. Noji smiled a strawberry red smile. Noji's father had run away four years earlier when Yata became pregnant. He said he was too young to deal with the responsibility of being a parent. *But my sister is doing a remarkable job of it—even if she can be as annoying as a nest of fire ants.*

"You do not take after your uncle, Noji!" Yata scooped stewed vegetables and scrambled eggs onto her son's plate. "Did you know Bok lived in the pigpen until he was seven summers?" Bok shook his head in mock embarrassment as Noji laughed.

Once the meal was done, Yata stood to leave the table. "Come, brother. Those horses aren't going to shoe themselves."

Bok scarfed down his last bite of bread. He faced a long afternoon—and the summer sun wouldn't make it any shorter.

The work was exhausting and by mid-morning, sweat soaked Bok's shirt. He wiped his reddened, dripping face with a hand cloth and dipped a ladle of cool well water from an oak bucket. Meanwhile, his sister and father kept pounding out the iron nails, the anvil ringing each time their hammers struck a blow. Bok admired their stamina and wondered how his father had kept such a pace for nearly 30 summers.

"HUMM!" Bok's father cleared his throat, a sure sign he was about to say something he didn't want to share.

"Bok... I appreciate your effort. But the nails need to be more like these." He held out his leathery palm with Bok's crooked nail side-by-side with a perfectly straight version hammered by Yata. "Do you think you could...?"

"No problem, Father. I'll bring in a load of wood for the furnace, too." As a blacksmith, Bok knew he made a fine country healer.

As Bok donned his gloves to resume his work, a horseback rider came down the dirt trail through the center of the small village, the stallion's hooves kicking up clouds of dust in its wake. The woman's store-bought clothes were far nicer than any in the village, as was her horse. Such a rider undoubtedly came from Ithenel, Imarina's capital city. Bok wondered why the rider would be coming through their small, out-of-the-way community.

"You Bok Omat?"

"That I am, ma'am." Bok removed his gloves and stepped out through the open doorway into the small yard separating the workshop from the dirt road. "How can I help you?"

The woman handed Bok a neatly rolled scroll, tied with a violet silk ribbon. "Her Majesty, Princess Isabella, requests your presence for an advisory meeting at the Royal Palace four days hence." The rider repeated the summons' wording, in the incorrect assumption that a peasant like Bok couldn't read.

Fin dropped his hammer and came outside. "B-But why? We mind our business and obey the King's laws. What could Her Majesty want with my boy?"

The messenger shrugged. "Those answers will be forthcoming at the Royal Council meeting. All I can tell you is Princess Isabella signed this command in her own hand."

Bok examined the scroll. It certainly seemed official, right down to the calligraphic script of Princess Isabella's signature.

Besides, King Isbiano isn't in the habit of jailing innocent people. And folks say the King's only child shares that sense of justice.

I hope they're right.

The messenger left as quickly as she had arrived, leaving Bok, Yata, and Fin to stare at the neatly printed scroll.

"Princess Isabella? Say—she's supposed to have a real soft heart for the Serving Class. Maybe she's looking for a Soleh Valley fella—someone like a blacksmith's boy!" Yata cackled. "They say she's as beautiful as she is rich. This could be your chance to marry up, brother!"

Fin shot his daughter a scowl. "This is serious, Yata. What could the Princess and the Royal Council possibly want with your brother? Perhaps that 'messenger' was some type of bandit."

Bok rubbed his finger over the wax seal embossed on the scroll. "I don't know, Father, but this summons looks authentic to me. If someone wanted to rob a poor country healer, surely there are easier ways to do it."

Fin furrowed his brow. "Son, I don't want you to ride into trouble."

"I don't believe I am, Father. If Princess Isabella meant me harm, she would've simply had me arrested, not asked me to show up at the Royal Palace."

"The Royal Family aren't who I'm worried about." Tana shaded her eyes against the bright morning sun with her hand. She shuffled her feet in the crunchy, dry grass. "But you'll be among the Noble Class, Bok. I don't want my son treated like a stray dog instead of a person."

Bok looked at the top of his scuffed brown boots. His mother was right—Imarina's strict class divisions meant people like him suffered insults and indignities from small-minded people of higher standing. *But what can I do? The only way to win a dispute with the Noble Class is to avoid one.*

Surely, this must be a mistake. A country healer—a member of the Serving Class, for goodness sakes—couldn't have much to say that could hold the attention of the kingdom's most important Nobles.

But not responding to a royal summons would only bring trouble.

"I don't want that, either. But we don't know the reason for this summons." He set his jaw and looked up to his parents. "There's only one way to find out—I must go to Ithenel."

The Royal Palace was nearly three days' journey, so he hurriedly packed to ensure that he met Princess Isabella's deadline. With Yata's help, he saddled Beki, the horse he took on his rounds as community healer.

Tana shoved a stack of griddle cakes, wrapped with a clean cloth, into Bok's hand. Then she hugged her son. "Be careful. You know how dangerous the city can be."

"You listen to your mother, Bok. Ithenel is no place to let your guard down." Fin pulled his son in for a hug of his own.

Yata waved, as if to swat away their concerns. "Pshaw! You two hens worry too much. Get me a present in the city, brother. And I can't wear anything ugly if I am to be the sister of a royal advisor—or the consort to the Crown Princess!"

"You could be King Bok!" Noji's joke got a laugh from his uncle and mother.

"I'll get you something nice, Yata—you too, little man. But don't make your plans for the Emissaries' Ball just yet." Bok climbed onto Beki's saddle. "For all I know, this is just a misunderstanding and I'll be home before week's end."

With that, he kissed Noji on top of the head, waved goodbye to his family and set out for Ithenel and the Royal Palace, still unsure of exactly why he was going or what exactly he would do once he arrived. He certainly had no idea that answers to those questions would alter his life's path—and that of Soleh Valley—forever.

CHAPTER 2

AFTER A THIRD DAY of hard riding, the dense forests thinned out and Bok found himself again among familiar-looking farm communities, even if he had never been this far north before. Miles upon miles of fields, dotted by the small homes of the field hands and the occasional manor house of the Noble Class property owner.

By late afternoon, Bok entered the sprawling city of Ithenel. The city seemingly sprang up out of the hills that guarded it. Millennia earlier, Ithenel's first settlers had built in the large, flat clearing between the cluster of hills, as the location's geography made it the perfect spot to fend off attackers.

The layout of the landscape also made Ithenel seemingly appear out of nowhere. Bok and Beki rode up a steeply sloping, wide dirt road and went around a bend. When they cleared the rocky hill, the city's skyline filled Bok's entire field of vision. Hundreds of buildings, from one-room shacks to multi-story towers, composed a man-made panorama too big for Bok to take in at once. Bok gasped at the sight, then blushed at his involuntary response. *Surely, everyone here will think I am a cornpone commoner.*

During his training, Weni Kon shared stories of Ithenel. Most of them centered on the city's sheer scope—the crowds in the Great Bazaar that surged and ebbed around the vendors' tables like a single living thing, the towers that stretched taller than even the red-tailed hawk dared fly, the sounds that hundreds of people generate while working, shopping, and talking on a single city block.

If anything, Ithenel was even more expansive than Bok imagined. Bok felt grateful to finally have seen the great city—and more than a bit nervous to travel into the gullet of this beast.

The Royal Palace loomed in the center of the metropolis, the light gleaming off its polished white marble spires like a second sun. Even from this distance, the palace stood out and above the rest of the city. It was built more than 600 years ago on Ithenel's tallest point, for reasons both strategic and symbolic. An artist's drawing of the Royal Palace hung in the single-room schoolhouse in Soleh Valley where Bok and Yata received their formal education. Bok stared at the picture on many chilly winter mornings. He wondered what it would be like to live in such opulence—how fortunate the Royal Family must be.

If I was that rich, I'd never have a care in the world. His parents would never have to cook again. Bok would hire someone to handle all that, as well as any farming his mother wanted done. Father and Yata could sell the blacksmith's shop and never have to lift a hammer again. And Noji would have every wooden doll he wanted, even the rare, expensive ones Bok's family only heard about from traveling merchants. As for himself, Bok would read all the books his imaginary wealth could purchase. As it was, he spent what few extra coppers he had on buying books from the traveling merchant wagons.

But he sighed as he shook the leather coin purse strapped to his belt. He had five coppers from performing healing duties in the village, and his parents were able to give him another seven for the journey—every coin they had in the house. However, Bok had never been outside of Soleh Valley, and he wanted to bring his loved ones something memorable to mark the occasion.

As luck would have it, his first encounter with the city was the one place in Imarina where virtually anything could be had for the right price. The Great Bazaar stood at the entrance to Ithenel and the main road into town ran through the middle of the marketplace, intentionally placed to ensure visitors had every opportunity to leave as many coins as possible in the capital city. Dozens of white canvas tents and makeshift wooden shacks formed a labyrinth, where buyers could purchase supplies, tools, livestock—and who knows what else. And the sales approach was aggressive, to say the least:

"Sir, would you like to buy a hammock?" a vendor asked, approaching Bok. "They're good for your back!"

Behind him, a stout woman with a kerchief around her head bellowed, "Fresh baked pastries right 'ere! Two fer a copper!"

Like a crow attracted to spilled corn, an old man crouching on a stool got in on the act. Beckoning Bok, he opened a battered black leather case. "We've got the finest jewelry right 'er! Surely, you've got a pretty girl back home. She would love to have one of these blue topaz rings, don'cha think?" Bok smiled and waved as politely as he could in hustling past the hawking vendors.

Bok pulled his arms tight into his ribs as he rode through the hornet's nest of activity. In Soleh Valley, you either bought what you needed at the village's lone general store, or you waited for the monthly supply wagon to come from Ithenel.

"Excuse me, sir? I'm sorry to bother you, but I need your help." Bok stopped Beki and looked down to see a young boy, no more than eight years old, standing at his side. The child's clothes were torn and dirty and he refused to meet Bok's eyes as he kicked at the dirt beneath his bare toes.

"What's wrong, little man? There's no need to cry," Bok said, dismounting from his horse.

The ragamuffin boy sniffed. "B... but I lost my mother! She was over there at the spice vendors' tent and I was looking at these pet snakes. When I went back, she was gone!"

"Don't worry. We'll find her; you just stay close to—" Beki whinnied and Bok wheeled around to see a young girl running away with Bok's knapsack.

"Hey! Somebody stop her!" But no one in the crowd attempted to stop the young thief. In fact, a few passers-by laughed at Bok's plight.

Bok considered chasing the girl, but she undoubtedly knew the bazaar far better than he did and could lose him in the dense maze of tents. Besides, he had to think about the young boy who lost his mother.

"Sorry about that. Now let's..." The boy was gone, too.

That's when Bok's stomach sank. The two children were working together and the mother, if she even existed at all, likely was waiting for them to return with their stolen loot. He took little comfort in knowing that all the children took was some spare clothing and a few snacks.

Stupid! I am just a foolish bumpkin. Five minutes in Ithenel and already, I have been robbed and mocked. Why did I leave Soleh Valley?

CHAPTER 3

AFTER ANOTHER TWO HOURS or so of slow riding through narrow, crowded city streets, Bok entered the sparkling center of Ithenel. There, at the heart of the metropolis, was the Royal Palace.

Bok first realized he must be close to the palace when the streets shifted from cobblestone to red brick, which gleamed from a fresh scrubbing. Glittering mansions, set far back from the road, lined both sides of the oak-shaded street.

The brick road dead-ended at a 15-foot high security wall made of granite blocks and reinforced by iron bars. Bok gripped Princess Isabella's scroll in a shaking hand and took a deep breath. *I doubt a peasant from the rural fringes of the kingdom is welcomed at the front door, no matter what official scroll I've got.*

So he went around back to the service entrance. Peering through the cast iron gate, he saw a small section of the sprawling Royal Gardens. The perfectly manicured shrubbery formed a pathway through rose bushes in a kaleidoscope of bright colors snaking up tall trellises. Neatly hedged boxes of zinnias, irises, and hydrangeas grew to the sides of the shrub-lined pathway. Bok could see as many butterflies and birds as flowers, too. He could putter in these gardens for days, putting his knowledge of Folk Magic to use.

But he came here on a different type of business. Bok approached the gate and straightened his loose-fitting shirt, then handed his official summons to the two Royal Guardians standing watch.

The woman and man served in the Royal Guard—Imarina's small military force that guarded the palace as well as the Royal Family when they ventured out of the castle. They were distinguished by their dark blue, red-trimmed coats and hats.

The male Guardian shook his head and handed the summons back to Bok. "No; this won't work. Turn around and go back."

"B-but this summons says I am to be here today. And it is signed by none other than the Princess herself!" *Just as I feared. Because I am Serving Class, they assume I'm lying.*

The second guard rolled her eyes. "Sure, she did. You are—what? The new candidate for Emissary of Commerce?"

"What exactly is your business with the Princess?" The first guard took an aggressive step toward Bok.

"I... I don't know!" Bok's heartrate raced. His pulse throbbed in his neck. "I received this summons, but I have no idea what this is all about."

"Come with me to Commander Coregan's office while we sort all this out. We can't have a strange man out here looking for Her Majesty." Both guards grabbed Bok's arms. The energy drained out of his body. He dared not resist two armed officers of the Royal Palace if he had any hopes of seeing his family again.

"B-but I didn't do anything wrong. I just reported here, as I was commanded to do!" Bok's breathing sped up. *They aren't listening! To them, I'm a peasant, not a person.* In Imarina, one's parentage determined social status for life.

It didn't matter how much the Omat family's neighbors respected them—they would always be Serving Class.

The guards jerked Bok away from the gate. But before they could take two steps into palace property, a voice behind Bok froze them in place.

"He's telling the truth, Corporal."

"Lord Amorinil!" The Royal Guards bowed, then snapped to attention. Bok turned to face a tall, brightly smiling man his own age.

Lord Amorinil was slender to the point of skinny and a head taller than Bok. A longbow and quiver of arrows hung casually over the man's shoulder and his curly black hair drooped low past his shoulders.

Bok recognized the name—the Amorinil Mercantile Company was Imarina's largest trading company. Their ships and caravans traveled all over the known world sending goods abroad and bringing treasures back home. Bok had heard it said that, save for the Royal Family, the Amorinil clan was the wealthiest family in the nation. Even if Bok hadn't known the name by reputation, the young man's bright blue silk shirt and eel skin boots marked him as a man of the Noble Class.

Avantil waved off the Guardian and continued to smile. "No worries. We appreciate your diligence. But the Princess did summon this man. And for good reason."

He clapped the shorter Bok on the shoulder. "I bet you could use a square meal and a cold pint after your journey!" That was the best offer Bok had heard since he arrived in the city. Having finished the last of his mother's griddle bread at breakfast, he feared he would have to spend a few of his precious coppers on a meal.

Bok couldn't meet the Noble's eyes but returned his smile. "That sounds wonderful, sir. But first, I must tend to my horse. Is there somewhere nearby I can stable her?"

Avantil waved over one of the numerous palace attendants roaming the grounds inside the palace gates. "You—young lady. I would appreciate you taking my friend's horse to the visitors' stables. She's tired from a long trip, so make sure she gets a good brushing and an extra treat along with her dinner!" He then pressed something into the palm of the young woman's hand.

"Oh, I will, sir! And sir?" She looked at Bok. "Please let any of us know when you need your horse and it will be our pleasure to retrieve her for you."

"Um, okay... thanks." *Sir? Our pleasure to retrieve her? This must be the treatment life affords those born into the Noble Class.* Normally, Bok would have made it clear to the attendant that, like her, he was just a member of the Serving Class, not a Lord like Avantil. But given how tired he was—and how exhausted he knew Beki to be—he thought it best to just remain silent. His horse could use some extra kindness, and so could he.

As the woman gently coaxed Beki by the reins down a long, brick-paved path, she flipped the object Avantil had palmed her into the air. *A silver! Avantil's tip is more money than we could scrape together for this once-in-his-life journey.*

A blush rose to Bok's face, and he bowed his head. "Th-thank you, Lord Avantil! I... I don't know how you know of me or my intentions here, but I appreciate your help."

"First of all, it's just Avantil. I grew bored with formalities long ago, as my exasperated parents will tell you. I heard you were coming because I'm going to be in the same briefing tomorrow. Goodness knows, I have plenty of free time on my hands, so I thought I'd come greet you in person."

Avantil lifted a lone finger in the air and grinned. "Oh, and because I promised my girlfriend I'd get you settled. What Princess Isabella wants, she gets."

Bok's jaw fell open. "Um, I see."

His girlfriend is Princess Isabella herself? Bok searched his brain for the right way to respond and came up with nothing.

Thankfully, Avantil filled in the awkward gap. "Have you spent much time in our grand city of Ithenel?"

"Well, uh, actually... this is my first visit." Bok looked down at his scuffed work boots. *At any moment, he will realize I am a simpleton from Soleh Valley and concoct a polite yet convenient excuse as to why his attention is suddenly needed elsewhere.*

But Avantil just threw his arms in the air. "Well, that's great! It means I get to share all my stories. Everyone else in Ithenel has listened to me tell those tales a thousand times and they are sick of them. But now, you, Bok Omat, get the pleasure of hearing them for the first time!"

He put his arm around Bok's shoulder and gestured toward the grand, four-story marble structure in front of them.

"The Royal Palace is the official residence of King Isbiano and Princess Isabella. But it also serves as the practical center of the Imarinan government. You'll get to meet the Emissaries tomorrow. Every one of them is an insufferable gasbag—probably why the rest of the country thinks we're all like that in the Noble Class! But don't let them intimidate you, Bok—they are all bluster and little brain."

Avantil stuck his index finger in the air. "There is one particular Emissary that you need to watch out for. Emissary Loronian leads the House of Magic, and she is as savvy as the rest are foolish. As you probably know, the House of Magic governs the practice of High Magic in Imarina. That gives them tremendous power, and Loronian isn't afraid to remind the Royal Council of it."

He cocked his head to the side as Bok listened. "Don't get me wrong—she's a loyal subject of the Crown. But she's got a way of getting her way—and she's blunt about doing it."

As they walked, Avantil continued his impromptu tour of the Royal Palace's facilities. The palace had numerous entryways beyond the main entrance used for ceremonial affairs—twin mahogany doors at the top of a grand white marble staircase. Several side doors seemed to constantly open and close to allow a veritable army of attendants, advisors and nobility to move to and from the palace. *It's like an ant hill where the ants wear nicely tailored clothing.*

Avantil took Bok through one of these side doors, then down a hall and through two swinging doors into a bustling dining room. Tables of various sizes filled the hardwood floor—four large rectangular tables for up to eight were in the center, with four square ones for four on each side. Unlike the lone tavern in Soleh Valley, the tables were stained and varnished, and patrons sat in matching chairs, not on rough-hewn benches. Most of the tables were in use by women and men wearing tailored clothes of fine materials—the type of clothing members of the Noble Class wore when conducting official business. Many patrons came with leather satchels stuffed with papers and books Servants half-sprinted through the double doors in the back of the hall to keep their plates and cups full.

"This isn't the main dining hall, but it's quieter and the servants are friendly," Avantil explained, almost apologetically. Two dining hall attendants scrambled from their posts to seat Avantil and his companion at a side table by the room's large panel window. A woman whom Bok assumed was the dining hall's manager, given the deference shown her by the other staff members, walked over as soon as she spotted Avantil.

"Lord Amorinil! Always a pleasure!" She clapped her hands, which brought her staff members running to her side. "Please seat our guests anywhere they like."

"Thank you. Anywhere will be fine—you know I'm not picky. Oh, and we'll have the usual, please!"

Within moments, a roasted chicken and bowls of steaming vegetables appeared on the table, along with a chilled carafe and two pewter flagons engraved with the Inishari family crest—a raven under a capital "I". Avantil thanked each of them and, as he had done earlier at the guard post, slipped each of the attendants a silver with an inconspicuous handshake.

"Drink up!" Avantil poured the amber drink into Bok's flagon. "They'll bring out another pitcher if we finish this one."

Bok sniffed, then sipped, the drink. The sweet aroma and flavor of honey tickled his nose and tongue.

"It's mead, my friend. Made with honey from the King's apiary. I come to this spot every day and they know what I like here." Bok understood why the Noble Class liked this drink so much. He took a deeper swig and savored its sweet taste.

Meanwhile, Avantil gnawed ravenously on a chicken leg. "So—you are from Soleh Valley. I've been through there a few times. Beautiful country. Do your people farm?

"Yes... no, well, kind of." Somehow, Bok couldn't help stumbling on on his words. "I mean, my sister and father are the community blacksmiths. That's what they do. But we live on a small farm that my mother runs. Only as much land as... as much as we're allowed to own." *There it is—the unspoken truth said out loud. I am Serving Class.* Bok exhaled and studied Avantil's face for a reaction.

But the young Noble appeared more interested in the dinner conversation than in any class differences. "And you're a healer? How did you get into that?"

Bok tilted his head back against the padded seat. "It wasn't a grand design. Weni Kon, my mentor, served as community healer all throughout my childhood. I did well in school and when I finished, she came to me and asked if I wanted to apprentice under her. I realized my options were to be a healer, get a job farming someone else's land, or be the third-best blacksmith in my own house. So it wasn't a tough choice." Avantil chuckled at that line through a mouthful of bread.

Bok continued, feeling relaxed enough to cut a small piece of bread for himself. The aroma made his mouth water. "So far, it's been going well—Folk Magic just makes sense to me. Weni said she knew I had 'the Acumen' for Folk Magic, and that's why she picked me to be her student. I'm glad she did."

"And I'm glad, too, by the Exalted One. Because we need your skills."

Bok bit the inside of his cheek. "What do you mean?" *Ithenel is the center of High Magic in the kingdom, the home of the vaunted House of Magic. Surely those trained sorcerers are better equipped to handle any problem than a country healer with six months of experience.*

Avantil looked around the tavern, then leaned across the table to whisper. "Have you ever heard of whole fields of crops just... withering into dust? In seconds?"

Bok rested his chin on his hand. "Like a flash fire? Such things do happen in the summer. A dry spell followed by an ill-placed lightning strike, and a whole farm goes up in flames."

"Like that. Except there wasn't any lightning—it was a clear night." Avantil helped himself to a refill of mead. "Just whoosh! A farm was there and then it wasn't. The trees, the house—even the family. It's all ash now."

Bok froze when he heard this. Osoh Creek was a farming community, just like the one he called home. *If this could happen there, it also could happen in Soleh Valley. My parents, Yata, and Noji all are in danger if something like this was happening!*

Seeing the faraway look in Bok's face, Avantil met Bok's eyes. "I didn't believe when I first heard about it a few days ago, either. I'm still not sure I do. All I know is a whole village packed up and came here from Osoh Creek asking their King for protection. I don't know what they saw. But it frightened them to the core."

Nothing Bok had ever seen in a lifetime of living in a farming community could cause such a calamity. He also wondered what he could do to help. Folk Magic was used by Serving Class healers to heal, cure, and protect. It could not be used as a weapon. On the other hand, High Magic—the type which only could be employed by Nobles born with the Acumen to use it—contained the power to create or destroy. This business sounded like High Magic to Bok, not anything he could counter. And surely there were Folk Magic healers here in Ithenel, if that's what the Princess needed.

"So why did she ask for me?"

Avantil shook his head. "I do not know. But she asked for you by name—I was there when she dictated the summons. Believe me, Isabella chose you for a reason."

Bok rubbed the dark beard on his chin. "I don't know what I can do. But whatever you and your... the Princess need, I am happy to help."

"I'm glad to hear that—and I know she will be, too," Avantil's familiar smile returned, and he refilled Bok's flagon. "Enough unpleasantry. We will sort this mess out tomorrow in Royal Council Chambers. Let's get back to you—tell me, is there a young lady or gentleman back in

Soleh Valley, sitting on their door stoop waiting for your return?"

Bok snorted. "Ha! You sound like my mother! She's been trying to marry me off since I became a healer." Avanti's grim story of the refugees and the strange incident in Naseem still ran through his mind, but as his new friend said, there was little they could do before the morning.

"No—I suppose I haven't met the right person yet. Besides, any woman I bring home must meet my sister Yata's approval, and I wouldn't wish that on anyone's daughter."

Avantil draped his arm over the back of his own seat, grinning like a mischievous child. "This Yata? She's tough, I take it?"

"She swings a hammer to feed her family, so yes, I'd say she's tough!" Mead spewed from Avantil's mouth at Bok's colorful description of his sister. "She thrashed me plenty when we were children. Believe me. I'm more suited to healing sick crops or sick children. Yata can handle the fighting for the Omat clan."

Still laughing, Avantil wiped his mouth with a linen napkin. "Ha! Sounds like some of the women I've known. Except thank the Exalted One they didn't own a hammer, or they probably would have swung it at my head!"

"Well, I doubt you have to worry about that with the Princess." *I hope I'm not overstepping my place. But*

Avantil doesn't mind talking about his romance with our Queen-in-waiting.

"No, not Isabella. I can't wait for you to meet her tomorrow, Bok." Now, it was Avantil's turn to wear a faraway look. "She's incredible, as you'll see. Isabella is scheduled to become queen in five years—and she has such plans for Imarina!"

Bok fidgeted with his silverware—made of actual silver, not like the iron versions his sister and father crafted back at home. "I'm sure she is amazing." *I just hope her vaunted reputation for kindness is deserved, too.*

"The stories do not tell the half of it, Bok! This isn't common knowledge, but Isabella has the Acumen for High Magic. She is being trained as a sorcerer by a private tutor, outside of the House of Magic."

"The Princess is a sorcerer?" Bok looked around the upscale tavern, realizing that despite being the poorest person in the room, he now was the member of a privileged club. "But she certainly is of Noble blood, and I've always heard talk of her intellect. I suppose she is as incredible as you say."

Avantil tossed the napkin down on the table. "Oh, do not misunderstand—Isabella does not make things easy for me! The first time she met my family, she visited our estate. Our chef worked all day preparing the finest roast you've ever tasted. We sit down and look to Isabella... who quietly informs me that she doesn't eat meat!"

"At all?" Around the Omat table, and those of his neighbors, meat was a once-per-week treat. He and Yata practically wrestled over chicken legs when they were children.

"At all. Now, she was so embarrassed, thinking she had ruined the meal. But my parents blamed me! They thought I had insulted the Royal Family. I suppose I should have noticed she never ate meat—but I thought she just fancied fruit and bread!" He tapped a nearly empty ceramic serving bowl. "Speaking of which, how are the palace's offerings?"

"To be honest? Nothing short of fantastic!" That wasn't a polite lie. Bok had tasted flavors he never knew existed in his palate. Had he not been so nervous at first, he probably would've eaten nearly as much as Avantil.

"Glad to hear it!" The Noble set his empty cup down and gestured to the rear of the establishment. "Excuse me for a second—I'll be right back."

As soon as Avantil walked into the privy at the back of the tavern, a middle-aged woman on the serving staff tiptoed over to Bok's seat.

"How'd you do it? I mean, I'm glad you did—but how?" she half-whispered, half-giggled.

"Wha—what do you mean? I'm here with—"

"Don't worry—you're fine. It's not like we ask you for your parents' names before we let you eat here, and besides, you're here with Lord Amorinil. But you're one of us, right?"

Bok understood. Imarina's laws didn't prohibit the Serving Class from fancy establishments like this tavern. But no one in his societal strata had the coins to dine in a place as fine as this.

"I... I honestly don't know," he said. "I've been asked to be here and Avantil—Lord Amorinil—is my host. I wish I could explain."

"Darling, enjoy it as much as you can for as long as it lasts!" The attendant left Bok to return to his meal and his thoughts.

The rest of the meal passed with easy laughter and leisurely conversation. After Avantil took his third helping, Bok couldn't resist—he reached for a second piece of chicken, perfectly seasoned with rosemary and salt.

"Need anything else, Bok? If so, I'll get someone to bring it over."

"Oh, no thank you. I don't want to be sick before by first Royal Council meeting!" He stretched his arms back, satiated by the rich food. Avantil waved at an older gentleman in a tailored robe who was leaving the tavern. Bok assumed the man, who returned Avantil's greeting, was a Noble of some sort.

"Does your family live here at the palace, Avantil? You sure seem to know everything about it and everyone in it."

"Ha! No, our family has a home just across the other side of the wall," Avantil replied between bites of chicken. "But I spend plenty of time here and know my way around."

"My parents, they aren't in Ithenel much these days." The lanky young man stared out the window into the courtyard. "They left six weeks ago for a voyage around the Balan Cape. In another month or so, their flagship, along with five other Amorinil Mercantile Company vessels, will load a shipment of sugar, rugs, spices—all the things the Noble Class here in Imarina will pay in gold to have. I won't see them again before summer's end."

Bok rolled his eyes. "I'm surprised your parents didn't make you go with them. Even now, at my age. I half expected mine to stow themselves in my saddlebags."

Avantil got quiet for the first time since the two men sat down. "Actually Bok... my older sister and brother went. But I... wasn't invited. I'm never asked to go on these trips, not since I was 14 summers."

He took a sip from his mead flagon and got quiet for a moment before he continued, "I probably wouldn't want to go, knowing it would mean leaving the palace... but it would be nice if they asked."

Avantil set his glass down and resumed smiling. This time, though, Bok realized his expression, at least in part, was a mask.

"By the Exalted One, why am I saying this? I'm sorry to make you uncomfortable, Bok. I should be telling all this to the barkeep; at least she gets paid to listen to rich layabouts moan and whine! I shouldn't weigh you down with my personal entanglements."

Bok pointed to his own chest. "Me? The country boy in his one almost decent set of clothes who isn't sure which fork to use? You're worried that you are making me uncomfortable? Believe me, Avantil, you have been far and away the highlight of the strangest day I have ever lived!"

"Ha! I knew I liked you, Bok Omat!" Avantil laughed. "You aren't looking to gain anything from me, be it money or access to the crown. Oh, and you laugh at my jokes!"

Avantil waved over one of the serving staff. "Excuse me, miss? What's for dessert tonight?"

CHAPTER 4

B OK SPENT THAT NIGHT in a guest room the size of his parents' home. He almost was afraid to sit on the four poster bed, with its smooth cotton sheets and down pillows aligned in a symmetrical formation.

After gingerly stretching across the brass-framed bed, he fully extended his legs—something he hadn't been able to do in his own mattress since he was nine. *How can a mattress be so soft to the touch yet so firm under my full weight?*

But rather than sleep, he stared at the ceiling and tried—with limited success—to sort the many thoughts competing for space in his brain. He'd had a wonderful time with Avantil, and he was convinced the young Noble's friendliness was genuine. But his mind returned to the incident in Osoh Creek. Maybe the wise old women and men of the Royal Council would offer an explanation and dismiss Bok to return to Soleh Valley.

But could it be something else? Something sinister that no one had an answer for, but that was only going to grow worse?

Surely, Mother, Father, Yata, and little Noji are safe at home. I wish I could know for certain.

This should have been the best night's sleep of his life. But Bok wrestled with his pillow, aware that sleep would come hard in the palace.

The next morning, Bok arrived in the Royal Council Chambers early. He squirmed on the cushioned marble bench, trying without success to get comfortable. Twenty rows of the ornate benches formed concentric circles in front of a dais at the far end of the room. Nine seats behind heavy oak benches stood on the dais, the middle seat being taller than the others. Portraits of Imarina's past monarchs lined the walls on either side of the seats.

Bok held his arms close to his chest, as if he could hide his simple, homespun clothes from the few well-dressed Nobles scattered in the seats around him. Their perfumes and colognes mingled in his nose with smoke from the oil lamps ringing the council chambers.

The only other Serving Class people in the room were a handful of palace attendants, who tried to remain invisible as they prepared the chambers for the meeting. Bok would have felt more comfortable among them as they did their work than he would sitting among Nobles.

A now-familiar voice behind his shoulder offered a lifeline. "You made it, Bok! In fact, you even beat me here." Avantil sat down beside him in the back row and offered a quick handshake. "I know this is your first Royal Council meeting. I'll explain anything you need to know, from the pomp to the players."

Seven women and men in formal robes soon filed into the chambers. Each carried hard-earned wrinkles under their eyes and various degrees of graying or balding hairlines. Bok correctly figured them to be the members of the Royal Council. They took their seats on the dais, a thick purple curtain behind them.

At precisely the appointed hour, four people wearing light gray jackets over finely tailored outfits and matching flat cloth caps strode through the front doors of the chambers. Bok recognized their uniforms as emblems of the House of Magic. At the head of the entourage was a short, stubby woman with white hair and no shortage of creases in her face. The youngest of the sorcerers, a young blond-haired man with a slight beard—not quite as tall as Avantil and considerably more filled out—threw his hat and gloves into Bok's lap as he walked by.

"Take care of this, won't you?" The man didn't make eye contact with Bok and kept moving.

"B-but I don't..." Bok's protests trailed off as the man continued walking to the front of the room. Three of the four sorcerers took seats at a grand table in front of the center of the dais, between the other Emissaries' seats and the benches for the audience. The older woman—obviously the group's leader—took the one of the two final vacant seats on the dais, leaving only the middle seat open.

One of the Guardians retrieved the hat and gloves. Avantil covered a laugh with his hand.

"C'mon—let's move up to the front." Avantil gestured toward the open row of benches directly behind the petitioner's table. "You'll want to be closer to the discussion, particularly when you are introduced." Bok's hands trembled at the thought.

Other observers, most of whom carried bundles of papers or thick leather-bound books, moved to the benches, leaving the front row open. By their plain dress and apparent familiarity with the procedural protocol, Bok guessed they were various royal bureaucrats, officials at the various Houses, records-keepers, and other agents of the Crown. Such staff members likely came from the Landowning Class—the middle strata between the Noble and Serving Class. People in the Landowning Class had more legal rights than those in Bok's class, but not as many as those in the highest tier. A few well-dressed employees may have been young Nobles learning their way in the Royal Court.

Bok followed Avantil onto the empty bench at the front of the room. They took seats immediately behind where the three male sorcerers sat a table. The bearded, blond young man in their group turned and glared at Bok with flinty blue eyes. "The hired help doesn't know its place these days," he muttered in a voice just loud enough for Bok to hear.

Avantil leaned over. "I guess you've encountered Kotarian. Consider this a welcoming gift. Everyone in Ithenel has a story about him. I certainly have a few."

"Kotarian? Is he a sorcerer?" Bok furrowed his brow. "He doesn't look much older than me."

"Yes, he's an acolyte, the final step before becoming a full member of the House of Magic. They're grooming him for a leadership role, which explains his presence here today. Lucky us who must deal with him." Avantil's eyes rolled to the ceiling. "They call him the 'House's Shining Light.' Or maybe that's just the story he tells. Regardless, Kotarian certainly believes it to be true."

He pointed to the white-haired sorcerer sitting on the dais. "Up there, that's Emissary Loronian. As the leader of the House of Magic, she serves on the Royal Council." Bok nodded, remembering the previous night's conversation, where Avantil had described Loronian as crafty but ultimately loyal.

Avantil then pointed to a square-jawed, gray-templed man at the petitioner's table. "That's Karagian." The man's tapping foot patted a quick drumbeat into the red rug covering the white marble floor.

"Karagian is Loronian's Chancellor, or second-in-command, and the person likely to take over leadership of the House of Magic one day. He's even more hard-nosed than Loronian. He protests every time the King asks the House to do anything. To listen to him, Imarina revolves around Sonorian Square." Avantil put his hand up to cover his whisper. "I'm also pretty sure he wears pads under his jacket and lifts in his boots!"

Bok couldn't help but smile. "So how are they allowed such... insubordination? Don't they have to do what the Crown commands?" That was the way the world worked in Soleh Valley. The Serving Class may not like it, but the Noble Class made the decisions. And the King ruled the Noble Class.

Avantil nodded. "Oh, sure—but it isn't quite so simple. Imarina's national defense is based on the power of High Magic. Any invading army is going to pay a heavy price before our Royal Guardians even get their boots muddy, thanks to Imarinan sorcery. The House of Magic is the reason Imarina has been at peace for more than 300 years.

"But with that kind of power comes haughtiness. The House of Magic needs to believe every good idea is one they thought up. Thankfully, King Isbiano is an expert in that dance."

Avantil pointed to the fourth gray-jacketed sorcerer who sat on the same bench as Bok and Avantil behind Kotarian and Karagian. The balding, bespeckled man fumbled with a stack of papers while the other two sorcerers ignored him and chatted amongst themselves.

"Anyway, our final sorcerer is Salandrian. He's the Dean of the House of Magic, meaning he oversees the House's vast repository of information. He's usually holed up in his study at the top of the tower doing who-knows-what type of research. Every so often, they dust him off and bring him before the Royal Council whenever there's a technical question on magic. The man knows his spells, but he couldn't care less about politics or power struggles. Leave him alone with his scrolls and books and he's as content as a fly on honey."

As with Loronian and Karagian, gold braids and medals decorated Salandrian's jacket, indicating his position within the House of Magic. Kotarian's jacket was adorned with neither a braid nor a medal, as he was still an acolyte. However, he wore a blue-and-white starburst pin on the breast of his gray tunic.

"That must be his 'House's Shining Light' medal. I bet he bought it at the Great Bazaar!" Avantil chuckled at his own joke, while Bok just nodded.

I still don't know where I fit in with these high-ranking officials and reality-shaping sorcerers. The only magic I know is Folk Magic—nothing compared to the vast arcane knowledge assembled at that table.

At least Bok knew this no longer could be a prank. People in positions this weighty would only gather for something of actual importance to the kingdom.

A thickly muscled Royal Guardian opened the door in the back of the room and held it open. The assembled crowd stood up. Bok did the same.

The most important woman in Imarina—Princess Isabella Inishari—entered the Royal Council Chambers. Bok had no way of knowing it, but she soon would become the most important person in his life, too.

CHAPTER 5

EVERYONE IN THE ROOM stood at attention as Isabella walked down the center aisle to the front of the room, neither hurrying nor pausing. Although barely five feet tall and petite in build, Isabella controlled the Council Chambers from the moment she entered. Clad in a sleek purple gown, she smiled at those assembled and offered a surreptitious wave to Avantil as she walked by.

Bok's pulse leaped through his chest the moment she passed them. She walked close enough for him to hear the click of her heels against the polished stone floor.

A peasant boy from Soleh Valley granted an audience with the Princess? This cannot be real.

She motioned for everyone to be seated when she arrived at the front of the room, then walked around the dais greeting each member of the Royal Council. The massive Royal Guardian followed her when she entered the room and always stood just feet from her, yet spoke to no one, his eyes constantly watching the room.

Before taking her seat at the center of the Royal Council, Isabella spoke briefly with an older man who had entered the room with her and who walked behind her down the Chambers' aisle. The man, who wore a red jacket in the same style as the ones worn by the House of Magic, carried a tall stack of notes and stood behind the dais.

"That's Tovano—Isabella's magic tutor," Avantil whispered.

Isabella's long, curly dark brown hair spilled over her silver tiara and onto her face. Pushing it aside, she began the meeting: "Thank you for coming to this emergency session. King Isbiano asked me to lead this meeting, which well could be critical to our nation's security."

Bok waited on every precisely pronounced word spoken by the young woman in the center of the dais. *I couldn't even speak before such a crowd. But the Princess is no older than I am, yet she leads this meeting as if she's done this for 30 summers.*

The Princess' dark eyes moved from side to side across the room. "A group of terrified citizens from the village of Osoh Creek, near the city of Naseem, has brought a report that I take seriously. Here is what they said:

"One week ago, a mysterious blight struck a farm in the village, which is less than a mile from our border with the Mosork Empire. An entire acre of farmland was reduced to black ash. Far worse, four of our citizens—Kam and Wot Yult and their young children, Tash and Von—were killed."

"So someone burned their property to the ground?" a Royal Council member asked.

The Princess shook her head. "No, Emissary—there were no signs of fire. More like... they disintegrated. And the affected area was a perfectly square tract of land—not the random destruction one would see in a blaze." Frantic whispering broke out around the room. Isabella restored silence by raising her hand.

"I immediately reached out to Emissary Loronian and have been in contact with the House of Magic ever since." She looked to Loronian, who returned a satisfied nod. *Smart; she made sure to acknowledge them.*

Loronian rose. "As you are aware, Your Majesty, I've asked Dean Salandrian to research any spells that could create such an effect. Salandrian...?" The man on the bench beside Bok shuffled a handful of papers as he stood.

"Let's see... my research hasn't uncovered any magics that, um, could cause such an effect." The man looked at one of his notes, then another. "Fire generation spells are common, of course, but as you said, um, there is no indication fire was used in Osoh Creek—either eldritch or natural."

Loronian nodded her satisfaction with this answer. "You see, Your Majesty—while this unfortunate incident may appear at first glance to be magical in origin, we believe it is the result of natural phenomena."

Tovano stepped forward from his spot behind Isabella. He was balding and slightly stooped, with a thin, uneven brown-and-white beard. "What about primitive magics?" He scratched his patchy chin. "From the time before the House was established and magic codified? There are stories that the old sorcerers had spells of great destructive force."

Loronian frowned. "Those are folk tales meant to frighten peasant children, Tovano. As you well know."

"But didn't Queen Imbiria form the House of Magic centuries ago largely to regulate such dangerous spells?" Isabella tilted her head to the side as she faced the sorcerers.

"Um, yes... er, no." Salandrian dropped a stack of papers. "You are correct that is why your ancestor formed the House... Your Majesty, that is."

Loronian froze the disheveled sorcerer with a glare. "Be that as it may, Your Majesty, our archives contain no records of any such spell. I highly doubt ancient spellcasters could do what the House of Magic cannot."

Isabella rapped her knuckles against ornately carved arm of her chair. "Very well then. If we do not know what caused this destruction, we at least should consider who."

This question set off a firestorm of arguing amongst the Royal Council. The Emissary of Security felt certain that Imarina's ancient enemies, the Mosork Empire, were responsible and pounded her fists into the table to make her point. The Emissary of Commerce was just as animated in noting he spent years establishing trade routes with the Mosorks and any military action would jeopardize that diplomatic progress.

"Enough!" The Princess stood and raised her hand, and the bickering stopped. "Esteemed Emissaries, please—let us not lose sight of our purpose."

She sat down once she had the group's attention. "We do not know who did this—or why. The kingdom has been at peace for more than 300 years. We cannot declare war on the Mosork Empire over guesswork and flimsy evidence."

"Agreed, Your Majesty," Loronian said. "The House of Magic believes any aggressive action would be premature, at least until we ascertain the culprits responsible… if they are any such culprits."

"What do you mean, Emissary Loronian?" The tone in her voice made the back of Bok's neck quiver.

"What I mean, Your Majesty, is that this assembly is placing great stock in the far-fetched tales of terrified, superstitious farmers. It could be that some Serving Class field hand got drunk, set fire to his own land, then passed out from the smoke and was consumed by the blaze. Yes, no one saw any fire—but perhaps they simply weren't looking."

Isabella's brown eyes narrowed; Bok even saw her fist clench, ever so slightly. "Whether you believe these people or not is your prerogative. But Emissary—and anyone else who doubts my resolve, I spoke with them personally. I heard the terror in their voices, the grief at losing their beloved friends and neighbors. They came to Ithenel to warn us—but also to petition their leaders for help. If this is some type of hoax, these poor people are no party to it."

Avantil nudged Bok with his elbow. The blacksmith's boy nodded. *Yes. I see why you called her incredible. Princess Isabella is every bit as capable as she is beautiful. Which is saying a lot.*

Isabella stood again and looked out over the room. "That is why I will lead an expedition to Osoh Creek to investigate this tragedy—and to help the people affected. A large force would arouse the Mosorks if they are not responsible and tip them off to our concerns if they are. So, a small task force, rather than a large army, is preferable for this mission."

"Accompanying me will be my personal tutor, Tovano." She gestured to the older man behind her. He smiled and waved to the audience in an informal way Bok could not imagine Loronian, Karagian, or Kotarian ever doing. The latter two sorcerers shook their heads and muttered amongst themselves in obvious disapproval.

Isabella raised her eyebrows to them. "Chancellor Karagian and… um, Kotarian, I believe it is?… I understand this mission requires the House of Magic's trusted counsel."

Avantil grinned. "Heh! She knew that blowhard's name! She wanted to remind them of who is in charge."

Isabella continued. "I propose that our group include a representative of the House to serve as our primary consultant on all things High Magic. Tovano will be there to help me continue my studies, and who knows? Perhaps a second set of well-trained eyes may be of value. Emissary Loronian, do you have a nominee?"

"Kotarian will represent the House." Loronian called the young sorcerer up to the dais. "He is our brightest, most accomplished acolyte."

"I will do my best, Emissary... and Your Majesty." Kotarian bowed to the Princess.

Karagian sat back with his arms crossed. "You will do better than that—you are representing the House. Success is an expectation; failure is not an option."

"Very well then. Welcome, Kotarian; I am sure your skills will prove useful on this expedition." Isabella motioned to one of the Royal Guardians at the back of the room—the same older gentleman who had helped Bok when Kotarian had assumed Bok was an attendant. The man strode purposefully to the front of the dais, where he bowed to Isabella.

Isabella took him by the crook of the arm and nudged him onto the dais. "Commander Coregan will coordinate our security. The Commander has dedicated more than 30 summers as a member and now leader of the Royal Guard. We could be in no safer hands."

Like all Imarinian schoolchildren, Bok had learned the Royal Guard's creed—"Loyalty above all." This man seemed to be the embodiment of those principles.

Isabella turned to the back of the dais. "Coregan will be joined by my personal Royal Guardian, Lieutenant Wingate, whom I trust with my life." The Guardian who had been at Isabella's side throughout the meeting bowed to the Princess, then stepped back and resumed his silent duties. Wingate was extraordinarily large—several inches taller than Avantil even. The broad shouldered man's dark brown arms were as large around as many men's thighs, and his own legs were equally muscular.

"Also accompanying us will be Lord Avantil Amorinil. For generations, his family has owned a vast shipping and trading empire. His knowledge of local customs will be valuable assets in our journey." Avantil jumped up off the bench and took his place on the dais, giving the crowd a quick wave while doing so.

"The final member of our party is a newcomer to the palace, but I believe he will prove to be a vital ally in our cause. Bok, could you please stand?" Isabella pointed to the startled peasant.

Bok folded his arms at his waist and stood. He hoped his legs didn't visibly shake, although they twitched under his pants leg.

Should I smile? Or wave? Say something?

Instead, he stood mute as a tree stump. Heat rushed to his cheeks.

"I give you Bok Omat, healer of Soleh Valley, an agricultural community south of Ithenel. I personally chose him to join our team." *Did I imagine it, or did Isabella emphasize the word "personally"?* If Bok's mind played tricks, the rest of the audience must've imagined the same thing. He expected snickers at his simple clothes and awkward demeanor, but no one muttered a syllable.

"Bok is thoroughly versed in Folk Magic and given the nature of this attack, we could need that perspective.

Thank you for coming, and for joining us on this important mission. You may be seated."

Bok nodded in acceptance of the invitation—he feared that if he stood much longer, his nervous legs would collapse underneath him, as if he was a newborn calf.

He also realized he would not be back home in Soleh Valley in a matter of days. Instead, he would be part of an official royal mission to the nation's northern border, where he would investigate an unknown yet highly dangerous situation of concern to Imarina's most powerful leaders.

Quite suddenly, Bok's life had become a great deal more complicated.

But before he could even begin to sort through the repercussions of Isabella's announcement, Karagian pointed to him. "Folk Magic? Is this necessary, Your Majesty? No offense to this... person, but do we need a country healer in a royal delegation?"

"I say we do. Any additional questions, Chancellor?" Isabella's curt response left no room for debate or misunderstanding. Karagian let the matter drop, something Bok doubted he did very often.

The Princess spoke for a few more minutes, mostly about the logistics of the upcoming journey, but Bok heard little of it. He still couldn't believe that he, of all people, had been picked for such an important mission. *I wish I could tell my family. But I'll be on the road to Osoh Creek by the time I could send word home.*

The meeting soon adjourned, and everyone stood as Isabella, followed by Wingate and Tovano, exited through a side door. The House of Magic contingent then got up and left as a group, walking past Bok and Avantil on their way out. Kotarian lingered behind his superiors to speak with his new travel companions.

"Well, Lord Amorinil, I'm delighted that you will be joining us." Kotarian snickered. "Tell me now—how does being the Princess's concubine qualify you for a paranormal inquiry?"

The young sorcerer then stuck a thumb in Bok's direction. "At least the peasant might be good for something—preparing meals, laundering clothes, excavating latrines. But you? A dilettante who spends his family's money? The lone function you serve is... well, I suppose only the Princess can attest to that. Or perhaps she finds you lacking in that regard, too."

Avantil jumped to his feet and leaned in close to Kotarian's smirking face. "You'll watch your tongue, jackal. Or you might find yourself picking it up off the floor!" He practically spat the words at the young sorcerer, who waggled his fingers in mock fear.

Bok grabbed his new friend and struggled to pull him back. Avantil's thin arms felt like hammered iron under his loose-fitting crimson-and-gold shirt.

"Come on, Avantil. Pay him no mind. He's trying to get you angry in front of the Royal Council—and the Princess," Bok said. "Let it pass."

Avantil stepped back. "Correct, my friend. This gray-coated worm wouldn't have the heart for a real fight. But someday, he might find himself in one."

Kotarian laughed as he strutted away. Bok watched the arrogant sorcerer for a moment, then turned back to Avantil. The redness in his friend's pale face dissipated as quickly as it surfaced, and the two men sat again in the now-empty gallery.

"I am sorry that happened, Avantil. I wish I could've done something more."

"No, my friend—you were right. Kotarian and I have never gotten along. He wanted to goad me into doing something impulsive to 'prove' to Isabella that I am too immature to be trusted on this mission. Maybe he's right!"

Avantil looked over Bok's shoulder and smiled. "Enough unpleasantness. There's someone who wants to meet you. Isabella! I've got Bok here!"

She turned. For a second, her eyes locked with Bok's. He forced himself to look down, lest his heart stop beating.

CHAPTER 6

"Um, maybe now isn't a good time, Avantil. I mean, I'm sure she's in the middle of something..." But Isabella excused herself from a conversation with the Emissary of Agriculture and came to the bench where Bok and Avantil sat.

Bok quickly rose to his feet and stood at attention as she approached. He smoothed his rough cotton shirt with his shaking hand.

She took a spot on the bench beside Avantil. "Please sit, Bok! You are not a member of the Royal Guard, after all!"

"I-I'm sorry, your Majesty. I..."

Isabella smiled, revealing perfectly straight, gleaming white teeth. "All of this pageantry and formality must seem bizarre and unnecessary. There are times I feel that way as well. Anyway, it is a pleasure to meet you, and I am thankful you agreed to join our group."

Isabella extended her hand to Bok without hesitation. The five identical gold hoops around her wrist jangled as she did. He responded with a handshake so limp that Yata surely would have punched his shoulder had she been present. He winced when his rough palms, calloused from years of work in his family's blacksmith's shop, touched Isabella's soft, manicured hand.

"I also apologize for the vague nature of my summons. But as you heard, it is a matter of national security that needed to be kept secret until today's meeting."

The healer bowed his head, still unable to meet her deep, dark brown eyes. "Ah, p-pleased to meet you, Your Majesty. I, um, am honored to take part in this trip."

Mother told me to "Make Soleh Valley proud." I'm not doing a good job of it.

"No need to be so formal, Bok. After all, we are going to be working together these next few days." She raised her eyebrows. "What do you make of all you heard today?"

Bok tucked his jittery hands in his lap. "Um... I do not know, Your Majesty. I am hardly in a position to—"

Isabella stopped him with a glance. "Bok, you are here because you are needed. This is neither a test nor a trap. I want to know what you thought about what was said. And please be honest." She touched his arm. He desperately hoped she did not feel his skin tingle through his shirt.

"Um, I know the Emissary of Magic disagrees and who am I to dispute what she says? But I believe these people—and nothing in the natural world can explain what they saw. It must be magic—and I suspect it is intentional."

Isabella put her hand to her chin. "Hmm... I suspect the same. But go on. Why would someone do such a thing?"

Bok inhaled deeply. He hadn't had a chance to ponder that. *How would I feel if Soleh Valley was attacked this way?* "If I had to guess, I would say to inflict fear."

"What do you mean?" Isabella pushed up her sleeves, making her bracelets clink together again.

"Crops represent life itself, Your Majesty. Without them, we die. Our families die—everyone in my community knows this. I believe the Yults were just unfortunate to be in the wrong location. This terrible crime was designed to create fear through the destruction of crops. And I suspect they will do it again."

"But what end would such a vicious act serve, Bok?"

He hadn't considered that, either. But again, the answer came to him from his experiences growing up Serving Class farming community. "Working the farms isn't easy, Your Majesty, particularly when you can't even own the land you work. But there is something to knowing your family will eat that day. You described how frightened the people from Osoh Creek were when you spoke with them. Desperate, fearful people will go to great lengths to protect their families. Even defy their King."

At this, Avantil leaned into the conversation. "Surely you cannot mean the Serving Class of Imarina would rebel against King Isbiano! I have traveled these lands extensively and found great affection for the King."

"Oh, absolutely—people in my village love their King and respect the Crown's rule!" Bok quickly added. "I simply mean that when pushed into a desperate situation, any people may respond in ways that don't make sense. I meant no disrespect to the Royal Family."

"And none was taken, Bok." Isabella nodded. "I appreciate your candor."

"Does... Does any of what I said make sense to you?" Bok fidgeted with the cuff of his sleeve.

She propped her chin in her hand. "It makes perfect sense. In fact, your thoughts mirror my own."

"But there is no way of knowing until we get to Osoh Creek, so why worry about it now?" Avantil stood and stretched his back "Enough of this dour talk—let us enjoy this time together before the hard work begins."

Isabella's smile returned. "My favorite merchant is correct—and I am being a neglectful host. Are you ready for the trip? Is there anything you need before we leave in the morning?"

Bok still halfway expected a crowd of Nobles to emerge from hidden doors in the council chambers at any moment. Of course, they would point and laugh at the country healer who dared speak to his better as an equal.

But in their brief time together, he believed in Isabella and Avantil's kindness.

"No, Your Majesty, I'm—" Bok exhaled, somehow finding the nerve to string together a few coherent words. "Actually, I do have one question... why did you pick me?"

She raised her hands and her shoulders. "It is as I told the Royal Council, Bok. Your experience nurturing crops may well prove valuable in halting the Blight."

"No... what I mean is... why me? Surely there are other healers in Imarina more qualified."

Isabella grinned and looked away, as if she was... embarrassed? *Is it possible for a Royal to feel embarrassment?*

"Bok, the truth is... we did not realize you had become Soleh Valley's healer. We reached out to Weni Kon, not realizing she had stepped down."

My presence here is a fluke. And why wouldn't it be? Why would the Princess need a blacksmith's boy from Soleh Valley? Blood rose in Bok's face again, and he looked to the shiny white floor jutting out from the edge of the rug.

Isabella quickly shook her hands. "No, do not misunderstand! After I spoke with Weni, I knew you were the healer we needed. She noted you rode two hours in driving rain to set a boy's broken arm. Slept in a barn for three nights tending to an ailing horse. And that you have never refused a patient who cannot pay." Isabella jabbed a finger toward Bok. "I want *that* person by my side."

Bok said nothing, but his face remained unmoved. She leaned forward so that only Bok could hear. He raised his head to look at Isabella.

"I am 19 summers, Bok—the same as you. This is the first true royal responsibility I have undertaken, and I am terrified that I am not worthy. It is why I wore a long dress today—I did not want the assembly to see my knees trembling!"

That has to be a joke. Her grin indicated it was, and he couldn't help but smile in return. Here he was, joking around with the Princess of Imarina, as if they were just two friends sharing a laugh, and not sovereign and servant.

"But we will succeed despite our fears. You and I both."

"Do you really think so?" Bok whispered.

"I do. I also believe I am a good judge of people. And I have the sense you are capable of so much more than you ever believed possible."

When Isabella says it, I can almost believe it, too.

Avantil placed his hand on her shoulder. "My sweet, I hate to interrupt, but your attention is needed elsewhere..."

Isabella's smile returned. "Here is a little something to cover any supplies you may need for our trip."

She called over an aide, who handed Bok a small purse of silver and gold coins. His eyes grew wide. The purse contained more money than his father and sister would make in a year of blacksmithing.

"Um, thank you, Your Majesty. But I couldn't possibly—"

"Don't worry about it, Bok; it's coming from the Treasury." Avantil slipped his arm around Isabella's waist. "Not like the Princess is spending her own hard-earned money. What is it you do again, anyway?"

"It seems my main responsibility is keeping you out of trouble!" She pushed his hand away. "And what did I tell you, Avantil? Not in public..."

He smiled and stage-whispered, "Then maybe we should go somewhere private."

Rather than maintain a stiff royal decorum, as Bok expected a princess to do, she giggled and raised an eyebrow.

"We will see you in the morning, Bok. Have a good rest of your day!" Isabella took Avantil's hand and Bok could tell he no longer was needed in the Council Chambers. But he left with this thought: He didn't know much about Princess Isabella—but letting her down felt like the most painful thing he could ever do.

The Royal Council Chambers cleared, save for a few servants cleaning up loose papers and sweeping the floors. "Give me one moment," Isabella told Avantil.

She then stepped into the anteroom separated from the dais by the purple curtain. King Isbiano stood there, his forehead creased under his silver crown. His closely trimmed graying goatee framed a frown.

"Isabella, I gave you permission to lead the Council meeting, not the expedition to Osoh Creek!" He bit his lower lip and shook his head. "Change your plans. You could be heading into danger."

Hands on hips, she looked up into her father's eyes. "What type of monarch would I be if I am not willing to take the same risks I ask of my subjects? I have assembled a loyal team, and we will prove ourselves up to the challenge."

"Oh, yes—you do have a fine group." Isbiano pulled down the hem of his loose-fitting purple tunic. "At least the members we know. But what about this Omat fellow? People talk about you welcoming a peasant healer into the company of Nobles—"

"Let them talk!" Isabella interrupted. "He wants to serve the Kingdom. Why is that wrong?"

Isbiano exhaled deeply. "You have so much of your mother in you. Her intellect. And her sense of justice. I love those things in you just as I did in her. Together, we raised a Queen whose achievements will dwarf my own."

He then put one hand on his daughter's shoulder and gestured in the direction of the council chambers. "But when you sit in that middle seat, every decision you make weighs heavy."

Her nostrils flared. "As if I do not understand that responsibility! In case you have not noticed, I am up before dawn. Every. Single. Morning. Pouring over reports, studying every aspect of commerce, security, international relations, even magic. And I am at my desk after the servants have gone to bed. No one makes me do these things. I do them to make sure I am ready to lead Imarina when that day comes."

"I know, my child. You work so hard. No one could be more prepared for the job." He pulled his daughter into a tight hug. "What I mean is that you sometimes must look beyond your personal sense of right and wrong and consider what is best for the nation. Your desire to help the Serving Class is honorable. Just make sure you consider the consequences before you upend our social order."

Isabella said nothing but returned her father's embrace and rested her head on his shoulder.

CHAPTER 7

Once again, Bok rose early the following day. After buying some new clothes from the tailor's shop in the palace basement, he had settled in his room early the previous evening. He wanted to make sure he was completely prepared and on time for the journey. He planned to be the first person at the meeting point at the West Stables.

But when he arrived, a sound rang out from behind the expansive building: *THNK! THNK! THNK!*

Longbow in hand and silver-and-white shirt tied around his waist, Avantil fired arrow after arrow at a small wooden target more than 100 feet away. Each of the arrows hit the middle of the board. But Avantil muttered and shook his head. Given the number of arrows on the ground and the amount of sweat on his face, he had been practicing for hours.

His frustrated demeanor changed as soon as he noticed Bok. "Hello, my friend! Good to see you!" He stopped his practice and walked over to Bok.

The country healer leaned against a wooden beam supporting the stable's roof. The familiar smells of hay and horses brought a smile to his face, as did Avantil's marksmanship. "That was impressive, Avantil. I had no idea you were so accomplished at archery."

"That? It was nothing. Just a hobby my parents consider a waste of time and money. But it gives me something to do other than get in Isabella's way." Avantil grabbed a clean towel from a hook on the stable's wall and mopped his face.

Bok jumped when someone brushed against his arm. A green-clad attendant hustled past him to hand Avantil with a cup of cool water.

"Oooh, that's good! Thank you." He drained the metal cup and handed it back to the servant, who bowed and left without saying a word.

He could be me. If I worked at the palace, it would be as a servant. And would Avantil notice me then?

"G'mornin', Lord Amorinil."

Commander Coregan's gruff voice interrupted Bok's thoughts. The Royal Guardian sported a gray mustache, a strong arm, and a face like leather. After nodding to Avantil, Coregan lifted a worn, scratched leather saddle, his biceps flexing under its weight.

Avantil put his hand on Bok's shoulder and gently pushed him forward. "And good morning to you, Commander Coregan. I'd like to introduce Bok Omat, healer of Soleh Valley. He will be accompanying us, as you know. Bok, this is Coregan, Commander of the Royal Guard."

"I'm honored to meet you, sir." Bok saw the Commander at the Royal Council meeting, but the two hadn't exchanged words until this moment.

"Y'need a sword," Coregan said without looking away from his chores.

Bok rubbed his forehead. "Excuse me, sir?"

"If you're goin' on this mission, y'need a sword." It was not a question. Coregan pulled a spare blade from a leather sack he brought with him and tossed it to Bok.

Bok unsheathed the sword and examined the blade. He had never held a sword before, something he felt sure those in the palace would find amusing. Villagers like him and his neighbors depended on weapons that doubled as tools, such as axes, knives and spears, for self-defense. And you can't kill a deer, chop firewood or clean trout with a broadsword, no matter how much it gleams.

Coregan then explained that the group would pose as a traveling merchant party, giving no official notice of their departure in Ithenel or arrival in Naseem. Along the way, they were to maintain a low profile, never appearing to be more than a routine, anonymous group of business travelers.

"Better that whoever did this not know about our comings and goings."

The Commander also had decided against sailing upriver to Naseem—a decision Bok appreciated. He had never sailed on a boat and was glad he wouldn't have to on this voyage.

Bok looked toward the palace—and ships, swords, and saddles suddenly left his mind. Because Isabella glided down the brick path, Tovano and Lieutenant Wingate in tow.

She had replaced the purple silk gown she wore to yesterday's briefing with white cotton pants, a loose-fitting tan shirt and polished riding boots that nearly stretched to her knees. A wide-brimmed black hat replaced her tiara, and her long hair was tied back in a ponytail.

Coregan stood at attention, while the servant who had given Avantil the cup of water bowed deeply when she passed. Bok merely folded his hands at his waist and shuffled his feet.

Isabella met him with a broad smile. "Good morning, Bok. Are you ready for our adventure?"

His heart thumped against his ribcage. "Absolutely, Your Majesty! I'm ready for anything."

It is a lie. But how can I say any different to the Princess?

After a quick but warm greeting to each of the other men, Isabella looked around the stables and frowned. "Where is Kotarian? If he causes us to delay our trip—"

"No worries, Your Majesty!" Kotarian ran into the courtyard at easily three times the speed of a normal man, pollen, dust and pine needles flying in his wake.

"Look at that fancy peacock!" Avantil muttered to Bok. "He used a wind whisper spell to push himself through the courtyard so he could make a big entrance. Big deal—Isabella can do that, too."

Kotarian didn't let on if he heard the comments. He dusted off the sleeves of his gray coat. "My apologies for being late, Your Majesty. But I know you wouldn't leave without me!" He shot a smirk toward Tovano. "After all, you'll undoubtedly need a skilled sorcerer before this mission is through."

Isabella fixed her eyes on the sorcerer's. "What I need is for you to be ready on time. Every member of this team is important. We all need to remember that."

"And yuh need to take off that jacket and cap," Coregan grumbled. "We're s'posed to be a trading group—why would a sorcerer be riding with a band of spice merchants? Might as well paint a target on our backs."

Kotarian pressed his hand to his chest as though wounded. "But I'm representing the House of Magic!"

"Listen to Coregan." Isabella spoke slowly and quietly. "Our security is his job—and he is expert at it."

Kotarian stuck out his lower lip. "Fine." He carefully folded the gray hat and jacket and tucked them into his saddlebag. First, though, he removed the starburst pin and affixed it to his shirt.

With that, Isabella signaled to Coregan to lead the traveling party out of the palace courtyard. Coregan rode in front of the Princess, with her bodyguard behind her. Avantil said the Royal Family trusted Wingate like a family member. The Guardian lived in the Royal Palace in a fourth floor room adjacent to the Princess' own.

Bok had decided to ride Beki rather than take one of the horses from the palace stables. He realized his plow horse looked out of place among the row of fine royal steeds and the Guardians' powerful war horses. But she was a strong, good-natured horse who could work from sunrise to sunset without tiring. Plus, Bok hated the idea of leaving her behind in the care of strangers.

"Good Beki." He stroked her head as she walked down the well-worn path leading out of the stables and through the palace's rear courtyard. This space behind the palace served as a working area, with numerous sheds, outbuildings, workshops, and storehouses to serve the practical needs of the large campus. The familiar black smoke of a blacksmith's shop curled up from behind a greenhouse. *So much activity. It's like a functioning city within the palace walls.*

Another section of the Royal Gardens jutted out into the rear courtyard. The expansive green space had to be many acres.

Isabella rode up beside Bok and pointed to a plaza just inside the gardens. "The Royal Gardens were my mother's favorite spot. She spent hours there every day the weather would allow, pruning, watering and otherwise loving the flowers into existence."

Isabella smiled at the fond memory. "Even after she... became ill, she spent many days there on that plaza, painting portraits of her beloved blossoms. I would bring my lessons and study at her side while she painted. In fact, Mother's grave is here in the gardens, just beyond that grove of trees."

Bok swallowed hard. He certainly remembered Queen Ipharina's death. He and Isabella were 12 summers, and the news was all anyone in Soleh Valley could talk about. The entire Kingdom observed a full week of mourning. Many of his classmates were thrilled to have those days out of school. But all Bok could think was that a girl missed her mother terribly. Hearing the catch in Isabella's voice now, he knew she still did.

He wished he could hug his own parents one more time before setting off for unknown lands.

CHAPTER 8

THE FIRST PART OF the planned five-day ride took them through a densely populated neighborhood north of the Royal Palace. Neatly kept two-story frame buildings, often with storefronts on the bottom floor and small homes upstairs, lined both sides of the street. The corners of each block typically housed businesses, temples, schools, or other larger, brick or stone buildings.

Single-level buildings crammed into the side streets. These structures were built from thin planks with gaps between each board. Childrens in threadbare clothes played tag in the narrow roads, darting out of the way when a donkey-drawn cart clomped through.

This must be where the Serving Class lives in the city. Bok set his jaw and continued riding.

He had to keep his eyes on the road to avoid trouble. People dashed in front of the riders, almost daring the horses to trample them. The spaces around the sidewalk tables overflowed with customers. Horse- and hand-pulled carts moved slowly down each side in the street, with impatient travelers sometimes creating an impromptu third lane in between.

They barely had been on the cobblestone road for an hour when traffic came to halt after an oxcart carrying a load of melons lost a wheel, spilling fruit into the streets.

"Are you joking? Such incompetence." Kotarian rolled his blue eyes to the sky and sighed loudly.

Coregan and Wingate dismounted and stood beside Isabella's horse. The Commander scowled. "Your Majesty, you may wish to dismount. It looks like this may take a few minutes."

Wingate stood with his back to the Princess to scan the crowd. Bok took that as an invitation and stepped down, too. *Beki could use the break as well.* He stroked his horse's mane as he waited.

Within moments, a short, balding man carrying a string of cloth flowers walked down the street to meet the stalled group. "Lord Amorinil! So good to see you! It's been a while—you weren't so tall then!"

Avantil squinted at the man. "Tartio Thanilar? It's been a while! Come, let's catch up. "He stepped forward to meet Tartio on the sidewalk, away from the rest of the group. Bok couldn't hear their conversation, but by the number of times Avantil slapped Tartio's shoulder, he could tell it was a jovial one between two long-time friends.

After a few moments, Avantil came back to the group, which still was stuck behind the broken-down wagon.

"Tartio owns a couple of garment shops here in this neighborhood. The Amorinil Mercantile Company has been his supplier for 20 summers. He wanted to catch up a bit—and he said this was for my 'lady friend,' as he put it." Avantil presented the string of artificial red, orange and white dahlias to Isabella.

"Well, your 'lady friend' thinks they are beautiful!" She tied the bouquet to her saddle, removed a single cloth flower, and placed it in the brim of her wide hat.

"What do I have to do to get flowers?" Kotarian said to Wingate. But the guardian refused to acknowledge the young sorcerer's attempt to start a conversation.

"Come on, Wingate. The love birds won't talk with me, the Commander already doesn't like me, and there's no way I'm talking to... him. He gestured with his eyes toward Tovano, who stood on the opposite side of the horses from Kotarian. "That leaves you and the peasant."

Wingate waved off Kotarian. "I have no time to placate your need for attention. Please do not bother me while I am on duty." With that, Wingate turned his back and scanned the streets for possible danger.

"Does he ever get off duty?" Kotarian sighed. "I guess that leaves you, oh mage of the mud huts. Enthrall me with your wisdom!"

Bok looked around in vain for someone to cut in. "Um, at least it looks like it's just a wheel. If the wagon had broken an axle, we could be here a while, but I think they should be able to get this fixed momentarily..."

Kotarian produced a brown glass flask from his saddlebag and threw back a large gulp. "Bok, you are inspiring. Given the choice of your insights and grain alcohol, well..." He took another deep drink from the flask and turned away from Bok.

"I just... I..."

I hope he didn't hear that. I wish Yata was here. She would punch Kotarian square in his nose.

⎯⎯⋈⎯⎯

"This melon is good." The True Leader sat at Tartio Thanilar's desk and sliced another piece of cantaloupe with a paring knife.

The merchant's smile turned into a shiver. He quickly glanced back into the store and closed his office door.

"Are you mad? What if someone saw you come in?"

"They didn't." The True Leader raised his hand. Blue-green magical energy glimmered on his fingers. He leaned forward; the melon dripped juice on the wooden desktop. "Did you get it done?"

"Yes." Tartio looked down at the floor. "Although I feel awful about it. Lord Amorinil's family has been good to me."

The merchant's hands balled into fists. His voice rose. "And I know who his traveling companion is. I could be charged with treason! Isbiano may be a merciful king, but how much grace would he show a man who conspired against his beloved daughter?"

The True Leader smiled and ran his hands through this thick hair. "You just handed your friend a necklace for his lady. You didn't do anything wrong." He stabbed a piece of melon with his knife. "Tell me, Tartio—do you think Imarina is losing its way? That we are drifting from traditions that have brought us centuries of peace and prosperity? Is that the Imarina we want for your children and their children?"

"Well, yes. But..."

"But are you aware that Princess Isabella advocates allowing the Serving Class to own more property? Perhaps as much as, oh, a garment store? That peasant your friend is traveling with—she would have him be your neighbor."

"Yes. I know." Tartio sighed. "And that's wrong—I agree that it must be stopped. But I don't want to hurt anyone!"

"And you didn't. No one is getting hurt here, my friend. Those cloth flowers have a minor enchantment allowing my associates to simply track the Princess and her party. That's all."

The True Leader fished a carved wooden token of a gray wolf from his pocket. He fidgeted with the token and placed his other hand on Tartio's shoulder.

"Trust me. In a few days, you will be glad you are on our side."

CHAPTER 9

AFTER THREE DAYS OF uneventful travel, the seven riders had slipped from the farmlands and villages into the North Country Forest. The dirt road narrowed into a thin, faint path through the dense pine trees, often veering around briar thickets and other natural barriers. The summer tree canopy was so thick that Bok had trouble seeing more than a few feet ahead of where Beki slowly trod.

As the sun began to set, the group stopped for the night in a small clearing near a stream. Since he had the most experience preparing meals, Bok agreed to handle the cooking.

Coregan and Avantil set up the campsite, while Wingate built a fire. Coregan and Wingate tried to convince Isabella to let them construct a tent for her, but she refused. "If the rest of the group plans to sleep on the ground, then so shall I."

Meanwhile, Kotarian begged off from helping with the chores, claiming he had to practice his spells. He spent the rest of the daylight pouring over his spellbook at the edge of the makeshift camp.

While he waited for the cooking fire to warm up, Bok spotted a thicket of blackberries. He could use them to whip up a simple cobbler and undoubtedly, his new colleagues would appreciate dessert after a hard day on the road.

He had just started away from the campsite when Isabella ran to his side. "Do you mind if I help?"

"Of course, Your Majesty." Bok handed her an oak bucket. Her request surprised him, but he hardly could decline it—even if he'd wanted to. Again, he felt his pulse thump in his throat as they walked to the thicket. He deftly plucked a handful of juicy, ripe berries and deposited them into the bucket with a thump.

Picking berries with the Princess? Oh, Bok... what have you gotten into?

The sweet aroma of honeysuckle vines, entangled with the blackberries, filled the hot, sticky air. Dry pine needles crunched under Bok's feet as he rocked back and forth to select the ripest berries.

"Owww!" Isabella pulled her hand back from the briars, a drop of blood pooling on her fingertip.

Bok flinched when Isabella yelped. He reached for his healer's bag, but she waved him off. "It is a thorn prick, not a dagger wound! I should have been more careful."

Bok handed her a clean rag. "Have you picked many blackberries, Your Majesty?"

Isabella peered inside her bucket and made an exaggerated show of counting her meager harvest. "Let us see... four, five... I have picked six in my lifetime! And you?"

Bok smiled a silly grin. "Oh, a few more than that. It's one of my daily chores back home, assuming I'm not out on healer duties. Soon, I hope to train my nephew to take over."

Dimples formed on Isabella's cheeks as she smiled. "I hope your absence does not create too much hardship for your family."

"No, I think they'll be able to manage without me."

They resumed picking side-by-side. "But my father worried about me traveling to Ithenel. I'm glad he doesn't know about this mission."

"A loving but fearful father? Yes, I am quite familiar with the concept." She chuckled. "Paternal fears are one thing we have in common."

Bok raised an eyebrow. Isabella's smile grew broader. "It's true! Just last month, I journeyed into town to buy Avantil a gift. Wingate and I arrive at the store, only to find it empty of any other customers. The shopkeeper explained that my father had ordered it closed to the public for 'my security.' I was so embarrassed."

"Okay, I guess you do know about an overprotective father." Bok's head grew dizzy. *As a member of the Serving Class, I wouldn't be allowed in these same stores.*

"They mean well, I know—are these berries ripe enough to pick?" She held up the bucket and Bok nodded that they were.

Isabella propped her hand on her hip. "Anyway, I want to hear more about your work. I know of Folk Magic, but I comprehend so little about it. As I understand it, you employ magic in harmony with nature. That is very different from High Magic, which manipulates mystic energies to achieve things not possible in the natural world."

Bok relaxed his shoulders a little. "I'm not sure how interesting it is. Last week, I used Folk Magic to help a mother goat deliver her kid. Not the stuff that fables are written about, Your Majesty."

"Ha! Point made! Well, the life of the Crown Princess can be tedious, too."

Bok couldn't hide his bemused grin at that statement.

Isabella playfully cocked her head to the side, tossing back her wavy hair. "Why are you smiling, Bok Omat? You think I do nothing but flit from state dinners to formal balls?"

Bok stopped picking and turned to her, his face flushing. "Not at all! I just found it funny to think my simple life could be of interest to someone like you. I have so little... and you have everything."

"I suppose we have a lot to learn from each other." She turned to face Bok. "I have been granted many unearned privileges. And our nation's customs are unfair to those in your class. For example, why should everyone assume you will be our cook?"

"Oh, I don't mind." Bok waved his hands. "It's no trouble, really."

Her voice became softer and deeper. "But the assumption is what bothers me. I suspect it bothers you as well."

Bok didn't reply directly; he didn't have to. He pressed his lips together, lest his voice crack, and took a deep breath.

"Okay, so you don't spend all your time in dress fittings. What do you mean about your life being tedious at times?"

"I simply meant... well, there are times I wish I could disappear into this forest, if only for an afternoon." She looked around at the canopy of tall pine trees surrounding them. To Bok, the location was as commonplace as his family's three-room home. But Isabella soaked in every sight and sound in the woods.

"It is an honor to be our next Queen, and I do not regret my life's path. But it has not always been easy. Would it surprise you to learn that before I met Avantil, there was no one in my life I considered a friend?"

"You... didn't have any friends?" As annoying as Yata could be at times, he'd had his sister's companionship his entire life. "Surely, there are young women and men of the palace..."

"And *they* are the ones flitting from state dinners to formal balls. The weight of a nation doesn't rest on their backs."

Bok shooed away a yellowjacket buzzing around the sweet berries. He couldn't understand that type of duty, but responsibility to others was something he knew. "I get the sense you wouldn't be content living an idle rich life, Your Majesty. You wouldn't have added magic to your duties if you were."

She smiled again, then turned her eyes downward. "Are you sure we just met yesterday? I am afraid I can never be prepared enough for my role. But I suppose worrying is what a Royal must do."

"No." Bok pointed his finger at her, momentarily forgetting their vast differences in station. "It is what a good Royal does. Believe me, someone in your position doesn't have to care about people like me. But you do."

To Bok's surprise, Isabella got silent for a moment. He held his breath. *I hope I didn't overstep my place...*

But she just blinked a few times. "Bok, you do not know how much those words mean."

HUH-HOO!

"What was that?" Isabella swiveled her head to scan the treetops.

"It's just an owl on the hunt. The sun will go down soon." *And our conversation must end, unfortunately.*

Bok dropped the last handful of berries into his bucket. "Well, this has been a wonderful time, Your Majesty. But I suspect the others will be grumbling if I don't serve supper soon!"

"Tovano will be for sure—that old man can eat his own weight and not gain an ounce! Oh, outside of the Royal Council Chambers, you are Bok and I am Isabella."

"Um, let me work on that... Your, um... That's going to take some time."

And spending more time with the Princess sounded wonderful to Bok.

CHAPTER 10

B OK COOKED A STEW using some vegetables they had packed, flavoring it with some wild herbs and mushrooms he found in the forest. He had helped his mother in the kitchen since had been old enough to stir a pot. While he wouldn't pit his culinary talents against Tana Omat's, he could whip up a decent meal. Still, he was surprised that his simple country cooking was met with approval from a group used to fine meals.

Isabella waved a spoon, which reflected the gleam of the fire. "This is exquisite, Bok! I am going to insist you share the recipe with the palace kitchen."

Bok hoped the light from the campfire masked his blushed face. "It's nothing special. Just something I grew up on."

"A peasant dish, then." Kotarian sneered. Of course, that hadn't stopped him from filling his plate with a second helping of stew.

"I appreciate your kind words, Your Majesty." Bok ignored Kotarian, content to bask in his other colleagues' praise.

After the meal, Tovano launched into a rambling yarn about a long-ago trip. Isabella and Avantil left the campfire to wash up, and the two Guardians followed behind them, leaving Tovano and Bok on one side of the fire and Kotarian on the other.

"I assume you are handling the dishes as well...?" Kotarian uttered a brief incantation and twisted his fingers awkwardly in an arcane gesture. His empty plate then floated across the campsite and into Bok's lap.

Tovano leaned forward, enjoying a bowl of blackberries drizzled with honey. "That's a push-pull spell, Bok. It doesn't mean our young friend shouldn't wash his own plate, but he demonstrated how High Magic can be used to move objects effortlessly. You see, High Magic manipulates energy—"

"Why bother to explain the inner workings of High Magic to... him? An outsider lacking in the Acumen?" Kotarian scoffed.

Bok winced. While he had the Acumen for Folk Magic, only Nobles could possess the ability to perform High Magic, as Kotarian had pointed out.

He continued. "And really, Tovano—a 'push-pull spell'? Its proper name is 'Tranogian's Territorial Transport'—but you know that."

"Well, that's what the House of Magic calls it." Tovano laughed as he scratched his thinly bearded chin. "Those gray jackets love to stamp their names on everything."

"You used to wear a gray jacket, too." Kotarian stood and stepped back from the fire. He then stomped away into the dark woods toward the creek. Tovano silently rooted around in his travel bag and produced a small pouch.

Bok watched Kotarian leave the campsite. "I-I'm sorry if I did something to offend him."

Tovano shook his head. "Nothing you did, my young companion. Kotarian's talents are only exceeded by his temper. He carries a great deal of pain inside him. One day, he will either reckon with it or it will destroy him. But still, I'm glad he is with us."

Bok placed another log on the fire. "Why? You have far more experience, and you've said Isabella is one of the brightest students you've ever taught."

Tovano fiddled with the pouch's drawstring, trying to pry it open. "Both true. But I've always been more of a teacher than a combat sorcerer. Isabella has a broader skill set, but she has never tested herself in a practical setting before. For all his bluster, Kotarian is a skilled young sorcerer with self-confidence and sharp reflexes. Those talents could come in handy if things turn ugly."

Bok wrapped his arm around his knees. "So you think we could be heading into danger?"

"I hope not. But I would be lying if I told you it wasn't a real possibility."

This wasn't what Bok had planned on when he answered that royal summons. Being over his head was one thing; losing his head was another. There was little he could do about it now, though, and something else the sorcerer said had intrigued him. "So, you used to be in the House of Magic?"

Tovano scooped dried root bark out of the pouch and into his cup. Then he added hot water from the kettle over the fire.

"Sassafras tea! My grandmother used to love that," Bok said. "I didn't know people in Ithenel drank it—particularly advisors to the Crown."

Tovano gave him a hint of a grin. "You might be surprised. And I'm not ignoring your question. Yes, I was once a full member of the House of Magic—long before Kotarian was there. He doesn't know the whole story as to why I had to leave, and at this late hour after a long day of riding, I don't feel like recounting it. Just know that I am happier at the Royal Palace than I ever was on Sonorian Square." He leaned back, closed his eyes, and sipped his tea.

Interesting. It certainly explains the tensions between Tovano and the House sorcerers, including Kotarian.

Bok hoped they would be able to co-exist on this trip—and he also wanted Tovano to share more of his knowledge in the days to come. But he couldn't shake the elderly sorcerer's warning of pending danger.

Bok scooped up the dishes from around the campsite, including Kotarian's, and washed them with the remaining hot water. No one save Kotarian had asked him to do this chore, but normally, such duties would be performed by one of his social rank. *Better to do it without being asked to avoid any conflict.*

The group soon settled in to sleep around the embers of the campfire, with Avantil offering to take the first watch.

Bok crawled into his canvas bedroll and closed his eyes. *"You are Bok and I am Isabella." As if we are friends, not Royal and Serving Class. Bok Omat, what have you gotten yourself into?*

While his brain raced, he covered his hand to stifle a yawn. A long day on the road and a lack of sleep the previous evenings had caught up with Bok.

I wonder what adventures tomorrow will bring.

He wouldn't have to wait long for an answer.

"Uh, we have a problem." Avantil's quiet but firm voice pulled Bok out of a shallow slumber. He struggled to grasp where he was for a second, until his hand touched pine needles and he saw the moon overhead.

A panorama of glowing lights appeared among the pine trees and underbrush surrounding the clearing, like a field of stars. Then he heard the faint footfalls of predators. Bok realized those lights were eyes reflecting moonlight.

His heart rate jumped when the animals behind those eyes stepped out of the trees. Two dozen wolves had surrounded the camp and closed in on the sleeping travelers!

CHAPTER 11

WHILE AVANTIL EDGED OVER to his bow and quiver, Bok rousted the others.

Wingate bounced to his feet like a startled cat. Broadsword in hand, he moved the Princess to the center of the circle, while Coregan drew his own sword and stood in front of her. Isabella hardly retreated in fear. Instead, she flexed her hands and slowed her breathing to prepare a spell.

Bok inched over to Kotarian's bedroll, never looking away from the snarling wolves. The campfire had burned low, but even in its dim light, he could tell the wolves' eyes were bloodshot and their fur bristled.

What's more, they moved in concert to completely encircle the camp and prevent Bok and his friends from fleeing. When one stepped forward, another filled the gap to its left or right.

"Wolves don't normally act like this. Something unnatural is going on!" Bok shook Kotarian's bedroll where the sorcerer's shoulder should be but found it empty. However, that was a problem that would have to wait.

As one, the savage wolves leaped into the camp. Coregan caught the first with a slash of his sword, but a second and third knocked the Royal Guardian to the ground. Before they could reach his throat, Wingate grabbed them by the backs of their necks and threw them off. However, three more wolves attacked the Guardians, one of which caught its jaws around Wingate's calf.

Tovano's claims to be more of an educator than a warrior unfortunately proved to be more than modesty. The sorcerer struggled to find the right words and gestures to help Coregan and Wingate fight off their attackers. Tovano used a variation on the push-pull spell—Kotarian would've called it "Phenarian's Featherless Flotation"—to levitate above them. But one of the wolves latched its teeth around his pants leg and pulled him down roughly. Only Coregan's quick swordsmanship saved him from death.

"The healer was right—it is as if these animals are being controlled by some outside force," Tovano said to no one in particular. He cast a spell at the nearest wolf. Lights dazzled in front of the animal's eyes, briefly making the moonlit campsite as bright as midday. The wolf stopped its advance, looked around as if it had just awakened in an unfamiliar place, then ran away into the thick expanse of pine trees.

Meanwhile, Isabella cast a flashfire spell. A bright burst of flame projected from the Princess' hands and incinerated two wolves mid-leap. She and Avantil stood back-to-back. She illuminated the dark campsite with bursts of fire and he placed arrows precisely between the ribs of approaching wolves.

Still, the mass of feral beasts grew closer, its ability to close ground superior to Isabella and Avantil's desperate efforts to fight them off.

Bok got caught watching the fight and realized that a wolf stood between him and his sword. He'd inadvertently left it strapped to Beki's saddle while preparing supper. His entire body tensed like an iron bedspring.

Wingate had piled their saddles at the edge of the clearing. *If I move carefully, perhaps the wolf won't see me.*

He took one step toward the saddle—and the wolf spun to face him, a violent mass of muscle, fur, and fang.

The wolf sprinted toward Bok. *No, not toward me—toward Isabella!* Her back was turned to cast another spell at the wolves attacking her from the opposite side.

"Bok! Stop that one!" Avantil yelled. Bok froze. Should he reach for his sword? Tackle the animal with his bare hands?

Before he could decide, the wolf raced past him. Bok made a feeble effort to grab its hind legs, only to come up empty.

The wolf now had a direct line on the unsuspecting Princess.

"Avantil, what—OOF!" Isabella hit the ground hard, knocked there by her boyfriend. The wolf's nails scraped across his back as it leapt over its intended prey. He dropped his bow in the scramble, and the blue-green aura around her hands vanished. Both laid among the pine needles covering forest floor and tried to push themselves up to their feet before the regrouping wolves could attack again.

"I'm coming!" Rather than taking time to go back for his sword, Bok instead grabbed a still-smoldering log from the fire as a weapon. He ran toward Isabella and Avantil—only to be knocked to the ground himself by another wolf.

The wolf mounted Bok in an instant, snapping at his face, its hot, fetid breath barely an inch from his nose. He grabbed the fur at each of the animal's shoulders and pushed up for all he was worth to keep its fangs from ripping his skin open.

His muscles strained and he gritted his teeth in a desperate effort to save off death. But the wolf was in a position of leverage, and within seconds, it would overpower Bok.

He closed his eyes. *I hope Avantil and Isabella escape. And I wish I could see Mother, Father and Yata one more time...*

"YOWLP!!" The wolf's fur stood on end as a blue-tinted lightning bolt ended its life. Bok's hands tingled like he had plunged them into a hive of bees. His heart raced like he had run the whole way from Ithenel. *But I am alive! And so are my friends.* Through blurry vision, he saw Isabella and Avantil were back on their feet.

Bok drank in precious oxygen in greedy gulps. He threw the wolf's charred carcass to the side, unable to stand and barely able to breathe. The adrenaline pumping through his veins blurred his vision and made it hard to think. A pang in his gut urged him to run away. But his legs were as heavy as the anvil in his family's shop.

After a few gasps, he was able to lean up and see his savior. He could scarcely believe what he saw.

Kotarian casually walked through the center of the campsite, eldritch energy exploding from his hands. One spell dispatched two of the wolves stalking Isabella and Avantil, while another blast sent more scattering.

"TSK! TSK! I go away for five minutes to clear my head, and everything falls apart!" His hands literally smoked—but were unburned—from the impressive display of High Magic's destructive potential.

No one could dispute that the boastful sorcerer had turned the tide. In moments, the remaining few wolves retreated into the woods, leaving the travelers frightened, but largely unharmed, save for Wingate's wounded leg.

"Here; let me take a look at that." Bok reached into his healer's bag. His face flushed both from the surge of energy expended in the fight and his embarrassment at having frozen when Isabella and Avantil needed him.

"No, I'm fine; there's no need," Wingate said. It was the most Bok had heard the giant bodyguard speak since the trip began, but the man's baritone voice threatened to shake the trees around them.

Isabella raced over to examine her bodyguard's injury. "Let him tend to your wounds, Wingate. We need you at full strength." With that, he relented and let Bok clean and dress his injuries.

Avantil propped himself against his longbow. "So, what caused these wolves to intrude on our good night's sleep? Did they think we would make an easy dinner? Or could they be rabid?"

The group turned as one to Bok. He wished he could crawl into a hole, rather than answer his friend's question.

"Um, I don't think so. Wolves usually go after a stray sheep or chicken, not a party of well-armed humans. And I see no signs that these animals were mad."

"Bok is right." Tovano nodded. "Those wolves didn't think we were prey—there was a purpose behind their attack."

"A purpose?" Isabella wrinkled her nose. "But these are mindless beasts!"

"Perhaps. But magic can make a beast—or a man—do strange things," Tovano said. "Did you see the reddish tint to their eyes?"

The sorcerer gingerly knelt on arthritic knees to check one of the dead wolves. "See? That red aura is gone now that the animal is dead."

"Magic? I've never heard of any spell that would control animal behavior. Not in any of my classes, anyway." Kotarian dusted off his sleeves as he walked into the conversation.

"Nor have I," the Princess agreed. "Bok, you know more about animals than any of us. Is there anything in Folk Magic that could explain this attack?"

"Not that I know of, Isa—Your Majesty. Folk Magic is used to heal, not to harm."

She turned next to Tovano, who still examined the dead wolf. "If magic was involved, can we find a spell signature on one of these wolves?"

"I don't think so." Tovano shook his head, then painfully returned to a standing position. Bok furrowed his brow and Tovano must've noticed, because he put his hand on the young man's shoulder. "Every spell leaves a trace of mystical energy that gives us a bit of information about the spell and the person casting it. Sort of like when you write on a table, you sometimes leave a faint imprint in the wood underneath.

"But in this case, we are too far removed from the original incantation to pull a spell signature. Perhaps if the wolves were still alive... but dead? We may never learn how this was done—or why."

His leg bandaged, Wingate resumed his normal stance without as much as a wince. "We could've stumbled into an area that was being guarded, for some reason. In which case, we shouldn't have any further trouble. Or maybe someone doesn't want us investigating the Blight. Although that still raises the question of how they knew where we were and where we are going."

Coregan nodded as he cleaned his sword. "In any case, we should alter our route a bit just to be safe."

"Very well." Isabella untied her hair and shook out her long brown locks. "Since we are not likely to learn anything else tonight, I suggest we get back to sleep. Standing around talking will not make tomorrow's ride any easier."

"I'll take watch," Bok volunteered. He wouldn't be getting any more sleep this night. *After my performance, I don't deserve any.*

The rest of the party went back to their beds and Bok crouched by Isabella and Avantil's spot around the fire. His fight-or-flight instincts had settled down, replaced by a nauseated feeling in his stomach. *My friends nearly died because of my inaction. I don't know if I can get rid of that feeling, but I have to address it.*

"Before you get to sleep, um, I... I need to apologize. I don't know what happened to me..."

"Bok, do not trouble yourself." Isabella reached up and took Bok's hand. "You never have been in a life-or-death situation before. Nor have I."

"But you and Avantil were in danger, and I did nothing. I just froze."

She gave his hand a squeeze. "Out of shock, not apathy. When you regained your senses, you ran to our aid despite the danger. No apologies are needed."

"Listen to her, Bok—about everything!" Avantil turned around and propped his head against his hands. "You'll get another chance. Now, go do the guard duty you volunteered for!"

And so he did. Bok still regretted his poor performance that evening, but thanks to Isabella and Avantil's grace, the sick feeling in his stomach subsided, just a little.

CHAPTER 12

THE PARTY LEFT THE forest the next morning. Soon, they entered the vast expanse of farmland that filled Imarina's North Country—the area around the city of Naseem between Ithenel and the border with the Mosork Empire. For days, the seven travelers saw little more than cotton fields—miles and miles of pure white as far as anyone could see. Were it not for the sweltering temperatures, one could have mistaken the scene for a winter snowstorm, the kind that rarely fell in the kingdom.

To Bok, the North Country looked a great deal like Soleh Valley, just with cotton instead of corn as the region's lifeblood. People here stooped over short cotton plants, cutting away weeds with handheld tools, just as tenant farmers did back home. Come harvest time, they would pick cotton in 50-pound burlap sacks, as his neighbors gathered corn. From there, the cotton blossoms would be hauled to Ithenel, where they would be spun into yarn, woven into cloth, then cut into clothes and shipped around the world—probably on a ship owned by the Amorinil Mercantile Company.

Such cycles were more than a way of life in places like Osoh Creek and Soleh Valley—they were life. Did the others, even Isabella, truly understand the threat they faced? Bok's mind again turned to his family. Even if they weren't directly impacted by the Blight, they would be in the path of any ensuing panic.

However, the peaceful time spent traveling through the North Country somewhat settled Bok's anxiety. Tovano shared stories of sorcerers from centuries past, the so-called Dark Era before the formation of the House of Magic. Avantil led the group in songs he had learned aboard his family's boats. Even Kotarian acted less abrasively, buoyed by the praise he had received for his performance in battle. Although he made the point that he would do no singing.

They passed a family working the fields. The parents were about the same age as his own. Their daughter wore a cloth headband to keep her bangs out of her eyes, the same way Yata did when she swung her blacksmith's hammer in front of their roaring forge.

What are my sister and little Noji doing now, I wonder? Will he still beg to play dolls with "Unca Bok" when I return? Or will he have moved on to something else?

Tovano's bony hand clapped the young healer's shoulders. "Thinking of home, are you? I've seen that look before."

Bok blinked. "That easy to tell, eh?"

"Consider yourself fortunate to have such a place to think of. Never apologize for that—it's something too many don't have."

Bok nodded in appreciation, but he wondered if the old man was perhaps speaking from personal experience. Tovano dragged his vowels like Bok himself did, giving the old man a hint of Serving Class accent. But that would be impossible. Tovano was a sorcerer, after all. Those in the Serving Class could not be born with the Acumen for High Magic.

***

The True Leader leaned back in a flimsy wooden chair and planted his shoes on the sawdust covered tavern floor. He sipped bourbon from a smudged glass. This show was getting good.

The remaining patrons inside the Knobby Hill saloon leaped over the still-warm corpse in the middle of the torchlit room. They skittered out the back door like barnyard mice as Coz Cosan waved his battered broadsword over his head.

"Ha! Ha! Ha! Any of you'uns wanna step up and try us, too?"

The other members of the Cosan gang—Jairs the Wicked, Brac Ranam and the 400-pound giant Silent Tig—laughed along with him and returned to their drinks. The True Leader nodded at the sight.

Coz pointed the tip of his sword at the bartender's chin. "Barkeep, me 'n my crew'll take another round of ale. On the house, 'course."

"Make mine a whiskey, mmm-hmmm," ordered Brac, a tall, skinny woman with long, greasy hair and a large red scar stretching like a hard country road from above her right eye to the bottom of her sunken left cheek. She, too, waggled a saber in front of the man's face. The dings and notches on their swords were grim, tangible reminders of how the Cosan crew earned their living. Each imperfection represented a cracked skull or shattered collarbone.

"O-of course, Mr. Cosan! Madam Ranam!"

Brac cocked her head back and drained the shot of whiskey in one violent swallow, slamming the glass to the bar in triumph. "Another!" she croaked. The bartender shuddered at the woman's raspy voice and nearly spilled his bottle as he scrambled to fill her drink.

The existence of criminals like the Cosan gang was a rare black mark on the otherwise peaceful society that King Isbiano and his predecessors tried to foster. For the most part, people in the cities and villages lived in relative safety from crime, but a scattershot of roving gangs followed the trading routes and skulked around the city slums, preying on merchants, business owners, and the unfortunate passers-by.

But Coz Cosan's existence as a successful, if somewhat low-level, street thug was about to move to an entirely new level, although Coz didn't know it.

"Impressive. The four of you did quite a bit of damage, I see." The True Leader leaned forward and applauded the cutthroats.

"What're you, some kinda funny man?" Coz looked up from his drink with an annoyed gaze. "I'd shut my mouth and walk outta here if I was you."

"Look at how he's dressed—pure silk!" Brac whispered excitedly. "Bet you he's got a fat purse under those fine clothes!"

"I say we find out," Jairs the Wicked replied, conspicuously not whispering. His hand moved to the dagger tucked in a pocket inside his long cloak.

The True Leader opened his arms to meet the hostile response.

"But if you kill me, you will miss out on a grand opportunity. A golden one, I might say."

The man stood and stepped into the middle of the barroom. He folded his hands casually behind his back. "I understand you... professionals like to earn gold. Nothing wrong with that—we could use more enterprising types like yourselves."

Coz furrowed a scarred eyebrow at the relaxed man now standing in front of his table. "Is there a point to this? 'Cause we're kinda busy right now."

The True Leader glanced around the blood-stained barroom. "What I have to say will be worth your time. I wish to employ the four of you for a special project. It will be the easiest money you will ever earn and you won't even have to leave Naseem to earn it."

"Izzat so?" Coz snorted. "You musta confused us with someone else. The Cosan gang don't work for nobody! Besides, I doubt you could afford—"

The clang of gold coins hitting the table interrupted the bandit's speech. He gawked at the purse the man had casually tossed on the table. Pulling the drawstring, he dumped its contents onto the table. A glittering waterfall of dozens of gold coins flowed out. Coz fingered one and held it to eye level.

"Those are... real!" Brac muttered under her breath.

As they spoke, Jairs the Wicked quietly slipped the dagger from his cloak and hid it behind his back.

With only a slight rustle of clothing to betray his movements, Jairs leapt from behind the table, intending to land on top of the man with the full force of his body weight behind his blade. But without even turning around, the True Leader waved his hand and quickly spoke a few words in a language none in the bar had ever before heard.

And Jairs simply stopped in mid-air.

Coz, Brac, and Silent Tig watched with mouths agape as their colleague dangled three feet above the floor. The little man hovered completely still, his face frozen in a voiceless scream. Tig tugged Jairs' leg in a vain effort to pull the man down, but the powerful man could barely nudge him.

Coz stared at the suspended Jairs. "Is he—?"

"He's alive. He is merely captured in Taermigian's Temporal Trap." Coz stared stupidly at the sorcerer. "That means he is frozen in time. As time moves forward for you and me, your colleague remains stuck in the moment when he leaped to attack me. But he's fine."

To prove his point, the True Leader stepped to one side and snapped his fingers. Jairs tumbled to the floor.

"What happened 'ere? Where did he—?"

Coz signaled for Jairs to stay his attack. "Okay, you're a spell-weaver. Prob'ly a powerful one at that. So what d'you need us for?"

The True Leader sat down at the table and indicated for the others to take their seats around him. They tentatively did as he requested.

"A group of merchants is heading into Naseem this evening, led by a young woman. I have had... bad dealings with her family and I need the four of you to send a message to her loved ones. A permanent message. In exchange, I'm prepared to pay you 500 gold—apiece."

Brac whistled and Silent Tig's eyes bulged. Such a sum would make them wealthy even by the standards of a prosperous nation like Imarina.

Coz scratched his chin. "Why not just kill 'em yerself? You could turn 'em into baby ducks or a pile of creamed potatoes with a wave of your hand."

The man nodded. "I appreciate your skepticism. The answer is simple—discretion. I do not wish to be connected to this crime. My magic could be traced back to me, so I need to take a more indirect role—at least for now.

"And it must look like a robbery. Feel free to take anything of value you like. Be aware that this woman is traveling with six companions, several of whom are dangerous. But you needn't concern yourselves with them, just with the woman. Of course, you may well have to kill her associates to get to her. If so, please enjoy yourselves!"

Coz looked around the table at his colleagues. Yes, they nodded, they all wanted in on this job.

"But we get paid up front."

"Of course. I trust you understand that taking the money without completing the job would violate the terms of our agreement and would result in... Well, as I said, you understand." The man leaned back in his chair, hands clasped behind his head.

Coz nodded, indicating he had no desire to cross such a sorcerer. "There 'as to be more to yer story. That's an awful lot of gold and a great deal of risk just to settle a score. What ain't ye tellin' us?"

"Well, there is one more thing. This woman is under the protection of two Royal Guardians. You knew one of them—he was a Lieutenant then, but he goes by Coregan."

Coz Cosan's eyes widened, and he drew a deep involuntary breath. Jairs and Silent Tig lurched forward and Brac grabbed the sleeve of Cosan's blood-splattered shirt.

"Coz! This is it! The chance we've wanted for." Brac whispered around the barroom table.

Jairs nodded vigorously. "Aye! The chance to finally put Coregan in the grave."

Cosan continued to stare silently. He pulled a heavy hunting knife from his belt and stabbed it into the scarred tabletop.

The True Leader drained his last sip of liquor and looked around the table. "Any questions before you go to work?"

"Just one." Brac's scarred face curled in a twisted smile. "Can we make Coregan scream before he dies?"

CHAPTER 13

B OK AND HIS COMPANIONS continued to ride through miles of farm country. In addition to the vast white cotton fields, they also passed small plots of corn, peanuts, and vegetables, where single families raised the crops.

Immediately following the wolf attack, everyone in the traveling party had been tense. Wingate rode with his head in a permanent state of motion, constantly scanning the fields and forests for any threats. Bok constantly checked the sword Coregan had given him. He didn't want to be without it again.

Bok spent much of that time riding with Isabella and Avantil at their insistence. Avantil told of his fabulous adventures traveling the five seas with his family, before their recent falling out. Isabella talked about life in the Royal Court, but many of her stories were about quiet times spent with her parents. Bok couldn't relate to being a Royal, but he could understand why she valued the time with her mother and father so much.

To his surprise, the two young Nobles seemed as taken with his stories of farm life as he was with theirs. Isabella nearly exhausted herself laughing at Bok's childhood tale of Yata locking him in the community root cellar.

"Yuh-Yata actually left you there?" Isabella wheezed, her eyebrows raised.

"Yes! She told my parents I'd run away!"

"That scoundrel! Did no one hear you?" Avantil leaned forward for Bok's response.

"Well, she told me I couldn't make a sound or the Mosork marauders would find me. Remember—I was barely six summers old. I spent the night in that damp, dirty cellar until a neighbor came for some sweet potatoes!"

The stories and laughter continued each night around the campfire. As the long hours on the trail wore on, and as they saw no signs of trouble, Bok—and nearly everyone else—started to get tired and more complacent.

Certainly, they encountered friendly faces along the road. Many of the tenant farmers tending to the cotton crops looked up from their perpetual stooped position to wave at the travelers as they passed by. "Hello, friends!" Isabella called back.

Those familiar-looking faces and campfire stories were bright spots in an otherwise exhausting journey. Bok's back stiffened from riding day after day. Even Avantil, who practically was born on horseback, drooped in his saddle.

No one complained, though—no one save Kotarian. The glow he wore after his performance against the wolves had worn off, and he resumed grumbling about the travel conditions.

One late afternoon, Isabella traded whispers with Coregan, then smiled. "My next announcement may please you, Kotarian. We could all use a night indoors."

"You mean *you* would like a night away from the bugs and humidity, Your Majesty?" Avantil teased.

A grin on her face, Isabella propped her hand on her hip. "Well, I am a princess. How can I look regal after sleeping on a bedroll in the woods? My people demand that I look my best!"

"By the looks of things, you've a long way to go." Avantil's banter drew a playful slap on the shoulder.

"Bok, please tell me I am not the only person here who would like a night in a real bed." Isabella pleaded her case as if they were back in the Council Chambers and Bok was a member of her Royal Court.

Bok raised his hands and joined in the laughter. "I am sorry, Your Majesty. Being from the country, I'm used to camping. You are on your own here."

"You men—always banding together!" Isabella gently poked Bok side, too. "Fine. You and Avantil can sleep in Beki's stall. The rest of us will enjoy a comfortable, bug-free night indoors."

Butterflies fluttered in Bok's stomach. He held his hands over his head in mock surrender. "Very well. We will stay inside, too."

Their travels soon brought them to Naseem, a city that formed to support the vast cotton farming enterprises in the North Country. While Naseem would never be confused with Ithenel in terms of size or grandeur, it offered travelers a chance to rest their horses, eat a hot meal, and sleep on something more comfortable than pine straw and pebbles.

Factories, workshops, and row houses dominated the center of the hard-working city. Laundry-filled clotheslines dangled over every grimy street. Black soot poured into the sky from cooking stoves and smokestacks.

Naseem had its Noble Class—someone had to own those factories and workshops. Their fine homes ringed the center city. The city's wealthiest neighborhoods were a short walk from some of its poorest. Most had tall wrought iron gates and staffed guardhouses to make sure those two worlds remained separate.

The river Narthalon ran along Naseem's western boundary. The river was the city's lifeline, carrying goods made in its factories down to Ithenel and, via Ithanel's port, across the five seas to markets around the world.

Bok found it no less intimidating than the capital city. Naseem may have been smaller and poorer, but it still crackled with activity. Too much for a young man who had never left Soleh Valley.

Still, Bok figured he should soak up the experience while he could, before the true work began when they got to Osoh Creek.

CHAPTER 14

T HE RAYBUN INN IN southeast Naseem was a basic, nondescript hostel. Every town of any size in Imarina had at least one, and the Raybun was one of a half-dozen in Naseem. It sat well off the main thoroughfares through the city—something Coregan noted would help them slip through the city unnoticed.

The Raybun sported a simple layout. To the left and right were symmetrical two-story wings. Both contained eight identical rooms—four upstairs, four down, with an open staircase at the entrance to each wing. The center of the inn housed the tavern and kitchen. The second-floor wings looked out over the tavern floor, which at this time of evening, was rollicking. Only a few tables and a couple of barstools remained unoccupied. The aromas of grilled meat and the sounds of conversation filled the space.

For the rest of the well-traveled party, securing accommodations was part of the routine and rhythm of being on the road. The others waited near the entrance while Coregan went to find the proprietor. But for Bok, it was an unfamiliar experience completely.

"Oh, it's nothing so special." Avantil shot a wave and a smile to the waitstaff. "These places all look, feel, and taste alike after a while. The same bare pine walls, the same lumpy mattresses, the same watery beer. Even the smells of cooking smoke and cheap soap intermingling. By the Exalted One, I practically grew up in these places!"

"Really? These places seem so... well, I just thought..."

Avantil laughed. "That a rich noble family wouldn't stay in a working person's inn? My parents stay at the finest hotels—unless they decide to stay in their ship's luxury quarters in dock. But they told us children, 'You have to earn your place at our table.' They made my sister, brother, and me stay at the same inns as their... our servants, once we were old enough to hold our own fork and spoon. We only could join them when we had proved our worth." He paused. "My sister and brother now stay at the 'Big Hotel' whenever they travel on business I am not entrusted to join."

A pang shot through Bok's heart. *Mother and Father had so little. But everything they had, they shared freely with Yata and me. How I wish I could tell them how grateful I am.*

"But why would they do that, Avantil?"

The noble pulled up a worn-smooth wooden bench and motioned for Bok to join him. "Just before my sixteenth summer, my parents offered to let me captain my first ship, leading women and men twice my age, on a month-long trading voyage. I refused, because a young woman had stolen my heart." He glanced over at Isabella, who moved closer to Avantil. "I didn't tell them that young woman was our future Queen. Still, it was a test—as are most things with my parents. And I failed, as I usually do."

Avantil sighed and slapped both of his knees." Anyway, that's why the Commander's choice of accommodations doesn't bother me."His now-familiar smile returned. "C'mon—let's find a clean table. Maybe Coregan can negotiate a late-night snack and some wine with the innkeeper!"

Unsurprisingly, Kotarian was less sanguine about the group's plans for the night. "I spotted at least three halfway tolerable hotels in the nicer part of Naseem—'nicer' being a relative term, of course. Why the Commander insisted on this fleatrap, I shall never know."

The commander walked back in time to hear Kotarian's complaints "This place is out o' the way—less likely that we'll be spotted in this part o' town. Just remember to check your mattress for bedbugs."

Kotarian flinched. "Brrr...! By Nawailian's Noxious Nodules, this place is a hellhole. I need a stiff drink... and soon."

The innkeeper, a bulbous man with a walrus-like mustache and a pronounced limp, wobbled from the inn's storeroom to the front desk.

"What'll it be? We're out of lamb stew, if that's what you want."

"Three rooms—side-by-side if you've got 'em," Coregan said.

The innkeeper rubbed his stubbly chin as he sized up the traveling party and made some mental calculations. "Well... we're pretty busy tonight. But I think I got two rooms on the east wing and one on the west. Seven silver apiece." It was twice the going rate, but he placed the coins into the innkeeper's eager hand and gestured to his colleagues to take a seat at one of the few available tables.

None of them paid much attention to the four people sitting in the back of the room, hats pulled low over their faces.

———◈———

"...Anyway, after that incident, we were so ready to leave Hahnizk, we agreed to buy 400 crates of purple trousers." Avantil gestured excitedly, as the rest of the table guffawed. "Thankfully, the General was willing to call it even. But how were we supposed to know he was allergic to goat's milk?"

"You do not know how lucky you were!"Isabella laughed. "The General is notorious for cutting out his enemies' tongues."

"If only we had been so fortunate..." Kotarian drained a glass of wine—hardly his first of the evening. He poured another, turning the wine pitcher upside down to allow every remaining drop to splash into his cup.

"C'mon, Kotarian. You have a better story to share? Then let's hear it!" Avantil said.

Kotarian rolled his eyes. "If you insist. Awhile back, we received a new crop of first-year apprentices—aspiring members of the House. This one boy only applied because his father is some Earl or some such and dear old daddy always wanted a sorcerer in the family. But the boy just kept to himself, afraid to talk to anyone, apologizing for getting in the way. You know the sort." Kotarian shot a look at Bok, who sat directly in front of him at the far end of the table. Bok tensed but continued to listen.

"We discovered he carried a torch for a girl his class, a young lady from a highborn family far too good for the likes of him. But this boy kept making big cow eyes at her. So one day, I took him aside and offered to help him win his lady love. I pumped him up full of courage, wrote him bad poetry to read, handed him some wilted flowers, and sent him to her dormitory."

Kotarian paused for another drink of wine. By this point, he giggled as much from the alcohol as the pending punchline to hisstory.

"S-s-so he goes up there and—" Kotarian paused to suppress a chuckle. "Knocks on her door. But he doesn't realize I've cast Uralian's Unseen Utility on his clothes! He may be wearing his finest outfit, but to everyone else, he appears to be stark naked! The poor boy dropped out the next day and returned to wherever he calls home. I suppose he wasn't House material."

No one else laughed. But Kotarian exploded in a rapid, almost wheezing, laugh.

Bok's face flushed, and his fists clenched. The gaze Isabella directed toward their end of the table let Bok know she was disgusted, too.

Tovano set his cup on the table. "Um, I believe this old man will retire for the night."

"I shall as well." Isabella stood to leave, Avantil and Wingate joining her.

"What? Can none of you appreciate a good joke?" Kotarian scoffed. "Fine; I will go to my room as well. Better than sit here with you milksops—Your Majesty excluded, of course!"

Kotarian muttered a few more drunken words and staggered up from the table, nearly tripping over his own feet in the process.

Tovano leaned over Bok's shoulder. "He's never going to make it up the stairs by himself. I'd better assist him in getting to his room. After all, we all would be lost without the Exalted One's personal gift to sorcery." Tovano put his arm under Kotarian's and steered the tipsy young sorcerer up the staircase.

"Sleep well, my friend." Isabella gave Bok a quick hug. Her jasmine-scented perfume electrified his nostrils, making his pulse jump.

She and her entourage climbed the steps, leaving Bok alone at the table with his thoughts.

Has it just been a few days? I feel like I've known these friends for years. But I have neglected to think of my family as much as I should. How I wish they were here. Including Yata—even if that meant taking a punch to the shoulder.

And then there is the Princess. It is all just fantasy, of course. Romances between different classes are frowned upon. And she loves Avantil. I'd never try to come between them.

When this journey was over, whatever its outcome, I will return to my normal life in Soleh Valley and they will remain in their world, which I can never be part of again.

Bok sipped his beer and stared into the mug.In some ways, it would be easier if Isabella and Avantil acted like the condescending elitists Bok once imagined all Nobles to be. But losing those friendships, after having experienced their warmth, would be heartbreaking.

Bok drained the last of his drink, then collected his friends' mugs and returned them to the bartender. *Might as well do a small kindness for a stranger before turning—*

"AIEEEE! Avantil!"

"Isabella!" Heart pounding, Bok sprinted for the stairs.

CHAPTER 15

THAT NIGHT, TWO YOUNG women entered the side door at the Mechedi Glass Foundry in Naseem. The pair wore leather aprons and padded gloves in addition to their thick canvas pants and long-sleeved shirts. Such attire was standard for employees at the glass factory, which at peak capacity turned out hundreds of bottles, windowpanes, dishes, and other items used in households throughout Imarina and beyond.

Their presence, like their appearance, would have been typical had the Mechedi Glass Foundry not closed six weeks earlier.

The women stepped inside the darkened building and into a dust-covered workplace. All the equipment and furniture had been removed. Only the dim light of a single fireplace broke the gloom.

When the door closed completely, an amber aura enveloped each of the women. They emerged from its glow wearing black jackets over unadorned red attire, dark hoods covering their faces. They stepped to the far end of the long foundry floor, where two dozen similarly dressed women and men formed a circle around the gleaming brick firepit.

The two newcomers took their places in the circle, neither speaking nor being spoken to. Moments later, the True Leader emerged from the shadows and stepped into the center of the circle. The others knelt at his appearance. No one dared move.

"Rise, my acolytes. We have much to celebrate!" As one, they did as he commanded. "But first, an update. Alaydrian, what is the latest from Osoh Valley?"

The young woman bowed her head. "I have excellent news, True Leader. The Blight is spreading. Peasants flee Osoh Creek, spreading rumors of calamity from Naseem to Ithenel."

The True Leader smiled. "Word spreads quickly among the Serving Class—farmers chatter in the fields, servants gossip in the kitchens. It won't be long until every community in Imarina wonders if their family will be next."

He faced the woman, who had been with him in Osoh Creek. "Alaydrian, you serve our cause well. What of our second front?"

Neuragian, the other acolyte who had helped destroy the Yult farm, spoke up. "Good news from here as well,

True Leader. We kindled a second Blight across the border into Mosork territory. Panic is setting in among their people as well."

"Yes. They undoubtedly will blame Imarina for the incursion—just as Imarina will blame the Mosork warlords." The light of the firepit behind the True Leader cast an eerie halo around his head. "All wars are founded on mistrust, and a border war with the Mosorks will foment panic and undermine support for Isbiano."

Alaydrian asked, "What of the Princess and her band of followers? They turned back our enthralled wolves and have reached Naseem."

"I have that under control!" the True Leader boomed, causing Alaydrian to flinch. "By morning, Princess Isabella will be off the board, and no one will be able to warn Isbiano."

He put his hands on Alaydrian's shoulders. "But I didn't get to where I am by neglecting details. Which is why I want you to return to Osoh Creek with a team. Should Isabella survive the night, I want you waiting on her."

"You will not be accompanying us, True Leader?"

"No, Alaydrian. I must stay here and continue preparing for the assault on Ithenel. But I trust you are more than up to the job, on the off chance it is necessary."

"Consider that traitor as good as dead!" Alaydrian cackled.

Daronian, a third acolyte, raised a trembling hand. "But True Leader—wouldn't such a direct attack on a Royal party reveal our existence to the House of Magic?"

"Yes, and that would necessitate accelerating our plans, which is not ideal." The True Leader paced around the circle, the heels of his boots clicking against the foundry's brick floor. "But the Princess cannot be allowed to take the secrets of the Blight back to Ithenel, as remote as that possibility may be."

"There is no other course—Isabella Inishari must die."

CHAPTER 16

AFTER SEEING THAT TOVANO got Kotarian safely to bed in their rooms at the far end of the hall, Isabella and Avantil went to their room at the opposite end.

The walls and floor were simple planks of unvarnished, knotty pine forming a 20-foot-by-20 foot box that smelled like resin in the summer heat, provided smoke wasn't pouring in through the window from the cooking fires below. The furniture—a bed, dresser, and small bedside table—were unadorned pieces held together by wooden pegs and sanded down to a reasonably smooth finish. A faded patchwork quilt and cotton sheets covered the straw-stuffed bed, topped by two pillows as flat and plain as a cake of Bok's griddle bread.

It was a far cry from Isabella's room back at the Royal Palace. By this point in the journey, though, she would consider bartering her crown for a hot bath, a mug of chilled wine, and a halfway comfortable bed.

"Ahh!" She opened her arms upon entering the room, as if to embrace the oversized crate. "All I want to do is get clean and sleep for a month!"

"I'll go along with that. But I hope you'll add one more thing to the list, preferably between bathing and sleeping. I'm not sure I can last a month!" Avantil muttered under his breath, where only Isabella could hear him.

"Shhh!" she put her finger to her lips, barely able to contain her laughter.

"I'll be outside the door if you need me." Wingate left the room. If he heard Avantil's remark, he was too discreet to show it.

Avantil laughed with Isabella. Once the door was safely closed, he whispered, "Need his help? I sure hope not. I think I remember what to do!"

Isabella squealed and stroked her lover's arm. "Avantil! You are awful!"

"I know—and that's why you love me." He grabbed her around the waist and pulled her into a kiss. She gave in, but only momentarily. The hot bath left for her by the inn's staff was too temping after a week on the road.

"I do love you, but right now, I think I'd love a bath even more. Besides, I will be more appealing once I am clean."

"I can't imagine you somehow being more appealing, Isabella."

"Well, there is something to be said for building the anticipation." She threw her hat on the bed. "But I will be back—I swear. Now, turn around—and no peeking! Promise?"

"You don't make it easy. But I promise, my sweet!" He flopped on the soft cotton mattress and exhaled a soft sigh.

Forget High Magic—this is true sorcery. Isabella closed her eyes and leaned her head back against the wooden edge of the tub. The grime slipped off her skin and into the pleasantly warm water, along with her stress.

Kotarian is a handful. But he is every bit the talented sorcerer he claims to be. And Bok is so kind and loyal. I still make him nervous, though. Is that solely because I am his princess? Or is more on his mind? I hope not... Surely, he realizes my heart belongs to Avantil.

The team is performing well. But I cannot shake the thought that the wolf attack was no coincidence. There are secrets in Imarina—as I am well aware. Perhaps someone doesn't want us to—

WHUMP! A muffled thud broke her concentration.

"Avantil? Are you okay?" Isabella jumped out of the tub and quickly threw on her nightgown.

She opened the door back into their bedroom to see Avantil holding his sword, surrounded by three armed assailants. Tiny feathers drifted through the air behind her boyfriend, where a sword had cleaved the pillow he'd been resting on in half.

Isabella's pulse spiked, but her hands glowed. Princess Isabella wasn't needed; Isabella Inishari, the trained sorcerer, was.

Upon seeing her emerge from the bathroom, one of the assassins' jowly face curled into a smile. "Evenin', Yer Majesty. This here's Brac Ranam. She's killed 17 men an' women in her day. The big fella's Silent Tig. On account o' the fact he don't talk. But his sword arm says plenty.

"Me? I'm Coz Cosan. But you and yer fella can call me death." He took one step toward Isabella, sword raised above his head.

That head was met by the flower vase from the dressing table, courtesy of Isabella's push-pull spell. She had far more potent spells in her repertoire, but she didn't want to risk using them in such proximity to Avantil. The vase shattered, leaving stale water, pink carnations, and a three-inch cut on Coz' face.

"GAAA!!" Blinded by pain, he grabbed Isabella by the arm and slung her hard into the wall. Coz then grabbed his wounded head and looked at the blood left behind on his hand. He glared and grunted at her as she struggled to her feet. No doubt—this man intended to murder her. She bit her lower lip and focused her energies in preparing a second spell.

The door then exploded open in a shower of wooden splinters, courtesy of Wingate.

"Your Majesty! What—?!"

Before he could fully assess the situation, Silent Tig met Wingate with a charge so rapid that it seemed impossible for a nearly 400-pound body. The man's sword aimed directly at Wingate's chest.

But Wingate caught the man's sword arm—barely. Any other member of the group would have been cut in half, but Wingate's power was such that he was able to stop the killing blow. Still, the momentum of the tackle sent both men tumbling into the narrow corridor outside the upstairs rooms. Only a fragile-looking wooden rail separated the top of the stairs from a nasty 20-foot drop to the inn's main floor below.

Wingate smashed into the rail back-first. The wood grimaced but did not give. At least not yet. But as Silent Tig pushed Wingate backward across the rail, that could have changed at any second.

Avantil couldn't possibly provide Wingate or Isabella with any help. Not when Brac's sword flickered inches from his face.

The villain smiled as she circled the young Noble. Avantil had been trained by some of the finest fencing instructors in Imarina. But sparring in a gymnasium and fighting for one's life were two completely different matters. As the two combatants danced in a circle, Brac calmly advanced while Avantil backed away.

Brac's sword flashed—too fast for Avantil to parry. "AAGGH!" The blade bit into his left bicep. Not deep enough to cause permanent injury, but deep enough to burn like fire.

Isabella swallowed a yell to her lover, not wanting to distract him. She and Coz faced off, each waiting for the other to make a move. But she couldn't focus completely on her opponent while Avantil was in mortal danger.

"Heh. It hurts, doesn't it? Don't worry—you won't feel the next one." Brac moved side-to-side, as a cobra would do to its next meal.

The next strike came quickly—hard and high. Avantil blocked the thrust, but when he tried to counter with a swing of his own, Brac darted backward, easily dodging the attack.

"Tsk! Tsk! Is that the best you have to offer?" Brac spun her sword playfully. She feigned a second thrust high and struck low. Her blade ripped through Avantil's thigh, even deeper than the first cut.

"AAAHHH!" Avantil yelped in agony. Isabella knew he couldn't take many more blows like that one. The assassin was a far superior swordswoman; Avantil could never beat Brac in a straight-up duel. She knocked Coz to the floor with a push-pull spell and turned to help Avantil.

But with their concentration on Brac, neither Isabella nor Avantil heard the dresser open behind them.

Now, with Brac on the defensive, Jairs the Wicked—who had been hiding in the dresser—struck. The diminutive cutthroat swung his dagger like an axe.

It hit Avantil in the back of the head. He collapsed to the floor and didn't move. Blood quickly—too quickly—began pooling beside him on the hardwood floors.

"AIEEEE!!! Avantil!"

Isabella fought for her own life, but her concern was across the room with Avantil. She couldn't be certain if he was still alive. Brac and Jairs moved to aid Coz, meaning the Princess now faced attackers on three sides.

"See what you done? You done got yer man kilt," Coz said. "Woulda been a lot easier if you hadn't tried to fight back." Brac's scarred face twisted in a sick smile.

CHAPTER 17

B OK SPRINTED UP THE stairs two at a time. Still, he couldn't get to Isabella's room fast enough.

On the landing outside her room, Wingate wrestled over a dagger with the largest man Bok had ever seen.

If anyone can take care of himself in a fight, it's Wingate. I have to get to Isabella and Avantil!

He raced through the shattered door. Three dirty, tough-looking rogues circled the Princess with blades drawn. Isabella backed against the far wall as the men closed in from all sides, her hands glowing with eldritch energy as she prepared to defend herself.

Avantil laid on the floor by the foot of the bed, bleeding badly and possibly dead. A surge of nausea hit Bok's stomach. *No! Please be okay, my friend.*

That fear quickly transformed into desperation, and desperation into action. "Get back, you devils!" Bok swung his sword wildly. He never had wielded a sword before, much less used one in a fight. But he was determined to protect Isabella and Avantil.

The unorthodox nature and untrained ferocity of his attack took Coz by surprise. Bok's blows didn't strike the assassin, but they came close. The bloodied Coz retreated to the open window to the right of the door, away from Isabella.

Coregan entered the room as well. "The Cosan Gang? Thought I was done with you 10 summers ago."

Brac turned to him and smiled. "Our old friend Coregan! Still the Nobles' guard dog, I see."

Coregan, as skilled with a blade as Bok was inept, paired off with Brac. She lunged at Coregan, but the veteran deftly dodged his attacker's thrust.

He struck low—toward Brac's calf. But Brac's sword flashed with remarkable quickness and parried Coregan's blow. And before Coregan could counter, Brac's sword swung back up, cutting the Guardian deeply across the right shoulder and even grazing his cheek.

"Ho, ho! You're good, old man. But I bet you aren't as good as you used to be, are you?"

Coregan steeled himself for the next exchange. "Perhaps not. But I'm still good enough to handle the likes o' you, assassin."

Brac was taller than Coregan, giving her a reach advantage. She struck. Once again, he defended the blow, but in turn, Brac quickly followed up with a strike that met its target, cutting Coregan across the shoulder a second time.

He stepped back. His shoulder dripped blood on the wooden floor at an alarming pace. Coregan's wounded sword arm dropped to his side. Sensing weakness, Brac put her full weight into a roundhouse swing at Coregan's neck, looking to separate the Guardian's head from his shoulders.

But Coregan ducked just as Brac's swing reached the point where the killer could no longer pull it back.

Mustering all his remaining energy, Coregan moved inside his opponent's reach. Before Brac could recover her balance, Coregan ran the assassin through.

"Huh... how did you...?" Brac gasped a dying breath and collapsed to the floor. Coregan nearly did the same, dizzy from the loss of blood.

Meanwhile, Jairs focused his attention on Isabella.

"Any last words before I cut your throat, missy?" He moved his dagger between his hands more quickly than Bok could follow. Not that he could devote too much attention to Isabella's plight, given that he had to duck and parry a series of strikes from Coz.

But the circumstances had changed, thanks to Bok and Coregan. Now, Isabella faced a lone opponent, with no one to attack her from the blind side should she cast a spell.

"Why, as a matter of fact, I do have a few words. Care to hear them?"

Isabella uttered an incantation and waved her hands in a deliberate but fast pattern—movements she had practiced hundreds, if not thousands, of times in Tovano's studio.

Lights flashed around the face of their attacker. Each flashing light left a corresponding red welt on the man's face, as if he was being stung by dozens of invisible, swarming hornets. He collapsed to his knees and swatted helplessly at the intangible insects.

"UHNN! I'm... UHNN... gonna... kill you!" Jairs grunted. The sores on his face ballooned to the point of giving his cheeks a grotesquely round and puffy appearance. The swelling constricted his breathing into rapid, shallow huffs.

Isabella stood over him calmly, speaking in a measured tone. "This is your only chance. Cease and live or continue and die." Jairs said nothing—by this point, he was no longer capable of speech. But his hand fumbled on the floor to recover his dagger.

Isabella only reply was a second incantation. She grasped the man's shaking wrist. His eyes opened wide and his body spasmed. Jairs the Wicked took one final gasp—and then breathed no more.

She then raced to Avantil's side, saying, "Exalted One please let him live or..." She couldn't finish.

If he was indeed dead, there was a good possibility that Wingate could soon join him.

The Guardian and Silent Tig continued their life-or-death tug-of-war over the dagger, until Tig kicked Wingate in the midsection, knocking his breath from his lungs. The blade clattered to the floor.

As Wingate lunged to retrieve it, Tig snatched him in a bear-like grip and fell forward, crushing Wingate's chest with his 400-pound frame. Wingate tried to draw breath, but none came.

He inched Tig over and inhaled a life-giving gasp. However, his relief lasted less than a second, as Tig, while still atop Wingate, placed his oversized hands over Wingate's mouth and nose to smother the Guardian.

Wingate pulled and scratched at Tig's wrists and hands, but with little effect. The assassin was too strong and had the benefit of leverage.

Smiling, Tig leaned over to place the full weight of his might on Wingate's face. Grabbing Tig's wrists, Wingate painfully and slowly drew his legs up, until his feet pressed against the man's abdomen.

Then, with all his remaining strength, he pushed Tig's body forward by extending his legs, using the man's wrists as a lever. Wingate's powerful thighs, built from thousands of hours of calisthenics in the Royal Guard gymnasium, expended every bit of force his body could muster.

Silent Tig moved. With the full weight of his own body now pushing him forth, he flipped over, crashing back-first into the guard rail separating the landing from the inn below.

The rail snapped and Tig fell to his death on the floor below. He didn't utter a sound all the way down.

As Wingate battled fiercely against Silent Tig, Bok's attacker regrouped.

Coz used his sword to block one of the healer's wild swings. Bok attempted another thrust; Coz sidestepped him and employed Bok's own clumsy momentum to shove him down to the floor.

THUD! The hilt of the assassin's sword smashed into Bok's skull.

Bok saw a bright flash of light, then black. He had to quickly regain his feet or die. But his legs and arms stopped responding to his mental commands, like a newborn calf flailing to stand. With adrenaline pumping through his veins, he crawled into the hall outside the room in a desperate effort to put some distance between himself and Coz.

"Just so y'know, I'm gonna cut ya bad enough ta bleed out, but ya won't die until ya seen what I'll do to the lady and the tall lad! And I've got something special fer my ol' chum, Captain—excuse me, Commander Coregan!"

"Help me..." Bok called out feebly. But his colleagues didn't hear him. They were too busy with their own battles to notice his desperate situation. Sweat poured off his face, and his open mouth gasped for air.

I... I've failed again. I've failed my family, my friends... and Isabella. This time, no one can rescue me.

Coz winked at Bok and theatrically raised the sword over his head, waggling his hips to mock the wounded healer. Without even thinking, Bok raised his hand and reflexively spoke the first words that entered his mind. They were the same words that Kotarian had spoken nightly around the campfire. *Move!* he thought.

Bok wasn't of Noble Class birth, as Isabella and Kotarian were. He was not able to use High Magic.

Except he did.

Power surged through the core of his body, passing through his arms and hands and exiting the tips of his fingers. He recognized the sensation as magic at work. But using Folk Magic was more like a mild tingle. This sensation touched every nerve ending in his body. He hairs on his arms stood on end.

"What the bleedin'—?" Before Coz could strike, an invisible hand raised him off the ground. It slammed him into the far wall, like a petulant child smashing his toys. The plank walls cracked from the impact, leaving a man-shaped imprint just inches below the ceiling.

The spell ended seconds after it began. Coz fell harmlessly to the floor.

Oh no! Please don't be dead... Then the man's chest rose and fell in a steady rhythm. Bok exhaled a relieved sigh when he realized the man wasn't dead.

"What did I do?" Bok stared at his hands, as if they could provide some clue as to how he accomplished the unthinkable. He blinked through the pain of his still-throbbing head and looked up at the now-quiet scene. Bodies, broken glass, and splinters littered the inn room's hardwood floors. The damaged wooden panel that Coz hit creaked and—*WHUMP!*—collapsed on the floor, an exclamation point to the violent episode.

"Yes—what did you do?" Kotarian staggered down the hallway, still wearing the same clothes from the night before. He and Tovano had been asleep on the opposite side of the inn and ran to the battle only to find it finished. His blond hair was now a tangled nest and spider webs of red blood vessels covered his eyes. But he was sober enough to realize that a Serving Class healer shouldn't have been able to cast the spell he had witnessed Bok employ.

"I said. What. Did. You. Do?" Kotarian spoke through clenched teeth.

"I... I don't know... Honestly, I don't." Bok pushed himself to a seated position on the floor. He put his hand to the back of his head; a knot rose under his hair where he had been struck. The room still wouldn't come into focus and his stomach swirled as though he may regurgitate his supper at any moment.

"What do you mean you don't know?" Kotarian yelled inches from Bok's nose. "No dirt farmer can do that kind of magic! You must be a Mosork sorcerer, sent to spy on us all!"

"No! I..." Bok's head hurt. *Please... shut up and leave me alone.*

"Don't be absurd!" Tovano thundered. He had come in behind Kotarian, although Bok hadn't noticed when he entered the hall. But then again, sorcerers had a way of moving around discreetly when they wished.

"If Bok truly was an enemy spy, why was he fighting to save Princess Isabella's life? And why did he get wounded himself?" Tovano truly was mad for the first time Bok had seen. "You may have gotten an education at the House of Magic, but they sure haven't given you any brains!"

Kotarian shook his head. "But that doesn't explain how he—"

"That's enough!" Isabella yelled, voice cracking, from inside her room. "Avantil needs help! Now!"

CHAPTER 18

ISABELLA WAS RIGHT, OF course. Bok's head felt like his sister had used it as an anvil. But he shoved aside the pain, bulled past Kotarian, and forced his head clear.

He knelt over his injured friend, whose head rested on Isabella's lap. His blood quickly stained her white robe. "Be easy, my love. Don't try to move—help is here."

To Bok's surprise, Avantil started to regain consciousness—a good sign, although he remained delirious and weak. What worried Bok now was the nasty gash on the back of his friend's scalp. Bok touched Avantil's head with his fingertips. The blow hadn't fractured Avantil's skull, but it had cut him badly. If Bok didn't act quickly, Avantil would bleed to death.

Bok carefully lifted Avantil's head and placed it on a pillow, as Isabella held his hand.

"Easy; you've taken a pretty good knock, my friend. Just stay still." He dug around his healer's bag as the

Noble groaned. Bok pressed a clean white rag hard against Avantil's wound to staunch the bleeding. He then rubbed some white powder on the cut to further slow the flow of blood.

"Ow!" Avantil cried.

"So you are in there!" Bok quickly swapped out a clean cloth to cover the wound. "If you can feel pain, that's a good sign. And you're about to get more good signs than you ever imagined!"

Removing a needle and a spool of thick thread from his bag, Bok sewed up the cut. Avantil winced with each new stitch. "AAAHH! That really hurts!" he yelled with all the force in his lungs, which wasn't much after the severe beating he had received. But the bleeding stopped, and Bok was able to stitch up Avantil's other wounds.

Avantil tried to sit up, but Isabella stopped him and gently put his head back in her lap.

"Shhhh. Rest, my love." She stroked the hair from his face as Bok finished treating the wound on his arm. Once he finished, Bok pulled another powder made from ground roots from his healer's bag, mixed it with some wine and handed it to Avantil.

"Ugh—this smells awful."

"You can't be hurt too badly if you are complaining about the yorka root. Back home, we string it up around the fields to keep the rabbits from eating our vegetables; they hate the smell that much. But you need to drink it.

It'll take the sting out of that headache and help you get some rest." Avantil gulped down the thick brown potion with a grimace.

When he came to Coregan, Bok could see the older man's legs trembling, even as his facial expression remained unchanged.

Bok pulled aside the man's bloody shirt and almost gasped. Brac's sword had slashed deeply and left ragged, uneven wounds in Coregan's shoulder. It would take more than a bit of knitting powder and some thread to repair these cuts. He needed to try his most powerful healing spells—the ones Weni taught him and that he had yet to completely master.

"Coregan... you're hurt. You need to lay down."

"I'm fine, Bok. Been cut far worse than this in my line o' work. Just sew me up like you did the boy."

Bok's hands shook. "I must prepare a healing spell. I'll need to gather some supplies. And you need to lay down while I do."

"No. I tell you—I'm fine." Coregan waved him off. "Besides, there's no time. I'll rest when we're back on safe grounds. I'm not arguing, I'm telling—"

Just then, Bok heard a second set of moans from across the room. Coz Cosan was reviving. Bok figured his conversation with Coregan would have to wait.

"What... where... am I?"

Wingate held the man's arms and Coregan stepped in to interrogate their would-be killer. But Isabella raised her hand. "Let me speak with him."

The Princess knelt beside the groggy, wounded assassin. Coz tried to push himself off the floor but slipped and fell face-first back to the hardwood and into a pile of down from Avantil's disemboweled pillow. She waved her glowing hand over his head and whispered a few words. Bok couldn't hear what they were, but he could tell she was casting some sort of spell.

"Should you speak an untruth, your tongue will swell until it literally explodes in your mouth. So think carefully before you answer my questions. Do you understand?" Steel crept into her voice where moments before, there had only been compassion for Avantil.

The assassin's eyes bulged. He nodded demonstratively.

"You need to say it—but be careful. Do you understand what I have done to you?"

"Y-yes!" Coz stammered. His hands gingerly touched the sides of his stubbly round cheeks.

"Good. Now, why did you attack us?"

"Wuh-we wuz hired to kill you, ma'am. We wuz tole you'uns is merchants carryin' gold, 'n to make it look like a robb'ry. We didn't know you'uns is sorcerers—honest!"

"Obviously not. Had you known, you certainly wouldn't have been so foolish!" Kotarian said.

"Enough," Isabella silenced the ever-smirking sorcerer with a single glance. "Now, I want you to tell me who told you this. And if you value your life, or at least fear an agonizing death, you will not leave out a single detail."

"I-I don't know, honest!" The assassin's once-steady hands trembled. "A man met us at a bar here in Naseem—said he knew we wuz int'rested in this kinda work."

"You mean they knew you were criminals who would mercilessly kill for money." Isabella fixed her gaze on Coz, who still laid stomach-first on the floor.

"Yeah, that's right." He looked at the floor to avoid her condemning stare. "Anyway, he tole us he would pay five hunnerd golds each."

500 gold! The entire village of Soleh Valley couldn't come up with 500 gold, even if they sold every home, animal, and stick of furniture in the community. And the agents behind this attack were willing to pay that to each of these hired killers. Bok looked around to see if anyone else was as astonished as he was, but no one seemed to be.

"If the others got in our way, we wuz to kill them, too. All 'cept for him, the blond feller." Coz pointed a grease-stained finger at Kotarian.

"Me? Why me?" Kotarian lifted his hand to his puffed-out chest. "Doesn't your master know what I can do? Why would he not want me killed?" Bok was surprised at his tone; he seemed offended that his name got left off the list of murder victims.

"I-I dunno," Coz sputtered. "I wunnered that myself, but he wouldn't tell me who you were or why he wanted you dead. The man just said we wuz sendin' a message if we took care of the lady."

Given how fast he's breathing and how his hands are shaking, I don't think he's lying. Magic can have that effect on people.

Isabella exhaled deeply. She took her time with the interrogation, making Coz sweat out every question and answer. "What can you tell us about this man who hired you?"

The anger behind her slow, soft voice scared Bok—and more than a little. The Princess Isabella he knew was kind, thoughtful, gentle. But threaten those dear to her—including her subjects— and she became as hard as the iron his sister and father forged in their blacksmith's shop. Even though the assassins had tried to kill them, Bok couldn't help but feel a touch sorry for the man begging for his life before him.

"Honest, I-I can't tell you nothin' about him!"

The Princess leaned over until she was merely inches away from the assassin. "You met him at a bar. Surely, you remember what he looked like, what he wore, whether he had any sort of accent that might identify his country of origin."

"Buh-but that's just it, I can't!" Coz squealed. "I remember exactly what he said, but when I think about the man... nothin'!"

Tovano put his hand over his mouth. "This fellow is telling the truth. His mind has been clouded by a powerful enshroudment spell. He truly cannot remember the man who hired him."

"Hmm... I suppose not." Isabella stood, but continued to watch the assassin, who dared not move off the floor.

Behind them, heavy footsteps, accompanied by even heavier breathing, lumbered up the stairs.

"What's the meaning of this? What have you done to my inn?" The innkeeper panted. "They come and get me out of bed—say it sounds like a riot is taking place in this room. And from the look of things, they are right!"

Isabella reached into an embroidered silk purse and pulled out a handful of coins.

"Sir, we simply wished to enjoy a delicious meal and a good night's sleep at your fine establishment. Then, with neither warning nor provocation, these four cutthroats broke into our room and tried to rob us."

She handed the coins to the innkeeper. His expression immediately changed from angry to astonished. "Here are five gold—this should cover any damages as well as compensate you for your troubles." Isabella then pointed to Coz, still on the floor. "Please contact the local constables and have him arrested—he will confess to his crimes. My friends and I will leave your inn immediately and spare you any further aggravation."

Isabella motioned to Bok and Wingate, who carefully put Avantil's arms over their own shoulders to carry the injured nobleman out of the inn.

The innkeeper pinched, scratched, and bit the coins to discover that, yes, they truly were gold. "But... how am I supposed to keep him here until the constables arrive?"

"Do not worry. He will not give you any trouble."

"If you say so, miss." The innkeeper looked askance at the assassin, who remained perfectly still on the floor as if his life depended on it. Because, as far as Bok was concerned, it did.

Isabella walked out of the disheveled room behind Bok, Avantil, and Wingate.

Bok turned to Isabella. "Believe me, I will care for him like he was my own family."

"I know you will, Bok. That was never in doubt. It is just... I knew this journey could prove dangerous. But coming so close to losing Avantil? To losing you all? That was more than I was prepared to handle."

Bok understood. "I feel the same way, Your Majesty. And I'm going to do everything I can to make sure neither of us feels that way again."

CHAPTER 19

THEY WENT BACK DOWN to the inn's downstairs tavern, which was closed and empty for the night, until they could get ready to depart. As Bok continued tending to the injured, Isabella ducked into the kitchen and changed into her riding clothes. Tovano gathered their horses, while Kotarian went out to buy a cart with which to transport Avantil, who was too hurt to ride. Spotting a delivery cart making its rounds to the shops and eateries on their street, Kotarian spoke a few words to the driver, then returned a few moments later with the cart (minus the donkey).

"I'm sorry, Your Majesty, but that fruit peddler charged us two gold for this rickety donkey cart." Kotarian gestured to the humble carriage outside the inn. "By Sacrilian's Stupefying Silence, I should know better than to do business with a... laborer!"

"Or maybe you demanded when you could have asked politely." Bok surprised himself with the tinge of anger in his voice.

Kotarian gaped at the blacksmith's boy's sudden show of feistiness. Bok walked away before the sorcerer could reply. "Come on; we need to get Avantil into this cart and then back to bed. He needs to rest—and so does Coregan."

"I'm fine; I'll help." Coregan sweated heavily and staggered as he rose from his chair.

The Commander is far from "fine." He has lost so much blood...

"No, sit down." To Bok's surprise, Coregan didn't argue this time and returned to his seat.

Bok and Tovano then helped Avantil into the straw-filled cart. "I will ride with Avantil," Isabella declared. Wingate strapped the cart's simple harness to his powerful warhorse. He tied the reins of Isabella's horse to his saddle, while Bok did the same for Avantil's stallion.

With Isabella in the cart, Coregan insisted on mounting his horse and riding alongside her. Wingate rode ahead of the cart, with Kotarian and Tovano in the back, taking care to avoid being too close to one another.

"Beki and I will ride beside the cart, too, in case Avantil needs further aid." Coregan grunted a muffled reply. *And I also want to keep my eye on you, Commander. You are hurting far worse that you let on... not that you would admit it.*

Thankfully, the streets of Naseem largely were empty, so the party, some of whom still wore bloody clothes, didn't attract much attention. Wingate examined every dark side street and alleyway for trouble. "We shouldn't stay at any inn—those behind this attack will be looking for us there."

Tovano scratched his chin. "Think so, eh?"

"Whoever sent this death squad knows who we are. They probably know where we are headed and why." Wingate replied. "Anyone who went to this expense and trouble won't give up just yet."

"What should we do, young fella?"

Wingate kept his eyes on the road as he spoke. "When we are able, we continue to Osoh Creek. Clearly, there's something there that our mysterious attacker doesn't want us to know. Find that secret and we will find who hired these cutthroats."

Bok turned his head to Isabella, who continued cradling Avantil. *She truly loves him. And my friend needs my healer's skills. That must be my focus.*

"But what about tonight? Avantil isn't in condition for an overnight ride—and neither is the Commander." On one hand, Bok badly wanted to continue the journey and stop the Blight before any more innocents were harmed.

Particularly now that they suspected the malevolent force behind the Blight was actively trying to stop them.

But Avantil and Coregan were his patients now, and as a healer, he had an obligation to put their care above his own fears for his family's safety. *If Mother and Father were here, they would tell me the same.*

Hands on his head, Avantil gingerly sat up in the back of the donkey cart. "Uhhh... I may be of some help. Assuming I can clear the cotton from my brain."

Isabella supported him with her arms. "Lie still, my love. Don't—"

"No, I have an idea. One of my family's trading partners, Grenuteral & Associates, is based here in Naseem. Lord and Lady Grenuteral happen to be on that voyage with my parents. Their home is in the heart of the city—and I'm fairly certain it will be empty. We can stay there for a few days, I think."

Isabella's dark eyes widened. "You mean trespass in their family home? As if we were criminals?"

"Like long-lost friends!" Avantil grinned. "They won't mind, particularly when they see the bag of gold we leave for their troubles. OW! Watch the cobblestones, Wingate!"

In less than an hour, the exhausted, bedraggled group arrived at the Grenuteral home. Bok whistled upon approaching the gate. The three-story home featured large stone columns in the front and a back garden secluded by thick rows of hedges. A wrought iron fence encircled the property, but otherwise, there were no signs of any security and no light came from the home.

"I'll open the gate. It appears to be a simple latch—WHOA!!" When Bok touched the metal latch, an invisible force threw him backward. He would've fallen had Wingate not caught him as he stumbled.

"An eldritch alarm." Tovano scratched his gray temple. "Figures they wouldn't leave such a nice home unguarded."

"Is there anything we can do?" When Bok looked closely, he saw the faint blue-green outline of the magic dome around the perimeter of the property.

Tovano nodded. "Certainly. This is a low-level alarm spell—hardly the type used to safeguard Sonorian Square or the Royal Palace."

Kotarian cracked his knuckles. "Botharian's Battering Barrage would shatter that low-quality shield instantly."

"As well as every window and half of the eardrums on the block." Tovano replied. "No, this takes nuance. Allow me..." The old sorcerer placed his hands at the side of his head and closed his eyes. He quietly spoke a few words and slowly, a small hole in the dome began to open, just big enough for a person to walk through.

Bok tried the latch again. This time, it opened. The group made its way into the courtyard and Tovano ceased concentrating. The hole in the dome immediately sealed behind them.

Hands on knees, Tovano took a moment to catch his breath. Bok handed the man some water and he eagerly accepted it.

"That's a disruption spell, Bok. It can temporarily negate another sorcerer's magic—but only for a brief time and only while the second spellcaster maintains her or his concentration. It is a great deal more difficult from outside the perimeter of the spell than it would be inside of it."

Getting in the house was considerably easier. The lock on the back door was mechanical, not magical. After Tovano recovered, he jimmied it with a basic turnkey spell.

Bok exhaled when they stepped into the quiet, empty—and hopefully safe—house. With his assistance, Avantil climbed the steps and into one of the five upstairs beds, with Tavano claiming another one. Bok applied a healing poultice to his friend's scalp and gave him another dose of the yorka root, hoping to grant his patient a long, uninterrupted night's sleep.

He returned to the kitchen. The rest of the group moved their bags and supplies into the house. Coregan insisted on carrying in his own bag. "'m fine," he said weakly. But after taking just two steps into the house, he stumbled and collapsed unconscious.

"Commander!" Wingate rushed to his mentor's side and found him muttering in a barely audible whisper.

Bok knelt to examine Coregan. "His wounds have reopened. I need to get these cuts closed or he'll bleed to death!"

Wingate lifted Coregan like he was a child and placed him on a bed in a lower floor bedroom. Bok pulled some items out of his healer's bag and pointed to the pantry. "See if they have any dried sage." It wasn't exactly the herb he needed, but Weni Kon told him sage could work for a healing spell in a pinch. Isabella jumped up and searched the cabinets.

"Kotarian, find me some clean rags—please." To his relief, Kotarian did as asked without complaint.

Bok then ripped open Coregan's shirt, cleaned the gory gashes on his shoulder, and stitched the wounds closed.

When Isabella returned with the sage, Bok tossed a pinch into the air, took each of Coregan's hands, and began his Folk Magic incantation. He closed his eyes and focused all his thoughts, all his energy on repairing Coregan's injuries. *Heal this man. Flesh become whole. Wounds knit and strength return.*

He held the spell for a full five minutes, until he could hold it no longer. With a gasp, he opened his eyes.

Such a spell was one of the most powerful in a healer's repertoire—but one of the trickiest. One small mistake and the spell could fail.

He dropped the Commander's hands and pulled back the man's shirt. The wound remained raw, but the bleeding had stopped. Bok then smeared the cuts with a salve to keep the wound clean. *I... I finally did something right.*

"How is he?" Isabella asked, Wingate looking over her shoulder

Bok wiped perspiration from his brow. "He's... better, but still not well. If I had treated him an hour ago, I'd feel much better, but—"

"You did the best that could be done under the circumstances, Bok." Isabella squeezed his arm again. "Wingate, please keep watch over the Commander and let me know if there is any change in his condition."

"But, Your Majesty, I must be at your side to protect you. What if we are attacked again?"

Isabella raised a single finger. "Currently, the Commander needs you more. You have pushed yourself this whole trip, always putting our concerns ahead of your own. Consider yourself relieved of your duty until tomorrow morning."

Wingate opened his mouth, but Isabella would hear none of it. "That is my decision and, as your princess, I command you to carry it out!"

They stepped back into the kitchen to find Kotarian rummaging through the Grenuteral's cabinets. With a satisfied "A-ha!", he pulled out a bottle of red wine.

"This day has been a complete disaster. I only can hope tomorrow brings better fortune—or a quick death." He walked up the stairs, bottle in hand, without a word to the others.

When Kotarian was out of sight, Isabella's shoulders slumped as she sat at the table. "He is correct, you know."

"About what, Your Majesty?" Bok put a kettle of water on the wood-burning stove.

"This day—this mission—has been a complete disaster, as Kotarian said. Avantil and Coregan were almost killed, we are fleeing for our lives—from what, exactly? They know us, but we know nothing of them." She closed her tired eyes and put her hand to her aching forehead.

"True, they have us on the run." Bok took a seat beside Isabella. "But that isn't your fault. We all were taken by surprise at the inn."

Isabella leaned toward him and shook her hands vigorously, tears now welling in her eyes. "It is entirely my fault! It was my idea to come here, and I asked each of you to follow. Ultimately, your safety—and the success of this mission—falls on my shoulders. I should have been prepared for every possible outcome."

"Now wait!" Bok held up his hands. "Prepared for every possible outcome? That is impossible. You can't hold yourself to that standard, Your Majesty."

"But... I am the Crown Princess. If I fall short in my duties, the whole kingdom suffers. Perhaps Kotarian is right, and I am not up to the challenge."

"Well, we must be close enough to the truth that our enemies are nervous. So you are doing something right." Bok offered her a soft smile. "I don't know anything about being royalty, but I know you have prepared for this your whole life. You are up to this challenge, Your Majesty. And that is the truth."

She sniffed, then chuckled. "You only say that because you must!"

He returned to the kitchen, lifted the hot kettle from the stove and poured it into the coffee press. "Remember, Your Majesty—I am just a Serving Class boy from Soleh Valley. I could flatter you for a month solid, and I still couldn't hold an estate or serve on the Royal Council."

Setting a mug in front of her, Bok sat back down. "So, believe me when I say we need your leadership, Isabella. Even Kotarian. He is a powerful weapon, but he still requires your guidance. I know strong women. Trust me when I say you are one."

Isabella stared into her mug. But tears no longer pooled in her eyes.

Me, of all people, providing counsel to our princess? I would have thought this one of Yata's pranks. Except it didn't end with me getting punched in the arm. Bok couldn't help but grin thinking about what his sister's reaction to this conversation would be.

"You're laughing at me!" Isabella looked up, trying not to succumb to laughter herself. "I must admit, that is not a reaction I normally receive!"

"No, no—it's not that, Isabella! I was just thinking about my sister."

"Again, that is hardly the response I expected!" Now, they both chortled.

"No! It's—you have to know Yata," Bok forced himself to say in between laughs. "If she were here, she would scold me for not thrashing that assassin more quickly. And then she would lift her hammer and stand beside us in this fight."

"It sounds like you are fortunate to have Yata for a sister. As I am fortunate to have you as a friend." Isabella wiped the remaining tears from her face. "Thank you, Bok. And do not think I missed that you called me by my name. I hope to hear it again."

CHAPTER 20

B OK GOT UP EARLIER than he wanted the next morning. While still somewhat tired, he was ready to get out of an unfamiliar bed. Yata would have cackled at that, for he always seemed to be the last one to his family's breakfast table. Of course, it didn't help that Kotarian snored as loudly as a hibernating bear in the next room over.

Bok first checked on Coregan, who thankfully remained asleep. Bok had looked in on the man several times during the night. The yorka root appeared to be doing its work in easing his pain. The Commander needed at least another week in bed, but Bok figured he had about as much chance of making that happen as a blacksmith's boy did of attending the Grand Merchants Gala.

Once in the hall, he noticed the door to Isabella and Avantil's room was cracked open. Inside, Isabella and Avantil cuddled together in their sleep, his arm draped across her waist. His face grew hot, and he quickly looked away.

Alone in summer morning quiet, Bok poured a glass of water and sat on the edge of his borrowed bed. Only those born to the Noble Class even had the potential to use that potent brand of magic—the type of magic that could create and destroy. *How was I able to cast that spell? And could I do it again?*

In the life-or-death excitement of the previous day, no one had pressed him on it. He had been more concerned with keeping Avantil and Coregan alive, and then Isabella needed him. And truth be told, he didn't want to consider what his actions at the Raybun Inn might indicate.

Because the only possible explanation he could come up with would be if, somehow, he was not truly the son of Tana and Fin Omat. He knew his grandparents well enough to know his parents weren't secretly Noble Class themselves. That led him with the uncomfortable conclusion that his parents had misled him about his own origins.

But Serving Class life—and his parents' love—was all he had ever known. Certainly, they would not lie about something so important. Someone who knew more about High Magic—Isabella, Tovano, or even Kotarian—surely could relieve those fears.

He couldn't avoid the question any longer—he needed answers. Bok went downstairs thinking about who could provide it when—

"Got a lot on your mind." Tovano's voice startled Bok, as if Bok had conjured the elder mage simply by thinking of him.

"I suppose I do," Bok whispered, not wanting to wake the others. "How did you know—? Did you perform some sort of spell?"

"Hardly." Tovano's wrinkle-creased face tightened into a smile. He took a deep sip of his sassafras tea. "If you've been around as long as I have, you learn to read people's faces. Yours tells me that you have many questions and few solutions. I think I know why."

"Come." He rose from his chair. "Let's go outside. I don't have all the answers you want, but maybe we can come up with some together."

The hot morning air stuck to Bok's skin as they entered the estate's enclosed backyard. The grass came up over the men's ankles when they stomped into the middle of the yard, away from the house. Tovano whistled an old folk tune and fished a green apple from his pocket.

"Am I supposed to do something with that apple?" Bok asked.

"Ha! No, not at all! This is my post-breakfast snack!" Tovano chomped into the apple. Between crunchy chews, he continued. "No, I want you to do something with this."

He tossed a small glass globe into the air as he walked into the yard and motioned to Bok to follow.

Tovano then slapped the top of an old oak stump with his weathered, skinny hand. "When you've been casting spells as long as I have, you can do plenty with a plain, everyday object like this." To illustrate his point, he threw the globe high into the air and quickly whispered a few words. It levitated at the apex of its ascent and took off sideways, zooming around the yard and slaloming between the backyard pine trees. Then, as quickly as it started moving, the glass ball stopped again as it returned to the sorcerer's palm.

"Now, if you get really old and bored, you can learn to do something like this!" Tovano spoke a different incantation, waved his other hand and the globe vanished. Tovano pointed at a large rock around 100 feet away. The sphere rested safely in the grass in front of the rock.

"That is amazing!" Bok exclaimed. While Folk Magic had its valuable uses, none of them were nearly as dramatic.

"That is a transmission spell—the user can move an object across short distances instantaneously. Even through walls! However, the spell can never be used on anything living," Tovano shrugged his bony shoulders. "Transmission spells are never completely precise—to be honest with you, I was trying to place the globe on top of the rock, not in front of it. If I do that with a person and they end up materializing inside a solid object... well, I think you understand why you can't transmit a living creature!"

Bok nodded. "I had no idea such things were possible, even through High Magic."

"Oh, this is just the beginning of what you can do with High Magic." Tovano finished the last bite of his apple and tossed the core into the grass. "But today, we are going to start with something much more basic. Do you remember the words to the push-pull spell you used last night?"

Bok shuffled his feet. His breathing sped up. "Um, I believe so. Do you want me to try to use it on that stump?"

"Oh, no!" Tovano chuckled. "This stump is rooted deeply in the ground; I would be hard-pressed to animate it and I've been doing this spell for more than 40 years!"

Tovano placed the crystal sphere on top of the stump. "No, what I want you to do is to simply animate this globe. Don't worry if you can't hold it long. Just get it moving—if you can. And if you can't, then we'll consider last night up to one of those mysteries of life."

The more Tovano talked, the more skeptical Bok became that he could repeat this incredible feat. He wondered if his actions back at the inn were some once-in-a-lifetime fluke born of desperation, an answered prayer, or even a spell cast unknowingly by Isabella, some sort of self-defense reflex of a trained sorcerer. *But I have to try the spell again. I must know for sure.*

"Just take it slowly, my young friend." Tovano encouraged in a low, soothing voice. Bok closed his eyes and pictured each of the words to the spell in his mind. Word by word, he spoke the incantation, carefully enunciating each syllable for fear of the sounds tangling on his tongue.

His eyelids remained shut, but Bok could feel the invisible tendrils of magical energy snaking forward from his fingertips. They crawled across the ground and through the air toward the glass ball. He had experienced this sensation once before, when he willed the dresser to move across the room to save himself and his friends from mortal danger. Except this time, he was aware of what was happening and controlled the magic. He could almost understand why Kotarian carried himself as he did.

Bok stretched his arms forward. The globe rolled, then dribbled, then bounced once—twice—and into the air. It hovered precariously an inch or two above the stump, like a baby bird pushed out of the nest to test its wings for the first time.

"Right, right." Tovano clapped softly. "Keep it going. Just a few... more... seconds."

Bok's strength ebbed. His outstretched arms ached under a phantom strain, as if he held Yata's hammer.

Bok opened his eyes. The connection instantly severed, and gravity took its course. The globe dropped onto the stump with a thud, shattering when it struck the wood.

"I-I'm sorry about your globe, Tovano," Bok sputtered, hoping he hadn't broken a favorite heirloom.

"Don't you worry about that! Cost me two silver at the Great Bazaar—they've got a whole table of them." He walked a quick circle around the globe, making mental calculations of the height it reached and the time Bok held it in the air. He shook his head vigorously. "I say, that was quite a feat, my friend! How did you—?"

"That's what you're supposed to tell me!" Bok flexed his arms, trying to bring feeling back to his stiff muscles.

Tovano continued to shake his head side to side. "By all rights, you shouldn't be able to do that, even if you are what I suspect."

"What I suspect?" I don't like the sound of those words. "What do you suspect? What do you mean?"

Tovano put his hand on Bok's shoulder. "Come; let's go back in the house."

Bok started to object, but Tovano cut him off. "I know you want answers, but Princess Isabella must hear what we are about to discuss."

"Bok, your life is about to change. Nothing you've heard about or experienced can prepare you for what you are about to hear. You are no longer a simple village healer. You soon will become one of the most important people in Imarina!"

CHAPTER 21

Tovano's gentle hand stirred Isabella from sleep.

"Tovano…? Is everything okay?" She rolled over to see Avantil still asleep and visibly relaxed when she realized he was fine.

"Oh, yes, yes, yes—everything is well, Your Majesty!" the sorcerer whispered. "But Bok and I need to speak to you. In private, please." Tovano's excitement—and the mystery surrounding his behavior—concerned Bok as much as it piqued his curiosity.

They went downstairs and Isabella rubbed her eyes in protest of the already-bright morning sun.

"Your Majesty, pardon the interruption. It's just—after what happened at the inn yesterday, Bok and I conducted an experiment, and it confirms my suspicions. Mister Omat here is a Noble and has the Acumen for High Magic!"

Nausea hit Bok in the stomach—just as it did when the wolves attacked. He began to hyperventilate and turned away so his friends could not see his panic.

Tovano had just confirmed his suspicions—and his dread. Only members of the Noble Class may be born with the ability to use High Magic. When the Nobles claimed they were born to rule, they offered this as proof. Such was the natural order of things, or so Bok had always been taught.

So if Bok could perform High Magic, he must be a member of the Noble Class. It was a simple matter of connecting the dots.

That also means I am not the son of Tana and Fin Omat of Soleh Valley. But... but how can that be? I have my father's green eyes and my mother's affinity for baking bread. Yata even remembers the day I was born—she calls it the saddest day of her childhood. She was used to getting all of Mother and Father's attention and when I came along, she had to share.

Isabella furrowed her eyebrows. "Why would you declare such a thing, Tovano? You have upset Bok!" Although groggy a moment earlier, Tovano's proclamation provided a bucket of ice water to her face. "Surely, in your decades of study, you must have encountered some other explanation for what Bok did."

"I know this is a shock, but I am quite certain." Tovano tapped his finger against a tabletop. "He displayed some remarkable Acumen just now."

Isabella shook her head forcefully. "No, Tovano! What happened last night was an act of desperation. Bok's life and those of his friends were in danger. He reached out with Folk Magic abilities that somehow simulated an effect resembling High Magic. But a lost Noble? That is a huge conclusion to spring on our friend."

Tovano looked into Isabella's rapidly blinking eyes. "Perhaps if last night was the only evidence. But just this morning, Bok reproduced the push-pull spell, this time under no duress—and with great effect! I dare say he did almost as well as you the first time you tried, and a fair bit better than me. There can be no other answer: Bok Omat is of Noble birth."

Isabella went quiet and looked away. Bok slumped into a chair, unable to stand

My parents lied to me my entire life. Were they secretly Noble Class, too? No—why would they work such hard lives as a blacksmith and farmer? How did I come to live with them—do I have another family out there? Does Yata know the truth, or was she lied to as well?

Too many questions. I wish I could run away, go back home to Soleh Valley, and forget I ever heard of sorcerers or Blights or High Magic.

Tovano gave no indication he noticed Bok's distress. "Don't take my word for it, Your Highness. Bok, could you please give the Princess a demonstration?"

Bok felt like a show pony paraded around for the lords and ladies at one of the Royal Palace's fancy equestrian events. The last thing he wanted to do was attempt another spell, after what the last one had brought him. But he would cooperate.

"Okay. Do you want me to... animate something again?"

"No, let's try something different." Tovano whispered some words into his ear. "Just a simple pyromancy spell, Your Majesty. Although I would advise stepping back!"

Bok nodded and licked his lips, then shook out his hands and jogged in place. At least focusing on the spell gave his jumbled mind a reprieve from sorting out all the conflicting emotions he was feeling.

He repeated the words Tovano had given him and followed the directions to the letter, speaking the words in their proper cadence and performing the hand gestures exactly as Tovano had shown him.

Bok could feel Isabella's eyes focused on his every movement. His tongue tripped and his fingers tangled. He pointed his hand forward...and nothing happened.

"I... I'm sorry. I thought I could do it." *I should be relieved. But part of me is... disappointed.*

Isabella bounced forward on the balls of her feet. "I told you so! Bok is who he seems to be. And that is plenty." She patted his broad shoulder.

Instead of comfort, pain stitched Bok's flesh where her hand had been. *Does Isabella pity me for being Serving Class?*

Bok gritted his teeth and tried the spell again.

At first, nothing happened. But then, Bok's fingertips began to throb and burn, as though he had touched his family's wood-burning stove.

He flicked his hand toward the kitchen—and a gout of eldritch fire shot forth from his fingers. The stream of flame struck a dishrag on the counter and set it on fire. Isabella gasped in what sounded like horror.

"Oh, dear!" Tovano mumbled. "Perhaps that wasn't the best choice of spells..."

Isabella numbly waved her hands and the fire soon smoldered and died, covered by an unseen blanket of magic. Bok's display dimmed her usual spark. Not so for Tovano, who practically skipped around the kitchen.

"You see? He must be a Noble! Such a man would be a powerful ally for the Crown, Your Majesty. A young sorcerer like you, whose loyalties lie with the King alone, not the House of Magic."

Tovano placed his hand on Bok's shoulder. "I'm sure we can arrange an appropriate title for you—the Barony of Nardru is vacant, as the former Baron died without an heir. You could fill that position and study sorcery with me in Ithenel. What do you say?"

"I... I don't know. I need to think..." Bok's brain whirled, unable to process Tovano's offer. "This would mean leaving my home... my family..." *But do I still have a place in Soleh Valley, after what I have learned?*

So he turned to the Princess, desperate for guidance. "Isabella, what should I do?"

Isabella said nothing—but she didn't have to. The fact she couldn't even look at Bok said it all.

CHAPTER 22

B OK THREW HIMSELF INTO chores the next two days. He cooked every meal, hauled water from the well, helped Wingate groom the horses, and ministered to Coregan. Staying busy helped some, but not a great deal.

When he wasn't working around the house, Tovano had him practicing spells in the backyard. He focused on the push-pull and pyromancy spells, as Tovano didn't want to overload his new student. Bok struggled to control both—a tiny flame exploded into a raging blaze; a gentle nudge became a rough shove. But every time Bok became frustrated, Tovano provided needed guidance, and focused his young student again.

On the third afternoon of training, Bok successfully raised one of Tovano's glass globes a few inches off the ground, then brought it back down softly, without damaging the fragile orb.

"I always knew you had it in you, Bok—or should I say, the Baron of Nardru?" Avantil stepped out from the back porch and walked down into the yard to where Bok and Tovano trained. He slapped Bok on the back. "Ow! Shouldn't have done that—my head is still throbbing! But I can endure a little pain to welcome you."

"Welcome me to what?" Bok crossed his arms to await Avantil's reply.

"The Noble Class! Honestly, Bok—we're not all snobbish elites. But you'll learn that for yourself."

No, I'll never be one of you. It was a statement of fact as much as defiance. He never could be Noble Class, no matter how many spells he learned or how much of the "Acumen" he carried. Bok had been raised in Soleh Valley, as far distant from the sophistication and bustle of Ithenel as one could get in Imarina. He was well-mannered, sure—his parents had raised him that way—but he knew little about the intricate customs of the Noble Class. *A blessing? More like a pox. I'd gladly give up the Acumen if people would never call me "Baron" again.*

But he wouldn't have that chance, not if Tovano had anything to say about it. And he certainly did. He had informed every member of the group that, without a doubt, Bok was a Noble, blessed with an open invitation to the Royal Palace and the Acumen for High Magic.

I wish Tovano would give me more time to process this. Most of all, I wish I could talk with Mother and Father.

Whatever the truth, I want to hear it from my family's own lips.

"Baron, are you in there?" Avantil waved a hand in front of Bok's face.

"Oh, um, sorry. I got lost for a moment. It's been a difficult week."

"I know—and I do not mean to make light of your burden, Bok. But that is why you have friends, to share that load."

Bok bit his lower lip and nodded. *Friends. Yes—at least I can trust my friends.*

After dinner, Isabella called Bok and Avantil back the kitchen table, where she sat with Wingate.

Wingate nodded to Avantil. "My apologies for disturbing you while you recover, Lord Amorinil."

"Not a worry. The Exalted One gave me a thick skull, perhaps with little inside it. What troubles you, my friend?"

Bok cleared the table but kept an ear on the conversation. *A new Noble or not, I still can't ignore a dirty dish.* He filled a gleaming white ceramic basin with clean water and deposited the plates in it. He then soaped up a clean cotton cloth and gently washed each item.

Wingate spoke softly and deliberately. "We know someone is trying to stop us from reaching Osoh Creek. Whoever it is, I believe they have found a way to track our movements through Imarina."

"But who?" Isabella drummed her fingernails against the table's dark mahogany surface. "The only people who knew of our mission were the Royal Council and trusted staff."

"And how? Avantil added. "Coregan has us on these back country roads, sleeping in fields, disguising ourselves. They can't trace us with magics, either. Everything we have with us, we brought from the Royal Palace."

"Except for one thing." Bok pointed to the string of cloth flowers Isabella received in Ithenel, which now rested on the kitchen counter, draped over a black and white vase. "We didn't bring that necklace. And our troubles started after we got it."

"Now wait a minute!" Avantil's face reddened. "Tartio Thanilar has done business with my family since I was a child. Granted, he holds traditionalist views on class structure. But that doesn't make him a traitor to the Crown."

"Perhaps not. But we must know for sure." Isabella whispered an incantation, and a greenish light filled the room. The cloth flowers immediately glowed red. Bok dropped the blue porcelain dish he was drying, and it shattered into fragments on the clay tile floor.

"Curse me for a fool—they are enchanted! This necklace has put our enemies right on our heels." But before she could examine the spell signature on the cloth blossoms, they flashed bright white—and crumbled into a pile of ash.

Avantil held his fingertips to his open mouth. "Remind me to buy you chocolates next time, my sweet."

Isabella sighed. "A counter-spell. Someone went to a lot of trouble to ensure we could not discover their identity. Someone far more powerful than a neighborhood shopkeeper."

"But we do now know two important facts: One, those conspiring against us possesses highly sophisticated magics. And two, they are operating from the heart of the kingdom itself!"

CHAPTER 23

GIVEN THAT KNOWLEDGE, ISABELLA decided they should resume their journey to Osoh Creek in two days' time. According to Tovano, the estate's security spell provided them some protection from discovery, but an enemy this resourceful surely would keep looking until they were found. Coregan still needed more time to recover, but Bok knew arguing with the Commander would prove fruitless.

They also resumed posting guards on their last night in the Grenuteral home. Isabella volunteered to take the first shift upstairs, while Bok remained in the downstairs den. While he kept watch, he settled into a red upholstered chair and studied the spellbook Tovano loaned him. The shield spell was the first—and perhaps most important—spell a combat sorcerer learned as a House of Magic acolyte. Spellcasters learned a nearly unlimited range of attack magics, but one general spell for defense. Tovano explained that mastering the Sonorian's Stalwart Shield could be the difference between life or death.

As he studied, Bok attempted to mimic the gestures and movements the sorcerer had showed him. But he couldn't quite get it right. He slapped his palm down on the chair's cushioned arm and groaned. *This is impossible. I'll never be able to do this.*

"No—you fold your index finger over your middle one and then snap your wrist, rather than waving your hand," Kotarian stood in the open doorway between the kitchen and den, waving another bottle of wine.

"Like this." He set the bottle on the edge of a bookshelf and cracked his knuckles. With a few muttered words and a quick hand motion, a textbook-perfect mystical shield appeared in front of him. Even with Bok's rudimentary knowledge of High Magic, he could tell it was more potent even than the ones Tovano could conjure.

He looked to Kotarian, who simply raised his eyebrows. Bok tried the spell himself, concentrating on the words and gesturing as Kotarian showed him. A blue-green field of energy appeared in front of him. He poked it with a finger. It gave a little but was solid.

"Thank you, Kotarian! You should be my tutor."

Kotarian scoffed. "What, you think I have time to spoon-feed magic to an absolute beginner less ready than the slowest, most ill-prepared first-year apprentice on

Sonorian Square?" He uncorked the wine bottle with his hands and tilted the bottle back for a deep drink.

"I-I'm sorry!" Bok sputtered. "I didn't intend it that way at all! I simply meant... that you are skilled at sorcery, and I appreciate the small fraction of your knowledge that you shared. Honestly—my sole intent was gratitude."

Kotarian took another slug from the wine bottle. "Humph! Well, I suppose that is understandable. Were I in your position, I'd be grateful if one with my talents shared their counsel, too."

Probably the nicest thing Kotarian has said to me on the entire trip. "Were your parents in the House of Magic, too?"

"No, my parents and I lived on our estate just east of Ithenel." Kotarian took a seat beside Bok and set the bottle on an ornately carved end table. "But I never wanted to be someone who managed peasants and attended masquerades. I wanted to do more. When I was 14 summers, I submitted my name to the House of Magic to be screened for the Acumen. To my great delight but hardly my surprise, I was found to be imbued with the ability to perform High Magic.

"I served my four-year apprenticeship, studying with such masters as Salandrian and even Karagian himself. I finished at the top of my class. It's why I wear this." Kotarian tapped the starburst brooch affixed to his shirt. "Upon completing my apprenticeship, I became an acolyte of the House and was given increasingly important duties. Once we return, I will be formally inducted as a full member of the House of Magic. The culmination of seven years of work and sacrifice."

Bok exhaled. "I can see why magic makes you so passionate."

"More than you can ever know."

The bed creaked in Coregan's room. Bok bolted up and checked on the resting Guardian. Still asleep.

He turned back to Kotarian but lowered his voice to a whisper. "I bet Karagian was a tough teacher. He seemed like a real fireball back at the council meeting."

Kotarian stroked his hand through his short blond hair. "Ha! A 'fireball'! He would like that country colloquialism. Yes, he is demanding. But I earned his complete respect. I am honored to call him a mentor."

Bok sat down and stared at the red-and-white striped wallpaper—something he'd never seen in Soleh Valley. He thought about bringing up Weni Kon, but he figured Kotarian might be insulted if he compared a Folk Magic healer to the House of Magic Chancellor. "What about Salandrian? He wasn't like the rest of you sorcerers. He seemed..."

"Inept? Hapless?" Kotarian laughed, gargling a mouthful of wine as he did. "Don't get me wrong—Salandrian is a fine academic and is an excellent steward of the House's collection of arcane knowledge.

But as a magic-user? He's not in the same class as Karagian, Loronian… or me, if I am being honest."

"From what I've seen, I can believe it." Bok closed the spellbook. "I'm glad you are here for another reason, Kotarian. Tovano's story about me being Noble born… it seems far-fetched, but given the evidence, I can think of no other answer. You know far more about High Magic than I ever will. What do you think?"

Kotarian's eyes went wide. "Of course it's far-fetched. The idea of you as some long-lost Noble? The heir to a legacy of magical ability? When you are so… Serving Class. The notion of you being one of us is absurd!"

Bok rubbed the back of his neck, reaching under his dark brown hair. "What you say is harsh, but not untrue. How then I can I perform High Magic? I'm hardly a sorcerer or your level or Princess Isabella's"—the comparison caused Kotarian to frown—"but you saw what I did just now."

"Sonorian's Stalwart Shield! Speak the name if you are going to use it."

"My apologies—Sonorian's Stalwart Shield. How could I cast such a spell if I am Serving Class, as I have believed my entire life?"

"Oh, you definitely are Noble Class!" Kotarian drained the last of the wine. "Just because what Tovano says is absurd doesn't make it any less true. Someway, somehow, you are of Noble Class parentage. Perhaps your mother…"

Kotarian laughed to himself, as Bok's ears grew hot. "Well, some jests are too pointed even for me."

Kotarian ended Bok's final hope of returning to life as he'd known it. *Perhaps it is time to stop fretting about what is past and start figuring out how to move forward.*

Bok stared out the window into the dark Naseem night, his mind returning to a decade in the past. When he and Yata were children, they pretended to be sorcerers on those days when their chores were done and their parents told them to get outside and play. But those were childhood fantasies—adventures that a young boy and his rough 'n' tumble sister spun to fend off the boredom of long summer days. This was real, as much as he wished it weren't.

I prayed that I find a way to protect my family and friends, and I have been granted that gift. I still need answers, but one thing is clear: I must use these abilities to help others.

The blacksmith's boy is a Noble and a sorcerer now, whether I want to be or not. Maybe I never was a blacksmith's boy at all.

"Thank you, Kotarian. I suppose Tovano and I have plenty of work ahead of us."

Kotarian threw back his head and laughed. "Tovano—ha! Tell me, Baron Blacksmith, do you trust Tovano?"

Bok nodded.

"That is your first and biggest mistake." Kotarian slammed the empty wine bottle down on the end table between his seat and Bok's. "Has he told you the circumstances of his departure from the House of Magic?"

"No. I don't know the exact story, but I get the sense he left in protest of certain House practices."

"Of course, that's what he wants you to think!" Kotarian spat. "The truth is, Bok, that your trusted mentor Tovano was expelled from the House of Magic. It was before my time, and as I am not yet a full member, I am not privy to the exact nature of the dispute. But I can say for sure that his departure was the decision of our leaders, not some lofty sacrifice by Tovanian—or Tovano, as you know him.

"While it is no concern of mine, I'd caution against putting too much faith in that charlatan," Kotarian continued. "Your 'friend' Tovano desires one thing—what is best for Tovano. Everything and everyone else are just collateral to purchase that reward."

Expelled from the House of Magic? Was Tovano a forked-tongue opportunist, rather than the kindly old teacher he appeared to be? Tovano has been eager to help, while Kotarian... well, has been Kotarian.

But the young sorcerer reinforced one idea in Bok's mind: If he listened, studied, and practiced as he had never done before, he could master High Magic. He cast another shield spell and this time, it was a bit sturdier and lasted a few seconds longer than his previous attempt.

"A bit better. But you have farther to go than you can even imagine." Kotarian pointed to the empty wine bottle. "Take care of that, will you? I'm going to bed."

Bok mulled over what Kotarian had said for a while, then decided his time would be better spent reviewing the spellbook, rather than pondering his now-uncertain parentage.

After another hour of study, he jumped when he heard a loud creak from the kitchen. Houses naturally settle at night. Surely, a groaning floorboard caused that noise. But Bok eased out of his chair and tiptoed into the kitchen just to make sure...

WHAM! Something hard and flat struck him between the shoulder blades, knocking the wind from his body and his body to the floor.

"Wot are ye doin' here, villain?! Answer me or I'll brain ye good!"

CHAPTER 24

B OK LOOKED UP TO see a scrawny young woman with long, stringy light brown hair wielding an iron skillet like a Royal Guardian would a sword.

"D-don't move!" she screamed. "I know how ta use this and don't think I won't!"

At that point, Isabella ran down the stairs. "Stop! Please—we mean you no harm!"

"Wait—you?" The woman gaped at Isabella and relaxed her aggressive stance.

"Do-do you know her, Isabella?"

"*Bok!*" Isabella's rebuke startled him, but too late. He had compromised her identity—and possibly safety.

"No worries, Yer Majesty!" A massive grin stretched across the young woman's long, narrow face. "I knew you was Princess Isabella! I recognized yer face from paintings I seen!"

Remembering her manners, she quickly curtseyed. "I'm a loyal subject o' the Crown, Yer Majesty. Name's Umra Sel. I'm the housekeeper an' caretaker o' this property. I been comin' by once a week since the Grenuterals has been out of town. You've nothing to fear from me—I'd never tell yer secret, honest!"

She then pointed to Bok. "And you! You must be an earl or baron of some sort. Are you Lord Amorinil, consort to Her Majesty? That's it! Figgered you would be a bit taller, sir—but 'tis my pleasure to make yer acquaintance!"

"No. I'm really... My name is... Bok Omat, a healer from Soleh Valley. I'm sorry if you find that disappointing, Umra."

"Not at all! Yer Servin' Class like me then? So whatcha doin' with Her Majesty?"

"I can answer that, Umra," Isabella interjected. "Again, I need your discretion—but as you said, I can trust you. Bok is assisting me on a secret mission of vital importance to the Crown. Knowing the Grenuteral family's loyalty to my father, we took shelter here as to remain undetected. But we are leaving in a few hours and—"

"I'll come with ye!" Umra threw her arms out to her side.

"Excuse me?"

"I could be a big help, Yer Majesty. I'm a great cook, can handle the horses. Whatever ye need me ta do!"

Isabella cleared her throat. "Umra, I am certain you are excellent at your job. But I must decline your generous offer. This mission could prove dangerous."

"Could?" We've nearly died twice!

"But Yer Majesty—I'm not afraid! I know my way 'round a scrap. And there's nothin' ta hold me here."

"Don't you have a job working for the Grenuteral family?" Bok asked.

"The Grenuteral family—pshaw!" Umra snorted. "Lord Grenuteral is a complete taskmaster. 'Clean this again, Umra. You haven't finished in the dining room, Umra.' And Lady Grenuteral? She looks down 'er nose at any of us not Noble born. Er, no offense, Yer Majesty."

"Oh, um, none taken. But—"

"Anyway, you both can go back to bed. We can talk about my place on the mission later. But first, I'm gonna fix you the best breakfast you ever et!" Umra shooed Isabella and Bok up the stairs. "Me, cookin fer Princess Isabella! If Mother was alive ta see it..."

Bok wasn't ready to completely trust their security to this young woman. However, she had more right to be in the home than they did. So, he went upstairs as she asked, but he doubted he would return to sleep.

—————✕—————

True to her word, Umra whipped up a feast of sugared pancakes, fresh fruit, smoked bacon, and scrambled eggs. Heavenly aromas practically carried Bok down the stairs to the kitchen. He couldn't help it—he cleaned his plate and went back for seconds.

"Umra, this is wonderful. I'm sorry I startled you earlier." She scooped eggs onto his ceramic plate until he held up a hand for her to stop.

"'S'okay. Not every day I get to whack a handsome fella with me skillet!" Umra winked at Bok, whose cheeks blushed in response.

After finishing his eggs, Bok insisted on helping Umra clean up before going out back for another training session with Tovano.

She washed dishes with a speed that belied her bony frame. "Can you go 'round back and fetch some wood fer the stove, Mister Bok?"

Bok agreed, but as he started to the backyard, he heard voices—Isabella and Tovano's. He started to turn away, not wanting to eavesdrop. But he heard the Princess speak his name and his curiosity took over. Bok stood behind the door and listened.

"—should not have told Bok such things, Tovano. Nor should you have offered to train him."

"Those decisions were out of my hands when he used High Magic, Your Majesty. Either those abilities serve the kingdom—or become a threat to it."

Bok peered through the cracked door. Isabella stood hands on hips, her shoulders slumped. "Very well. I swore to my father I would not let my personal feelings jeopardize the safety of the realm. Train him well, Tovano. But know this—I will be watching you."

Why do they think I could become a risk? I would never do anything to harm the kingdom or its people. Surely, Isabella realizes that.

"Speaking of watching, I think Mister Omat is here to join us!" Tovano rubbed his hands together briskly. Bok's stomach jumped into his throat. Had Tovano seen him eavesdropping?

Bok stepped outside, brushing his hand across the back of his long, straight hair. "Oh, um, I was just coming out for firewood."

"Please, come down for your next lesson." Isabella's familiar warm smile was back. "I shall leave you to it. But I might check in later." She looked in Tovano's direction as she spoke.

Bok welcomed her return—perhaps she would shed some light on this mystery. In the meantime, he was eager to demonstrate his improvement. He concentrated, positioned his fingers as Kotarian had shown him and a translucent blue-green shield appeared before him—solid and stable.

"Very good!" Tovano clapped enthusiastically. "We'll make a sorcerer out of you yet."

Tovano certainly wants as much. But what do I want? And what does Isabella know?

At this point, the questions seemed too numerous for Bok to count.

CHAPTER 25

Early the next morning, a clanging bell at daybreak jolted Bok out of bed. Wingate dashed up the stairs and went to the large window overlooking the front of the house.

"Two young people—revelers, by the looks of it."

Outside the front gate, a young woman and man shouted, "Hello in there!" and "Anybody home?" as they rang the iron bell posted outside the defensive spell's perimeter.

Isabella and Avantil emerged from their room. He slipped on a shirt and gazed around Wingate's wide frame. "Who are they? They don't live here, at least to my knowledge."

"I dunno know 'em either, but I'll go see!"

"Umra—wait!" Isabella cautioned. "They could be—."

"No worries, Yer Majesty! I know what ta do." And she bolted out the front door to greet the visitors at the front gate.

"Any idea what they're saying?" Avantil peeked around the edges of the drawn curtains. Bok couldn't hear the discussion outside, but Wingate drew his sword from its scabbard, nonetheless.

After a few moments of animated conversation, the two revelers walked down the street and Umra returned to the house.

"What did they want?" Wingate returned his sword to its sheath. The others also crowded around, awaiting her answer. Only Kotarian remained asleep through all the excitement.

"Just a coupla young folk who lost their friends at a pub last night. Oh, and these friends they was lookin' fer—an odd bunch o' characters fer sher. Lessee... One fella is tall, real thin but good lookin'. Another has collar-length brown hair, powerful build, and short—sorry Bok! There's a blond fella who they called a name I won't repeat."

Isabella put her arm around Avantil as they listened intently. *Perhaps it is his lingering injury, but did Avantil pull away from the Princess?*

"Then they mentioned two older fellas—one real fit, but ailin', and the other kinda scrawny..."

"I resent that!" Tovano reached for a leftover piece of cheese on the counter. "I am naturally trim!"

"I kin believe it! I bet you could eat the Grenuterals inta the poorhouse—not that I'd mind much. Oh, and there's a young lady with curly brown locks."

"Anyway, I tole 'em I'd seen no such folk and that I was here all by myself, as the Lord and Lady of the house are absent and I'm just the servant girl meant to clean the place. That sent 'em on their way—I reckon they was askin' at every house on the street."

Umra tied her apron around her waist to finish cooking. She smiled as she tapped her long index finger on the kitchen counter. "Y'know, there was one funny thing. Did I tell you I've worked at a pub or two? They was still tipsy from their night on the town, talkin' real loud and slurrin' their words. Just yer average drunkards... other than they didn't smell o' alkeehol a bit and fingered the daggers hid under their shirts while we was talkin'."

She looked around at the group, her smile having vanished. "I never went ta school, but I ain't stupid. I know yer in a whole lot of trouble. If I'd let 'em in, they woulda slit all our throats—mine included. Am I wrong?"

Isabella made eye contact with her companions, then spoke.

"No—you are completely right, Umra. We are in terrible danger, and there are bad people who want us dead for reasons not completely clear even to us. But we know it involves a situation in Osoh Creek. Family farms have been attacked; villagers killed. By what? We do not know—and that is what we intend to discover. I believe it is safe to say our two visitors are part of the mystery behind this crime."

Umra whistled. "Whew! I reckon it's a good thing I run 'em off, then. Princess Isabella and her friends, on the run and hidin' out with ol' Umra. That is quite...?"

"Frightening?" Bok offered.

"Naw—amazin'! I can't imagine anythin' more excitin'! Now, siddown, all o' you—I'll have breakfast on the table in a minute. I've got a hot mug of coffee fer Yer Majesty, and I made sure to cook an extree helpin' o' sausage fer Lord Tovano."

The sorcerer stroked his chin. "I like this young woman!"

———⋈———

A few hours later, they made their final preparations to continue the journey to Osoh Creek. Avantil strapped his bow and quiver to the saddle of his stallion and secured his sword to his belt. Wingate helped Coregan back into his saddle. The injured Commander was determined to ride again today. Bok applied another round of his curative poultice, but he could see the redness of infection setting into Coregan's wound. He tightly bandaged the man's shoulder, and prayed his measures would suffice.

Isabella pulled on a pair of riding gloves and her wide-brimmed hat. Despite the hardships and danger they had encountered, she looked as pulled together as she did the day they left Ithenel, wearing a flowing cotton blouse over tight tan pants and black riding boots polished to a bright shine.

"Wait! Yer gonna need this!" Umra ran into the brick driveway carrying a canvas satchel. "I've made you some lunch fer the trip!"

Isabella smiled. "How thoughtful, Umra. I will make certain your kindness is rewarded once we return to Ithenel."

"Sure there's not room fer me on this trip? I mean, this is my one real chance of getting' out of Naseem."

Isabella leaned forward and took Umra's hand in her own. "My sweet friend, I wish I could. But I cannot put you in harm's way—even though I know your courage is up to the challenge. I tell you what, though: Go to the Royal Palace in two weeks' time and ask for the Head of Housekeeping. I will make sure you have good employment and quarters within the palace waiting for you."

"A generous offer, indeed. Thank you, Yer Majesty." Umra curtseyed again. But her chin sank to her chest as she returned to the house.

They made their way through Naseem's quieter side streets heading north of the city. Just days earlier, these streets had been active with people going to their jobs, delivery carts bringing in new goods, and early shoppers looking for the freshest produce, meats, and fish. But on this morning, Bok only noticed a few stragglers moving in and out of buildings quickly. Scattered horseback riders shared the streets, but nothing like what he would have expected.

Bok didn't like the normal cacophony of city life, but he liked this eerie quiet far less. That didn't stop Wingate from watching every home and storefront for signs of trouble. Bok rode up beside him, slowly as to not alarm the Guardian.

"You are good at your work, Wingate. We all feel safer with you on guard."

"Be watchful yourself—I cannot monitor every corner. Those cutthroats who attacked us are not working alone. And we will be near the border."

Wingate's warning hardly seemed an idle threat. Bok grew up hearing stories about the cruelty of the Mosork warlords. The Mosork Empire had been crushed trying to invade Imarina 300 years ago. The Imarinans, under the command of Queen Imbiria and the legendary sorcerer Sonorian, destroyed the Mosork army and the country's central government.

Since then, a loose consortium of warlords, who were more criminals than leaders, ruled the remnants of the Mosork Empire. The warlords had an uneasy truce, with each controlling their piece of territory via their marauders—private armies that terrorized the Mosork citizenry, collected protection money, and occasionally fought with rival gangs of marauders.

Bok's mind returned to the quiet streets of Naseem and the ride to Osoh Creek. Their business wouldn't take them across the border—and as dangerous as the Mosork marauders could be, they weren't foolish enough to invade Imarina. Or at least he hoped. *In any case, I'll be glad when we finish our business in Osoh Creek and get on the road back to Ithenel.*

Meanwhile, Kotarian rode beside Isabella that morning. "The streets are unnaturally quiet, Your Majesty. Something has changed in the past three days—for the worse," he said.

"Agreed, Kotarian, and I suspect the reason has to do with our mission to Osoh Creek, But that isn't what you want to speak about, is it Kotarian?"

"Quite true—your reputation for perceptiveness is well-earned, Your Majesty. And I respect that and you." He made a point of bowing in his saddle. "What I have to say is of a more personal nature, and I suspect you aren't going to like it. Nevertheless, I must say it for the sake of the mission—and for your own good."

He continued: "Your generosity toward the Serving Class is commendable, Your Majesty. Sometimes, I fear you are too kind to them."

"What do you mean?"

"I mean—they envy those of us in the Noble Class. We have everything that they want, all they could dream about. Yes, they fulfil a vital role in our society—in their rightful place. But if I may be so blunt, do not confuse loyalty with love, Your Majesty."

He jabbed his thumb over his shoulder as he bounced on his saddle. "Take that servant girl, Umra. Yes, she kept our confidence. But how many servants would have jumped at the chance to earn a reward at our expense? It could have ended badly, you know."

Eyes wide, Isabella turned her head to Kotarian. "But it did not. Umra was put to the test—and she proved her character. That is all any of us can do."

He pulled his flask from his jacket and took a sip. "Perhaps. Just remember: Nobility isn't something that can be donned like a cloak, you know."

Isabella's face trembled, then froze. She beckoned Kotarian forward with her index finger. When he leaned to her in his saddle, she put her hand to his ear and whispered.

"I understand your meaning Kotarian. So, consider this a request from a friend: Do not hurt Bok. Please."

Isabella pulled away from him and rode ahead, to leave Kotarian with his own thoughts. But she turned her head to deliver one final message: "And if we must speak of this again, it will not be peer-to-peer, but Crown Princess to royal subject. That is not a conversation you wish to have."

CHAPTER 26

They arrived in Osoh Creek mid-afternoon. Cotton fields blanketed the land with white as far as Bok's sight extended. But that was all he could see or hear.

"Anyone else notice something strange about this place?"

"Yes," Tovano replied. "Where are the people who should be tending these fields? At this time of day, field hands should be working. But we haven't seen another soul for miles."

The answers to those questions came a half-mile down the road. The group encountered two dozen or so people carrying children, livestock, and any possessions they could transport by hand. By their homespun clothing, Bok recognized them as Serving Class—probably the very farm hands he noticed missing. They walked as fast as a group this large could manage.

Isabella waved. "Hello, good people! Is something amiss? And may we help?"

But the group didn't stop to talk. "You and your fancy friends need to turn around!" one man said.

Maybe they'll listen to one of their own. Bok climbed off his horse to meet the travelers at eye level. "Why? Because of what happened at the Yult family farm? We heard about something strange happening there, but we know nothing more."

"No, you don't!" A woman laughed bitterly. "This land is cursed. We've lost everything save our lives. If we stay here jabbering with you any longer, we'll lose those, too."

The farmers hurried on, leaving Bok, Isabella, and company confused, and concerned.

Unfortunately, the situation became clearer when they cleared the next hill and saw black ash where lush fields should have been. The Blight had spread far beyond the Yult farm. Scores of acres, fields and farmhouses now were dust.

An invisible fist slammed into Bok's midsection. He rubbed his eyes in a failed effort to blot out the emptiness before him. *All those farms... They weren't all empty when the wave of destruction hit. I would bet on it.*

"By the Exalted One..." Avantil whispered.

Isabella dismounted. Her hands shook, but she took command. "Come. We have no time to waste. Bok—begin your assessments. Tovano and Kotarian, the three of us will prepare further spells depending on his findings. Avantil, help Coregan and Wingate with the horses and return here as soon as you can." The others quickly followed her lead, heads down to the devastation in front of them.

Kotarian's voice cracked. "I... I never imagined it would be this bad." No one else spoke, but they scrambled into action.

With shaky hands, Bok handed Beki's reins to Avantil. His chest drew tight.

If we can't learn the truth about the Blight here and now, it may be too late for anyone else to do so. Too late for my family, too.

Bok unpacked his healer's bag on a patch of unaffected ground. "Stay back; we don't know if it may still be dangerous."

Avantil crossed his arms. "How do we know this Blight won't come back while we're here?"

"We do not," Isabella replied. "So we must move quickly. Bok, your talents as a healer of the land will guide us as we cycle back through the devastation done here."

"I will try." Despite his lingering questions about Isabella's conversation with Tovano, her supportive words swelled his heart.

He donned his heavy riding gloves for protection, pulled a strand of sage out of his bag, and scattered it across the nearest piece of the blighted soil. After a deep breath, Bok began his incantations.

When working with farmers, one of Bok's Folk Magic spells assessed the soil to determine how it had changed over time. The answers helped him decide how best to replenish and heal the land. But it was a tricky process—and the damage he examined here was far more extensive and mysterious than flooding or locusts or any of the other natural ills he normally encountered.

Bok closed his eyes and listened for the Folk Magic to respond. He felt the spell flow out of his hands, through the air and across the ground in front of him. Like fingers, the magic sifted through the ruined soil, probing it. The rest of the party undoubtedly watched him intently, but he forced that uncomfortable thought out of his mind and focused on the spell. One lapse in concentration and it could be ruined.

He remembered Weni Kon's guidance as she trained him in the art of Folk Magic. Wagging a wrinkled finger, she'd said, "The magic knows the answer, Bok. But you have to give it time to speak."

Bok heeded that wisdom, and the Folk Magic responded with the answers he needed.

He stood and dusted off his gloves. "One bit of good news—the blackened soil is no longer destructive and is safe to the touch. Whatever evil caused this devastation has passed."

Isabella exhaled. "Do you know the cause of this Blight?"

"No—but I know what didn't cause it. No fire caused this, nor is it the result of any poison or insect or anything else occurring in nature. That leaves one possibility."

"Magic." Isabella nodded, Bok having confirmed her long-standing suspicions. "Tovano, Kotarian—join me and see if we can determine its origin."

The three sorcerers formed a triangle around the patch of ground Bok had probed. Each of the three then began an incantation to reveal the spell signature cast on the blighted ground. Tovano had described a spell signature to Bok as being "as unique as any fingerprint. Find that spell signature, and you will reveal its caster."

Three circles of dark blue light appeared on the ground, as if cast by invisible candles. The three spellcasters each stepped into one of the circles. Runes and letters appeared in the light, but to one untrained in High Magic, they appeared to be simply gibberish. Thanks to the rudimentary training Tovano had given him, Bok spotted an occasional pattern in the marks. However, the spell was far too complex, and its revelations coming too fast, for him to make sense of it.

So he waited. While his spell had taken 30 minutes at most, Isabella, Kotarian, and Tovano continued their magical inquiry for one hour, then another. They remained within the circles of blue light, unaware of anything going out outside of its diameter, unable to communicate with their colleagues in any way.

"This is the downside to having a sorcerer for a girlfriend." Avantil nudged Bok's shoulder. "You spend lot of time doing nothing while they look at light shows." He pulled some bread and cheese from the basket Umra had prepared that morning and sat cross-legged on the black ground. "And I seem to do a lot of nothing."

Bok's attention focused on Coregan, however. The Guardian had said little in the past few hours. Bok noticed the man's gait grew increasingly shaky and his face wan.

"Let me check your wounds." Bok took his healer's bag and approached the trembling Guardian.

Coregan attempted to beg off, but Bok insisted he recline on the ground for an examination.

He placed his hand on the man's forehead and it was hot to the touch. When he unwrapped Coregan's bandages, Bok recoiled at how puffy and red his shoulder had become.

He pressed his knees together while he regained his composure. Bok cleaned the wound, administered a poultice, and wrapped it again.

But my skills as a healer mean little if my patient won't rest.

Wingate approached once Coregan had drifted off into a light sleep, aided by a double dose of Bok's yorka root. "How is he doing? And please be truthful."

Bok rubbed his tired eyes. "Most men would not be able to stand—I have no idea how he keeps going. His wound is infected. Still, I believe he can recover if we can get him off the trail and into a bed for a few weeks."

"That will not happen until the mission is complete," Wingate offered. "But I will take care of him the rest of the way. And Bok? Thank you."

Halfway into their third hour of scrying, Tovano ceased his spell, prompting Isabella and Kotarian to do the same. The blue lights blinked off, taking with them the cryptic messages that the sorcerers had been decoding. Craning their necks, Bok and Avantil waited for their friends' report.

Isabella panted and hunched over to catch her breath. Black dust stained her pants legs and dulled the sheen of her riding boots. "As expected, the spell signature of the sorcerer—or sorcerers—behind the Blight was shrouded by a second spell." Bok handed her a water jug. She knelt and took a long drink before continuing. "But Tovano guided Kotarian and me in unraveling the camouflaging spell. Once we did, we found the true author of the Blight."

"The Mosorks," Kotarian sneered. "More specifically, an old Mosork sorcerer named Wunebo-Pran."

Avantil nodded. "They have long wanted to avenge their crushing defeat at Imarina's hands 300 years past. But the Mosork Empire doesn't have the magical capabilities to launch a large-scale attack."

"Wunebo-Pran is regarded as a competent enough sorcerer—for a Mosork," Kotarian said. "But I wouldn't have thought him capable of High Magic of this magnitude!"

"Nor would I." Isabella shook her head. "Truth be told, I would not think even the most powerful sorcerer could harness these forces. Something does not feel right about this result. Almost like the answer was too easy to come by. I... I fear we are being led astray."

Kotarian threw his hands above his head. "By Tregainian's Turgid Torment! Your father sent you to get an answer about this Blight. But you didn't get the answer you wanted. So now, you don't want to accept it? I regret my bluntness, Your Majesty. However, I must say that may be how things work in the Royal Palace, but in the House of Magic—"

Bok stepped between Kotarian and the Princess. "Trust your instincts, Isabella." He knew little of High Magic, and even less about the centuries-old tensions between the Crown and the House of Magic. But he trusted Isabella's judgment. If she had doubts, they should be explored.

Avantil put his arm around her shoulder. "Bok's right—trust yourself, my love. And Kotarian, by the Exalted One, must you always be so insufferable?"

He continued, "The real question, I suppose, is how do you know for sure? If the spell you just cast didn't give you the right answer, and if Bok's prodding and poking didn't unearth the truth, what else can we do?"

Isabella stood back up. "I have one idea. When I was a girl, I used to watch my mother paint in our garden. She could sit at her easel for hours. Sometimes, she would start over, covering one painting with a fresh layer of paint to create a new picture. But in certain spots, if you scratched at the outer layer of paint, you still could see a vague outline of the original work."

Expelling a deep breath, she dusted off her pants. "I say we keep going, push past the spell signature we unlocked. It will not be easy, and we may find nothing. But the truth is too important."

"This is absurd!" Kotarian moaned. "All three of us arrived at the same answer—including me! There is no need for us to continue."

"Well, no one said you had to be a part of it, grayjacket!" Avantil snapped. "You can pout, while Isabella and Tovano do the work!"

Tovano nodded in agreement. "Your Majesty, what you say makes a great deal of sense. Any sorcerer powerful enough to create such a force may be skilled enough to create such a sophisticated falsehood.

"But such an exercise in collaborative magic will require precision, care, patience—not raw mystical power. We must disrupt the enchanted soil as little as possible, slowly peeling back the events of recent weeks. The forces who cast this spell did so consciously to hide their tracks, and we must be even more deliberate in uncovering them."

Kotarian raised his hand above his head. "You aren't restarting this spell without me! By Subanian's Subtle Scream, you need my expertise if you have any hope of success. Just give me a moment and the House's Shining Light once will again lead the way."

Isabella finished her water and grinned. "Indeed, my friend. Lead on!"

After a short rest, the trio recast their discovery spell. They had to start over from the beginning, taking the same care as before to ensure the incantation's path remained on course. The conjuring went on for hours, until deep into the night.

Bok wished he had the knowledge and training to help. His companions' heads drooped and shoulders slumped within the greenish circles of eldritch light. But he could do nothing for his exhausted friends, except wait and watch.

The landscape provided little stimulation. Just an ocean of dark ash that ended at the edge of a nearby forest. Bok missed the normal sounds of birds chirping and small animals rooting for food. He looked at the pine trees a hundred yards away or so. The shift from black to green, death to life, sent a shiver down the back of Bok's neck.

He, Avantil, Coregan, and Wingate maintained a vigil surrounding the three sorcerers, protecting them from outside harm and awaiting some definitive answers as to what entity brought them to Osoh Creek.

Those answers came a couple of hours before daybreak. The three spells ended almost simultaneously. Tovano collapsed to his knees, kicking up a cloud of black ash around him. Wingate rushed to give the man water.

Kotarian staggered off into the dark field, his eyes glazed over. He clutched his stomach as though he might vomit.

Isabella stood in place, neither speaking nor moving. Her dust-streaked face didn't change expression.

"My sweet! What happened? What did you learn?" Avantil put his arm around her, and she leaned into the tall Noble. A single sob escaped her throat, but her eyes were too dry for tears.

"A Mosork sorcerer did not cause the Blight. This atrocity... was a House of Magic spell," she whispered in a parched, raw voice. "Salandrian cast the Blight."

CHAPTER 27

"SALANDRIAN? THE DEAN OF the House of Magic? The short, balding fellow with the ill-fitting clothes and the pile of dusty books? Are you certain?" Avantil's questions echoed the thought running through Bok's mind.

"Completely certain. We all saw it—even Kotarian." Isabella's hands trembled. Bok handed her a cup of coffee from the campfire and she took it eagerly. "There is no doubt."

She looked up at her lover and her friend. "We must get back to Ithenel as soon as possible. My father—the very kingdom—is in terrible peril!"

"I understand. We should wait until the sun rises. Besides, we all need a rest—as short as it may be. But we will be ready to leave soon." Avantil then stepped away to speak with Wingate and Coregan.

Bok started to follow, but Isabella grabbed his arm. "Come. Sit with me. I need someone to talk with."

"Of course." He unwrapped a package of Umra's crusty bread and sharp cheese.

Isabella gobbled two pieces of cheese. "I appreciate your good work, Bok. We could not have found the truth—unpleasant thought it may be—without your efforts."

"Thank you, I... I'm sorry you had to receive such bad news. But we will do everything we can to defend your father—I promise."

She nodded and sipped her coffee. "I know. I could not ask for a more loyal group. It is just... I never would have thought one of our Nobles—a man who has worked with my father in the council chambers for years—would betray us." She set her cup on the ground, folded her hands at her waist, and sat slump shouldered.

"I recognize that look, Isabella. But you must not blame yourself. No one could have ferreted out Salandrian's treason. He's probably been planning this for years, and he covered his tracks well."

"Are you certain mind reading is not a Folk Magic ability?" She smiled a little, the light of the campfire reflecting off her face.

Bok laughed, then looked skyward. "No... but snooping may be. I... I may have listened in to your conversation with Tovano yesterday." She looked up, her eyes wide.

Bok scrambled to add, "I apologize! I should not have eavesdropped. But when I heard the two of you discussing me, my curiosity got the best of me."

"Well, that is understandable. I would be curious, too, if my life had been completely upended." She fished a square of chocolate out of the picnic bundle. "Do not make eavesdropping a habit, though."

"Thank you... and I certainly won't!" Bok exhaled. "But I have to ask... what did Tovano mean that I could become a risk to the kingdom? Surely, you do not think I could ever turn against you or your father!"

Isabella stared incredulously. "Oh, Bok. Is that what you thought we meant? That I no longer trust you, now that you can use High Magic?

"I trust you with my life, Bok. What Tovano meant—and what I agreed with—is that High Magic can be dangerous if the user does not know what they are doing. That is why he wants to train you. But I never doubted your loyalty, my sweet friend. Not for a second."

Bok swallowed past the lump in his throat. "Good. I may not understand exactly what is happening. But I absolutely want to be here, to protect my family and defend the kingdom. You are our leader and I am with you. All the way."

Finally, Bok again saw the smile which had made his heart skip a beat back in Ithenel. "So that was the extent of Tovano's concern? There's nothing else about my past or my powers that I need to know?"

"No... nothing." Isabella pulled him into a jasmine scented hug. But she did not look into his eyes. "You are a good friend, Bok Omat. Better than I deserve."

She took his forearms in her hands. "The princess and the blacksmith's boy—together until the end!"

"Until the end." Bok hoped those words wouldn't prove literal in the days to come.

He also knew for certain that Isabella was keeping something from him.

From across the dusty field, Avantil hailed Isabella. "Hey—if you are done with Bok, I could use you over here." She waved good-bye and went to join her boyfriend.

Bok stood up and stretched. Whatever she was hiding would have to wait. For now, his friend had more than enough to deal with—and so did he. His family and the Kingdom were in peril, and he and Isabella would face that threat together.

Bok squinted. Something moved through the sky. Coming in from the direction of the forest, four greenish-blue globes—were they stars? No—they were too big and moved—floated up, up and then arced down, toward the makeshift campsite.

Isabella ran toward him, screaming. "Bok, take cover!" She could say no more before the night exploded in a silent flash of green-blue light.

CHAPTER 28

*C*OUGH! *COUGH!*

The explosions kicked up choking clouds of black dust. Bok struggled to clear his eyes and throat. His ears rang from the thunderclaps of the blasts.

Through the haze, Isabella crawled toward him. Black dirt streaked her olive complexion. A trickle of blood ran down her forearm, sticking out through a ripped sleeve.

"Isabella!" Bok's throat closed, as his fists clenched the dark ash.

"B-Bok! Shield now!" she sputtered. As one, they cast defensive spells in time to deflect another wave of magical attacks. Four sorcerers clad in the black jackets of the Scions of Sonorian stepped forward from the edge of the blacked field.

Isabella could barely stand, and Bok was less than a week into his High Magic studies—he hardly was prepared to battle four skilled sorcerers.

"Leave me, Bok! Go to Ithenel—warn my father!" Isabella blocked a third attack. Bok doubted she had the reserves to counter a fourth.

"No! They'll kill you!"

She pushed him away with her left hand, while her right glowed faintly with her remaining magical energy. "You must. For the sake of the Kingdom!"

"I won't abandon you to die!" Bok looked toward the approaching sorcerers. They walked steadily, blue-green auras shining brightly. One even wore a smile. Bok's heart thrummed against the walls of his chest. A reptile voice in the back of his brain urged him to run. But he ignored it and planted his boots on the ash-covered ground.

Whatever happens, I'll stand here, beside my friend.

Before the final blow came, an arrow flew between Bok and Isabella and struck one of the sorcerers in the neck. He collapsed dead in an instant.

His three partners turned to him, and away from Bok and Isabella. The distraction broke the spells they had been preparing.

"Get away, you bloodthirsty jackals! By the Exalted One, I have three more arrows to bury in your hearts!" As if to prove his words, Avantil fired again

This time, though, the Scions of Sonorian were ready. His second arrow transmuted into a harmless bouquet of flowers and fell to the ground. One of the sorcerers, a young woman, pointed in his direction. "Kill the bowman first!"

But before they could make good on that threat, a burst of hurricane force wind pushed the evil trio backward, forcing them to shield their eyes from the dust storm.

"Alaydrian! What are you doing?" Kotarian held his hand in front of him palm first, as if he literally pushed the wind toward his former House of Magic colleagues. "Your actions bring shame to our House!"

Alaydrian extended her own hand and Kotarian's spell abruptly stopped. "I wondered when you would make your grand entrance! That Bognonian's Bellicose Breeze spell needs work, though. Our teachers would've awarded you unsatisfactory marks had they seen how easily I countered it."

"You betray our teachers and the House!" Kotarian spat. "They taught us to use magic for the good of Imarina. Instead, you serve... what, exactly? Chaos? Treason? Death?"

"The House's Shining Light isn't gleaming very brightly, is he?" Alaydrian flexed her fingers, which continued to glow blue-green. "Our True Leader did nothing but reveal the True Path! Imarina has strayed from its traditions, allowed outside influences and decadent beliefs to taint our once-great nation. But those of us who follow the True Leader—the Scions of Sonorian—will lead it back to greatness!"

"You are insane. Absolutely insane..." Kotarian whispered.

The Scions of Sonorian prepared to renew their attack, but Avantil and Kotarian had given Wingate time to act. He rode furiously through the black dirt, pulling the reins of the other horses behind him. Without slowing, he scooped Isabella up with one arm and deposited her behind him on his horse. She repaid the favor by blocking another exploding globe of blue-green light headed directly toward Wingate.

"Hold on, Your Majesty—we must retreat!" Wingate dodged yet another mystical projectile. Bok, Avantil and Kotarian quickly mounted their own horses and rode toward Wingate and Isabella, away from the fight. The Guardian headed for the trees at the edge of the destroyed farmland.

They met Coregan at the edge of the field and raced into the still-dark woods. Flat patches of soil gave way to thick clusters of pine trees, green undergrowth, and more than a few tree roots jutting out of the ground.

The chances of a horse tripping or twisting its leg in the woods weren't small. But Bok knew those odds were better than remaining within range of the spellcasters' deadly magics.

The pine trees formed almost an umbrella over the forest sky. They could no longer see or be seen by the Scions of Sonorian, but that didn't stop the rogue sorcerers from launching more wide-range attacks into the woods. Magic globes floated through the night sky.

One of them struck a tall pine just yards from Bok. It exploded into a shower of bark and splinters, filling the air with the brisk smell of resin. Beki flinched and Bok eased her reins to sidestep the shattered, smoking stump.

Sizzling bolts of magical lightning streaked past them through the trees. One of them singed the elbow of Bok's sleeve. A tremor ran through his body as he patted the smoldering fabric. *That would've taken my arm had it been an inch closer.*

"Keep the horses focused—straight ahead!" Coregan called. "Don't let 'em be scared!" The same advice applied to the riders. At the Commander's urging, Bok focused on moving as quickly as possible out of the field of danger.

Bok held his breath and whispered silent prayers. After a few uneasy moments, the explosions behind them stopped. The group slowed their pace to a more cautious trot. Still, they continued to move, in case their enemies pursued them. Beki grunted but reluctantly kept going when Bok gently shook her reins.

He looked ahead at the others—the night was so dark it was hard to see more than a few yards ahead. The tree canopy blocked off most of the ambient light. But one of their number appeared to be missing. "Wait—where is Tovano? He wasn't there for the battle. I thought he was with you, Coregan!"

"Haven't seen 'im in a half-hour. Thought he would be with the Princess 'n you."

"What? We must go back!" Isabella brought her horse and the rest of the group to a full stop. "We cannot abandon Tovano!"

Avantil nudged his horse beside hers. "My love, we must keep moving. Your safety—and the outcome of this mission—are too important, even for Tovano. Believe me, he would be the first to agree."

Isabella pumped her fists at her side. "No! I refuse to accept that! Avantil, do not ask me to betray a mentor and friend."

A rustle in the brush interrupted their argument. Through the still-gloomy early morning, Bok thought it might have been deer. But then a woman's voice boomed, "Drop your weapons and dismount! This will be your only warning!"

The group turned to see one, then two, then a half-dozen armed riders emerge from the woods into the clearing. Although he had never seen Mosork marauders before, Bok knew he was in their presence. The half-dozen iron swords pointed at him and his friends merely confirmed that fact.

CHAPTER 29

PINK AND BLACK DYES streaked both the riders' hair and the manes of their horses. The same colors adorned their clothes. The male riders were shirtless, and the women wore tops that could better be described as sashes. Regardless of gender, each rider sported multiple silver and gold necklaces. Such outfits indicated the wearer's membership in a particular outlaw group. And if they made their enemies afraid, all the better.

Pushing Avantil aside, Isabella strode to the front of the group. "We are a traveling party of merchants on official business of King Isbiano! You are trespassing on Imarinan soil. Turn around now and avoid a serious conflict between our two nations."

A tall woman rode forward. She never stopped holding her sword toward Isabella. "That remains to be seen. But if you are a peaceful band of merchants, explain why you were engaged in magical combat on the other side of these woods?

"And as for trespassing, you entered the Glorious Rejah-Lahr's divinely granted territory five hundred yards ago."

Oh, no! The muscles in Bok's legs went weak. *We were in such a hurry to escape that we didn't realize we crossed the border.*

Hearing no explanations, the Mosork soldiers forced the group to walk deeper into their territory.

After a while, the forest gave way to a grass-covered clearing that extended as far as Bok could see. The rising sun baked him and his friends. Within minutes, sweat soaked his tunic.

The conditions proved particularly brutal to the injured Coregan who, after an hour of walking, stopped and slumped to his knees. He gasped for breath as perspiration poured down his face. Bok stepped out of line to help him and was shoved back by the flat of a Mosork sword against his chest.

"'m fine, just gimme a moment." Coregan waved off his fellow prisoners.

"Get up now or we leave you here!" The Mosork leader shoved Coregan's back—near his injured shoulder—with the point of her steel-toed boot. He winced and slumped forward.

"You devils!" Avantil struggled toward the Commander. But two Mosork soldiers grabbed his arms and wrestled him back in line.

Wingate picked Coregan up in his arms. "I will carry him from here." The Mosork leader said nothing, but she pointed her sword, indicating they should continue walking.

Fortunately, the forced march ended soon, when they arrived at a large temporary encampment on a riverbank. Dozens of marauders moved in and out of makeshift lean-to huts constructed from pine branches, toting water and supplies into the campsite.

The pink-and-black-haired leader of the Mosork group stopped them at the entrance to a spacious, empty hut near the center of the camp. "In here." She pushed Isabella hard in the back, and the Princess stumbled forward. Bok grinded his teeth. Protesting would only make matters worse.

Inside the tent, soldiers bound each Imarinan with rope and ordered them to sit on the straw-strewn floor.

Coregan could barely sit up, but he still did so, seemingly in defiance of his physical plight as well as his captivity, Avantil breathed in short, angry bursts like a mad bull and stared directly at the half-dozen Mosork soldiers in front of them. Bok had no doubt his fiery friend would have fought the entire group single-handedly if given the opportunity. Isabella, on the other hand, took deep, slow breaths. Bok recognized it as Tovano's technique for sorcerers to clear their minds in a time of crisis.

Kotarian writhed and struggled helplessly against his bonds. "What do these awful people want with—?"

"Silence!" The Mosork leader and the other soldiers knelt on a single knee and bowed their heads. Bok did as well, just to be safe.

"I present... The Glorious Rejah-Lahr!"

Bok looked up and beheld a man Yata undoubtedly would have described as a "banty rooster." Barely taller than Isabella, the bare-chested warlord sported a thick, powerful build. His matted pink and black hair hung nearly to his waist, as did his matching beard. Salmon-colored silk ribbons festooned the man's ebony trousers, and ten or more gold necklaces hung around his neck to his protruding belly. He shoved a greasy piece of meat in his mouth when he entered the hut, then licked his fingers clean with loud slurping sounds. Two muscular bodyguards, swords and daggers dangling from their belts, stepped inside the hut to either side of the man, and a servant girl knelt by his feet.

"Ho, ho! Princess Isabella Inishari of Imarina! So nice of you to visit my kingdom!" In truth, Rejah-Lahr was one of twenty or so warlords who controlled relatively small pieces of territory within the Mosork Empire. But each claimed he or she was the rightful monarch of the entire nation.

"Come to see your father's handiwork in person, villain?"

Isabella scrunched her eyebrows. "My father's handiwork? Glorious Rejah-Lahr, I do not know of what you speak. We were sent here to investigate a bizarre phenomenon on the Imarinan side of the border. We were attacked—not by your soldiers, to be clear—and during the battle, we accidentally trespassed across your nation's borders. If you would graciously allow us to proceed on our way, our kingdom will send you a generous restitution of gold and goods—plus a handwritten letter of apology from me."

"Leaving?" He chortled. "Forget your father and the Royal Council, little Princess—you have much more important matters to answer for here." The warlord's soldiers nodded their silent agreement.

"I do not know what you mean. We literally just crossed into your land mere moments before your soldiers captured us."

Rejah-Lahr snorted, then snapped his fingers for the servant girl to bring him another plate of meat. "'Just crossed into your land...' Tell me, little Princess—do you take me for a complete fool? You have been here for days, if not longer, seeking to assassinate me!"

Isabella recoiled at the accusation but otherwise maintained her calm demeanor. "Again, Glorious Rejah-Lahr, we apologize for our brief intrusion. But on my word as a fellow sovereign, I promise we have done no such thing."

Sweat dripped down Bok's face. The canvas hut trapped the summer heat like his father's brick stove. The hard ground made his back ache; the golden straw covering it provided little padding. But he dared not move.

The Mosork warlord sneered at Isabella as he handed the plate back to the servant girl. She popped up from where she knelt on the floor, took the plate, and returned to her kneeling position, all without lifting her face. He turned his back to the prisoners and folded his arms across his chest. His deep, angry breaths bounced off the hut's walls.

I've heard that sound before—when a bull is furious and ready to charge the first creature it sees.

After a full minute of silence, he pivoted, eyes building. "Then why have five acres of our land been reduced to black ash? Three days ago, no more than two miles away. And you just happen to be nearby with three sorcerers among you?" He snatched a full cup of wine from the lone table in the hut and flung it across the room. The purple liquid soaked into the straw.

"And you think we are responsible?" Isabella responded.

"What else am I to believe?"

"Believe this, Glorious Rejah-Lahr—we came to Osoh Creek to investigate this very thing! We call it 'The Blight' and it has infected our land as well. Whoever attacked you also attacked us." Isabella tried unsuccessfully to make eye contact. Despite the incredibly tense nature of the conversation, Bok couldn't help but be impressed by her poise.

Rejah-Lahr stroked his wild beard with grease-covered fingers. "And the identity of these attackers? Are you telling me that Imarinans did not cast this spell upon our land?"

She paused. "That... is a complicated answer, Glorious Rejah-Lahr. Yes, these villains are from Imarina. But they do not represent our nation, my father, or me. We believe them to be a rogue faction within the House of Magic."

"The House of Magic?" Rejah-Lahr raised a ring-pierced eyebrow. "The same House of Magic that answers to King Isbiano! How could sorcerers concoct such a plan without your father's approval?" Rejah-Lahr stood over Isabella, shouting down at the diminutive Princess.

She waited for him to finish, and only then spoke. "I... I do not know. But we believe my father is in terrible danger from these rebels. That is why we must return to Ithenel!"

Rejah-Lahr grabbed a piece of meat from the plate held by the servant girl and gulped it down in a single bite, again licking his fingers afterward. "You will go nowhere! You and your friends have attacked my nation and will be treated accordingly."

Isabella's eyes flared. "Are you threatening me, Glorious Rejah-Lahr? I am Imarina's Crown Princess—harm me and our forces will destroy your marauders by week's end."

"Oh, no—I am not threatening you, little Princess!" Rejah-Lahr's belly shook as he laughed. "You are far too valuable as a hostage.

"Your friends, on the other hand, will hang at sundown."

CHAPTER 30

WE'RE GOING TO DIE! I'm going to die. And my family would never know what happened.

Bok strained against his bonds. The ropes bit into his wrists, cutting his flesh. But they would not budge.

Not that escaping was much of an option. Rejah-Lahr, his entourage, and most of the soldiers left the hut following his death sentence proclamation. But two soldiers, including the leader of the Mosork band they encountered in the woods, stayed behind to guard the group until sundown. At that point, they would be escorted—carried, if necessary—to makeshift gallows at the edge of camp, where they would be hanged one after another until all five were dead. Bok's chin fell to his chest, as his heart continued to race.

The Mosork leader patted Isabella on the head. "And you will be there to watch your friends die." The Princess defiantly jerked away from the guard's hand.

The male guard pointed at Bok, a vindictive grin on his face. "Look at how that one shakes!"

Bok tried to stop his hands from trembling to no avail. *Yes, I'm scared. I do not want to die!*

Turning away from the hostages, the guard then produced a deck of cards from his boot. "Care for a game?"

The woman commanding the raiding party sat down across the table. "Typical Imarinan coward. They all deserve to die like dogs! And, yes, I would love to take your share of the reward money the Glorious Rejah-Lahr has promised!"

The man laughed, then dealt the cards.

"What are we going to do?" Kotarian whispered. "I've been betrayed by a girl I've known since I was 14 summers, and I cannot perish in this backwater before I avenge that slight!" He shook even worse than Bok and his eyes bulged. The sorcerer's haughty veneer of arrogance had been stripped away by the promise of imminent death.

"By the Exalted One, he's right—we can't give up!" Avantil added. "Isabella, if you can get a finger under my bonds, maybe I can loosen yours and we untie each other."

With one eye on the guards, they started to move ever so slowly, inching across the straw floor until they were back-to-back.

Bok's heart pounded as the lovers struggled to loosen the other's ropes. Like them, he kept a close watch on the guards. When the woman turned to check on her prisoners, Bok quickly interjected, "Lost enough money yet?" to draw her attention away from Isabella and Avantil.

"Silence, cur!" Her gold and silver chains bounced as she snapped.

When the guard turned back around, Isabella gave Bok the slightest hint of a smile in recognition of his quick thinking.

She and Avantil continued to work on each other's bonds and after ten excruciating minutes, he partially freed one of her hands—hands that commanded the immense power of High Magic. Bok licked his lips. *Come on, Avantil!* With a few more minutes' work, he hopefully could loosen the ropes enough for Isabella to cast a spell. *Those guards might not be so arrogant then.*

But everything changed on a cruel fluke. The Mosork guard dropped one of her cards. When she leaned over to retrieve it, she noticed Isabella's ropes drooped off her wrists. The pink and black-clad marauder jumped from her chair.

"You dishonorable dishrag!" She grabbed the Princess by the collar of her shirt and lifted her off the ground. Isabella's feet dangled six inches off the floor as the Mosork leader pulled Isabella's face into her own.

"There is no escape from here. Do that again, and you will join your comrades on the gallows!"

Isabella's voice rose in pitch. "I'd rather die beside my brave friends than live as your captive!"

"Your fate already has been decided by the Glorious Rejah-Lahr. You must live... but he never said I had to be gentle." The Mosork flung Isabella across the room, away from Avantil.

"UGH!" she cried as her back hit the floor, the thin layer of straw providing minimal cushion. She laid there unmoving.

Although still bound, Avantil bolted to his feet and raced toward the fallen Princess. "Devils! You can—!" The other guard's heavy boot slammed into his midsection. He, too, collapsed to the floor gasping.

Isabella gained enough strength to lift her head. Her long hair spilled wildly around her face. "S.. stop! Don't hurt him."

The Mosork woman pointed at her. "You stay on that side of the room—away from your concubine. If either of you move again, he dies."

The guards sat back down and resumed their game. "Hah! I take your bard again!" the man exclaimed, causing the woman to throw her cards to the table in disgust.

Bok's body went slack, all air leaving his lungs. *Our one chance of escape—gone.*

The laughs, shouts, and other exclamations from the guards' card game provided the only sounds for the next few moments. The serving girl slipped back into the tent carrying a heaping plate of meat and a sloshing jug of red wine. She sat both items in the center of the table and poured each of the guards a full cup.

"Ha! Better eat as much as you can," the man taunted through a full mouth. "The way I'm going, you won't be able to afford dinner for some time!"

"Shut up and drink your wine." The Mosork woman roughly pushed the servant with the hard toe of her boot. "Keep this coming. I worked up a thirst tossing around the flower-smelling girl."

The servant simply nodded and knelt by the table, head still down toward the floor. The card game—and the accompanying silence of the prisoners—continued for a few minutes, allowing Isabella and Avantil to sit upright again to reclaim at least a little dignity.

"Bok, there is something... I must tell you." Isabella spoke quietly as their captors stared at their cards.

I hope it is a plan to escape.

The Princess paused, swallowed, then signed heavily. She opened her mouth to speak. But before she could continue, Avantil nudged her shoulder.

"Hey, that guard is falling asleep!"

Sure enough, the guard who had kicked Avantil moments earlier now rested his head on the table, eyes closed.

"'L'sy b'sterd... think y'can get outta losin' by fallin'..." The woman didn't even finish her thought before her eyes rolled to the back of her head.

The servant girl checked both guards to ensure they were deeply asleep. Then, she put her hands on her hips and giggled. "I gotta tell you, I done some doozies in my life, growin' up on the streets an' all. But nothin' quite like this!"

As one, Bok and Isabella looked at her, eyes wide. "Umra!!"

She took a dagger from one of the guards and cut the bonds holding each of the prisoners. They all rose to their feet and stretched, save for Coregan, who remained seated. Wingate collected the guards' weapons and used the ropes to bound their former captors.

"Isabella! Are you hurt?" Avantil ran to her side as soon as Umra freed him. But the Princess waved him off.

"I am fine." she insisted.

Avantil recoiled. "I just wanted to make sure you weren't hurt, my sweet."

"I said I am fine, Avantil. And I do not appreciate you always treating me like a porcelain doll!"

Isabella bit her lip. Bok could tell she regretted the angry words the instant she spoke them. Avantil froze, then stomped to the other side of the hut. "Point made! Forgive me for being concerned."

"Avantil, wait—!" But he had turned his back, crossed his arms and withdrawn from the conversation.

"Best let 'im be, Your Majesty," Coregan cautioned. "His pride's hurt. But he'll calm down."

She sighed. "I am sure you are correct, Commander. For now, let us focus on escaping this awful place."

Isabella massaged her bruised wrists. "Do not misunderstand, Umra—we certainly are grateful—but how did you find us? And how did you... well, how did you do all this?" She gestured around the canvas hut at the guards sleeping on the table and severed ropes now on the floor.

Umra grinned. "I've always been one ta push my luck. I been followin' since you left Naseem. I wasn't ready to give up and figgered I might prove myself along the way. Reckon I was right about that!"

"I'll say!" Bok rubbed the back of his sweat-soaked hair. "But I'd still love to get my healer's bag back."

"I might be able to help with that, too. They's storin' all yer things with the horses in the stables out back. As fer how I got in, I been a servant since I was old enough to hold a tray an' pour a drink. We got a way o' bein' invisible around important people, and I've gotten real good at it. 'Twasn't hard to blend in, 'specially once I snagged this uniform and put some color in my hair."

Isabella put her hands on the young woman's shoulders. "You are amazing! But all those soldiers we saw—?"

"Weren't lookin' fer a lone servant girl. They keep their eyes open fer important folks like yerself. But every city, every palace, every camp has a servants' entrance 'round back, so that folk like me can come 'n' go without gettin' in the way."

Umra then held up a small, green glass vial. "As fer the guards, Yer Majesty, Lord Grenuteral takes these sleepin' powders every night. Mix 'em with wine, it'll knock a body right out."

"That is incredible." Isabella voice barely rose above a whisper. "Umra, I promise your courage and loyalty will be rewarded once we return to Ithenel."

Umra looked away from the Princess. "About that, Yer Majesty... it ain't like I'd turn down a big pile o' gold, but... I didn't do this fer any reward."

She paced around the hut, collecting herself and her next words. "Y'see, I seen how you treated Mister Bok like he was one o' yer own. I been an orphan since I was six summers—sleepin' in doorways and beggin' strangers for scraps of food. As soon as I could, I got a job warshin' pots and scrubbin' floors for a Noble Class family that thinks I ain't fit ta be scraped off their fancy shoes. I don't know... I just hoped... maybe there was a place fer me, too."

Isabella said nothing—she just wrapped her arms around Umra's neck and let the servant girl rest her face into her shoulder. Bok felt tears well up in his own eyes when the Princess said, "And you do, dear girl. You will never leave my side again, Umra Sel."

Avantil gently interrupted with a hand on Isabella's arm. "Yes... well, we are indebted for your help, miss... Umra. But shouldn't we be getting out of here before Rajah-Lahr returns?" He peeked around the hut's canvas flap into the compound's yard.

"Yes, we should." Isabella let go of Umra and wiped her own eyes with a lace handkerchief. "Kotarian, you and I will use illusion spells to temporarily disguise all of us as Mosork marauders."

Kotarian flexed his fingers. "Your Majesty, do you have one good reason why I shouldn't burn this miserable place to the ground?"

"Because inadvertently or not, we are trespassers on foreign soil, and doing so could be considered an act of war. Do you understand, Kotarian?"

He sighed. "Fine. But what if we are discovered?"

"In that case, Kotarian, just save something for me to burn, too."

CHAPTER 31

I SABELLA AND KOTARIAN GATHERED the group in a circle and chanted. When they finished, Bok's companions didn't appear any different. But when he looked closely at his own body, it shimmered slightly, as if his eyes were out of focus.

Kotarian explained. "To those outside the spell, we will appear as Mosork soldiers. We need to move quickly, however—Germarian's Generative Guise will only last for fifteen minutes—twenty at the most."

The group split in two and headed in opposite directions. "Yer horses and things are right over 'ere." Umra pointed toward the stables. "Ol' Rejah-Lahr thinks yer still tied up back there."

"Yes—for now," Isabella said. "But if he discovers we are free, the Mosorks shall lock down the camp. We need to get far away from here before that happens."

They stepped out of the hut, Umra in the lead. "'S'all clear!" she called back after making sure no additional guards loitered around the hut's entrance.

They walked in a straight line toward the stables, passing Mosork soldiers, as well as family members, camp servants, and various hangers-on. Some were working—cooks prepared meals, armorers sharpened swords—but most of the crew seemed content to drink, gamble, and gossip. Impromptu shoving matches and belching contests broke out across the patchy grass field. Bok had never seen anything quite like it. The whole camp seemed to be a hornet's nest of heavily armed, intoxicated, and unsupervised criminals.

Bok took a deep breath and shook loose his wrists, which still hurt from where he had been bound. *Act natural and call no attention to yourself.*

That plan lasted all of thirty seconds.

"Hold it right there!"

A voice boomed behind them and they all stopped. Bok's heart raced. Even with Isabella and Kotarian's magic, plus Wingate's sword arm, fighting their way through this mob would be suicidal.

They turned to see a single Mosork marauder, thumbs tucked in the waist of his pants and a giant grin on his face. And it was directed at Isabella: "Don't walk away so fast! Are you new? I know I would remember your face."

Color rose in Isabella's cheeks. "Well, I actually— "

Isabella's formal speech patterns would give her away if she said too much. "Yeah. She's new, and I'm showing her around," Bok interjected.

"Maybe I want to show her around. Who are you, anyway?" The marauder slid his hand down to the knife tucked into the top of his tight pink-and-black trousers.

Bok considered his words carefully, knowing the wrong response could bring the entire camp down upon them. He also noticed Avantil's coiled posture.

But before anything could happen, Wingate stepped beside Bok, hands empty but powerful arms crossed. The marauder eyed the mountainous Guardian. Although though he had a weapon and Wingate didn't, the Mosork took the first step back.

He frowned and backed away. "This isn't over. I'll see you again—when you don't have your giant friend to help."

Not if I can help it. The man continued to glare but let them continue on their way.

"I'm sorry to interrupt you!" Bok told Isabella once they were out of earshot from the marauder. "It's just—"

"No, I am pleased you did! I can fend off suitors at the Royal Palace with practiced ease. But a shirtless cutthroat is beyond my training, Bok."

"We're almost there." Umra pointed to the stables. While guarded, the lean-to's sentries faced the perimeter of the camp, expecting trouble to come from the outside.

They didn't realize their apparent colleagues instead were Rajah-Lahr's prisoners under a magical disguise. Still, one of the guards scowled at the people moving horses and equipment from under his watch.

"What're you doin'? Who sent you here?"

"The, uh, Captain sent us to bring the prisoners' horses and things," Umra promptly replied in a voice completely unlike her Naseem-born Serving Class accent. "Er, the Glorious Rajah-Lahr wanted him to see if there's anything we could use for ourselves."

At the mention of their leader's name, the guards posture stiffened. "Oh—carry on, then." He walked outside, giving the group free run of the stables.

Bok's face lit up. "That was great, Umra! You had them completely convinced."

She cackled. "I've had to talk my way out o' a few jams! I'll tell you 'bout 'em over a glass when we get ta Ithenel!"

They quickly collected their belongings and unhitched their horses. Bok sighed in relief to find Beki not only unharmed, but also well-fed and with fresh water. *Mosork marauders may be ruthless warriors and bandits, but they clearly care for their animals.*

Wingate helped Coregan onto his horse and they navigated their way through the campsite and back to the trail, just as the spell wore off.

They raced through the pine forest, back the way they came. Hooves clomped down the narrow trail worn through the woods by centuries of travel. The sticky, humid air clung to Bok's already sweaty clothes.

Isabella urged her horse forward. "Only a few more miles to the border. Then we can return to Ithenel—and find Tovano."

They had not ridden five minutes, though, when the sound of hooves echoed behind them, faint but growing louder.

"Blast! They have discovered our absence!" Kotarian moaned.

Coregan drew his sword. "No sense 'n running. We'd never get back to Imarina before they catch us."

Isabella slowed her horse to a halt. "Then we make a stand."

Avantil chose an arrow, while Kotarian prepared a spell. Not sure what to do, Bok readied a push-pull spell and watched as the cloud of dust moved closer. Within less than a minute, the dust cloud became a Mosork raiding party—and this time, Rajah-Lahr led the group.

"Ho-ho, little Princess!" He called his group of a dozen soldiers to a halt just yards away from the Imarinan group. "Our camp is back this way." He jabbed his finger over his shoulder. "Fortunately, Wunebo-Pran was able to track you." A man with long, graying but still pink-and-black-streaked hair and a matching wild beard nodded.

Kotarian cracked his knuckles. "Wunebo-Pran. You are a sorcerer of some repute. Of course, everything I've been taught has turned out a lie. Perhaps your reputation shall be as well."

"Your spell signature tells me you are Kotarian, acolyte of the Imarinan House of Magic," the raspy-voiced man replied. "But I do not know your reputation."

"You will, Mosork." Kotarian's hands crackled with blue-green mystical force. Seemingly from nowhere, a strong wind began to gust at Bok's back and the skies around them darkened.

Hurricane gusts blew at Bok's back, nearly knocking him to the ground. "Let's see how these Mosork ruffians like Caelian's Calamitous Cloudburst." Kotarian moved his arms back and forth to gather strength for the storm.

On the other side of the stand-off, Wunebo-Pran calmly spoke similar words and conjured his own version of a contained storm. Whether it was as strong as the one Kotarian had prepared seemed irrelevant; at this short distance, it would be more than sufficient to blow away Bok and his friends. The storms kicked up golden brown pine needles from the forest floor and whipped them into the air. Skinny trees swayed violently.

Bok's eyes moved from Kotarian to Wunebo-Pran and back. The two sorcerers engaged in a deadly staring contest, each waiting for the other to cross an imperceptible threshold before they unleashed their destructive spell.

"Kotarian, please!" Bok insisted. "Don't make this any worse than it already is."

"My friend is correct, Glorious Rajah-Lahr!" Isabella yelled over the sound of the gale. "We share an enemy—and a problem. If you allow us to stop the evildoers behind the Blight, you will protect your people as well as ours."

Rajah-Lahr scratched his hairy belly absentmindedly. "Perhaps you are telling the truth. But I have a squadron of Mosork marauders beside me. If I allow you to leave, I risk losing face with them."

Isabella gestured to the riders flanking the Mosork warlord. "Ask them, then. They may understand that mercy can be wise and blind violence foolish."

The warriors said nothing, but neither did they dispute what Isabella had said. At her signal, Kotarian slowly powered down his spell. Wunebo-Pran did the same in response, although neither sorcerer ceased their spellcasting completely.

Isabella continued. "Now, I will tell you something that shames me deeply. I told you a rogue group of Imarinian sorcerers is to blame for the Blight. Well, we have discovered their leader is Salandrian, Dean of our House of Magic. One of my father's top advisors is behind this assault on both our nations."

Wunebo-Pran's eyes grew wide. "Glorious Rajah-Lahr, I know of this Salandrian. He is the keeper of Imarina's magical knowledge. If he has turned against them, he poses a grave threat to your empire."

Isabella jumped in. "If the Blight is such a threat, why not allow us to risk our lives—instead of Mosork ones—to stop it? Or the Blight and those behind it may prove too dangerous for us to defeat. If so, your death sentence will be carried out. You win either way."

Rajah-Lahr thought quietly for a long moment. No one on either side of the stand-off dared to speak a word.

Finally, he broke his silence. "Very well, little Princess. Had you slain any of my soldiers in your escape, I would have been forced to exact revenge. But you spared my sleeping guards who, despite their inept performance today, remain respected members of my mighty army. Go and fight these evil sorcerers killing both our people."

"And little Princess? I hope you win. For all our benefit."

CHAPTER 32

THE CIRCLE OF BLACK-CLAD sorcerers gathered once again inside the glass foundry in Naseem. Salandrian—the True Leader—paced around the center of the circle, his arms folded behind his back. The Scions of Sonorian stood with their heads down, hands clasped at their waists. No one spoke.

Finally, the three young sorcerers who had fought Bok, Isabella and the others entered the foundry. Again, the spell masking their true forms peeled away once they closed the foundry door. This time, however, they dragged a heavy canvas sack, which they slung across the stone floor toward the circle.

"So... you failed."

"Salandrian... True Leader..." Alaydrian stammered. "How did...?"

"Magic? No! I could tell by your faces that you failed! Princess Isabella and her mixed-class band of idealists still live. Tell me what happened—and spare no detail."

"We... we attacked without mercy, as you have taught us." Alaydrian's lower lip shook as she spoke. "We almost had them, but they escaped into the forest. We lost their trail near the border."

"And Daronian? I assume he is dead."

"Yes. Killed by the rich boy with his bow and arrow."

"Tell me—and this is perhaps the most important question you shall ever answer, Alaydrian. Did they uncover the extent of our plans?" Salandrian stood in front of the young sorcerer, his face inches from hers.

"I... I do not know, True Leader." She turned away, then looked to the floor, only to be jerked into the air by a violent variation on Tranogian's Territorial Transport.

Salandrian thundered, "If you don't know, then why should I let you live?" Alaydrian dangled 10 feet above the foundry floor. Her legs kicked involuntarily in mid-air and her hands clutched at the tendrils of translucent blue-green energy wound around her neck and chest.

"Buh-because..." Through the crushing pain, Alaydrian gestured to the canvas sack, her fingers twitching as she pointed to the bag. "I buh-brought someone who can tell us!"

Her two companions pulled away the bag to reveal Tovano. The old man moaned as he drifted in and out of consciousness.

Salandrian set the gasping young sorcerer back on the floor. "You may have redeemed yourself after all, Alaydrian!"

He stepped over to Tovano and knelt over the delirious old man. "Good evening. I trust your journey wasn't too uncomfortable."

Tovano blinked to clear his head. "Salandrian? But how...? This isn't an illusion spell—you truly are different, changed."

"Indeed I am. Younger. Stronger. More vital. As for how, I will just say the old scrolls and dusty tomes at Sonorian Square contain ancient secrets that my small-minded so-called 'superiors' could never imagine." He pushed back the sleeves of his jacket. "But you could and did, didn't you?"

Tovano covered his mouth with his hand and coughed. "I warned King Isbiano that the House of Magic had become too powerful, too corrupt. I suspected one of you might be responsible for the atrocities in Naseem. But I needed proof."

"And did you and the Princess find such proof at Osoh Creek? Will she be able to reveal my conspiracy to the King?"

Tovano shook his head. "I'll tell you nothing. I've lived a long enough life and I'll die knowing I helped purge the kingdom of you and your empty-minded followers."

Salandrian stood and gestured for the Scions of Sonorian to pull Tovano into the middle of the circle.

"My acolytes, I have an unexpected lesson for you: How to extract information from an unwilling mind."

He leaned over, so only Tovano could hear him. "This is one of those old, forgotten spells you feared someone might uncover. Thankfully, Tovanian, it is an effective and highly pleasurable enchantment.

"Pleasurable for me, that is. For you, it will be severely painful."

CHAPTER 33

B OK AND HIS COMPANIONS crossed back into Imarina that evening. They intended to retrace their route back to Ithenel as quickly as they could. They had to return to the King and the Royal Council before Salandrian and whatever corrupt forces he had assembled within the House of Magic had a chance to strike from the inside.

But they could only go so far so fast and needed to rest their horses—and themselves—on Naseem's outskirts. Wingate found a barn left abandoned by farmers fleeing the Blight. He tied their horses up and the group went inside for a few precious hours of sleep.

This gave Bok a chance to minister to Coregan's injuries again. His infection remained severe, despite Bok's attempts to treat it on the road. Coregan even winced when Bok changed his bloody dressing—something the young healer doubted he would ever see.

Coregan drifted off into an uneasy, Yorka root-induced sleep. Bok stretched out on a bare patch of dirt beside his patient. Using his rolled-up shirt as a pillow, his eyes quickly became too heavy to keep them open.

He woke to find the others already stirring, even Coregan, although the sun had not yet risen. Umra lugged in a bucket of water from a nearby stream and filled everyone's cup as Isabella gathered them together.

"This is where we must divide our group."

"Divide our forces?" Avantil looked up from his drink. "But why?"

"We must get word back to my father—that is our mission and my priority. But I cannot abandon Tovano. If there is any hope of rescuing him, I must try."

Bok nodded. He wanted to get back to Ithenel, stop the Blight, and protect his family. *But Isabella is right—we can't leave Tovano. What if he has fallen into the clutches of the Scions. I couldn't face Mother and Father having abandoned a friend.*

She looked to the two Royal Guardians. "Wingate—I need you to ride on to Ithenel. Coregan, we are going to get you to a healer in Naseem."

Coregan flexed his wounded shoulder, testing his arm. "Your Majesty, the King put me in charge o' your safety and I intend to see that job through."

Isabella held up her hand, as if she anticipated his answer. "Commander, you are the embodiment of

'Loyalty above all.' But I am here, and my father placed me in charge of this field mission. That means my orders countermand his instructions back in Ithenel, correct?"

"Aye, Your Majesty," he softly grumbled. "That they do."

"Very well then. You may ride with Wingate into the city, where you are to go to the first reputable healer you may find. May the Exalted One ride with you."

The group stepped outside the barn just as the first rays of daylight cracked the sky. The two Guardians saluted their Crown Princess and rode away toward the city. Their horses' hooves kicked up dusty clouds as they raced toward Ithenel.

When they were out of earshot of the Guardians, Kotarian cornered Isabella, his hands waving above his head. "We should go with Wingate. Returning to Ithenel immediately is our *only* goal. You have said so yourself!"

Isabella didn't raise her voice to match his animated ire. "Of course, the Kingdom's safety matters most. But I believe we can accomplish both goals here. If you were held captive, would you expect us to attempt to free you?"

Kotarian looked to the sky. "Well, the House's Shining Light wouldn't have been captured by those back-of-the-class nitwits! But if I was, I would expect you to follow your father's orders."

Not now, Kotarian. Why must you always assert your opinions at such unwelcome moments? But Bok didn't know what to say that wouldn't make the situation worse.

Besides, Isabella was more than capable of expressing her own authority. She spoke slowly and softly. But her small hands clenched into fists at her side. "Careful, Kotarian. Do not forget who is in command here."

"Exactly! Your. Father. He sent you to carry out his wishes, just as the House sent me to represent our order."

Isabella waited until Kotarian had finished, then paused briefly to take deep, measured breaths. "My father appointed me to carry out his wishes *under my leadership*. The goal is the same, but the means to achieve it are mine. That means the King trusts my judgment, and my decision is—"

Kotarian interrupted the Princess. "If the King was here, he would agree that your affection for Tovano clouds your judgment. If you weren't so—!"

"That's enough!" Avantil grabbed the startled sorcerer's collar. "Shut your smirking mouth!"

"Let him go, Avantil!" Isabella tried to wrench his hand away from Kotarian's throat to no avail. But the sorcerer squirmed away.

"The jealous boyfriend act! How predictable!" Kotarian laughed in Avantil's face. "The Princess and I are two trained sorcerers engaged in conversation. This is far above your intellectual level, rich boy. Stand aside until the

Princess gives you something to keep you busy while we do the important work. I suppose she learned that tactic from your parents."

WHAM! Avantil delivered his response with a hard right to Kotarian's jaw.

Mouth agape, Bok watched the sorcerer slump to the ground, momentarily dazed. Blood and saliva dribbled from his mouth. When Kotarian recovered his bearings enough to realize what had happened, he touched his bleeding lip with his fingers and ran his tongue under his lower lip to make sure he hadn't lost any teeth.

Bok stepped in front of Avantil, who shoved him away. But the merchant's son didn't advance toward Kotarian. Instead, he stood where he was, fist drawn and waiting for the sorcerer's response.

"Stop it!!" Isabella cried. "Please... do not fight!"

But if Kotarian heard her, he did not care. "Oh, you are going to regret that, rich boy." He flipped the blood from his fingertips to the ground and wiped his hand on his trousers. "I'd almost forgotten how much I hated being struck. Almost."

Kotarian slowly sat up. The lack of inflection in his voice terrified Bok. Kotarian sounded like someone resigned to performing a horrible but necessary task, the way Bok's mother spoke before slaughtering a chicken.

Kotarian stood and dusted off his clothes. He whispered an enchantment, and a halo of blue-green energy engulfed his body. His hands no longer were visible, encircled by his mystic power. Even his eyes turned blue-green, transformed by the mighty forces that gathered around him.

"Kotarian—! I'm sorry for hitting you. Truly, I should not have done that." Avantil backed away. "Hit me back if you must, but please... This has gone too far!" But Kotarian listened to nothing except the rage racing through his mind.

He stopped his advance and raised a glowing hand. He meant to kill Avantil—Bok was sure of it. And if bloodlust consumed the battle-trained sorcerer, even Isabella could do little to stop him.

All Bok could do was appeal to Kotarian's higher instincts. He hoped they listened.

"Wait, please!" Bok placed his own body between the sorcerer and his intended target. "This mistake would overshadow all your hard work and sacrifice. You could never undo it."

"Step aside, Bok," Kotarian warned. "You meddle in things that are not your affair."

"But they are. These matters—this mission—concern all of us. Every single person in Imarina. And we need you, Kotarian. That isn't an appeal to your vanity—it is the truth."

Kotarian wouldn't look at Bok or drop his still-charged hand, but he listened. "Perhaps. But I once swore that I would never again be a victim."

Bok met Kotarian's eyes. "Avantil is not the rightful target of your vengeance. No, he never should have hit you. And you never should have spoken to him the way you did. Or the way you have to me or to Umra or so many others who have done nothing to threaten you." Kotarian cocked his head to the side, awaiting Bok's next words.

The young healer set his jaw. "Yes, you have made yourself powerful, Kotarian. But don't forget what it feels like to be powerless."

Kotarian looked away, then lowered his hand. The blue-green aura around him quickly dissipated.

"I suppose you truly cannot complete this mission without me." Kotaran then turned to Avantil. "Rich boy, consider yourself lucky to have a friend as loyal as Bok. I wish to be alone now. But when it is time, I shall be ready."

He walked away, down a path toward the nearby creek. The rest of the group exhaled the tension they had been holding in.

"Bok, that was amazing—and brave!" Isabella rushed to his side. "Your compassion has served us well this day."

He smiled at her kind words, despite his racing pulse. "Everyone else has put themselves in harm's way on this trip. I suppose it was my turn!"

Isabella took his left hand into both of hers and held it for a moment. As nice as her soft hand felt in his, Bok realized it was a gesture of friendship—nothing else.

But Avantil shot them both a stern glance. "By all means, attend to Bok. No need to concern yourself with my well-being, Isabella. I'm fine, especially for a man who was nearly reduced to a pile of fine particles by a lunatic."

Isabella spun, her feet planted wide. "Whose fault would that have been? You hit him, Avantil!"

"By the Exalted One! You act like he was justified in trying to murder me!"

"Of course not, foolish boy!" She practically spat the word *boy*. "Kotarian did everything he could to goad you, and you were oh-so willing to bite at the bait. He challenged your precious manhood and nothing else mattered."

Bok's fingers tingled. *Please—both of you. Don't do this.*

Avantil rolled his eyes. "Let's be honest, Isabella. You don't want a partner. You want someone who will do anything the Crown Princess asks without question—like Bok does. No offense intended, Bok, but we all know that is the truth."

Bok said nothing—because it was, in fact, true. Even if she was withholding information about his past. *But hearing Avantil frame my loyalty to Isabella in such a pathetic light hurts. After all, the merchant's son is my friend, too.*

"This is not about Bok—it is about you, Avantil. You hardly are the only one whom Kotarian has taunted. But rather than act the bigger man, as Bok has done, you behave like a pub hooligan brawling over a card game!"

Avantil's pale face flushed crimson. "You truly are angrier with me than with Kotarian! Whose side are you on, exactly?"

"Yes, I am angrier with you. Whatever he is, Kotarian will not be Prince Consort one day. This is not some rich boy's game—actual lives depend on our efforts. I know you are just a month shy of 19 summers, but it is time that you grew up, Avantil."

Just stop it! Bok did not want to see such anger between two people he cared for so much. The stress of their plight weighed on them all; now, it seemingly tore them apart.

"Oh, is that right, *Your Majesty*?" he sniffed, letting her formal title hang in the air. "You don't think I'm aware of the stakes? On a mission I volunteered to serve on, so that I could be by your side?"

His voice cracked. "I know being Crown Princess is a difficult job and you are devoted to duty. But sometimes, I wish you realized the rest of us have our own burdens to carry."

CHAPTER 34

I SABELLA AND AVANTIL WALKED in separate directions. Like Kotarian, they needed a moment alone.

Bok knew they would return soon. Too much was at stake for them to dwell on personal feelings for long. *But we're falling apart when we needed to band together most. At this rate, we're doing Salandrian's work for him.*

Sure enough, the group soon reassembled. But Avantil wore an unfamiliar frown. Kotarian stood cross-armed when Isabella called for their attention. She didn't look in Avantil's direction, nor would he stand near her.

"We only can allow ourselves a few hours to find Tovano—at that point, we must return to Ithenel as well. Bok—you will come with me and patrol the area north of the river."

"Gladly. But what are we looking for?" Naseem wasn't the size of Ithenel, but it wasn't Soleh Valley, either.

Finding a clue about their lost friend in the city in such a short time wouldn't be easy.

"I... I am not sure, my friend," she admitted. "I only know that we must try."

Umra provided a voice of optimism among the stunned and somber group. "I know these streets as well as anybody, Yer Majesty, an' I got contacts in every corner of the city! If yer teacher is stowed away anywhere in Naseem, we'll find that hidey-hole."

When Isabella announced Kotarian and Avantil would be paired together, the young nobleman pointed a gloved finger at his lover. "What? You are aware that he tried to kill me just this very day!"

Kotarian laughed as he uncorked yet another bottle of red wine he pilfered from the Grenuteral's wine cellar. "That's a bit of an exaggeration, rich boy. Did I want to kill you? Eh... perhaps, perhaps not. Did I think of killing you? I suppose I did. And... that took the situation farther than it should have gone."

He took a drink and let his eyes linger in Avantil's direction. "But had I truly tried to kill you, we wouldn't be having this conversation."

"Kotarian, enough!" Isabella said. "Umra says there has been an unusual volume of activity in the manufacturing sector near the river, with unfamiliar faces coming and going for reasons not readily apparent."

"I tol' you—Servin' Class folk talk to each other!" Umra grinned broadly.

"And you, Umra, shall accompany Avantil and Kotarian in patrolling that area. They need your keen eye and local knowledge." Isabella added, "And if you can keep their pridefulness in line, all the better."

Avantil simply grunted and paced in a circle. "Fine. I'll work with the sorcerer. For Imarina and King Isbiano."

He walked away without a farewell for Isabella and mounted his horse. She watched and waited but refused to speak first.

"Well, this should be fun." Kotarian returned to his mount. He pulled his gray jacket from his saddlebag, carefully smoothed out the wrinkles, and put it on, replacing the star-shaped pin on his lapel.

"No need for subterfuge at this point; I'll stand or fall representing the House. Wait—who are we talking about? I'll stand representing the House!"

Isabella waved her finger. "Remember—we meet back at Queen Imbiria's Square in four hours. At that time, we will return home, with Tovano or not."

"That bag of bones will owe me dearly," Kotarian said. "I still say the best way to find him is to drag a fruit pie through the middle of town. Ah, well. I bid you farewell—for now."

CHAPTER 35

"PLEASE—STOP THIS AT ONCE! Have you lost your mind?"

A few blocks away, Isabella asked that question of a mustachioed middle-aged man who, given his flour-covered apron, appeared to be a baker by trade. But instead of baking loaves, he heaved rocks through a neighboring store's window.

"Sorry, lady! You'll have to fend for yourself!" He stuffed cured meats and wheels of cheese into a canvas sack. Isabella and Bok had ventured into a residential area of Naseem looking for the missing Tovano. Instead of clues, they found only chaos.

The baker-turned-bandit ran off with his treasures while down the street, two men engaged in an impromptu tug-of-war over the reins of a donkey cart. Bok thought he should intervene before the dispute became violent, but before he could, the larger of the men wrested control of the reins and rode off.

"Come back!" the other man yelled. "That's my vegetable wagon, you thief!"

Bok rode to the man's side. "What... what is happening here? Where are the constables?"

"Constables," the man sneered. "They was the first ta leave town. Like a fool, I stayed behind. Well, the Blight may not get me, but it looks like my neighbors will."

The man pointed at Isabella. "Y'know, you look just like—"

"Princess Isabella. Yes, I know—"

"Haw!" the man chuckled. "Yer a fine-lookin' young woman ta be sure. But do you think our princess ever leaves the Royal Palace without runnin' a comb through her hair? Or puttin' makeup on her face?"

"Well, um, I am certain there have been occasions… perhaps if she was in a hurry?" She smoothed out her hair with her fingers.

"Naw, yer no Princess Isabella. I was gonna say you look like a couple o' them fugitives those strange folk was lookin' fer the other day."

"Strange folk?" Bok asked.

"I mean, they seemed awful serious! They stopped me in the street as I made my morning rounds. They acted like they come from Ithenel on behalf o' the King. But they gave me a bad feelin' and I didn't tell 'em nothin'… 'Course, even if ye are those fugitives, I don't guess it matters. Not with all this happenin'." He gestured at the burning buildings and unchecked looting around them.

Bok wondered if the Scions of Sonorian remained in Naseem. And if so, was Tovano even still alive? At some point, they would confront the Scions again. Bok hoped it would happen before it was too late for Imarina.

The fires had spread to a nearby boarding house. The building hadn't been extensively damaged yet, so Isabella cast a spell and the flames quickly burned out.

"At least that is one problem I can solve." She and Bok continued riding down the street, dodging the occasional pile of broken glass or smashed crates.

They paced their journey through the neighborhood, carefully looking around for clues, but also aware that their time to find Tovano was limited. But the streets framing Naseem's factory district all held the same mix of isolated fires, broken windows, and the occasional looter or frightened straggler who had not fled town with their neighbors. Bok found a sameness in the chaos, as incongruent as that seemed.

"I wish there was something more we could do, Bok. I never thought this could happen in Imarina. In my family's kingdom."

"I know." Bok pulled his horse close alongside Isabella's and, from his saddle, put his arm across her shoulder. She rested her head on him and closed her eyes to the devastation around her.

Bok grieved at the destruction, too, knowing what it meant for the people who had lost their homes, their jobs, and perhaps more. But he also hurt for his friend, who took the widespread devastation afflicting their country as a personal failure of her leadership.

"The best way we can help these people is to stop Salandrian," Bok assured her. "He's the root of this evil. But first, we find our friend." She straightened up and Bok pulled his arm away so they both could resume their search.

However, the next two hours proved fruitless, only extinguishing a few fires and breaking up two fistfights.

Wherever Tovano is hidden, it might as well be a thousand miles away.

Bok paused in front of a three-story grain mill, where the river powered a giant wheel to turn the millstone that every day, ground hundreds of pounds of corn from the nearby fields into meal. He snapped his fingers. "If we could get up on the roof, we probably could see the entire street."

He looked around the side of the mill. "Maybe we can find an open door; there should be stairs inside."

"No need for stairs!" With a wave of Isabella's hand, an invisible wind swept her and Bok off the ground. Like all children, Bok and Yata had pretended they could fly. Once, Yata even climbed to the top of their house, stretched her arms wide, and leaped into a pile of straw. "Watch me, Bok! I'm a red-tailed hawk!" Her antics earned her a month of extra chores from their parents, but Bok still laughed every time he thought of his sister, suspended in mid-air in his imagination, diving into that hay pile.

"Tovano taught me the gentle float spell when I was a child. You will learn it soon. I used to employ this spell to sneak out of the palace tower and into my mother's gardens. My father was furious when he discovered. Tovano had to pretend he was disappointed as well. But as soon as my father left the room, Tovano admitted he was proud of me for mastering the spell."

They reached the sloped roof of the mill, and the sense of weightlessness ended. "Your father—the King—does he have the Acumen? Or did your mother?"

"No—neither was born with the Acumen," Isabella peered over the edge of the roof and pointed to a man moving through a side street below. "Who is that skulking about down there?"

Bok looked down. "I can't say for certain, but he appears just to be trying to get somewhere safe without encountering any of that rough crowd we saw." Bok turned back to the conversation. "So where does your Acumen come from?"

"Well, my grandmother on my father's side—Queen Iladalya—had the Acumen. But she never bothered to develop it. She became too comfortable with the trappings of royalty to commit to something as challenging as High Magic. When I learned I was endowed with the Acumen, I promised I would not let it go to waste.

"But what about you, Bok? Do others in your family practice Folk Magic?"

Bok shook his head. "They don't. But when I was young, Weni Kon tested all the children in our community—and I suppose she saw something in me. And like you, I didn't want to let that opportunity slip by. In my case, I didn't care for farming and while I have done my share of blacksmithing... well, I'm terrible at it, if we are being honest! Becoming a healer seemed a better path for me."

He looked across the city. They could see the entire street—and more—from their third-story perch atop the slanted wooden roof. Construction workers had used pine resin to seal the cracks between the shingles. This kept the grain and meal inside dry even on the rainiest of days. Bok admired the craftwork. He wondered—would the Baron of Nardru have a similar appreciation of skilled labor? If so, how long would that last around the courtly people of Ithenel?

"You were right, Bok. We can see forever from here," Isabella shielded the late afternoon sun from her eyes with her hand. "Any sign of Avantil, Umra and Kotarian?"

He sighed. "No. I'm sure they are too far away. There are a few people out on the streets, but none of them appear to be likely to bring us closer to Tovano and the Scions."

"Yes... That's been the story of this mission, hasn't it? Every step we take puts us farther and farther from our goal."

"No! Don't say that, Isabella—please. We uncovered Salandrian's plot and once Wingate informs the King, he will put an end to this uprising. Your father will be proud of you—he is proud of you. And if I know Avantil, he will—"

Isabella rolled her eyes. "Avantil. I believe I have lost him, too. Truth be told, he will consider himself grateful, if he does not already. My duty to Imarina will be—and must be—my first love."

"I... I'm sorry." In recent days, Bok recognized that Isabella's presence made his stomach flutter and his thoughts scatter. He figured she had that effect on plenty of people.

But he also knew that no matter what the truth may be about his origins, he was Serving Class raised. Imarina's Noble Class never would accept their princess having a romantic relationship with someone from his background.

Far more importantly, she and Avantil are my friends. Their happiness means more than a teenage boy's fever dream.

For the same reason, he wouldn't press Isabella about the secret he suspected she kept. *Whatever it is, she would never hurt me, and right now, she needs my support, not an interrogation.*

"I know you mean a great deal to Avantil. And he to you, Isabella. Perhaps the final chapter in your story together has not yet been written."

"Perhaps." She smiled, then quickly turned look for signs on Naseem's streets that might lead them to Tovano. "It truly is beautiful up here—despite the circumstances. I have not spent much time in Naseem. I suppose I always thought it paled when compared to my shining city of Ithenel. But the ancient buildings, the symmetry of the center city, the old oak trees lining every street—I need to spend more time here, and throughout the kingdom. I will return soon if we succeed."

"*When* we succeed," Bok's mouth curled into a smile.

"Yes, that's it!" Her hands smacked together. "When you say it, I believe it. Tell me, Bok, why do I inspire so much faith in you?"

"Because I see you for how you truly are." He became aware that his breathing and heartrate both had sped up, as if he had jogged up the side of the grain mill. "I hope I can help you see it, too."

"You have a way of saying exactly what I need to hear, Bok." Isabella turned her eyes to him and back to the horizon again. "But I am not the only one struggling with unanswered questions. Have you thought more about what Tovano shared with you?"

Bok nodded. "Accepting a Barony and becoming his next pupil? An incredible opportunity, but it doesn't seem real and true. Kotarian says that while I have the Acumen and am Noble Class born for sure, he is skeptical of my potential to be a sorcerer. Even an intensive course of study can't overcome 19 summers in Soleh Valley, or so he tells me."

"It is not Kotarian's decision to make, though, nor that of the House," Isabella brushed the long, curly brown hair from her face. "My father alone has the authority to award Baronies. Given the courage and loyalty you have displayed; you can be the Baron of Nardru if you choose."

This presented Bok with a clear path of opportunity. Accepting the King's offer would make Bok a wealthy man, to the point that his parents, Yata, and even Noji never would need to work again. He could give them the lives they deserved. It also provided the opportunity for Bok to develop his new-found skills in High Magic and use those talents to their highest purpose. But most of all, it would mean there was a place for him with Isabella and Avantil.

However, accepting this offer would mean leaving his family behind in Soleh Valley. They would never agree to join him in the city, and he would miss out on his parents growing old, on Noji growing up, and on Yata reaching her full potential as a blacksmith, a mother, and a community leader.

"So what should I do?'

"Follow your heart." His confusion must have been clear on his face, as Isabella threw her arm over his shoulder, her gold bracelets clinking.

Where does my heart lead me? Choosing between my family and my friends seems an impossible decision.

But that it was a choice for another day. For a moment, he forgot about the mystery of his parentage, the questions about his future, the danger facing Imarina, and the life-or-death battle that undoubtedly lay ahead. He and

Isabella stood on the rooftop, each silently supporting their beloved friend.

In that moment, all was right in Bok Omat's soul.

CHAPTER 36

"Isabella!" Avantil's voice called out from the street below.

Bok looked down to see their three companions standing below. As long as he lived—and he hoped that would be far longer than the trip back to Ithenel—he would cherish this time spent with Princess Isabella on the roof of a Naseem grain mill. But now, it was time to refocus on the job at hand.

Isabella nudged his arm. "I can get us back to the ground the same way we came up." With a gesture, they floated down from the roof to the street.

Isabella's shiny black boot kicked the dusty road. "I hope you three had better luck than we did. We found nothing, save a city on the edge of self-destruction."

"We did—on Queen Inderia Avenue! We must hurry to the glass foundry." Avantil pumped his fist, a small smile creeping back to his face.

Kotarian shrugged. "The rich boy insists he spotted some clue. He won't tell me what. But I am inclined to believe him."

Avantil hustled back to his horse. "By the Exalted One, I will show you!" The young Noble rode toward the foundry a few blocks over and the others followed.

They arrived at the brick building, which from the outside, appeared as silent as every other building on the street.

"Tovano is in there. I'm certain of it." Avantil slammed his fist into the palm.

Isabella squinted through the foundry's darkened window. "How can you be so sure? I see nothing out of the ordinary."

Avantil took the group to the side door. "Because Kotarian and I saw two glass factory workers go inside, dressed for a day's work in a dangerous environment. They wore thick aprons and heavy gloves—exactly the type of thing you would wear if you made glass for a living."

"Yes, and so?" Kotarian wondered. "Even in this madness, we have witnessed people attempting to go about their routine lives. If these two are glassmakers, why wouldn't they go to work?"

Avantil smiled and raised a finger knowingly. "Yes, it would be normal to see workers entering a glass-making factory. But I know something you both don't—the Mechedi Glass Foundry closed more than a month ago. Its owners have kept this news a secret, as they are trying to sell the business and fear that knowledge of their financial hardship would drive down their asking price to sell."

Umra raised her thin eyebrows. "Yeah, I bet they's two of those folk my barkeeper friend Lefi was talkin' about! Strange folk showin' up here in the factory district in recent months, dressed ta work but not minglin' with the other workers."

"Hmm... that actually makes sense, rich boy. How do you know the old bag of bones didn't simply get lost?'

"Tovano is too resourceful for that." Isabella shook her head. "He would've found us by now, if he was able."

Kotarian shrugged. "Well, if we are dealing with Salandrian's jackals, they will have shielded the door with magic. So how do we get inside?"

Isabella bit her thumbnail as she concentrated. "A good question Kotarian. Umra, I do not suppose there is a servant's entrance here, too?"

"No, Yer Majesty. Most of the workers just go in this door here. But I do have an idear! As ye no doubt know, every wagon an' cart that leaves a fac'try like this one must pay a tax ta the Crown."

"That's right," Avantil said. "The House of Commerce levies a tax on every load of goods made in Imarina."

"Aye. But this foundry is real old. Centuries ago, places like this here in Naseem used ta get around payin' the tax by sneakin' goods through underground tunnels an' out o' the city. Until one day, the river overflowed after a heavy rain. The tunnels flooded—an' over a hunnerd folk died! Even though they was Servin' Class, that was more than could be ignored."

"That is when Queen Imbiria—my ancestor—ordered the Naseem tunnels closed," Isabella interjected.

"Absolutely, Yer Majesty! But them tunnels is still there. When I lived on the streets, me an' my friends used 'em ta hide from the constables—an' for other purposes I'd rather not mention in Noble company. Remind me ta tell ye about them days, Bok! We never came down the tunnels this far down Queen Inderia Avenue, but we may can get inside that way!"

Avantil threw up an open hand. "Slow down, Umra. That's if the entrance hasn't been bricked over. Or the tunnel filled in with dirt."

"One problem at a time," Isabella responded. "We must try the tunnels. They may be our only way to save Tovano!"

Umra took the group to a boarded-up brick building down the block. Umra explained that the constables covered the windows and doors covered with boards, which would get pulled off by people looking to get inside... until the boards went up again.

"Sometimes, folk without homes come 'ere fer shelter." As Umra spoke, Bok and Avantil pried back the heavy boards across one of the broken windows. Kotarian begged off from helping. "A splinter could impact my ability to cast spells, and then where would you all be?"

Once they cleared the window, the group crawled through the opening, with Avantil and Umra leading the way into the darkness of the abandoned factory.

Isabella and Kotarian spoke lantern spells. Cones of light sprouted from their upturned palms, revealing dozens of wine bottles and piles of discarded rags on the well-worn, dust-coated bricks. The factory floor itself contained no sign of its former use, with anything of value having long disappeared. Spider webs hung everywhere—Bok walked through one and frantically pulled the strand off his face.

SQUEE! A mouse ran by the group to its hiding place between two loose bricks, running across the toe of Isabella's boot on its way. The Princess didn't scream or complain, but Bok saw her entire body shudder.

Umra ran to the back of the dark factory and yanked up a pile of canvas tarps. "We're in luck! The entrance is still 'ere!"

She pointed to a stack of old planks uncovered when she pulled away the tarps. When Bok pulled the boards away, dozens of roaches scurried across the floor, fleeing the light being cast by the surprised sorcerers. He heaved the boards to the side and revealed an ancient stone hole in the floor of the factory. The dank, rotting odor wafting up from the tunnel nearly knocked Bok to the ground.

Kotarian grimaced. "By Hadranian's Horrifying Halitosis! Could you have taken us to a more dreadful place, Umra?"

"I didn't build these tunnels, nor did folk like me want 'em built."

"No—that would be my ancestors, or those like them, sadly." Avantil stood in the entrance to the tunnel. Despite the near-total darkness, Kotarian and Isabella's spells revealed a small flight of stone steps leading down to a water-covered floor.

"Musta flooded durin' the last storm. Doesn't look more than ankle-deep, though. We should be able ta wade through ta the foundry, 'slong as the tunnel isn't blocked."

"Then what are we waiting for? All in!" Avantil bounded down the steps and splashing into the fetid water.

"You heard him—no point in waiting." Isabella gingerly stepped off the stairs and into the water. The algae-coated tunnel was only about five feet tall, which wasn't much of a problem for Bok, Isabella and Umra. But Avantil and Kotarian had to crouch uncomfortably low to avoid banging their heads on the ceiling.

The group moved forward as quickly as they could through the narrow darkness. "You might wanna watch out fer snakes."

Bok cringed—when he was around seven summers, he and Yata were playing in a creek when he encountered a cottonmouth viper. Had Yata not scared it off with a stick, he likely would've been bitten. *But I can't hide behind my older sister now.*

"We're here!" Umra pointed up another set of steps to a boarded-up entrance in the tunnel's roof.

Avantil tested the weight of the boards. "It's too heavy to lift, and we'll need to move fast, in case they hear us."

"I can move it." Kotarian's hands glowed blue-green. "Anything to get out of this swampy, stinking crypt!"

Avantil nodded and nocked an arrow. Bok started to draw his sword but figured his rudimentary magical skills may be of more help than his rudimentary swordsmanship.

"Okay—now!" Isabella whispered.

Kotarian's spell deftly lifted the heavy wooden cover over the mouth of the tunnel. They carefully stepped out into the basement of the foundry. Stacks of crates filled with jars and bottles stood taller than a man's head and created a labyrinth leading to the stairs up. Other than a small amount of light coming from the stairwell, the basement was nearly as dark as the shoe factory—and just as unoccupied.

Bok exhaled. "With any luck, maybe we can get Tovano out without a fight."

"You obviously have never been a sailor, my friend!" Avantil patted Bok on the shoulder. "If you were, you wouldn't tempt the gods of fate and luck."

Unfortunately, that warning proved prophetic. As they were about to climb out of the basement, a voice behind them cried, "Over here! Someone's over here!"

A man rushed toward them across the dark basement. Bok spotted the distinctive glint of light on metal and heard the unmistakable sound of a blade being drawn from a scabbard.

Avantil shot an arrow, which found its mark. The man died instantly. But his momentum carried him into a stack of crates, which crashed the stone floor.

He groaned. "If they didn't know we were here before, they certainly do now. Up the stairs!"

They did as he said, only to find two more guards standing at the top of the stairwell on the foundry's main floor.

"Intruders! Kill them!" One of the guards threw a spear down toward the group.

Bok instinctively flinched, but Isabella flicked her wrist and an eldritch ribbon of energy, almost resembling a translucent blue-and-green hand, snatched the spear from the air and snapped it like a small twig. Avantil then dispatched one of the guards with a second arrow, while Kotarian cast a spell on the other. The man's mouth and eyes opened wide. In seconds, he was dead—encased in a thin layer of ice, his body completely frozen solid.

"Falarian's Frigid Fatality—I've been waiting for a chance to use that one."

"Admire your handiwork later, Kotarian! We must go now!" But even in the chaos, Isabella turned to Umra and said, "Sweet girl, I need you to stay here. For all your courage, you are neither a warrior nor a sorcerer—and if you are in the battle, I shall be distracted."

"Will do, Yer Majesty. Now go get them bastards!"

With the need for subtlety gone, the group raced up the steps and into the main factory floor. There, they found the Scions of Sonorian waiting. Alaydrian stood flanked by two other sorcerers. Two burly guards, swords drawn and shields up, stood between them and the stairwell entry. Oil lanterns ringed the perimeter of the dust-covered floor, casting gloomy shadows on stacked wooden crates and empty worktables.

Kotarian's face wrinkled into a snarl when he saw the Scions, one tall, gangly young man and the other a short, squat young woman with close-cropped blonde hair.

"Spalonian. Neuragian. Two more traitors! How dare you turn your backs on your country? Your house? Your siblings?" His hands crackled with magical energy. In response, the three scions prepared their first wave of attacks, too.

"We are the loyalists here, Kotarian. Loyal to Imarinan customs, not to some misguided House that lost its way many years ago or a Royal Family that openly carouses with... servants." Alaydrian practically spat the word "servants." "You could have joined us. But Salandrian knew you couldn't be trusted."

Kotarian rolled his eyes. "Join you? You three pretenders are about to get a lesson in magic. From the Shining Light of Imarina's House of Magic."

Kotarian lashed forward with a wave of pure mystical force. At first, it appeared he could overpower the trio of

Scion sorcerers, but Alaydrian, Spalonian and Neuragian countered and not only stopped the momentum of Kotarian's spell, but reversed its momentum, pushing the wave back toward Kotarian. Avantil fired a series of arrows at the trio, but they deflected the shafts, even as they drove Kotarian backward.

Isabella turned to Bok. "We need to help him! But first, we must deal with the guards. If they catch us casting spells against the Scion sorcerers, they will cut us down."

Bok remembered the pyromancy spell that he and Tovano had worked on. Flames danced forth from his hands—but the guards were ready. Their iron shields blocked the blast of fire, which dissipated when Bok's confidence waned.

But Isabella kept calm and spoke an incantation as the guards charged her with swords raised above their heads. Lightning shot forth from both her hands. While the guards' metal shields proved an effective defense against fire, they were a deadly liability against electricity. Both men dropped to the floor dead, just feet from where Bok, Isabella and Avantil stood.

"Remind me to never argue with you again!" Avantil joked. For a split second, Isabella returned his warm gaze for the first time since their dispute, then steeled herself for the remaining battle—which promised to be far more difficult.

"They have three sorcerers and we have three sorcerers, plus the best archer in Imarina. The odds are in our favor."

"Um, I'm not truly a sorcerer—not yet," Bok offered.

"You are now. Consider it a battlefield promotion. For Imarina! For King Isbiano!" Isabella sent a spell of pure magical force toward the trio of Scion sorcerers, who had Kotarian pinned against the foundry's brick wall, his defenses nearly exhausted. The attack threw Alaydrian and her co-conspirators off-balance, allowing Kotarian to regroup.

"Well, Princess Pretender has joined the fray!" Alaydrian crowed. "I'm surprised you aren't busy ministering to peasants—that is your favorite pastime, I believe. But if your master was any indication, breaking you won't be a problem. We'll even let your Serving Class friends bury you in the Royal Gardens beside your mother!"

Isabella's nostrils flared. A wave of fire, far bigger than the one Bok had been able to conjure, rushed forth and nearly engulfed Alaydrian. She barely threw up a mystic shield in time to avoid being incinerated by Isabella's spell.

Bok paired off with Spalonian, the tall man, while Kotarian battled the short young woman, Neuragian. Avantil stood back, waiting for his opportunity to strike.

"EEEK! GET YER HANDS OFF ME VILLAIN!" Umra's leather-lunged scream echoed up the stairwell.

"Go help her, Avantil! We can handle these three."

Bok heard his friend's feet clomp against the foundry's brick floor. But he dared not turn his attention away from the Scion across from him.

You told Isabella you would stand with her until the end.

He pushed up his sleeves. *Time to put that promise to the test.*

CHAPTER 37

I SABELLA FOUND HERSELF TOO concerned with fending off Alaydrian's relentless attacks to notice Avantil's disappearance. A hurricane spell threw Isabella across the factory floor. From a seated position, she had to dive for cover from the razor-sharp pincer appendage Alaydrian conjured next.

Bok fared even worse. He tried to replicate the attack that had served him so well against Coz Cosan. But when he hurled a crate of magic jars at Spalonian, the sorcerer smiled and reversed the spell, sending the crate flying back into Bok's midsection. He sprawled across the brick floor, as the breath left his body.

Dazed, Bok pushed himself back up onto his hands and knees. He couldn't beat Spalonian at High Magic. The more skilled Scion sorcerer could counter any of Bok's spells.

Now, he smirked as he stood over Bok. "I do not know who you truly are or how you learned to cast spells. peasant. But it matters not. You and your friends came all this way, fought so hard, only to fail." His hands began to glow.

Bok crawled across the brick floor looking for some way to prolong his life. Then, the most curious thought—in perhaps the most inopportune time—ran through his mind.

He spotted three maple sprouts growing between the aged bricks of the building. No doubt, someone walked in with a seed pod stuck to their pants leg, then the seeds fell between the cracks between bricks. Notoriously hardy, maple seeds could sprout just about anywhere.

Nurturing plants was one of his main duties as a healer. A foundation of Folk Magic involved encouraging plants to grow. That is exactly what he did to the maple sprout under Spalonian.

Except this time, he imbued High Magic into the Folk Magic spell.

The result proved even more spectacular than Bok dared to hope. In less than a second, the two-inch seedling expanded into a fully-grown maple tree—fifty feet tall! The tree—and Spalonian—smashed through the foundry's tin roof, leaving a massive, tree-filled hole in the ceiling. Bok hoped the sorcerer hadn't been killed, but he felt sure the fight had been taken out of the man.

Not bad for a beginner! After days of feeling overwhelmed and confused by his new abilities, his chest swelled as he examined the fully formed tree growing through the factory floor.

Meanwhile, Alaydrian kept Isabella on the defensive. The Princess had a dozen or more counterattacks at the ready—but Alaydrian's all-out assault wouldn't allow her the opportunity to use any of them. Instead, Isabella focused on blocking the spells that came one after another. Sweat streamed down her face and matted her hair to her forehead.

"Mind if I interrupt this dance?" Despite being in an intense battle with Neuragian himself, Kotarian walked up behind Isabella and spoke to her over his shoulder.

In between his jousting with his former classmate, he found time to throw a white globe of magical energy at the foundry's ceiling high above Alaydrian's head. The globe exploded into a flare of light—creating the effect of staring directly into the sun on a bright summer day.

"AIEEEE!" The spell broke Alaydrian's concentration enough to give Isabella a brief respite.

"Okay, Your Majesty—I want us to switch; you go on the offensive against Neuragian. Leave Alaydrian to me."

"No! Alaydrian said—!"

"Exactly—Alaydrian said." Kotarian turned his back to Neuragian and forced Isabella to block the Scion's incoming attack, lest Kotarian be struck by

Sonorian's Sublime Spear. She gasped at her colleague's fearlessness—or perhaps foolishness.

"Tovano gave you plenty of magical knowledge, Your Majesty. But he failed to impart a predatory instinct. I was schooled in an eat-or-be-eaten environment, and I've dealt with bullies most of my life. To the point where I may have become one, I am sorry to say."I heard what Alyadrian said about your mother. As verbal warfare goes, it was hopelessly crude, but she knew it would make you careless. Let me deal with my former classmate. Believe me, there's nothing this dolt can say that I haven't already heard a thousand times before." He stepped forward to meet Alyadrian before Isabella could reply.

Neuragian smiled as she waved her hands above her head to cast another spell. The Scion stood between towering stacks of loaded crates. "What an honor! I get to slay Imarina's Crown Princess—the beloved and beautiful Isabella. But don't worry, Salandrian will allow you a royal funeral when I—"

"Be silent." With a wave of Isabella's hand, the heavy crates beside Neuragian toppled, crushing the Scion under hundreds of pounds of glass and wood.

For once, Kotarian didn't want to fight. Keeping his shield spells up, he engaged his opponent with words, not sorcery.

"Alaydrian, I plead with you—do not do this. Not that I particularly like you, but we have been classmates since our time as apprentices. Doesn't that bond mean anything to you?"

Alaydrian threw back her head and laughed. "Ha! The House of Magic has rotted from the inside! The Scions of Sonorian don't wish to destroy the House—we want to restore it to its rightful glory. And with it, Imarina—dragging it by the neck, if need be."

A bolt of energy sizzled toward Kotarian, illuminating the massive wood-and-brick space. His shields brushed the attack aside and it shattered a stack of crated jars into a cloud of wood and glass splinters. The scent of thunderstorms filled the space around him.

"Yes, yes—the 'True Path' and all that retrograde nonsense. But you lived in Sonorian Square for years. You studied in our libraries, learned under our teachers, grumbled with your classmates in the commons—just as I did. Your actions betray the House and all of us who sacrificed beside you!"

"Betray... you do not know of what you speak. Kotarian, the House turned its back on us long ago—you more than anyone. If only you knew..."

"Enlighten me." He lobbed a blue-green globe of energy toward Alaydrian's shields. She blocked the spell with a nonchalant gesture, continuing their cat-and mouse standoff.

She prowled the wood plank floor, eyes focused on her former classmate. "Kotarian, my dear classmate, why were you chosen for this mission?"

"Why? Because I am the House's Shining Light!" He tapped the pin on his chest vigorously. "I'm the top sorcerer in the acolyte class. Why else would they have chosen me above all my classmates?"

"You really don't know, do you?" She propped her hand under her chin to demonstrate her incredulity. "Kotarian... you were picked because you were deemed expendable! The House leadership knew this mission could turn deadly—they were deeply worried by our actions at Osoh Creek, despite what they told naïve King Isbiano. If one of our ranks had to die, Kotarian, they wanted it to be you."

Kotarian's eyes narrowed. "Salandrian! He sent me to die because he sees me as a threat!"

Alaydrian laughed again. "Salandrian wasn't even consulted about this decision. No, Loronian and Karagian decided that if any of our number had to die, it should be you."

"Impossible!" He dropped his shields. "Didn't... didn't you hear what I said? I am the—"

Alaydrian waved her hands around her face. "The Shining Light. Top of the class. Yes, we've heard you crow for years. But dear Kotarian, we never liked you. No one would care if you died."

With that, Alaydrian projected a beam of solid magical energy at Kotarian—Bahlerian's Barbarous Bolt. The beam caught him squarely in the chest and knocked him backward into a pile of crates.

Kotarian had been able to generate a last-moment shield spell. That alone prevented his sternum from being crushed.

As it was, though, his torso screamed in excruciating pain. The force of impact knocked all the wind from his body. He laid on the hard floor and forced his brain to remain conscious.

"You... you got me with that one..." he coughed out. Rather than reply, she unleased a second beam of energy. Kotarian didn't have the chance to use a shield spell but dodged the fatal blow using a wind whisper spell—or Juvanian's Judicious Jump, as it was known by the House.

He crawled on his hands and knees behind another stack of crates. An undignified tactic for the House's Shining Light, but necessary. Kotarian needed to recover his wits before reengaging with his former classmate.

"Reduced to hiding behind boxes? For shame, Kotarian!"

He heard a high-pitched whine and a half-second later, a stack of crates ten feet to his right exploded into a mist of wood and glass splinters. If he had still been behind those crates when the spell struck...

Kotarian inhaled deeply and soaked his lungs with stale air. He then jumped to his feet, firing Malenian's Momentous Meteor at Alaydrian. A pebble-sized rock, engulfed in a tiny flame, appeared from the tip of his index finger. It grew exponentially as it surged toward the surprised Alyadrian, eventually reaching a full diameter of three feet.

Unfortunately for Kotarian, she split the burning hunk of rock into fragments with a counter spell.

He was not so fortunate on her next attack. His attempted counter missed, and her blast destroyed the crates directly in front of Kotarian. His shields held—mostly. It protected him from the brunt of the explosion, but glass shrapnel sliced through his right cheek, shoulder, and thigh, staining his gray tunic and pants with blood.

He touched his bleeding face, which burned and throbbed. He tapped his star pin and muttered. "Think, you stupid man! Why did you spend all those late nights studying if not for this moment? The answer is there—you must be smart enough to find it!"

And then he did.

Kotarian stood up from behind the last stack of crates still standing, his hands in the air. "Hold, Alaydrian! You are... improved, to be sure. Certainly better than I gave you credit for. But before I remove this pin and place it on your black jacket, I have one final question. Think back to

Session Four, Weeks Three and Four. What did we learn about then?

She cocked her head to the side. "What in the stars above are you playing at, Kotarian? Do you think this some academic exercise? This is life or death—and we know which card you have pulled."

He shrugged. "Ah, well. It doesn't really matter." Kotarian quickly dropped his hands and expended the last bit of energy he could muster to generate a giant iron javelin from the ether and shoot it at Alaydrian. She gasped—but then knocked the deadly missile above her head and behind her with a last-second shield spell.

"That was your final chance, Kotarian. And it was a good one. Palaxian's Preeminent Projectile. It failed and now you—!"

Alaydrian only had a second to look down at the giant iron javelin protruding point-first through her chest, having circled back and struck her from behind. She fell face forward and landed on the foundry floor with a pronounced *THUMP*!

"Not Palaxian's Preeminent Projectile." Kotarian wiped blood from his cheek. "Dolarian's Devilish Deceit. Session Four, Weeks Three and Four, we learned misdirection spells. I suppose one of us paid attention."

CHAPTER 38

B ok and Isabella ran to Kotarian following their individual battles, but he waved off their concerns.

"I am fine." He pressed a rag to his bleeding cheek. "I was given a needed reminder about trust. It was a lesson I will heed in the future." He walked off to the far side of the foundry floor, again choosing to set himself apart from the group. But before Bok and Isabella could follow, they heard a commotion from the opposite end of the floor.

"Look who I found when I went to help Umra!" Avantil stood in the stairwell doorway with his lean but strong right arm propping up Tovano. Umra followed and carried Avantil's bow.

Tovano's eye had been blackened, his mouth bloodied, and the man had trouble standing. But he was very much alive as he clung to Avantil's neck for balance.

"They kept him in a crate, of all things. By the Exalted One, I cannot fathom such cruelty."

"Tovano!" Oh, thank you, my... Avantil. My mentor, you are injured." Isabella pulled a handkerchief from her pocked, doused it with cold water from Umra's handy flask, and dabbed it on his forehead.

"Bah! It's... *cough! Cough!* It's nothing I can't shake off!" Another, longer coughing fit prevented Tovano from speaking any further. They set the elderly sorcerer down on the foundry floor, with Avantil supporting him into a seated position and Isabella holding his hand. Then Bok examined his wounds.

Bok gently applied pressure up and down Tovano's arms and legs. The man did not complain, but when Bok pressed on the right side of his chest, he cried out.

"That one... I may not be able to shake off so quickly." His voice trembled from pain and coughing.

Umra handed Bok a cup of water. He mixed it with some yorka root and gave it to Tovano to drink. "He has suffered broken ribs. They will heal, but he cannot ride back to Ithenel. He risks puncturing a lung if he tries."

"My friend Lefi can keep him safe 'til this madness ends," Umra said. "Let's take him to Talim's Pub. Lefi's got a secret compartment in the back o' the storeroom—don't ask! Anyway, he can hide Tovano there 'til he recovers—or 'til you can return fer him, at the least."

Isabella nodded in agreement, then turned to Tovano. Her mentor had recovered enough voice to speak in complete sentences without coughing.

"There is something important you must know, Your Majesty. Alaydrian and the others were left here to guard me—and deal with you, in case you found me. They tormented and tortured me until... until I talked. I am so sorry, Your Majesty."

"Nonsense, my teacher—you have nothing to apologize for." Isabella gripped his hand tightly in hers. "Those demons forced you. But tell me all you know."

He took a deep sip of the medicinal beverage Bok had prepared. "They now know that we discovered the truth—that the Blight was caused by Salandrian and a splinter group of rogue sorcerers from within the House of Magic, rather than by any outside enemy. They also are aware we plan to expose their scheme to your father, the Royal Council, and the leadership of the House of Magic. Because they know we are coming to Ithenel, they have accelerated their timetable for moving against the King.

"Salandrian and the bulk of his force—around twenty or so sorcerers—already have left for Ithenel. They left hours ago. These villains intend to overthrow your father and the House of Magic and install Salandrian as the True Leader of Imarina! Their goal is to establish a mageocracy in which the Serving Class is kept in line by fear and brutality."

Bok held back the urge to cry out. "Is there any chance the Commander and Wingate can reach Ithenel ahead of them?"

Tovano sighed. "Unlikely. The detour into Mosork territory delayed us long enough to give Salandrian an insurmountable head start."

"Curse them!" Isabella cried. "If they beat us back to Ithenel, how can we stop their plan before they set it into motion?"

This time, Avantil put his hand on her shoulder. She reached up to hold it. "I have an idea. The Amorinil Mercantile Company keeps ships in Naseem Harbor to transport goods into Ithenel. If we take command of one of these boats, we should be able to make up some time."

Bok knew that what Avantil didn't say was that if the Scions of Sonorian still were tracking them and spotted their ship on the water, they would be fat targets for their enemies' magics. But it was a risk they had to take.

"Yes! Quickly, let us depart for the harbor." Isabella stretched to her full height. "Umra, I need you to stay and care for Tovano until he is ready to travel. This old man is precious to me—and I only would ask this of someone I trust completely."

"I'd be honored, Yer Majesty. You can count on me."

"I know, sweet girl."

As they walked out of the building, Bok noticed the maple tree had returned to its original size as a seedling. Bok's hybrid spell apparently only lasted for a short duration, meaning it would have no practical purpose in his role as a healer. There also was no sign of Spalonian, meaning he survived and fled the scene.

That is a relief. With everything else swirling around my brain, I don't need to add the guilt of taking a life.

He looked around at his friends walking down the otherwise deserted street. *Isabella, Avantil, Umra, Kotarian, and Tovano are all safe. We've survived our biggest test to date—and I did my part. High Magic still makes me uneasy. But maybe it and I can come to an understanding.*

"Bok, you will have to teach me that most impressive spell after we return to Ithenel." Isabella mounted her horse, as Bok checked Beki's saddle.

"Honestly, it was born of desperation. That seems to be my best source of inspiration these days—get in a place where I am in mortal danger and figure out a spell to save my life!"

She laughed. "I would not make a habit of that, but it was quite resourceful."

"It's nothing compared to what Kotarian was able to do. You were incredible." Bok turned to the sorcerer, who did not acknowledge the compliment and rode ahead of the group.

"I know these past few days have been hard on him, learning of his classmates' betrayal," Isabella said. "I hope he can find some comfort—we will help him, if we can."

They rode toward Naseem Harbor. Tovano sat at the front of Avantil's horse, with the young merchant supporting him.

"What about you?" Bok asked Isabella. "You seem to be holding up okay, given the circumstances. If my father was in danger... I wouldn't even be able to think straight."

She gripped her horse's reins. "It comes down to trust, Bok. My father is under the protection of the Royal Guard—I trust them to protect him. The majority of the House of Magic are loyal to the Crown. I trust they will defend the kingdom. I trust that the people of Imarina will support their neighbors, even during these dark times."

Bok nodded. "And in return, we, the citizens of Imarina, trust that you will lead us with wisdom."

"That is my role. I have a part to play, as does everyone in Imarina. The system does not serve the Royal Family—the system serves the Kingdom, of which we all are part. And... if I am being truthful, Bok, I am not always as strong as you believe. Sometimes, your 'powerful princess' is scared and lost. Mother died when I was far too young. If I lose Father as well..."

Bok put a hand on her shoulder. "And that is why your friends support you. Have trust in us, too, Princess."

Isabella said nothing. She didn't have to.

They quickly stopped at Talim's Pub, where a plump man with long gray hair and a tattered tan shirt wobbled out to greet them with a smile and a wave.

"This is Lefi—he's the friend I was tellin' you about; the one who helped me outta that terrible sit'ation. He owns this saloon an' I was hopin' he would still be 'round."

Lefi's wrinkled face turned up in a wide grin. "You always were me best barmaid, Umra! And 'course I was going ta help you—you had a shift ta work the next day!"

Umra and her friend hustled Tovano through the back entrance and into the hidden saferoom. Lefi insisted on giving the party two big sacks of provisions for their return trip. "Not like we're expecting many customers these next few days anyway. Better to give this food away than let it go to waste."

He grumbled a bit when Avantil tried to hand him a sack of 50 gold, but Umra encouraged him to accept the generous payment. "You can finally fix up this dump! Place ain't had no class since I stopped waitin' tables."

Lefi also agreed to house the group's horses at the stable behind the pub. Bok walked with Umra, Beki's reins in tow, to make sure his family's horse would be kept safe among the panic suffocating the city.

"They'll be jus' fine here. Lefi put in a tall fence with a padlocked door. Too many horse thieves in this part o' Naseem not to be careful!"

Bok stroked Beki's nose and Umra fed her a carrot she pocketed from Lefi's kitchen. "Don't let yer horsey pals see you got a treat."

"Umra—thank you. For everything. I'll always remember this adventure for friends in the most unexpected places. If we live long enough to have memories, that is."

Umra wiped her hands on her homespun dress. "One step at a time. Yer alive today and that counts fer somethin'. Worry 'bout tomorrow when tomorrow comes. Besides, you ain't forgettin' any part o' this adventure once ye get back ta Soleh Valley! Like yer gonna be too distracted by watchin' the corn grow?"

He laughed. "You're right about that, I suppose." *Perhaps I should take my own advice about leaning on my friends.*

They went back inside. Bok gave Umra the last of his yorka root for Tovano, while Isabella had a brief farewell with her mentor.

"Remember—do not underestimate Salandrian," Tovano warned from his makeshift cot in the storeroom. "He has access to spells of great power. There have long been whispered rumors of books containing ancient magics—from the lawless days before the House of Magic—hidden in the House's archives. The Blight is just one of these magics. If anyone knows of their existence, it would be Salandrian." Another round of violent coughing ended his warning.

"We shall be as careful as we dare be when the kingdom's security is at stake. Rest and heal, my mentor. Your Crown Princess commands it."

From there, they rode to the harbor, where true to Avantil's word, a gleaming red sailing ship—with the words "AMORINIL MERCANTILE COMPANY" painted across the bow in bold white letters, along with the family's crest—was docked.

He slapped Bok's arm. "Well, how about that? I wasn't entirely sure it would still be here! Looks like our luck is holding out, my friend!"

They loaded the supplies into the ship's hold, dropped the sails, and hauled up the anchor. Their next stop would be Ithenel—hopefully, in time to save the king and the nation.

Umra waved from the dock. Slowly, she faded into the horizon along with the sun. Bok found he already missed the loud, animated housekeeper, just as he did his family.

"Be careful and, er, good sailin'!" Umra called. "Tovano and I'll join you as soon as 'e's hearty enough fer travelin'!"

By then, Bok realized there won't be a safe place in Imarina, from Naseem to Soleh Valley, if they didn't succeed.

CHAPTER 39

F OR A GROUP HEADING toward their likely death, the next few days were remarkably pleasant. Much of that positive morale came from Avantil, whose love of sailing became apparent as soon as they hit the water. If he wasn't singing sea shanties, he caught fish for dinner or expertly adjusted the sails to maximize the boat's speed.

Bok, on the other hand, was ready to make landfall—matters of his aforementioned likely death aside. He had never traveled on a boat, and its constant motion made him queasy.

This sensation got him out of bed in the middle of the night. That and Kotarian's incessant snoring. He, Avantil, and Bok crammed into hammocks strung up in the ship's galley—a concession to the limited space below deck. Isabella slept in the lone bedroom. Even though she and Avantil again acted civilly to one another, he didn't ask to join her at night.

Bok wandered out onto the deck. He carefully held one of the guide ropes surrounding the top deck, a safety feature in case of a sudden lurch. Not a strong swimmer, he didn't want to test his fate in the dark river.

"Beautiful night—best time to enjoy the water. You don't have to worry about the sun or the heat. It's you, the river, and the sounds of the night."

"Avantil! I didn't realize you were up here, too." Bok jumped at his friend's voice emerging from the deck's dark corner.

"Just had to check the sails. And I suppose you needed some fresh air!"

"Yes. I am afraid I do not share your affinity for sailing!"

"You get used to the movement." Avantil put his hands on the boat's wooden edge and breathed in the night air. "The love of the water grows on you. I find it peaceful. I become aware of being part of something far greater than myself."

Bok didn't join Avantil in leaning over the rails to look at the river. He wasn't sure he had an herb in his bag strong enough to cure that much motion sickness. But seeing his friend back in a tranquil, pleasant mood pleased him—and he appreciated a respite from the seemingly constant threats on their lives.

"Sailing comes naturally for me, Bok That comes from spending half my childhood on a ship. I wish matters of love were as simple."

"You are asking the wrong person about that!" Bok laughed. "I can heal just about any injured body part—except a broken heart."

"If you solve that mystery, please share the solution with me." Avantil shook his head as he tossed a handful of breadcrumbs to a passing school of fish.

"I'm sure Isabella will come around," Bok offered. "The two of you are speaking again—that is something, right?"

Avantil thought for a moment. "Perhaps. But we are not as close as before—and it is my fault. Sure, Isabella may be frustrating. She is overly serious, entirely too busy, and despite owning a thousand pillows, always steals mine. But she is wonderful—for reasons having nothing to do with the crown she is in line to wear.

"Believe me, Bok, a long line of suitors lined up at the Royal Palace, all of whom she turned away in her unfailingly polite manner. Isabella told me she knew from our first meeting that she wanted to be with me. And I am grateful she did. But my pride and temper have driven her away."

He loves Isabella as much as ever—and she still loves him. Now, I must prove my friendship to them both.

"You sound like a man who wants to find a way through the impasse you spoke of. Talk with her, Avantil. You might be surprised at how receptive she is to what you have to say."

The Noble looked up from the rail and for the first time in days, Bok found the glimmer in the man's eyes that he saw at the Royal Palace. "You know, for a man who has never left Soleh Valley, you have plenty of wisdom."

He clapped Bok on the shoulder. "I'll talk with her—and thank you, Bok."

Bok quietly returned below deck and climbed into his hammock, careful not to disturb Isabella. He felt sure nothing short of a hurricane could awake Kotarian.

As often was the case late at night, Bok thought of home. He had not yet bought Noji the gift he promised. The child loved creating adventures with the wooden dolls Tana Omat carved for him. Maybe he could get his nephew one of those painted wooden dolls from of those fancy Ithenel shops. Noji would love that.

Images of the little boy's exuberant face made him realize he couldn't be happy without his family, no matter how they may have deceived him. Yes, he needed the truth—but he would make amends with his parents, no matter what.

But how could he leave his friends? Or reject Tovano's generous offer to develop his amazing new gifts? For days, he had struggled with the idea that he did not know where he belonged. But that was not the case. The problem was that he now had two families—each completely incompatible with the other.

CHAPTER 40

AFTER LONG HOURS OF steering the boat, Avantil asked, "Could you mind the wheel for a bit, Bok?"

"Of course. Go below deck and rest—I can keep us pointed in a straight line." Bok climbed up to the bridge and took over the captain's seat. He welcomed the chance to sit in an actual chair and as long as the winds didn't shift, he would be fine and Avantil, the only true sailor on the boat, could enjoy a well-deserved break.

"I am going below deck as well." Isabella stretched her arms over her head. "I shall be back before long, though—and I shall bring some of the bread and fruit Umra sent. By Queen Imbiria's scepter, I am famished!"

When his companions left, Bok looked down from his perch and spotted Kotarian standing immediately below, leaning across the deck rail with a half-empty wine bottle in hand. Bok swallowed hard and considered his next words carefully.

"Kotarian! Come join me up here—it's a spectacular view of... well, nothing really. But I'd appreciate the company."

"Not interested." He didn't bother turning around. "Don't talk to me, Bok or Baron or whoever you are, and I'll act in kind."

"Yes, I understand you are upset. The situation back in Naseem with your House of Magic companions—"

At this, Kotarian spun to face Bok. "You understand nothing!" His eyes flared. "You never set foot in a High Magic class on Sonorian Square. Never spent hours straining your eyes by candlelight to prepare for an exam. Never known fluttering in your stomach at the knowledge that you would be called to demonstrate your prowess, to succeed or fail, in front of all your classmates."

"I... there is so much I do not know about High Magic," Bok admitted.

Kotarian looked out over the water and sighed. The tension left his body with his exhaled breath. "I know you do not understand; I do not blame you for that. How could you, given your upbringing?

"But I worked for years to become a member of the House of Magic. I dreamed of it. Until what I heard at Nassem. No, I do not blame you for not understanding. But forgive me if I do not revel in your new-found glory."

While he couldn't excuse Kotarian's behavior, Bok at least could understand its source a little better. "Well, I'm sorry if I've caused you any pain. But unlike you, I never asked for these abilities. Also, you don't have to worry about me being any type of competition—I will not be joining the House of Magic."

Kotarian touched the back of his neck. "You—you won't?"

"No. I have no idea what I'm going to do with this new-found knowledge. But the House isn't the place for me—no offense. Can you imagine me, with my homespun clothes and Soleh Valley mannerisms, in the Commons Room you've spoken about? Besides, I don't look good in gray!"

Kotarian chuckled under his breath. He started to respond, but Bok stopped him. "Don't say it! I know... I don't look good in green, brown, red, and so on." They both roared. For the first time, they shared a laugh together, rather than Kotarian laughing at the Bok's expense.

As if reading Bok's mind, Kotarian continued, "Unlike the rest of you, I've not shared much about my upbringing. I suppose I owe you at least that much."

He leaned against the boat, elbows propped on the rail. "My father owns an estate just outside of Ithenel; he's a minor Lord in the hierarchy of the Noble Class. It isn't the same as being a princess or the heir to the largest merchant enterprise in the known lands. But my family did well enough in days gone by, I suppose."

Bok nodded. "You briefly mentioned as much back in Naseem. Obviously, you must be from the Noble Class to practice High Magic. I'd say your family is still doing well, from where I'm at."

"Yes, well—that perspective may not be accurate." Kotarian drank more of his wine. "I said my father is a minor Lord. What I didn't mention was how 'minor' he is, in both land and honor.

"My family once owned four hundred acres of fruit orchards, employing some hundred peasants to work the estate. But managing such a complex operation never interested my parents, nor did any other professions. Instead, Mother held elaborate parties and Father his regular card games. At first, they mortgaged just a few acres to pay their debts—a short-term solution that would right itself when the summer crop came in, they said. But that windfall did not materialize, nor did the next summer's or the one after that. But did they cut back on parties or gambling? Bok, I trust you are intelligent enough to discern that answer.

"When I was 12 summers, the lenders from Ithenel came calling. We lost more than ninety percent of the estate—ninety percent! That left us with a token estate by the standards of the Noble Class, and a manor house quickly falling into shambles. Of course, Father and Mother spent more time keeping up pretenses than in finding a solution. They have lost even more land since I left to become an apprentice seven years ago. If they lose their remaining tract, they will be landless. And what do we call Nobles without land, Bok?"

"I... I am not sure."

Kotarian swallowed the last drink from his bottle. "We don't call them Nobles any longer, that's what."

"Anyway, against that backdrop, young Kotarel Jonaro had to go to school, go to social functions, attend Mother's parties with children from Noble Class families who owned more land, who held loftier titles—and who were aware of my family's struggles. They never let me forget them. No matter how I excelled in academics or athletics, I was the outcast.

"I once won an oratory competition at school. But when the judge handed me the bronze cup, a dozen or so copper coins spilled out. At that point, the second-place finisher announced to my jeering classmates that he had 'taken up a collection to help the struggling Jonaro family.'"

Bok clasped his hands together as the boat continued moving down the river. "And when Avantil hit you, it brought you back to that point. What those other children said and did." *That's why Kotarian is a bully. Because he first was a bully's victim.*

Kotarian continued, "So at age 14 summers, Kotarel Jonaro begged a ride into Ithenel and knocked on the door of the House of Magic. On that day, Kotarel Jonaro ceased to exist." He gestured to his gray jacket. "And Kotarian came to be. I had a place where I belonged. But Alaydrian ended all that back at Naseem. I may have won our battle, but we both were stabbed through the heart that day."

Bok involuntarily shivered at Kotarian's grim analogy. The breeze continued moving the boat forward, as it swished the pine trees on the riverbank.

"You felt betrayed by people you thought were friends. But Alaydrian, Salandrian—they don't speak for the House of Magic."

"Loronian and Karagian deemed me expendable!" Kotarian roared. "They sent me here, thinking I might die and not caring if I did. You cannot possibly relate to the sense of betrayal I now feel."

"You are right—I can't. If Weni Kon ever betrayed me in the way your mentors did... well, I'm not sure I could ever fully recover. But I also know that there are good people, just as there are bad. For all your bluster, I know which category you fit into. Yes, Alaydrian planted a dark seed in your mind, but you can choose not to nurture it."

Fishing birds flew over the boat. Bok looked Kotarian directly in the eye. "Had they asked, would you have done it? Would you have joined the Scions of Sonorian?"

Kotarian scoffed. "Of course not. My loyalty to the Crown and the kingdom has never been in doubt."

"No, it hasn't," Bok continued. "And would you have murdered the Yult family? Or stood by and watch Salandrian slaughter them in his mad experiment?"

"No—not a chance. I may not have much use for your—for the Serving Class. But murder? Never."

"Well, there's your answer. You weren't expendable—you were invaluable. Salandrian knew you would oppose him and that scared him. He and his underlings realized you wouldn't betray what the House of Magic stands for and they tried to kill you for it."

Kotarian turned away from Bok and stepped back to the rail, exhaling deeply. "What is wrong with you, peasant? After how I have behaved, you remain kind to me. You must be as simple-minded as you are ignorant of the world."

He paused. "Either that, or I have been wrong about you from the beginning, and the blacksmith raised a better man than I could ever hope to be." Thinking of Fin Omat, Bok's lower lip quivered for a moment.

Kotarian then turned back to Bok and smiled. But this time, the condescending sneer was gone. "Of course, we know I could never be wrong!"

They laughed again. "I'm sure that despite their flaws, your parents are proud of you, too. They should be."

Kotarian flung the empty bottle into the river. "Perhaps. I do not know. I have not spoken with them in seven years."

Bok leaned down over the edge of the bridge. "It's okay, Kotarian. If you need me—"

"Don't push your luck, plowboy." Kotarian turned to Bok. "Now, let's show those dung beetles what it means to cross the House's Shining Light!"

"And his friends?" Bok asked hopefully.

"*Sigh.* Very well, the House's Shining Light and friends. Satisfied?"

—◆—

That evening, Isabella brought a tray of dried fruits and assorted nuts up to the deck and invited Bok to join her.

"Have you ever had an apricot?" She held out the snack tray. Bok shook his head and picked one of the sweet, dehydrated fruits.

"Mmm! Almost as good as the dried apples my mother makes. So... did you and Avantil talk things through when you both went below deck?"

"We did, and I understand I have you to thank." She took a sip of sparkling wine and poured some for Bok. "That man can be stubborn, proud, hot-tempered... but I love him with all my heart. I can be all those things as well. I suppose we both needed a good friend to break the impasse and get us talking with, instead of yelling at, each other."

"I'm happy to help." *And I truly am. Isabella doesn't need another unwanted suitor. She needs a good friend. And so do I.*

Bok smiled. "Are you two... good again?"

"We are. Avantil and I know we both need to listen to each other more." Isabella touched Bok's muscular forearm, again sending a shiver through his body. *Some things are difficult to change.*

This time, he felt sure Isabella noticed. "Bok... you will find someone, and she will be an incredibly lucky and loved woman."

"You think so?"

"I *know* so. And I am always right—just ask Avantil!" They both laughed, and Isabella leaned back to look at the darkening sky. The river breeze felt good on Bok's face, but not nearly as good enjoying this quiet moment with his friend.

Which is why he hated to voice the question he was about to ask.

"Isabella, can you teach me the death touch spell? The one you used in Naseem? I have a feeling I may need a secret weapon when we get to Ithenel."

She sat up and looked into her cup before she spoke next. "Bok... that... that is a difficult request. On this trip, I have been forced to kill. I likely will have to do so again. But my gentle friend, know this: If you take a life, you also lose something you can never get back. Please consider this before you go down that path."

Bok nodded. "I understand. But I still need to know this spell. Just in case." He hoped he never would have to use it, but he figured he needed any edge he could find if they had to confront Salandrian and the Scions.

So Isabella pushed the tray aside and reluctantly taught him the spell. "Remember—you want to point your hand down and then start the incantation. And focus your energy to your palm, not your fingertips." Bok followed as she instructed, soaking in every detail.

After the tutorial, Bok thanked Isabella and sighed. *Could I intentionally kill another person? Knowing it goes against all I believe—even to save the lives of my friends?* He didn't know the answer, but he was glad to have the incantation as a last resort.

After they went below deck, Bok noticed that Avantil joined Isabella in the ship's cabin. He even heard giggling from behind their closed door—and this time, he had the propriety not to listen in.

CHAPTER 41

"MEMBERS OF THE ROYAL Council, I appreciate you coming on such short notice this morning. Believe me, I would not have summoned you so abruptly were the situation not so grave."

From his seat on the Council Chambers dais, King Isbiano surveyed the Royal Council. The normally opinionated Emissaries now looked to their king for leadership and guidance. But another watched the proceedings—Salandrian, who grinned as he peered through a cracked side door.

Once more, Emissary Loronian sat at the petitioner's table in front of the dais. Four Royal Guardians—one at each end of the dais, and one at each side door—stood stiffly at their posts.

"I nearly didn't make it," Pilano Samari, the Emissary of Commerce, said. "Frightened peasants and laborers accosted my carriage on the road into the city. I thought they might shake the blasted thing apart!"

"Yes, hundreds of refugees from Naseem and Osoh Creek have arrived in our city overnight. Those who have nowhere else to go are camped on the outskirts of Ithenel," Isbiano replied. "These people claim the Blight spreads. They are terrified—and who can blame them?"

"All the more reason we must take action now!" Corona Piari, the Emissary of Security, pointed a sharp finger toward the King.

"What would you suggest, Emissary? Beyond providing shelter and food for the refugees—which we are doing?"

"Your Majesty, a decisive strike against the Mosork warlords is needed. Rejah-Lahr has terrorized citizens at our northern border for years," Piari said. "If we deliver a powerful blow against his forces, it will force them to withdraw the Blight."

King Isbiano sighed. "Emissary Piari, we have gone over this before. Of course, Rejah-Lahr is a murderous criminal who would do the world a favor if he dropped dead. But we dare not risk a war without proof!"

"And your daughter was sent to find that evidence," Piari retorted. "There is still no word from the Princess?"

The King came close to shouting his reply. "Do not try me, Emissary. Not in matters concerning my daughter's safety. I eagerly await her return more than anyone. But until she comes home, we will stay the course."

Isbiano then looked down from the dais to the petitioner's table. "Emissary Loronian, where is Chancellor Karagian? I requested his presence at this meeting."

"I... do not know, Your Majesty," Loronian admitted. "Like you, I expected him. I assure you—this absence will be addressed upon my return to Sonorian Square."

"My apologies!" Salandrian stepped through the side door. "I had some important business to attend to before the meeting. But do carry on, my good women and men."

Salandrian sauntered over to the petitioner's table, as Royal Council members muttered amongst themselves. He sat beside Loronian in the chair reserved for Karagian, smiled at his Emissary, and waved at the assembled Royal Council.

Loronian whispered sharply, "What in the world are you doing, man? Interrupting a Royal Council meeting? Embarrassing me in front of the King? Have you lost track of what meager senses you once possessed?" Loronian's normally pale face turned a dark shade of burgundy.

"Have I upset you? My heart breaks, Emissary Loronian!" Salandian put his hand over his own heart, then slapped his leader between the shoulders.

"Oh, my mistake—that would be your heart that is broken... 'Ruptured', if we are precise in our language." His hand glowed on Loronian's back and her eyes grew wide, her body stiffened.

She made an involuntary sound not unlike a mouse's squeak, then slumped dead onto the petitioner's table. Her head thumped against finished walnut surface.

The grumbles and mutters from the dais turned into shrieks of outrage and terror.

Salandrian stood. The light around him shifted and blurred. In an instant, his normal image—that of a stooped, pale academic in an ill-fitting gray jacket—was replaced by that of a tall, handsome, dark-haired man in a neatly tailored black coat adorned with red piping, worn over a red shirt.

After barely a second's hesitation, the four Guardians ran toward Salandrian, drawing their swords mid-stride.

They may as well have been turtles returning to the lake on a scorching summer day.

With one motion and a quick incantation, Salandrian lifted all four Guardians high into the air, to the point where their heads were inches from the Chamber's vaulted marble ceiling. He then flung them across the room to the far walls with a flourish of his hand.

The Emissary of Transit moved toward the door. Before he could get a half-dozen steps from the exit, two dozen mystic blades appeared in mid-air and struck down the helpless Noble.

"We call that one 'Caelian's Cleaving Contrivance'. Care for another demonstration?"

Emissary of Security Piari, a former Guardian herself, had kept her combat skills sharp even in her administrative role. She pulled out the dagger she hid under her tunic and hurled it directly at Salandrian's head from the dais. Her throw was true and under virtually any other circumstances, she would have scored a clean kill. But Salandrian deflected the knife with a shield spell, then incinerated the astonished Emissary with Iledonian's Immaculate Immolation.

"Does anyone else wish to try their luck?" No one did—the remaining six Emissaries took cover under the dais. Sobs of "Please spare us!" and "I can make you a wealthy man!" echoed across the chamber. But Salandrian's eyes locked on the only person who did not hide—King Isbiano.

The King's voice remained clear and calm. "I would ask, 'What is this?' But it is clearly a revolt, and one that poor Emissary Loronian knew nothing about. I assume you are the cause of Chancellor Karagian's absence as well?"

"Yes, well, Karagian asked too many questions about spellbooks unaccounted for in our archives. A shame... I always liked the old battle sorcerer."

Isbiano cut him off: "Spare me the story—your issue is with me. So let the others leave, then you and I can discuss whatever demands you intend to make."

Salandrian walked to the front of the dais and looked at the trembling Emissaries cowering behind their desks.

"Very well. I will spare them. A leader needs followers, after all. And I will need seasoned administrators to ensure that our laws are upheld once more."

Isbiano scoffed. "The people of Imarina will never bow to a tyrant. Kill me if you must, but the Crown cannot be taken by force. It may only be earned through the respect and admiration of the Imarinan people. You will never be our nation's king!"

Salandrian turned his back to Isbiano, as if daring the King to challenge him physically. "You think I want to be king? I have no interest in your mundane job or your gaudy little headwear. Why would I want to be a mere king when I can be a god?"

Salandrian turned back to the dais and Isbiano. Magical energy now crackled in his eyes and around his hands, throwing a greenish-blue reflection off the polished marble walls of the Royal Council Chamber.

"Now having said all that, the last thing I need is the sad old king getting in my way. Farewell, Isbiano…"

He raised his energy-enrobed hands to deliver the killing spell. Isbiano closed his eyes… then two strong arms yanked him backward through the curtain behind the dais.

The King opened his eyes to view his unexpected rescuer. "Lieutenant Wingate! I was making my peace. I suppose the Exalted One sent you instead!"

Wingate hoisted Isbiano over his shoulder like a sack of grain and bolted for one of the doors off the anteroom.

Salandrian stomped up onto the dais, as terrified Emissaries scrambled from under their desks and dashed for the exits. But when Salandrian pushed through the curtain, he found no one in the anteroom. Wingate and Isbiano could have escaped through four separate doors, each leading to a different area of the palace.

"The Guardian is resourceful, I will grant him that," Salandrian muttered. The energy streaming from his body ebbed and his eyes returned to their normal brown color.

At that point, the front doors to the Royal Council Chambers burst open and the Scions of Sonorian—twenty strong—rushed into the room.

A tall, gangly young woman with long red hair stepped to the front of the group and stood at attention. "True Leader, we saw the Emissaries run out of the chambers. Should we track them down?"

"No need, Donlandrian. I already broke their spirit. But Isbiano is proving to be more trouble than I anticipated. I looked forward to transmuting his blood into rancid water. Those ancient sorcerers were imaginative in their cruelty!"

"We will bring him back to you, True Leader," Donlandrian offered. The other Scions of Sonorian surged forward to strike on Salandrian's command. But he waved his hand and instructed them to stand down.

"The King and his Guardians won't be going anywhere—our previous preparations will that they cannot leave the palace grounds. They are exactly where we want them to be."

"They are in the Royal Gardens?" Donlandrian asked. "Then it is time…?"

"Soon, my eager acolyte. We have a final player left on the board: Princess Isabella. She, my former student Kotarian, and their assorted group of misfits are back in Ithenel, according to our community sympathizers. They will come here."

"Should we—?"

Salandrian held up his hand. "Leave them to me, Donlandrian. In the meantime, take the others downstairs to the main dining hall and begin preparing our next spell—something for King Isbiano to remember the Scions of Sonorian by. I have everything you need right here."

He reached inside his jacket and produced a fresh red rose, a sprig of nightshade and a lump of charcoal, and placed them on the petitioner's table, beside Loronian's cooling body.

Donlandrian smiled. "We will prepare the Blight right away, True Leader!"

CHAPTER 42

THE AMORINIL MERCANTILE COMPANY ship pulled into Ithenel Harbor that morning as well, sailing past the encampment of refugees from Naseem and Osoh Creek.

"The problems from the North Country have followed us back to Ithenel." Bok's stomach sank at the sight of the people now crowding the riverbank, with nowhere else to go.

"Let's only hope our good fortune did as well." Avantil steered the boat toward the dock.

"Good fortune?" That was enough to turn Kotarian around. "By Patharian's Pungent Perspiration, we have encountered nothing but trouble on this entire mission!"

"True," Avantil admitted. "But we survived it and returned home. I say that counts as a victory, my friend."

"Don't notch your victories too soon," the sorcerer grumbled. Bok had to admit he spoke true—the next challenge would be the most dangerous by far.

Avantil quickly tied up the boat, while the others gathered only their most necessary possessions.

The terror and lawlessness Bok experienced in Naseem hadn't completely consumed Ithenel—yet. Sailors worked hard bringing ships into the harbor and preparing them to go to sea. Dock workers unloaded ships. Horse-drawn wagons hauled goods away from the waterfront and into the city.

One glum wagoner caught Avantil's eye.

"Ahoy, my good man! Is your wagon open for work? We're prepared to pay up front."

"Afraid not—though I wish it were." The wagoner propped his elbows on his knees and his chin upon his palms. "I was supposed to receive a load of fresh corn. But the boat bringing it was coming from Naseem and I reckon they got caught in... in whatever madness going on up there. So here I sit. Looks like a day of lost wages for me, but I gave my word I'd unload this cargo and take it to the city."

Avantil smiled and raised a finger in the air. "Fortune may smile on you yet, sir! You won't have to load our cargo—just take it into town. Even if your client does arrive, you'll be back in time to meet it."

This offer grabbed the man's interest. "So what is your cargo?"

Avantil gestured to Bok, Isabella, and Kotarian. "You are looking at it!"

The ride into the city's center was hot and bumpy. The wagon normally transported vegetables, not people. Sitting on its hard wooden bed, every divot and rut in the road burrowed into Bok's spine. He and his friends barely heard each other above the cart's wheels clattering over Ithenel's cobblestone streets.

So they mostly just sat in silence, each preparing in her or his own way. Avantil checked and rechecked the tautness of his bowstring and inspected each of his arrows for the tiniest of flaws. Kotarian rolled his neck, flexed his fingers, stretched his arms, and quietly repeated spellcasting mantras he had first learned before he was old enough to shave. Isabella sat with her knees pulled up against her chest, eyes closed, deep in thought.

I wonder whose mind is racing faster—hers or mine? There wasn't much Bok could do to get ready for what was to come. Even if there were, he was too nervous to do it.

The streets of Ithenel were as crowded and cacophonous as ever. Some things never changed, even in the face of a national emergency. People and work animals moved up and down at a deliberate pace, oblivious to the importance of the weather-beaten vegetable wagon moving through the crowd. At one point, they had to stop for five full minutes as a cart carrying a heavy oak bookcase stopped in the middle of the road to unload its cargo.

Bok was torn between complete fear at the prospect of facing Salandrian and the Scions of Sonorian and the unbearable sense of waiting for the inevitable. Bok's mother used to say, "The dread usually proves worse than the reality." But the likelihood of that being true here wasn't good.

Finally, after two full hours of uncomfortable, anxious riding, they made it to the center of the shining city and the Royal Palace. They instructed the driver to take them down King Isanaro Street, toward the back entrance to the palace and past Sonorian Square. But when the tall oaks lining the street cleared, they did not expect what they saw.

"Look! What on earth is that golden aura covering Sonorian Square?" To Bok, it looked like a giant pine tree had leaked sap onto the gray stone campus, trapping the people inside like bugs preserved in resin.

Avantil dropped a bag of coins in the wagoner's lap and instructed the man to stop. But Kotarian already stuck one leg out of the wagon and leaped to the ground before the cart came to a complete stop.

Plenty of Ithenel's residents continued about their business as though nothing was wrong, paying no attention to the giant magical dome or the people trapped within in. To them, this undoubtedly was just another bizarre magical experiment conducted by those odd and aloof sorcerers on Sonorian Square.

But many others gathered around the square. One well-meaning fellow tried to push his way into the field and reach a trapped man inside the edge of the spell. Instead, the stasis field engulfed the would-be rescuer, where he became another motionless mannequin in a pool of dark yellow syrup.

The concerned onlookers included a half-dozen uniformed constables. While they could do nothing about the spell, they tried to keep any more victims from being swallowed by the stasis field.

"Step back. This is a dangerous spell," one constable said to Bok, Isabella, Avantil and Kotarian as they approached.

"I appreciate your dedication to public safety, constable. But I assure you—if anyone can help, it will be the four of us."

"P-Princess Isabella! I-I am sorry, Your Majesty!" The constable stepped away.

"Do not apologize for serving the kingdom admirably. Please continue to keep onlookers at a safe distance—there could be more trouble. Just know that we are working to solve this problem."

"Yes, Your Majesty!" The constable gave Isabella a crisp salute and stepped away to let her and the other examine the dome.

"I've never seen anything like it!" Bok said, as he, Isabella, and Avantil followed Kotarian in racing toward the spell-covered campus.

Kotarian stopped in front of the amber done and stared agape at the immobile people inside. "I have. It is a stasis spell, of some type."

He pointed to a bearded man inside the sphere. The man had been stepping out of a classroom building and into the campus yard when the spell struck. A bird likewise was caught in mid-air some ten feet over his head.

"That is Panadrian—one of my first-year teachers." Kotarian didn't take his eyes off the scene in front of him. "Panadrian wasn't much of a spellcaster, but he was a fine teacher and a kind man. One of the few instructors who showed me any patience or understanding as an apprentice."

He pointed to a young woman, who wore a jacket just like Kotarian's, who was taking a break between classes to enjoy a cold drink in the afternoon sun. Her contented smile now was frozen for eternity—unless the spell could be lifted.

"On the bench there—that is Sumakian. She and I had numerous classes together as acolytes. She was preparing for a career serving the House in magical logistics. One of the few classmates I didn't find annoying."

He then pointed at a short man picking up litter from the grounds. "Even the Serving Class fellow there—I never knew his name, but he always was cheerful and diligent in his work. He greeted me with a wave every time he saw me... Perhaps I should have been equally polite to him."

"You'll have that chance," Bok said. "You said yourself you've seen this type of spell before. Surely, you know how to counter it."

"Oh, I am familiar with stasis spells and their counters," Kotarian replied. "Except that such spells typically are employed to immobilize one person or creature—an unruly prisoner, for example, or a mad dog. But such a spell applied to an entire city block? The power that such a spell would take is beyond my comprehension. Tell me, Baron Blacksmith—how does one counter a spell like that?"

Bok had no answer, but Isabella offered a thought. "Salandrian must have found this in those ancient spellbooks! The sorcerers from the time of Queen Imbiria were said to have developed spells of amazing power and destructiveness. This... stasis dome must be one of them."

Bok stared up at the done, completely unable to move. *This... this is way beyond anything Tovano can do. Beyond anything I ever thought possible.*

"Well, what then? We let this stand forever? These people will be frozen in place for the rest of their lives!" Avantil exclaimed.

Kotarian put his hand to the back of his head. "No, there is a way to bring it down—take down the people who cast the spell. Even with the arcane knowledge Salandrian has collected, something this complex would require conscious thought to maintain. My highly informed assumption is that after casting the spell, he assigned some of his acolyles to maintain it.

"So all that means is that we have to defeat the most powerful sorcerer in the kingdom, if not the world, as well as an unknown number of other highly trained magic-users. Just a small task."

As the others continued to examine the dome, Bok walked over to the edge of Sonorian Square near the Royal Palace, hoping to clear his mind. He looked inside the gardens and saw something that made his mouth tighten and brow furrow.

"Um... Isabella...? You need to see this."

The others raced across the square to the sidewalk outside the palace. A greenish blue wall enclosed the Royal Gardens. Unlike the dome covering Sonarian Square, this wall was a standard spell—much like the one protecting the Grenuteral estate in Naseem. But it kept people out of the gardens as well as in.

And then it was Isabella's turn to have her heart skip a beat or two.

"There is Father! And Wingate! They are safe and well. Oh, thank the Exalted One!" She waved frantically, but the King and his Royal Guardians did not see her, and the magical wall barred any sound from passing through.

She clasped her hands together in front of her chest. "Salandrian and the Scions must have forced them out of the palace and into the gardens, only to hem them in with this spell."

That means Salandrian and his rebel band have control of the palace. Defeating them would require an assault on the center of Imarina's government and Isabella's family home. Salandrian had managed to do what the Mosork Empire could not three hundred years before—unseat the Royal Family of Imarina.

But Bok knew Isabella cared nothing for the historical or political implications of their plight. Her only concern was rescuing her father and his Royal Guardians.

She raised her hands to the barrier and repeated the spell Tovano used in Naseem to enter the Grenuteral estate. The wall shimmered and blinked out of existence—but only for a split-second, reappearing exactly as it was.

Isabella redoubled her efforts, this time shouting the spell's incantation. But again, the barrier quickly reappeared as soon as it had vanished, and as strong as ever.

"No! This must work!" Isabella raised her hands to try a third time.

Then Kotarian put his hand on her wrist. "Your Majesty; the spell is too strong. We cannot disrupt it."

"B... but Father is trapped inside! Until we free him—and the others—they are at Salandrian's mercy!" She wrestled her hand away from Kotarian, tears pooling in her eyes. "I had relied on aid from the House of Magic, only to find them already defeated. Then I see Father in danger, and I can do nothing to help him. We have traveled so far and come so close..." She could not finish before the sobbing began. She put her hands over her face and wept into them in deep, ragged breaths.

Tears appeared in Bok's eyes, too. *She's hurting so much. We depend on her leadership and courage. I have to pick her up until she is ready again.*

"We just have to find a different way." He repeated himself, more forcefully this time: "We will save your father and the kingdom with it."

Avantil put his arms around Isabella and pulled her into a warm hug—the first time Bok had seen him do that since their argument. She leaned into his chest and put her arms around his waist. She still cried, but more calmly than before.

"Bok is right, my love."

Bok hoped he could back up his bold words. He was ready to fight to save everyone he and Isabella cared about. He was willing to die, if necessary. But how could they breach Salandrian's defenses to even challenge the power-crazed sorcerer? Folk Magic wouldn't do much good in this scenario, and if even two skilled sorcerers such as Isabella and Kotarian were flummoxed by Salandrian's magical defenses, what hope did an absolute beginner have?

But Avantil had an idea. He let go of a now-calmer Isabella. "Follow me! I think I can get us inside the palace gardens."

"Don't tell me there are swampy, bug-infested underground smuggling tunnels under the Royal Palace, too?" Kotarian rubbed imaginary insects off his arms.

"Not exactly, but there is a back way in!" Avantil's hands gestured excitedly down the hill the palace stood on.

"Remember, I talk to everyone in the palace, including the kitchen staff and housekeepers. The palace was built on the highest point in Ithenel."

Bok nodded. Even students in Soleh Valley's one-room schoolhouse learned that much.

"Well, down on Queen Imbiria Avenue, there is a narrow passage at the bottom of the hill. King Imbrileo had the House sorcerers of the day cut it through the bedrock so that the servants from Westown have a more direct path up the hill, on days when the weather was nasty. It's only wide enough to walk single file up the passage, but it opens inside one of the outbuildings, right beside the West Gate. The door inside the outbuilding is locked, except during shift changes, so your father could not use it to escape on his own. Still, though, we should be able to get inside Salandrian's wall and unlock the door with a spell—unless he is aware of the servant's passage."

"I wasn't even aware of this passage!" Isabella laughed through the last of her tears. "T-thank you, Avantil—that is incredible!"

"Isabella, how do you not know of an entrance into your own home?" Bok joked and she laughed some more.

"Well, my home is the Royal Palace, you know! It is not exactly a cottage."

Isabella then gathered the three men in around her and looked them each in their eyes before speaking. "My friends, words cannot describe the love I have for you. You three are here when I need you the most."

"We are all here for each other," Bok said. "And for the people of Imarina."

Avantil nodded firmly and even Kotarian tilted his head in a manner that indicated he didn't completely disagree.

Isabella smiled. "For the people of Imarina. Now, let us go save my father and our kingdom!"

With Isabella in the lead, they ran down the hill to Queen Imbiria Avenue and the below-ground passageway. The West Gate was closest to Westown, the nearest Serving Class neighborhood to the Royal Palace. Many of the workers employed at the palace or on Sonorian Square lived here in rows of modest two- and three-story apartment buildings.

The passage entrance stood at the foot of hill, where Westown ended. Bok saw people gathered outside of every building. No doubt, most of them had family members trapped inside Salandrian's snare. These people weren't his intended targets, but they would suffer all the same, as the Serving Class always did in times of war.

Unless we can do something to help.

Avantil yanked the bronze handle of the passage's heavy oak door—it swung open.

"By the Exalted One, our fortune holds! Old Worm-Face didn't put a barrier on this door. We may well be able to get inside the gate yet."

Countless thousands of boots had worn the granite floor smooth. As the passage was completely cut off from sunlight; mounted torches every twenty-five yards lit the space.

Isabella insisted on going first into the tall, narrow walkway, followed by Avantil, then Bok and finally Kotarian. Unlike the long-abandoned tunnels under the glass foundry, the passageway leading up the hill was well-maintained and frequently used. Thick pine beams had been mounted floor to ceiling and across the roof for support. The small, confined space made Bok's skin crawl as though a legion of spiders had taken residence under his shirt.

But the real horror is what waits on the other side of the tunnel.

"What will we do once we are inside?" he asked Isabella as they hustled through the passage.

"To kill the dragon, cut off its head," Kotarian interrupted. "Once Salandrian is dead, the Scions of Sonorian will crumble. We should strike while we have surprise in our favor."

The Princess turned her head, but kept moving forward. "No! Our objective right now—our only objective—is to rescue my fa... the King and his Royal Guardians. We will lead them out of the Royal Gardens through this passage and retreat to a safe distance. Then, we will recruit any House sorcerers who were outside of Sonorian Square when the stasis spell took effect, as well as any additional Guardians and local constables. We will raise an army and only then will we confront Salandrian. We will have one chance to win this battle, and we must fight it when we are prepared."

Kotarian had opened his mouth to offer another comment when the air shimmered blue-green fifteen yards in front of them. They stopped; Avantil pulled his sword and the others stood ready. Bok's pulse throbbed in his neck. Sweat beaded on his face the blur took shape.

"My! Aren't we a resourceful bunch? I am impressed that you have managed to get this far. But we need to have a conversation."

There, hovering in front of them in the passageway, was a translucent, greenish-blue image of the True Leader, Salandrian!

CHAPTER 43

"WHAT—WHAT IS HE?"

Bok stared open-mouthed at the glowing image floating in the tunnel.

"It's an astral projection—a spell that allows sorcerers to communicate across distances. Isabella does this sometimes and I hate it even then! He can't attack us nor we him. Let's listen to what he has to say. It's not like we can sneak up on him at this point."

Avantil's explanation provided little comfort. Every hair on the back of Bok's neck stood up. He looked around and over his shoulder, fearful that the Salandrian's projection was a distraction for the Scions to sneak up the narrow stone passage behind them.

"You look different, Salandrian. I suppose treason and murder must agree with you," Kotarian scoffed.

"I appear as my true self now. As for treason, I now control Imarina! From my perspective, you four are the traitors." He folded his hands behind his back and paced as he looked over each member of the group individually.

"Let's see... we have the Little Princess. Look at her, trying so hard to make her father proud. She wants to be a leader. She wants to be a sorcerer. She wants to be a social reformer. And yet she has failed so miserably at them all..."

He turned his eyes to Avantil. "But at least she's not the empty suit that is Lord Avantil Amorinil. A disgrace to his family, his entire self-worth rests upon the Princess's favor. You know, we used to laugh at you behind your back."

Bok put his hand on his friend's shoulder. "Now we know where Kotarian gets it from. He's just talk—let him blather on."

Salandrian continued, "Yes, Lord Amorinil, we all used to mock you, including this one—my old student Kotarian. But he never realized he was the butt of the joke, too. For one who has accomplished so little, your inflated sense of self-worth is legendary."

Kotarian yelled back, "Well, there is one thing I will accomplish—kill the worm who betrayed the House of Magic!"

Salandrian didn't look at Bok. "And I'll not even comment on the Serving Class peasant in your group."

In his eyes, I don't belong among my betters. He doesn't know what I have learned about my parentage. And why should that matter? Bok's rough hands formed into fists.

Isabella's hand swept in front of her "Are petty insults all you have? The people of Imarina will not allow this treachery to stand!"

The apparition leaned back with a broad grin. "Allow? Do you believe the wishes of the rabble—like the young healer back there—matter to me? Such creeping sickness is why Imarina now rots from the inside. High magic made our nation the most prosperous in all the five seas, and High Magic shall lead us back to prominence."

"With you at the head of the table, of course!" Avantil pointed a finger at the self-proclaimed True Leader.

"The exercise of power determines who makes the rules," Salandrian crowed. "With the knowledge I have accumulated, I have earned the right to lead."

"One thing I do not understand," Kotarian asked. "Where did this confidence and this zealotry come from, Salandrian? When I knew you, you were content to stay in your books and wipe your greasy fingers on your jacket."

"Just as I wanted you to believe." Salandrian lowered his chin to look down on his former student. "Playing the absent-minded academic was easy. I suspected the true power of the house lay in its ancient reserves of knowledge. But while you and your colleagues patted each other on the back, oh 'Shining Light of the House,' I have brought the House, the Crown, and soon, an entire nation to heel."

Kotarian's eyes flashed fire. "Your ambition greatly surpasses your ability, worm! Loronian and Karagian will be free and end your days upon your stolen throne!"

"Loronian? Karagian? Do you not...? You really do not know, do you? Oh, you poor, naive lad..." The projection's slightly hollow voice echoed off the passageway walls. "Loronian and Karagian are dead, Kotarian. I killed them just moments ago—personally."

Kotarian's mouth dropped open and his arms went straight at his side, "No! That is another of your deceptions!"

But Bok knew the evil sorcerer spoke the truth. His breath grew even shakier than before. Isabella's plan made sense—rescue the King, avoid confrontation, find a way to free the House, and then, with a replenished force, retake the palace. But they had been discovered and two of their strongest allies killed. The situation grew worse by the moment.

"If you believe it is a deception, so be it." Salandrian waved dismissively. "I have no time for debate with an acolyte. I have no time for any of you."

"So why are you here?" Avantil said. "Why bother taunting us with an astral projection?"

"Why, to say farewell, of course." His sneer lingered—at least in Bok's imagination—but the greenish-blue image slowly faded and disappeared.

The passageway became quiet again, save for the sounds of four people nervously breathing in the confined space.

"Shhh!" Isabella hissed. She craned her neck listening for a sound Bok could not hear. Then she turned to Kotarian and screamed, "Be ready! They are—!"

But she did not finish. Then a *BOOM*! jarred Bok to his core. The roof of the passageway collapsed!

Hundreds of tons of rock and soil buried Bok, Isabella, Avantil, and Kotarian before they could scream.

CHAPTER 44

Salandrian strutted into the Royal Palace's main dining hall. "Kotarian and the princess will bother us no more."

Most of the Scions stopped their work, stood beside their tables, and bowed their heads to their True Leader. A half-dozen did not, only because they maintained the stasis spell entrapping the House of Magic. After two hours of constant spellcasting, these six sorcerers would be replaced by six fresh colleagues and given a chance to rest. And so it would continue until Salandrian disposed of the helpless House sorcerers.

He was in no hurry to do so, though. He ordered a terrified member of the palace's kitchen staff to fetch him a cup of wine. The man sprinted to the kitchen to obey, as other palace servants stood motionless at attention around the vast hall, trembling faces fixed on their conqueror.

Donlandrian spoke first. "We knew it would be so, True Leader! The preparations for the next Blight are nearly finished."

"Good; inform me when the spell is ready. I shall be upstairs in the Royal Council Chambers. Tell me—what wine should we serve at our victory feast?"

⸺◇⸺

COUGH! "We are okay! We are safe!" Isabella's spell-enchanted left hand lit up the small space around her and her friends. But her statement consisted entirely of wishful thinking and was not true in almost any appreciable way.

The two sorcerers, along with Bok, had been able to project shield spells around the group. Those shields held up to the avalanche. The rock and debris formed a small pocket as they fell, carving out a space no bigger than five feet in diameter in which the four friends now crammed. Piles of dirt and stone blocked them in on all sides, unable to move forward or back the way they came.

COUGH! COUGH! Isabella cleared her lungs again. She had inhaled a face full of dust, and a falling rock cut her right arm. A layer of brown dirt coated all four. But they had much bigger problems.

An invisible hand throttled Bok's throat, panic making him fight for each dust-filled breath. Blood pulsed through every vein, to the point he could hear his own heartbeat.

He examined the huge chunks of granite jammed together above their heads. "The rocks are stable for now, but who knows for how long? The whole passage could collapse at any second!"

He took a deep breath, trying to hold his terror at bay. "But that may not matter. The air in here could run out before the roof collapses. Isabella, we have to get out of here, or..."

She raised her hands to the pile of rock blocking the passage in front of them, whispered a silent prayer and spoke the incantation for the push-pull spell. The rocks shifted and trembled, kicking dust into the small nook. But the massive pile did not move.

After a minute of pushing against the stone with all her mystical might, Isabella stopped, her energy momentarily depleted. She slumped over with her hands on her knees, taking in the thinning air in deep gulps.

We're going to die. I'll never see Mother, Father, Yata, and Noji again. And if Salandrian has his way, I might be the luckiest in the family.

No! If Bok died, it would only be after giving everything to save himself and his friends.

"Let me try." Instead of focusing his magic toward the front of the tunnel, he directed it at the rubble blocking the passage behind him. That may mean leaving the captured King, Wingate, and his companions at the mercy of Salandrian. But Bok didn't see any other way for them to escape the Scions' trap.

He reached out with his mind and focused on the largest piece of fallen granite he could find. A greenish-blue tendril of energy emerged from his hand and encircled the broken piece of stone. He latched onto it with his spell, got firm control of it, and pushed. And pushed.

But as with Isabella, nothing happened. Some dirt and small rocks fell from the roof above them. However, the tons of stone and dirt blocking the passage was too heavy to move.

"Help me! With your power, we may be able to move the stones!" Isabella and Kotarian joined in the spell. Two more tendrils of blue-green energy extended forward and combined with Bok's in surrounding the biggest piece of granite.

"On my command—now!" Kotarian yelled. They pushed forward as one. Their combined efforts placed incredible force of the pile of dirt and soil; the mound became indented where their magical energy pushed forward.

But it would not move.

The three tried again.

And again.

And a fourth time, pouring every bit of their energy and essence into each attempt. But the pile of rock entrapping them would not budge, no matter how hard they pushed. Bok, Isabella, and Kotarian stopped casting, completely taxed by the effort. Bok gasped for air which did not fill his lungs. He became lightheaded and dizzy and collapsed to one knee.

Kotarian dropped to the ground as well, his hands limp at his side. "It... it is no use."

Avantil, who stood behind the three spellcasters watching intently, took Isabella into his arms and pulled her close to him.

"Isabella, if... if our good fortune has run its course, just know... I love you. Now and forever."

She looked up weakly, as if she could barely lift her head. She rested her face against his cheek, her eyes closed. "And I love you, Avantil. Even when we were angry with one another, I never stopped loving you."

She then opened her eyes and lifted her head. "Bok, there is something—"

Bok staggered back up to his feet. His legs nearly buckled underneath him, but a profound fear of dying—and failing his loved ones—gave him the strength to rise again. "I know. And I value your friendship, too. But we need to try again to move these rocks!"

They would die within minutes if they could not force a way through the rock. What would that mean for the Omat family? They had to find a way out.

"If we focus our efforts, concentrate all our power, we may be able to move—"

Isabella stopped him. "You are not a secret child of the Noble Class, Bok.... We lied to you, my friend."

CHAPTER 45

Isabella... lied? Why would she do that? Despite the dust filling his lungs—and the impending death teetering above his head—Bok could think of nothing else. She knew how troubled he had been by Tovano's revelation, how painful it was to think his parents had deceived him his entire life. His head spun as though he might faint, for reasons beyond just the thinning air.

Isabella sighed deeply. "Avantil and Kotarian knew nothing of this, so please—do not blame them for my deception. Tovano and I lied to you to protect one of our kingdom's oldest secrets.

"For centuries, our people have believed that only those of Noble Class birth can be born with the ability to perform High Magic. Such a belief has been foundational for our society—we, the Noble Class, rule benevolently because we were endowed with a potential that others do not possess. Everyone has an important role to perform, and all classes are valued parts of our society. But the Noble Class leads because we earned that right, and our control of High Magic is proof of that mandate. That is what we all were raised to believe."

She looked down, even more defeated than she had been looking at her father imprisoned by Salandrian's spell. "But the truth is, Bok, that people from *all* classes, including those of the Serving Class—may be born with the Acumen to perform High Magic. You were.

"We in the Royal Family have hidden the truth for generations. It is shameful and wrong. My ancestors believed allowing non-Nobles to practice magic would undermine Imarina's strict social order. And every king and queen since that time has kept that secret, for fear of upending that system."

Kotarian exploded at Isabella's revelation. "By Chalendrian's Chaining Chastity! Do you realize what you are saying? The entire foundation of the House of Magic is built on a deception! How do you know these things, when I have never even heard such whispers?"

"Forget your House of Magic! Isabella, how could you keep such a terrible secret from me?" Avantil looked to Isabella, who kept her eyes turned to the stone floor.

"My father told me in private—and only within recent weeks," she said. "It is the most closely guarded secret of our Kingdom. The only people who know are my father, the Emissary of Magic, and Tovano—who apparently discovered the truth on his own, many years ago. Because if this became public knowledge, if the people knew their monarchs had lied to them for centuries, it could rend Imarina apart!"

"But by the Exalted One, why now?" Avantil exclaimed. "When we are in such a life-or-death predicament?"

"Because I owe Bok the truth." With a shaky finger, she pointed to the stunned healer. "I should have told him—told everyone sooner. But after all the four of us have experienced together, I cannot go to my death having lied to the people I love."

Bok put his hands over his face, unable to process what he was being told. He was not a Baron, not a long-lost son of some distant Noble. He was who he had always believed—a blacksmith's boy from Soleh Valley. Serving Class yet born with the Acumen for High Magic.

Impossible. But it also seemed impossible that his friend—the woman he had fallen in love with over the course of this journey—would betray him so deeply.

"So I'm not...?"

"No, Bok. I am truly sorry... This is why I was upset when you discovered the ability to perform High Magic. I knew I would have to lie to you, and I did not want to do that. Please forgive me, my friend."

My friend? What type of friend lied about something so important? How many others in the Serving Class had lived and died never knowing they possessed the Acumen for High Magic? How would their lives, and the lives of their families and communities, been better if they had known?

And what does it say about me that I was tempted to accept such a falsehood? To turn my back on all that I am? To believe the worst about my parents? Isabella isn't the only one who should be ashamed. Bok took a low, ragged breath, his hands still covering his face.

Isabella tugged at his sleeve. "Bok... say something—please! Hate me if you must, but please talk to me!"

He was not willing to give her comfort. Or forgive himself. What he had to offer, however, was a desperate plan of escape.

"Listen—none of this matters. Not now, anyway. We need to get out of this deathtrap. If we don't, no one will be around to care who lied to whom."

"Obviously," Kotarian said. "But how do you propose we move that heap of rock and rubble when all three of us failed before?"

"We use the transmission spell." Bok slammed his fist into the palm of his hand. "Tovano told me about it. It's our only hope of escape!"

"The transmission spell? Ritovian's Rapid Relocation? Bok, that only works on non-living matter. I realize you don't know—?"

"I do know, Kotarian—and it will work on living beings. It isn't used because of the risks. At this point, that's a chance I am willing to take. I do not want to die in this hole!"

"Bok is correct, Kotarian." Isabella finally looked up. "This will be dangerous—we could transmit into a solid wall and die instantly. But we must try. Oh, Bok... you have given us hope!"

Bok didn't respond to Isabella directly. "So what do we do now? I don't know the spell—just that it could work."

Kotarian exhaled deeply. "I... I am ashamed to admit, but I do not know this spell, either. I could perform a hundred and one different spells flawlessly, but the one spell we need, I do not know."

"I know it." Isabella slapped the dust-covered stone floor, her jaw set. "Tovano taught me the transmission spell. Obviously, I have never used it on any living being—much less a person. But I can cast it."

Kotarian smiled. "I can assist you. I may not know the spell, but I understand the concepts well enough to provide support. But to transport all four of us, you will need Baron Blacksmith to provide us with additional energy, too."

Bok nodded, then stepped back as far as he could in the small space. Isabella and Kotarian did the same, forming a triangle around Avantil. The merchant's son looked at the mass above their heads. The trickle of dirt and pebbles falling from the ceiling spilled faster. "Whatever you do, we need to do it now—the roof is starting to give!"

"Think of the place you know better than any other; the place where you feel most safe and comfortable," Isabella said, to herself as much as anyone.

She then moved her hands in an elliptical pattern and spoke words older than the kingdom itself. Greenish-blue energy filled the small nook. Kotarian added a few words and energy flowed from his body into Isabella's. Bok repeated the words that Kotarian chanted and transmitted his own magical energy to the princess, who used it to power her developing spell.

Bok immediately felt weak and light-headed, both from the lack of oxygen and the drain of the spell. But he forced himself to stay on his feet and continued to pour his dwindling supply of energy to Isabella.

Then, the rocks and dirt disappeared. Even the smell of earth vanished, as did the sensation of being buried alive. The dark passage transformed into a brightly lit tunnel with smooth blue-green walls. Isabella, Avantil and Kotarian were there, but bathed in a bright white light that quickly grew more and more intense. Within moments, he could not see his friends, only the auras surrounding them. Bok wondered if he had blacked out.

Isabella—or the bright light containing her—then shot down the tunnel at rapid speed, pulling Avantil with her. Kortarian followed closely behind. To Bok, his friends appeared to be three streaks of light, growing smaller by the instant.

He willed himself forward. To his surprise, he moved rapidly through the tunnel. Bok assumed that if he could see himself through the glare, he would see that he, too, was surrounded by an aura of white light.

He didn't even need to steer himself down the tunnel. As Isabella turned and moved, so did he, joined as they were by the spell's bond. Bok lost all sense of time and distance. He had no idea of how far he traveled or how long the journey took.

But within minutes—or perhaps just a millisecond—the tunnel's end appeared. It took the shape of a swirling gray mass, bright but completely without form or detail. Isabella and Avantil disappeared into the gray, followed closely by Kotarian. Bok raced forward. He couldn't stop or avoid the tunnel's end, even if he wished to. The shifting cloud of energy drew closer and then...

He disappeared.

CHAPTER 46

Bok rematerialized in a bright, sunlit place, staring at the most ornately carved marble wall he had ever seen. Artists had chiseled images of Imarina's monarchs from centuries past into the white stone. The detail and beauty made Bok gasp.

Then, he realized he wasn't viewing a wall—he was staring up at a ceiling. And now he fell.

He flailed his arms and kicked his legs, as if trying to swim—without success.

Fortunately, a giant bed, covered in a mountain of pink and teal silk pillows, broke his fall. Bok hit the bed, bounced three feet into the air, and landed backside-first on the white marble floor.

The landing was painful—not to mention undignified. But he was alive and unhurt. Either that, or the afterlife looked just like Isabella's bedroom.

Oil portraits by Imarina's most notable painters and hand-woven tapestries that covered dozens of square feet filled the room's marble walls. A giant mahogany wardrobe loomed over one side of the room, and rich red rugs covered most of the floor.

But Bok's attention went to the far corner, beyond the edge of the bed. There sat a plain desk piled high with papers and books. In addition to spellbooks, the stack included volumes about history, geography, art, literature, and science. They shared space on the desk with a well-used oil lamp. A small, framed portrait of Queen Ipharina hung on the wall over the desk.

It's not hard to understand where Isabella finds her determination.

He looked around; Isabella, Avantil and Kotarian stood around the room, having had smoother re-entries. He put his hand on the floor and pushed his way to his feet, taking care not to betray any signs that he was in pain.

Kotarian dusted off his gray jacket. "I have to say, Peasant-Once-More, your mad scheme worked! Somehow, we are safe—at least until Salandrian and his minions discover our presence. Assuming they were not already alerted by our spell."

Avantil shook his fist. "Then we must take advantage of the time we have and surprise them! Strike now before they discover we have escaped."

"But we are just four," Kotarian sat on a large pillow and pulled his legs close to his chest. "Four against... an entire cadre of trained spellcasters and like-minded allies who, while not sorcerers, are undoubtedly highly armed. And then there is the matter of Salandrian himself. Even without his minions, he would be an incredibly formidable foe."

"Kotarian is correct." The three men all turned to Isabella. "We cannot hope to defeat Salandrian and the Scions of Sonorian in direct combat... But we can disrupt their spells long enough for the House of Magic and the Royal Guardians to come to our aid!"

"Do you mean disrupt them with magic?"

"Exactly, Avantil! Just as I tried to do to the spell blocking my father's exit from the Royal Gardens. Except now, we are inside the perimeter of the spell. It should be more susceptible to disruption. A powerful enough counter-spell could neutralize both that spell and the stasis spell entrapping our sorcerers. If this work, we still can turn the tide in our favor!"

Kotarian continued to grip his knees and mused about what she was saying. "Perhaps—it will be a tall order, but one within the realm of possibility. A spell that powerful will require time to prepare. As soon as we begin casting, Salandrian will sense what we are doing and will be upon us before we have time to complete our spell."

Bok stepped forward. "That is where I come in."

He pointed to Isabella and Kotarian. "You two cast the disruption spell. Avantil and his bow will hold off any attackers who come down the hall."

The young Noble held his bow high above his head: "Aye! That they will!"

Bok continued, "As for Salandrian, he won't be able to attack you if someone keeps him occupied. That someone must be me. I will confront Salandrian while the three of you stay here."

Avantil ran to the door as if to physically block Bok from leaving the room. "Bok, he will kill you!"

"Avantil is right—you cannot fight him alone." Isabella gently grabbed Bok's sleeve. "I know you are angry with me. Please do not let that anger cause your death."

"Wait!" Bok held out both hands and backed away from Isabella and Avantil. "Believe me, I have no wish to die today. But we need you and Kotarian to cast the disruption spell. Unless we can bring down the barriers, we are doomed anyway.

"Kotarian is right—as soon as Salandrian knows what we are doing, he will come here to stop us. I'm a Serving Class son of a blacksmith, not a hero of legend—and I have no intention of dying a hero's death. But if I can divert his attention, just for a few minutes, that hopefully gives enough time to free our allies. It isn't just our best chance—it is our only chance."

"I'll go with you!" Avantil insisted. "Together, we can take this snake down together. With both of us—"

"With both of us gone, Isabella and Kotarian will be unprotected," Bok replied. "Someone must hold the line here."

Isabella's voice cracked. "Bok is right. This plan will work... but only if we all play our roles." Kotarian and Avantil then stepped back, saying nothing more.

As Bok checked his healer's bag, Avantil gave him an unexpected hug. "May your aim be true."

Kotarian took the pin from his jacket and handed it to Bok. "Wear this—and be inspired to greatness."

Bok pinned the medal to his own shirt. "With you as a role model, how could I not?"

"Ha! There may be hope for this one yet. Remember—I want that pin back when you are victorious."

"Agreed. There can be only one Shining Light." Bok tapped the medal and smiled. "I will bring this pin back to its rightful owner."

He hoped his forced bravado wasn't too obvious. Isabella was right—this likely was a suicide mission, and he badly did not want to die. But he could see no other way to protect his family, friends and the innocent people who would be crushed by Salandrian's cruel reign.

Isabella approached Bok with open arms, looking to hug her friend, possibly for the last time.

"No." Bok held up his hands and took a step back. Where once he had been too shy and intimidated to meet her gaze, he now stared directly into her brown eyes.

"I just want to protect my family and my people from the threat of Salandrian and the Scions of Sonorian. I don't care about the House of Magic, the Royal Palace, or your precious Kingdom."

"Does your scorn—understandable though it may be—extend to me as well?" Isabella shook her head vigorously and turned away from Bok. "No—do not answer that. I may have earned it, but it would break my heart to hear you say as much."

Bok paused. *I can't hate Isabella. How could I, as kind as she has been to me? And yet, how could she lie about something so important?*

He took a step toward her. "Isabella, I..." Every second they waited gave Salandrian another chance to discover their hiding spot and end their fragile hope of success before they had a chance to try. *My jumbled feelings and confused thoughts must wait.*

"Fire up the forge—I have a job to do." He turned, drew his sword, and walked toward the door, where a hallway and a flight of steps would take him to the Royal Council Chambers—and his confrontation with Salandrian.

"As do we," Isabella said. "Just know that I pray for your safe return... my friend."

CHAPTER 47

A SAFE RETURN WAS Bok's foremost concern as well as he raced down the hall toward the stairs leading down from the Royal Family's residential quarters to the Royal Council Chambers and the more public areas of the palace. He hoped he could somehow delay and defend against Salandrian's attacks long enough for help to arrive.

But that seems an unlikely wish.

He walked down the long white marble hall, hurrying but not rushing. Isabella and Kotarian would give him a few moments before starting their spell, and he didn't want to mistime his entrance into the chambers. Hand-woven rugs absorbed his footfalls; the only sound he heard was his nervous breathing.

Small tables, hand-carved by artisans from across the kingdom, had been placed at regular intervals throughout the hall. Each displayed a few decorative items—a vase of fresh-cut flowers and some small potted plants. As he passed, Bok yanked a small cactus from one of the tables and stuffed it into his bag.

Bok took another in a seemingly endless series of deep breaths. Then he walked down the polished stone steps to the antechamber of the Royal Council Chambers. His hands trembled as he touched the rail.

No building in Soleh Valley even had stairs. He hadn't walked up or down stairs until he was 14 summers—when Weni Kon took him to the closest town to purchase supplies. The store they visited barely qualified as a two-story building, and it wouldn't stand out at all in Ithenel, but young Bok thought it was the grandest place in the kingdom. He remembered the sweet store-bought candy he took home for his parents and Yata.

Strange and even funny that now, of all times, such a mundane memory would pop into my head.

Fingers tingling, he swung the double doors open carefully—in case any Scions stood guard in the antechamber. But they didn't. The room was quiet and empty. He exhaled, but that only stirred up the butterflies in his stomach even more.

He reached out for the handle of the front doors, then paused. *Maybe going in through a side door would take the Scions off guard. Besides, I'm Serving Class—I'll use the servant's entrance.*

Bok stopped in front of the heavy oak door and closed his eyes. No amount of calming breaths could force his mind and pulse to slow down. Salandrian waited inside the Royal Council Chambers.

Nowhere else such a power-hungry despot would be. My death could be on the other side of this door, too. This literally could be the last room I ever enter.

He inhaled deeply one last time, wiped his sweaty palms on his pants, and pushed open the door.

Bok rushed in, head low and eyes up, looking for Scions. He found none. His footsteps echoed off the white marble ceiling of the expansive Royal Council Chambers.

The room was empty. Except for one tall, handsome man in black and red relaxing in King Isbiano's chair in the center of the dais.

"You! What...? You are supposed to be dead!" The man tipped over his goblet when he bolted upright in his seat. Red wine spilled onto the floor.

Bok turned to his right and locked eyes with Salandrian.

The time for introspection had ended. Now, Bok would have to fight for his life.

⋈

Upstairs, Isabella and Kotarian waited nervously to start the disruption spell. They heard no signs of commotion after Bok left the residential floor, which was good. At least they still had a few moments of peace to prepare to cast the most important spell of their lives. Isabella's stomach churned with anxiety. *If this did not work...*

No. She would not dwell on failure. Her father depended on her. She thought of King Isbiano trapped outside their home, helpless to protect himself or their kingdom. She imagined his expression when he placed her mother's crown on her head in five summers' time. She already knew she was going to cry, regardless of royal etiquette.

She then thought of Avantil, who had taken his bow and quiver into the hallway outside her room. He did not know this yet, but at some point, when the time felt right, they would have a grand royal wedding. She would wear a purple dress made by her favorite tailor and carry a bouquet of flowers from her mother's garden. Their children would have their father's good humor and she would love them dearly.

And she thought of Bok. Sweet Bok—the boy whose only mistake was daring to trust his princess. She wanted so much to tell him how much he meant to her, even if it was not the way he may have hoped. She wanted to tell him how sorry she was for causing him any pain.

But to get that chance, she had to make this spell work.

"Take the lead, Your Majesty—I will be ready when you are."

Kotarian began calling forth the magical energies at his command. She did the same, and bluish green forces swirled around them like a summer storm.

CHAPTER 48

“I KILLED YOU! How are you here?” Salandrian thundered. “Never mind. I will just have to kill you again!”

Bok didn't respond with banter. Instead, he extended his hands and launched the most powerful flashfire spell he could conjure. The flame's size and intensity surprised him.

The spell caught Salandrian off balance. He blocked the blast with a shield spell—barely. "How did you—?"

Bok had hoped to end the fight quickly, but he didn't hesitate when his first attack failed.

He stuck his hand in his bag, retrieved the small cactus he'd grabbed in the hall, and threw it on the floor. When he used his combined magics on it, the plant instantly expanded and filled the space around the dais and Salandrian.

Again, the sorcerer projected a shield spell, but this time, he only partially deflected the attack. Several of the rapidly growing spines ripped his black coat and slashed his arm and chest, knocking him to the floor in the process.

"AAAGH!! Curse you!" From a seated position, Salandrian gestured and eight spouts of fire—like miniature comets—streaked across the chambers in an arc. Bok projected a shield spell. To his surprise, the shield held. The small, fiery projectile exploded in a ball of flame against the shield; Bok could feel its heat even through his protective spell.

The plant returned to its normal small size. Bok's attack had injured the sorcerer, but not nearly enough to incapacitate him. If anything, it made Salandrian more bloodthirsty than ever.

"Who are you? How are you able to do this—you, who are nothing but a Serving Class commoner?"

Salandrian tapped his finger to his temple. "Ah. I have it. The 'healer and practitioner of Folk Magic' story was just a ruse! You must be an agent of Tovano—I see his hand in the spells you cast. I bet he had you hiding and training in the far reaches of Imarina. Well played, my old colleague. It is too bad Tovano didn't teach you enough to survive!"

Salandrian lashed out with a push-pull spell, ripping an entire row of marble benches out of the marble floor and hurling them toward Bok. No shield spell Bok could conjure could stop thousands of pounds of flying stone, so he ducked to the side, barely avoiding being crushed.

He landed awkwardly against a marble column and hit hard. For a moment, his vision turned hazy. Only the sharp pain streaking down his left arm jolted him back awake and alert.

Still, he needed time to recover—time Salandrian wasn't inclined to grant him.

⋈

As Bok fought for his life, Isabella felt more alive than ever.

High Magic swelled inside of her, building until she could feel it bursting from the pores of her skin. In the corner of her sight, she glimpsed herself in the mirror. Without realizing it, she had levitated several inches above the floor, lifted off the ground by the power of the counter-spell. She and Kotarian moved their hands in circular patterns, repeating the incantation in barely a whisper.

Isabella continued to build and build the magic until it became painful, until it practically forced its way out of her soul. She now shouted the words to the incantation but did not stop chanting.

This... this is marvelous! I understand why magic can seduce a man like Salandrian. But such power must be used for the good of all.

Finally, she could take no more. She nodded to Kotarian and he unleashed the force of his spell. She did the same and a blue-green wave pulsed across her bedroom, lighting it up like a flare.

The magic swept through the palace and beyond, stretching across the entire block.

Then something truly incredible happened. The wall enclosing the palace blinked, then vanished.

Likewise, the stasis spell imprisoning the House of Magic disappeared. The people who had been frozen in place resumed their movements, although confused by what they had experienced. From the courtyard, she heard a Guardian shout, "The barrier is down! To the palace!"

Isabella laughed out loud as she looked out her bedroom window. *The spell worked! Bok's courage granted us enough time. Hold on, my friend. Help is coming.*

Now, she and Kotarian had to sustain the spell long enough for their allies to enter the fight.

As she had done in so many lonely study sessions, Isabella bit her lower lip, clenched her fists, and concentrated anew.

———⋈———

Bok's left shoulder took the brunt of the landing. After the shock subsided, he touched it and winced.

Dislocated at best; probably fractured. His left arm would be useless in the rest of the fight. If there even there was much more of a battle. The blow also dislodged both his healer's bag and his sword, which lay on the floor between him and the dais, leaving Bok weaponless.

Salandrian floated down from the dais, a greenish-blue aura filling the spacious chambers. He looked every bit the angry god he claimed to be.

Bok lashed out again with another flashfire spell. But Salandrian was prepared this time and slapped it aside, as effortlessly as a horse would swat a fly with its tail. Any advantage Bok had gained through surprise now was gone.

Salandrian stepped forward slowly—not from caution, but with total confidence that he now had the situation under control.

"So, who are you, really? I know everyone in the kingdom who has the Acumen for High Magic, and I don't know you." He sauntered over to take a closer look at Bok, who staggered to stay upright after being slammed into the benches. Salandrian furrowed his forehead and squinted, then shook his head.

"No, never seen you before." Salandrian smiled at the quivering young man before him. "You carry the stink of the Serving Class upon you, no matter your true origins. Again—who are you? The quest for long-lost information fascinates me. Reveal the secrets behind your mysterious appearance and I shall show you mercy. Now, I must be honest—you still are going to die. But tell me who you are, and I will make your death quick."

Salandrian's hands began to glow greenish-blue, as he prepared his next spell.

Bok's entire body trembled. Images, not words, ran through his mind in those next two seconds, as Salandrian intended to deliver the fatal blow up close.

He thought of his family's simple home in Soleh Valley. Mother, Father, Yata, and Noji sat at their unpolished pine table, staring at bowls of food they could barely touch. At one point, his father put his hand over his face, while his gray-faced mother turned away, unable to look at her grieving husband.

Then, his mind went to Avantil, Tovano, Kotarian, Wingate, and Coregan. After Bok fell, Salandrian turned his attention to Bok's friends. They all fought valiantly—they put up much more of a struggle than a fledgling High Magic user from the Serving Class did. But they still died under the might of Salandrian and his Scions.

And then his thoughts went to Isabella. She, too, would die. Unless Salandrian decided to keep the princess as a prisoner. He imagined her in a filthy prison cell, dressed in ragged, dirty clothes, her already small frame shriveled from the lack of food. All her spark had been extinguished as she mutely gripped her cell's iron bars.

I can't accept any of these outcomes. I don't know what to do, or if I have a prayer of winning. But I will do everything I can to save the people I love.

"Who am I?" Bok stood as tall he could through his pain, fatigue, and fear. "Just a blacksmith's boy."

Salandrian rolled his eyes to the ceiling. "Ha! A liar until the end. We both know a simple 'blacksmith's boy' could not possess the Acumen. But while I am a curious person, I also have grown bored of this game. So I will now..."

Salandrian held his hands in front of his face, his mouth open. He stared at his fingers, as if they held a secret clue to an unsolved mystery.

"What... what is happening...?"

The blue-green energy around him dimmed, blinked, and then disappeared. The most powerful practitioner of High Magic in the Five Seas now found himself unable to tap into the source of his might. Isabella and Kotarian had disrupted his magic.

My friends... they did the impossible!

And now, it was Bok's turn to smile.

CHAPTER 49

GIVEN A SECOND OPPORTUNITY, Bok charged the True Leader before the man could regain his composure.

He slammed into Salandrian with his full might. The impact sent waves of agony through Bok's injured shoulder, but at this point, desperation and hope fueled his body and he focused past the pain. He had to restrain Salandrian before the sorcerer regained his magic.

The men tumbled to the stone floor and Salandrian's face struck the white marble tile, bloodying his cheek.

Meanwhile, Bok's hand slammed hard into the floor. He yelled as hot pain ran up his arm, as if he had stuck it into a hornet's nest.

His hand swelled almost instantly. Bok grabbed his right hand with his left and gingerly felt the small bones. *Broken.*

Then, something hot stung him below the ribs—and sucked the air from his lungs.

Bok looked down to see the hilt of Salandrian's dagger protruding from his side. A red circle appeared on his white tunic. Small at first but spreading quickly.

Bok gasped for breath as he stumbled on fawn's legs. His eyes squeezed shut, then opened widely. A moan might have escaped his lips—he wasn't sure.

It's not fair! I cheated death from Salandrian's magic, only to die from a stupid dagger!

He touched his hand to his side, and it came back warm and wet. He looked down. His loose-fitting white tunic turned red at an alarming pace. The damp fabric stuck to his skin. Nausea flooded his abdomen as he clutched his wound.

From his back, Salandrian then kicked Bok in the face, sending him sprawling backward.

Salandrian grabbed the edge of the dais and pulled himself back to his feet, albeit unsteadily. The would-be world conqueror stared at Bok through swollen eyes, blood trickling down the side of his face. His chest, like Bok's, heaved for air that would not come quickly enough. Instead of an easy slaughter, as Salandrian had predicted, he'd received an absolute war.

Unfortunately, Bok's wounds were far worse. Still on his back, he grabbed the blade's hilt, his face snarling in pain as he pulled it from his body. He tried pulling himself up, but his mind went dark. He rested his head against the chamber floor, leaving a red puddle on the white marble.

D-don't think it got any internal organs. But I'll still bleed to death. Bok closed his eyes, unable to move and waiting for darkness to engulf him.

Then, he heard the most astonishing noise—one that opened his eyes and forced him to an upright seated position. He strained his ears. The sound was faint at first and he had trouble being sure it was real above his gasps for air.

But the noise became louder and louder until he was certain. He heard the House of Magic sorcerers and Royal Guardians storming the palace: the shouts of encouragement and instruction, the concussion of impact spells hitting their target, and the Scions' cries of surprise at the attack's ferocity.

Salandrian heard the sounds, too. He turned his attention away from Bok and looked out the room's gold-framed panel window. Bok couldn't see what Salandrian saw. But the sorcerer's hand covered his mouth at the sight. Happy tears swelled in Bok's eyes.

"I have said before—I'm not some great warrior or even a real sorcerer. I'm just a country healer from Soleh Valley. But my loved ones will be safe, and nothing you can do will change that."

Salandrian frantically looked from side to side, but no solution was forthcoming. Bok was correct. Even with

Salandrian's vast powers, he and his Scions of Sonorian could not defeat the combined forces of the House of Magic and the Royal Guard.

"Y-you have ruined everything!" he raged. "Everything!"

Still woozy from their battle, Salandrian stumbled toward his downed opponent. Bok inched backward in a vain attempt to put additional distance between himself and Salandrian, a slick red trail trailing him.

"I was supposed to rule! I deserved it—not that back-stabber Loronian or that half-wit Karagian! But you took that from me, and I am going to kill you for it!"

Salandrian's hands once again crackled and. The disruption spell had done its job—but it also had run its course. Magic once again functioned inside the palace walls, and Salandrian quickly was regaining his might.

He raised both fists over his head. The magical energy surrounding his body molded into the shape of a giant mallet.

Now on his hands and knees, Bok could not defend against such a blow. Salandrian's attack would crush even his best shield.

I have but one chance—if I can bring myself to do it.

He spoke the brief incantation for the death touch spell, just as Isabella had taught him. His broken right hand screamed in agony when he grabbed Salandrian's left thigh, sending mystic energy surging into the sorcerer's body like so many lightning bolts.

Salandrian again had underestimated the young man's resourcefulness and resolve. For when he cast his attacking spell, intending to crush the life out of Bok, he, too, was unable to cast a shielding spell.

The hammer spell dissipated. Defenseless, Salandrian spasmed, his eyes wide for a second. Then he crumpled to the floor, oblivious to all around him.

There, Salandrian's face and body shimmered and blurred. When the cocoon of magical energy disappeared, Bok saw the man had resumed the form he had worn in the Royal Council meeting. The True Leader's square chin and thick head of hair morphed back into a pasty, jowly face and patchy bald scalp—his real appearance. True to form, Salandrian had proven to be a deceiver until the end.

But was it the end? Salandrian deserved a hundred deaths for the cruelty he had inflicted. But Bok did not want to deliver that judgment. Killing would never be comfortable to him.

That is why at the last second, he held back on the amount of energy he had sent coursing into Salandrian's body.

He crawled over to the fallen sorcerer. The unconscious man's chest still moved up and down. Salandrian still lived. Bok had defeated him without taking his life, just as he intended.

B... but he'll be the only survivor if I... I don't get help soon. Bok touched the cut in his side again; it still bled rapidly. His vision blurred and he found it difficult to even lift his chin off his chest.

My healer's bag. In it were bandages, clotting powders, salves to slow the bleeding, And the satchel lay on the floor, only fifteen or so feet away. It tempted and taunted Bok through the fog of his failing eyesight.

Bok lunged toward it, then crumpled when his arms gave out. He collapsed on the hard chamber floor like a child's doll whose owner has lost interest in playing.

Fifteen feet away. Might as well be fifteen miles.

No. I'll... get it. Just... just as soon as I close my eyes an' rest for a moment...

CHAPTER 50

"For Imarina! For King Isbiano!"

The Royal Guard burst through the front doors of the palace and spilled into the main dining hall. The Scions of Sonorian took positions behind overturned tables. But the sorcerers of the House of Magic also entered the scene through the side door and outflanked the Scions.

Wingate charged to the front of the line. He dodged underneath a projectile spell and deflected a sword blow with his shield. He leaped over a table and cut down a Scion sorcerer with one blow, opening a hole in the Scions' line of defense.

King Isbiano insisted on accompanying his Royal Guardians in their effort to retake the palace. "It is my home. and I cannot ask anyone to risk their lives in an effort I am not willing to undertake myself." Sword in hand, he yelled words of encouragement to Wingate and his well-trained Guardians.

The Scions, all of whom were acolyte-level sorcerers, floundered against experienced House spellcasters. The Royal Guardians skillfully picked their opportunities and struck when the Scions were preoccupied with defending against magical attacks.

Within moments, King Isbiano's forces reduced the Scions' to just ten sorcerers and soldiers.

"Fall back! Fall back!" Donlandrian screamed to the remaining Scions. Still casting a shield spell, she pointed the dwindling band of insurgents toward the stairwell.

"The True Leader is in the Royal Council Chambers, and he has the power to destroy all our enemies! We will still—"

A blue-green lightning bolt cut her final words short. Isabella stood at the top of the stairs, her hand glowing with magical energy.

Two armed Scion soldiers spun toward the stairs, shocked by the attack coming from their rear. One of Avantil's arrow zinged through the opening in one man's helmet. Kotarian froze the other to the spot with Falarian's Frigid Fatality. He then looked around at his colleagues routing the Scions with a variety of magics.

"At least there are others who remained true to the House. Perhaps I should be nicer to them upon my return."

With that, the final members of the Scions left standing dropped their swords, raised their arms, and surrendered. Members of the Royal Guard quickly shackled them and led them away to the Ithenel Constabulary, where they would be held under tight security until they could be brought to trial on charges of treason.

The rebellion against Imarina had ended. The victory came at a cost, however. Six Royal Guardians and two House of Magic sorcerers died in the battle. Another twenty suffered injuries of various degrees, from sprained ankles to life-threatening burns.

Kotarian pointed to a neatly arranged ring of roses, nightshade, and charcoal in a corner of the hall. "Look at this. They were preparing another Blight spell when we arrived."

Avantil put his hand to his face. "And the King and his Royal Guard were its intended targets! Had we not broken their spell..."

"But we did, my rich friend. See? The King is hale and healthy."

After ensuring that the wounded were receiving care, Isbiano pushed his way through the ruined dining hall. Isabella ran down the stairs to meet him.

"Oh, Father! I... I feared that..." Unable to finish, she buried her head into his chest and pulled him in tightly.

"You know I could not do that to you, dear daughter." He brushed the princess's hair from her face. "I am proud of you, Isabella. You and your friends have saved our kingdom."

"That means more to me than you can know, Father. But unfortunately, our work is not yet done."

"Salandrian," Avantil hissed, "Yes, we cannot celebrate our victory until he is brought to justice."

"And until we know Bok is safe!" Isabella insisted.

Isbiano pursed his lips. "Bok? The young healer from Soleh Valley? What does he have to do with all this?"

Isabella's voice trembled. "Everything, Father. I pray his courage did not bring about his sacrifice."

At the King's command, the small army of sorcerers and guards stomped up the steps, with Isabella, Avantil, and Kotarian leading the way. When they entered the anteroom of the Royal Council Chambers, Isabella and Avantil, bow in hand, ran to the double doors. But Kotarian raised his palm: "Wait! Behind those doors is the most powerful sorcerer Imarina has known in 300 summers. We must remain cautious—and believe me, I do not say that lightly."

"You accursed spellweaver! Bok is in there with that demon! If there is a chance he still lives—"

"Believe me, Avantil, I take no pleasure in saying this. But we must assume that our... our friend already is gone." Kotarian folded his hands at his waist and sighed heavily.

CREAK! One of the double doors slowly opened. The Guardians drew their swords as a single unit.

Every sorcerer chanted, illuminating the anteroom with blue-green magical energy. The King held up his fist, waiting to give the command to attack.

And then a young man in blood-soaked servant's clothes wobbled out into the light.

"Bok!" Isabella shrieked. "Oh, praise the Exalted One—you are alive!"

Avantil grabbed Bok's arm and gently lowered him into a chair. "You are a most welcome sight, my friend! But Salandrian...?"

"In there—unconscious," Bok croaked. "Might... want to bind his hands and gag his mouth before... he wakes."

Good thing I reached my healer's bag. Still, I'm getting blood on the King's good furniture. Probably shouldn't do that...

Having ducked into the council chambers, Wingate stuck his head out the open door. "He is correct, Your Majesty. Salandrian is in Royal Guard custody—and we have Mr. Omat to thank."

"By Loronian's Laborious Lectures! The peasant won." Kotarian put his hands on his knees and chuckled. He even smiled at Bok.

At Isabella's direction, a Guardian brought Bok a goblet of cold water. Although thirsty, Bok almost was too exhausted to drink. He visibly winced when he reached for the cup with his broken right hand.

"Get this man to the infirmary!" Isabella grabbed a Guardian by his uniform shirt. "You there—take him now!"

"W... wait. Please." Bok's mind remained foggy, but he focused his thoughts as best he could. "I need... to say something first."

Isabella crouched beside him. "Go on—I am listening."

"No... not to you, Isabella. To your father." He pointed at the King.

"To me?" Isbiano raised his eyebrows. "Very well, young man. What do you wish to say?" The King joined Isabella, Avantil, and Koregan in crowding around Bok, waiting to hear the young peasant's words. The others kept their distance, out of respect for the King's privacy.

Bok paused. I am a Serving Class boy—who am I to make demands of the King? *But Isbiano has to hear this, in case I don't survive.*

He cleared his throat. "Tell the truth, Your Majesty. Tell the truth to the kingdom... about the Acumen for High Magic."

Isbiano looked to his daughter, who locked eyes with his. "Let Bok speak, Father. He has paid for that right in loyalty." The King simply nodded in agreement for Bok to continue.

"I am Serving Class, yet I was born with the Acumen—as I proved just now. And I used those abilities to defeat Salandrian—and save your life, Your Majesty.

There are others like me, working in the factories and on the farms. They deserve the same opportunity."

"What... what you say is not a simple thing." Isbiano spoke in a low voice, so that the others in the room could not hear. "Surely, you must recognize—"

Isabella interrupted the King. "Bok is right, Father. I defied you to represent the Kingdom on this mission so that I may learn to lead. But I also received a lesson in the potential of the Imarinan people. All of them. We discussed this issue before, and I deferred to your judgment. Now I am asking you to trust mine."

She took Isbiano's arm in her hand. "For generations, our family has feared a threat that did not exist—that the Serving Class would rise against the Crown if they knew the truth about High Magic. In doing so, we ignored the real danger growing right inside these walls. Salandrian is a Noble and a Dean in the House of Magic. Yet he tried to kill us all. And a Serving Class man from Soleh Valley would have died to protect us."

Isbiano placed his hand on his daughter's shoulders. "Your words shame me, Isabella. I should not need my daughter to remind me of what is right and what is wrong. But you have and for that, I am grateful."

Isbiano then turned to Bok. "Which is why I vow I will take care of you and your family, young man. And your community—we will devote more resources to Soleh Valley and the Serving Class in general. I promise, I will work toward fairer, more equitable conditions for all our citizens."

He then looked away, not able to meet Bok's eyes. "But I am afraid what you ask is not possible. Perhaps one day it will be, but today is not that day. Revealing the truth about the Acumen would divide our society and threaten our prosperity. I truly am sorry, Bok... but my answer is no."

I save his life, save his crown... and still, I am just a peasant to our King. It is all I will ever be to him or those like him.

Bok wanted to look Isbiano in the eyes and tell him as much. But the king's face began to swirl, and Bok's vision became clouded. *Perhaps I am hurt worse than I thought...*

CHAPTER 51

THE BATTLE OF ITHENEL was done, but the Crown Princess of Imarina had never been busier, starting immediately after the battle.

Her first responsibilities were to the wounded and dead. She and her father spent hours in the infirmary visiting with the patients well enough to receive them and the families of those who were not. In the days to come, they would receive the grieving survivors of those killed in the battle, which they learned included three staff members slain by the Scions for refusing to cooperate.

Such a small request is the least we can do for them.

Then there was the matter of the Royal Palace itself. The main dining hall and the Royal Council Chambers sustained significant damage during the battle. Workers already were busy to ensure the building remained structurally safe, with extensive repairs taking place in the weeks to come. Isabella admittedly knew nothing about building construction, but while her father held emergency meetings with the remaining members of the Royal Council, he tasked her with overseeing this important job. She put in long, late hours to learn it.

And finally, she volunteered to help rebuild Imarina's House of Magic, which lost all its top leaders in the revolt. Isabella decided to schedule a meeting later in the week with some key House sorcerers—those who were more open-minded than many of their peers. She had a few ideas she wanted to share with them.

So much to do. By the end of the evening, Isabella's head throbbed and her feet ached. She knew she would be asleep as soon as she crawled under the covers. Her bedroom next to her study called to her. As she rubbed her temples and mustered the energy to stand up from her desk, there came a soft knock at her study door. She acknowledged it and Wingate stepped inside the room.

"Lieutenant—it is good to see you. All is well here. So you and your colleagues can resume—oh, Wingate... I am so sorry."

The giant man's expression never changed, but somehow, she knew what he had come to tell her.

"Yes, Your Majesty... it is my sad duty to inform you that... a messenger just arrived from Naseem. Commander Coregan has been found nearby, along with Coz Cosan...."

"Loyalty above all," she whispered. Coregan had been a constant presence around the palace since before she was born. Isabella grew up under his watch. As a young girl, she feared the gruff Guardian, but as she got older, so did her appreciation for his role in making the Royal Palace a safe, comfortable home for her family.

And now he was gone. She realized when Coregan had not returned that this was the most likely outcome. But having it confirmed brought a lump to her throat.

To her surprise, after a brief pause, Wingate continued, "Your Majesty, I... I realize this is a difficult time for your family and the kingdom. But with your permission, I wish to go to Naseem and recover Commander Coregan..."

Isabella squeezed his taut forearm—any greater show of affection would have made Wingate uncomfortable. "Bring him home, my friend."

※

Meanwhile, Bok recovered in the infirmary—an entire wing at the back of the palace's second floor. After receiving treatment from a healer, he received his own room—an honor typically reserved for the highest-ranking Nobles—rather than being housed with the other wounded patients in the ward. He normally would have balked at the special treatment, but feeling as poorly as he did, he accepted the gift.

He already began to get stronger within a few days. Before long, the boredom of staying in bed for hours on end outweighed the pain of his stab wound, injured shoulder, and broken hand.

Isabella and Avantil came by regularly to check on him. The way she clung to his arm and how he leaned his body against hers made it clear their relationship was stronger than ever. *And I couldn't be happier. Because my friends are happy.*

Kotarian also visited. "Please understand, peasant-turned-patient, I am not making any extra effort to see you. I just happened to be on this floor..."

Bok grinned. "Of course. But since you are here, a kind nurse delivered a bottle of wine in that bag, along with two glasses. I would offer to share, but if you are in a hurry..."

"I suppose my business here could wait a few more moments." Kotarian raised his eyebrows and reached into the bag. "You were telling me the other day about the first spell you employed against Salandrian. Not a bad choice—for a novice. But let me explain what you should have done instead..."

———※———

Late on the fourth evening of his infirmary stay, Isabella came alone, bringing a small wooden chest with an ornately decorated lid.

"Bok, I am sorry it has taken me all day to visit." She sighed as she pulled a chair to his bedside. "Many things require my attention. And I never have enough time. But I suppose that is my duty."

"Isabella, you don't always have to carry the burden of Imarina's national morale." Bok pushed himself up to a seated position. "It is okay to get frustrated. Just don't let it become a defining characteristic. as with Kotarian!"

"Ha! Well, in that case, in the strictest of confidences… I have no idea why it should take so many months to complete the repairs. The first floor of the palace will look like a rock quarry for the foreseeable future."

Bok grinned. "Maybe we go back to the old ways. You could order the foreman hung by his ankles in the Great Bazaar."

"The thought has crossed my mind—do not dare repeat that!" She laughed. "In truth, I should be grateful—"

Bok put up his hand. "Stop right there. You expressed your frustration. How do you feel?"

Isabella put a knuckle under her chin. "Surprisingly better. Thank you, my friend. I hadn't expected to receive the gift of clarity, but I did bring a surprise for you."

She held out the box for him, and Bok set it on his lap. Inside were five hand-crafted highly detailed wooden dolls, each representing a monarch from Imarina's past. The paint on the dolls was worn in spots where little fingers had played with them.

"They were mine as a child. My parents gave them to me in my sixth summer. I thought your nephew Noji might like to have them."

Would he like to have them? I cannot imagine a more priceless treasure for a small child. On their own, they cost far more than his family could afford. That they were a personal gift from the princess only magnified their value exponentially. Not that any of the Omats would entertain an offer for them.

Bok gently closed the lid. "I... I cannot accept such a gift! What if you and Avantil have children one day? Won't you want them to have these toys?"

"I have no shortage of treasures to pass down to future generations, Bok. It is one of the benefits of being a princess."

"You certainly have enough pillows to share with Inishari descendants for centuries to come!" Bok joked. "You have but one head. Why do you need enough pillows on your bed to supply all of Soleh Valley?"

Isabella waved a finger at him. "If I recall, those pillows saved your life! Perhaps you should buy me a few more as a thank-you."

Their laughter, uneasy at first, became an uncontrollable roar, to the point that the knife wound in Bok's side barked at him to stop.

"OW! Well, Noji will cherish them as much as you did. These dolls may even earn me a brief reprieve from Yata's sharp tongue!"

"I need to meet Yata. As an only child, I used to dream about having a companion with whom I could share adventures, as you did with your sister."

Bok rolled his eyes. "Well, be warned—big sisters play rough. But yes—I would love for you to meet Yata, and I know she would be honored."

"As would I." Their laughter subsided, and Isabella looked up at the ceiling to consider her next words.

"Oh, Bok... I never meant to hurt you, my friend. But I deceived you, and I am so—"

"Wait. Do not apologize." Bok hugged his knees to his chest. "Please, Isabella. That apology already has been given, accepted, and forgotten."

He leaned up in his hospital bed and pushed a pillow under his back for support. "Do you remember what happened at the start of this adventure? When those wolves attacked, I became paralyzed with fear—precisely when you and Avantil needed me. You had every right then to send me home in disgrace. Or, at a minimum, to never trust me again. Instead, you remained kind and supportive. As you have treated me from the beginning.

"Then I find out you are not a perfect princess after all. You made a mistake in not telling me the truth. Yes, I was upset. But you did so to protect your father. Would I also lie to protect my family? I suspect that I would.

"And I have little to lose by sharing a secret that would shake Imarina to its core. You, on the other hand, have been entrusted with our nation's safety. Of course you would be conflicted by such a choice.

"So if you aren't perfect, what is left? A loyal daughter. A brave defender of the kingdom. A scholar who never stops learning. And the best friend I could ever hope to have."

Isabella hesitated before speaking. "Bok... I... I do not know what to say. Other than I am more grateful than you can ever know for those words. But I do not wish to avoid responsibility for my actions because I am the Crown Princess."

Bok smiled warmly. "Believe me—I will never tell you what you wish to hear just to curry favor with our monarch-to-be, It's not like I'm on the invitation list for the Grand Merchant's Gala!

"Isabella, you never held your status over me. How could I ever hold it against you?"

A healer timidly stuck his head inside the room, waiting until Isabella invited him to enter. When she did, he gave Bok a chalice of bitter herb tea to drink. Bok decided it was best to quaff the brew quickly, rather than linger on getting it down.

"This will help him rest, Your Majesty." The healer bowed to Isabella as he backed out of the room.

Isabella leaned back in her chair. "I am glad we had this chance to visit—just us two. Without fending for our lives against magic-crazed wolves or Mosork marauders."

The herbal tea took effect quickly. Bok grew drowsier by the moment.

"I know—and I am glad, too..."

"Shhh." She took his hand in hers. "Just rest."

They sat in silence as Bok became increasingly groggy. He fell asleep with Isabella still holding his hand.

CHAPTER 52

BOK WAS DISCHARGED FROM care after a week. He remained at the infirmary for two additional weeks, working alongside the palace's healers to tend to the women and men wounded in the Battle of Ithenel, as it had been named.

The infirmary's healers practiced Folk Magic. But unlike Bok, they were from the Landowning Class and had been trained through a formal course of study in Ithenel. He worried they would look down on a country healer, but the crew readily welcomed his help. He even learned a few new techniques, such as a specific healing spell for burns—which proved invaluable in treating victims of fire spells. If he could ever find a place in the capital city, Bok could see it being in the palace infirmary.

There also was the solemn matter of Coregan's funeral.

One afternoon, Avantil came to the infirmary to inform Bok that Wingate had returned and the burial would take place two days hence.

"I know you didn't bring clothes for a funeral. I'll have something sent to your room."

Sure enough, when Bok returned to his quarters, he found a long, dark green robe draped across his bed. Dark green represented the natural cycle of inevitable death and renewed life in Imarinan culture. Bok lifted the fine garment to examine it. *Yet another kindness from Avantil. I'm still not sure what I've done to deserve such friends.*

The funeral took place early in the morning—another Imarinan tradition. Bok was thankful for it on the day of Coregan's burial. Autumn was coming and the summer heat soon would ebb a bit. But the last days of summer still could be miserably hot.

The early morning funeral also meant Bok had to rise before the sun to travel across the city. He walked to the stable to retrieve Beki, who had returned to the palace as healthy as ever.

He fed her an apple and brushed her mane. Bok marveled at how the farm animal, used to pulling plows and hauling corn, had performed on their adventure. *Ha! The people of the palace probably say the same about me.*

He took Beki to the front of the palace, looking to orient himself in the still-confusing cityscape. He knew the funeral was to the north and—

"There you are, Bok! Come ride with us." Avantil trotted down the red brick street riding his prized stallion, as he and Isabella waited in front of the palace's main gate. She wore a simple forest green dress; a tiara threaded with green ribbon pulled her hair off her face. Her familiar five bracelets hung around her right wrist. If anyone could look radiant at a funeral, it would be Imarina's Crown Princess.

Wingate and two more Guardians rode behind Isabella and Avantil—the final time he would serve as her personal bodyguard. Following the funeral, he would become Commander of the Royal Guard, as Coregan intended.

"We wondered where you were," Avantil added. "We didn't want to leave without you." He motioned to Bok to join the group.

"With you? And the Princess? I have no formal standing in the palace... I will just be out of place."

"Nonsense! First off, despite Her Majesty's presence, this is an informal procession. We both want you to come with us. But most importantly, you were a friend of Coregan's, as was I. He would want you to ride with us."

So Bok did.

"Shall we leave now, Your Majesty?" If anything, Wingate was quieter and more reserved than usual.

"Just one more moment, Wingate. We still await one more..."

As if on cue, Kotarian rode around the corner. "We can depart now. I have arrived." He had traded his gray jacket for a dark green robe but still wore his House pin.

"I'm glad you are here, Kotarian." And Bok meant it with full sincerity.

"Of course you are. You may gaze upon me with wonder, Baron Blacksmith!"

With that, they went on their way, Bok's emotions tangled in mourning for their fallen friend, relief at having survived, and elation over their victory. Regardless, he was glad they could be together again.

The slain Royal Council members received lavish funerals, with their caskets paraded through the streets of Ithenel and proclamations honoring the dead by King Isbiano himself. Coregan, on the other hand, was buried in a simple graveside service at a small hillside cemetery on Ithenel's north side.

The King attended but did not speak. He and Isabella stood at attention as numerous Guardians honored their fallen commander with brief, unscripted remarks.

Concise and honest—Coregan would have had it no other way. Bok watched silently as the plain casket was lowered into the ground.

As he prepared to return to the palace, a loud, shrill voice immediately behind him made him jump. "'Ello there, Bok! You ain't leavin' 'til I get ta hug the hero o' the Battle of Ithenel!"

"Umra?" He turned to meet her. But at first, he wasn't sure he saw the same servant girl from Naseem. She had traded her threadbare work clothes for a dark green dress similar to Isabella's. Her normally wild hair was combed and pulled back from her scrubbed-clean face. *She looks... well, breathtaking.*

"Look at you all fancied up! I reckon we both present okay when we borry clothes from our rich friends." She flashed a broad smile. "Tovano an' I got inta town this mornin'. Just in time ta get changed and come over 'ere. Can you believe it? I've got my own room in the Royal Palace. An' I'll be workin' on the fourth floor. Me!"

"Ha! The Royal Family has no idea of the hurricane that is incoming!"

"Careful, Bok—or you might get caught in the storm, too." She put a fist up to his chin in a mocking threat. After a shared grin, they looked around the well-kept lawn of the cemetery, at the freshly dug grave and the flower-covered casket beside it. "Poor Coregan. I didn't get ta know him well, but I wish I had. A brave soul, that one."

Bok nodded. "He was a difficult person to get to know, but I learned so much from him. I leaned on the wisdom he shared when we faced Salandrian."

Umra clapped her hands against her thighs. "Now that's a story I want to hear!"

Bok shared how the King and the House of Magic had been imprisoned, how the group nearly died in the passageway leading to the Royal Palace, and how they had worked together to defeat Salandrian and the Scions.

"Anyway, I got extremely lucky that day."

"You were more than lucky, Bok—you were brave, too. I must be truthful—I didn't know you had that in you. Yer full of surprises, blacksmith's boy."

His face blushed. "W... well, I recall a barmaid-turned-housekeeper saving all our lives. So I'm not the only one capable of surprises."

"No, you certainly aren't." With that, Umra placed her hand on the side of Bok's neck and kissed him. She closed her eyes and her lips lingered on Bok's. "Don't lose that spark. D'you hear me?"

Bok's heart raced as he took Umra's hand. He scrambled to think of a response. Then Tovano hobbled up, leaning on a plain wooden cane for support.

"Umra, if you would be so kind as to wait for me at the wagon. I would like a word in private with Mr. Omat." Bok couldn't help but roll his eyes at the sorcerer's terrible timing.

Umra walked away. "This was a nice moment. You owe me another one soon." She winked over her shoulder at Bok, who waved to the palace's newest royal assistant.

I certainly hope so.

Tovano then motioned to Bok to sit with him on a bench near a cluster of graves.

"I am still regaining my strength. Salandrian and his Scions took great delight in tormenting me. And they were quite efficient in their work."

Bok didn't look at the sorcerer, choosing to stare across the fenced-in graveyard. "I truly am sorry for that, Tovano. That should not happen to anyone."

"I'm glad you feel that way, Bok. I was worried that you might try to finish the job the Scions began!" Tovano joked. "I know you are angry at me for deceiving you. But you must understand I had good reason—"

"You're Serving Class, too. Aren't you, Tovano?" The words hung in the humid air for a moment. Now, it was Tovano's turn to look away from Bok.

He sighed. "Serving Class... I haven't been called that in more than 50 summers. But yes... I am. Just like you, Bok Omat. I have never told anyone this story. Not King Isbiano, not Princess Isabella, not my colleagues when I was a member of the House of Magic. But I shall tell you now."

He leaned back on the bench and cleared his throat. "I grew up in a farming community in eastern Imarina, not far from Fossett. My mother worked as a servant in the house of a minor Lord who owned the farmland surrounding it. I was raised in the manor, helping my mother with her long list of daily chores. I did well in school, but I ceased my formal education at 10 summers because the Lord needed an extra set of hands—preferably one he didn't have to pay like an adult servant. Still, I figured it was better than working the fields, and he didn't mind if I borrowed books from his study as long as I had finished my daily work."

Tovano's rheumy eyes stared across the graveyard as he continued to reminisce. A songbird perched on a nearby tombstone. Its cheerful chirps took Bok's mind to Soleh Valley. But he continued to listen.

Tovano scratched his beard and tapped his cane against the lawn. "I assumed I'd found my lot in life. I would work in service to this Noble until I was too old for physical labor. But fate had different plans, I suppose. Although not born with the Acumen, the Lord of the manor had a fascination with High Magic. So he would pay a hefty honoraria to House sorcerers to travel to his estate and demonstrate spells.

"One of these demonstrations took place when I was 14 summers. The sorcerer, named Jalithian, began her presentation with Palonian's Prodigious Presence. It's a spell that allows the user to grow to heights of more than 20 feet tall. The room we were in had a vaulted ceiling. But once she cast the spell, Jalithian's head brushed against the ceiling's apex.

"When Jalithian spoke the incantation, the words, which must have seemed like so much nonsense to everyone else in attendance, made sense to me. Like pieces of broken glass forming a mosaic. I said nothing, but I knew I shouldn't understand."

Bok shuffled on the hard stone bench and nodded. Few Serving Class people had the Acumen for High Magic. But they all understood the need to hold their tongues around Nobles.

"After everyone left, I recreated her spell in the empty room, carefully repeating each word precisely as she had said it. And WHOOSH! I shot up to the ceiling, bumping my head so hard that I nearly passed out But I did what the Nobles said was impossible. I, a young man of the Serving Class, performed High Magic."

Just like I did at Naseem. He must've been as confused as I was. Bok smoothed out the wrinkles in his robe. Its smooth, cool fabric hung awkwardly on his body.

"Unfortunately, in my youthful excitement, I didn't pay nearly as much attention to the counter-spell Jalithian used to shrink back to her regular size." Tovano chuckled until he coughed into his hand. "I yelled for help and both my mother and the Lord of the manor came running. The spell wore off momentarily and I returned to normal. But the Lord saw what I had done, and knew I was a threat to the social order.

"So he immediately took me to Queen Iladalya—King Isbiano's mother. She ordered that papers be drafted creating a backstory to cover why I had been raised in a Serving Class home. Something to the effect that I was born to Noble Class parents, who died in a tragic accident and my Serving Class mother agreed to raise me as her own. No one in the Royal Palace bothered to investigate—and why would they? The explanation validated their view of the world, so they asked no questions.."

Bok furrowed his brow. "But why wouldn't you say anything? Why did you go along with this... this lie?"

Tovano shook his head, looking away from the young healer. "At first, I went along because the Queen quietly made sure my mother lived a comfortable life. She received a small piece of land and a generous pension—payment to ensure her silence. To be honest, I didn't visit as much as I could have after I entered the House of Magic and a life in the Noble Classes..." His voice trailed off momentarily. "I enjoyed my new life too much to be bothered thinking about the one I left behind."

Bok clenched his fists in his lap. "But you didn't just lie to yourself, Tovano. You lied to me, too. Knowing how much your deception would hurt me."

"I did." Tovano exhaled deeply and slowly. "I am not proud of it, but you speak the truth."

"The truth? Do you believe that you can declare yourself an honest man now and that erases your past lies?"

"No... I don't believe it erases the lies I've told—to you and to many more before you. Nor do I expect you to forgive me. But at the moment, honesty is almost all I have to offer."

"Well, you should have offered it back at Naseem." Bok stood up from the bench to face Tovano.

With a grimace, the old sorcerer leaned up on his walking stick. "That would have been the right thing to do by you. But would it have been the right thing to do by the Kingdom? I still do not know. And while it may be too late, I offer you my honesty now. That... and a renewed offer: I can teach you High Magic as I have done with Isabella. There is much more for you to learn. But once you do, young man, your opportunities are endless."

He fished a small glass globe from his pocket and held it out for Bok to accept. "What do you say?"

Bok raised his eyebrows. His own eyes reflected off the globe's shiny exterior.

The opportunity is as generous as he claims. But it doesn't tempt me.

"No—you may be a great teacher. But I will not be your student." Bok waved his hands to accentuate his certainty.

Tovano leaned forward on his cane. "Bok, please reconsider. Do not let some stubborn grudge against me rob you of the chance to develop those skills."

"I don't intend to." As Bok walked away, he added, "I already have someone to teach me."

At least I pray I do. I just hope Kotarian says "Yes."

CHAPTER 53

T HREE DAYS LATER, BOK packed his meager but growing possessions and left his room at the Royal Palace for the final time.

His work as an emergency healer in the palace infirmary had ended. The patients wounded in the Battle of Ithenel either had recovered enough to be discharged or they would require daily care for the rest of their lives. The infirmary's normal staff could manage without his assistance.

The night before, Bok announced his intentions to return to Soleh Valley at an informal dinner gathering on the fourth floor. Isabella and Avantil were there, as was Kotarian. Wingate and Umra also attended in their official capacities, but Isabella made sure they joined in the meal and conversation. Tovano declined the invitation, which relieved Bok. He needed time and distance from his one-time mentor.

In Isbiano's absence, Isabella shared some good news. Although the House had not yet named a new Emissary of Magic, at Isabella's recommendation, Kotarian would serve as a liaison between the new Emissary and the King. In that job, he would foster better relations between the Crown and the House of Magic.

"It's the obvious choice." He smiled as he swished his full glass of red wine. "Who would be better suited for such an important role?"

The gathering didn't break up until late in the night. No one wanted it to end. Finally, though, Bok stood up to leave, knowing he had a long ride ahead of him the next day.

Isabella grabbed his arm. "Wait! There is something I must give you. You will be at the stables early tomorrow morning?"

"At dawn's first light. But a gift? You owe me no reward."

"This is something I want you to have. Sleep well, my friend."

"Good night, Isabella."

What type of gift does one receive from the Princess? I'm sure I'll never be able to guess. Might as well wait until morning to find out.

Isabella waited for Bok at the stables early the following morning, just as the sky began to brighten. She sat on a bench outside of Beki's stall, sipping a mug of coffee. Steam curled up around her face as she brought the cup to her full lips.

"Good morning, Bok. I brought you one, too." Isabella handed Bok a matching ceramic mug emblazoned with the Inishari crest. He thanked her and she stood up in front of him, always taller than her diminutive height suggested.

"Mmmm... perfect!" Bok smiled in response. "Thank you. This will give me a boost for the ride back to Soleh Valley!"

"I believe this will have the same effect." Isabella reached into her silk purse and produced a tightly rolled scroll, sealed in wax with her royal seal and tied with a purple ribbon. It appeared similar to the message Bok received at his family's blacksmith shop, the summons that started him on this unreal adventure.

"I don't understand," he said.

"Just read it. You will."

And so he did:

Let it be known that from now forth, the practice of High Magic is open to all classes in Imarina. The House of Magic shall devise and submit a written proposal for incorporating apprentices from the Landowning and Serving Classes in its recruiting and training processes.

This is the word of Princess Isabella Inishari, eighty-seventh monarch of Imarina.

With a knowing wink, she drank from her mug. "As we speak, messengers are on their way across the country to deliver this news. There's even one heading to Soleh Valley."

His hands shaking, Bok read and reread the scroll, making sure his mind interpreted the words correctly. She had defied centuries of tradition and revealed the royal family's most painful secret—and created new opportunities and greater equality for Imarina's Serving Class. Finally satisfied that he had read it properly, Bok tucked the scroll in his healer's bag, lest his tears smudge the ink.

"Isabella, I... Thank you, my friend." *This is a gift beyond measure. Serving Class children will never know an Imarina where the House of Magic has a closed door.*

But beyond that, she heard what I said about my people. She listened and cared enough to make it right.

"To paraphrase my father, I needed a country healer to remind me of what is just."

Bok put his hand to his forehead. *Her father! What type of trouble will Isabella be in when he realizes what she's done?*

Isabella laughed. "I know what you are thinking, Bok. I am certain Father will not be pleased!'

She swung her feet out in front of the bench. "But deep inside, he knows I am right. Plus, he cannot be too mad with his only child!"

Bok felt the tension drain from his body. He leaned against one of the stable's sturdy wooden support posts. "Particularly when that daughter and her friends just saved his life and the entire kingdom."

"Exactly! With that settled, I do not understand why you must leave Ithenel, Bok. Can you not reconsider your decision?"

"It is as I said: Soleh Valley needs its healer. I have a duty to my people."

Isabella nodded, then looked down into the swirling light brown liquid in her cup. "Of anyone, I understand the burden of duty. I will miss you, Bok Omat."

"And I you, Princess." He started to move toward Beki, paused, then turned back to Isabella. "Of course, I never said I couldn't visit. I would not miss Avantil's celebration of nineteen summers in a few weeks. Oh, and Kotarian has agreed to train me in High Magic. His exact words last night were, 'There is so much Bok doesn't know. I am not sure he is capable of becoming a competent sorcerer. But if anyone can break through his lifetime of ignorance, it would be me.'

"Anyway, I am to come to the Royal Palace every third week to have my confidence shattered and parentage insulted. I shall have time for a royal consult in between humiliations. So get used to seeing me around your house."

She laughed—perhaps even guffawed, if a princess may do such a thing. "Bok, you deliberately waited to tell me that! Do your parents know what a mischievous son they have raised? If so, I may have to tell them in person."

"In person? You mean you plan to visit Soleh Valley?"

Isabella nodded. "If I am to be queen, I must see Imarina beyond the majestic city of Ithenel. I thought Soleh Valley could be an appropriate place to begin this exploration. That is, if you might recommend a knowledgeable local guide..."

"I believe that can be arranged, Your Majesty."

"That also will give me the chance to meet little Noji—and to compare notes with Yata. I suspect she has some interesting stories to share."

With that, they hugged one more time—and this time, any conflicted feelings Bok may have once had were gone. Only warmth remained.

I came to Ithenel as a country healer, and I leave changed in so many ways—but none more important than having gained a beloved friend. Along with my family's love, Isabella's friendship is the greatest gift I have ever received. And I don't have to choose between them.

He rode away from the Royal Palace with that friend—the Crown Princess of Imarina—waving farewell until she faded into the distance. Bok already missed her.

Bok patted the saddlebag on Beki's side. He felt the wooden box with Noji's dolls under his fingers. It hadn't all been a dream.

The road back to Soleh Valley gave him plenty of time to think, and he would take full advantage. But on this already humid morning, a lone thought dominated his thoughts:

How in the world am I ever going to explain all of this to Yata?

Acknowledgements

Wow—where do I even begin? I have so many people to thank in helping me bring *The Blacksmith's Boy* to life. It's no exaggeration to say writing a novel has been a wish list item for most of my life, and it couldn't have happened without a ton of help.

I'll start with the people most important to me--my family. Amy, thank you for being my go-to advisor and most trusted counselor on... well, pretty much everything. I couldn't have done this without you. Jackson, I'm proud to share this book with you, best kid. And Mom—I can't say enough about all the love and support you've given me all these years.

But this book would have remained in the unfulfilled wish stage if I didn't have a publisher. Thanks to everyone at Wild Ink Publishing for making this happen. Abigail Wild and Brittany McMunn—you believed in me and my book, and I'll always be grateful.

Every writer needs a good editor—and I've been lucky enough to have two great ones for this book. Dante

Medema edited *The Blacksmith's Boy* before I took it out into the publishing world. Her guidance was invaluable in getting this book where I wanted it to be. And Andie Smith edited it for Wild Ink. I wanted to work with her for a long time, and I'm grateful I got that opportunity. Can't say enough about her wonderful work. In addition, I'd like to thank Ian Tan, who proofread the manuscript. Ian edited the *UnCensored Ink* anthology for Wild Ink, and I'm proud to have written a story for that collection.

I'm also indebted to the writing community. Amy Nielsen helped me get my foot in the door at Wild Ink and is just one of the best champions for writers I've ever met. S.E. Reed had no reason to help a writer struggling with a rough draft, but she did and I'm forever thankful. Her guidance helped me get this book on the right track, and she's been a tremendous friend and mentor at all steps of my writing journey.

I greatly appreciate Tamara Horton for providing the outstanding illustrations found throughout the book. Your drawings brought these characters to life!

Finally, I'd like to thank everyone who reads this book. I sincerely appreciate your support, and I hope you enjoy it!

ABOUT THE AUTHOR

Bruce Buchanan is the communications writer for an international law firm and a former journalist. But he's been a fan of fantasy and heroic fiction for most of his life. His influences range from the novels of Margaret Weis & Tracy Hickman and Terry Brooks to the Marvel Comics stories of Stan Lee, Jack Kirby, and Steve Ditko. He lives in Greensboro, N.C. with his wife, Amy Joyner Buchanan (a blogger and the author of five non-fiction books), and their guitar-playing teenage son, Jackson. Learn more at https://brucebuchananauthor.com/.